D0038098

Gregg

(continued on next page . . .)

THE BRIDE NOVELS

THE SHERBROOKE BRIDE • THE HELLION BRIDE •
THE HEIRESS BRIDE • THE SCOTTISH BRIDE

"Coulter is excellent at portraying the romantic tension between her heroes and heroines and she manages to write explicitly but beautifully about sex as well as love."

—*Milwaukee Journal*

THE VIKING TRILOGY

LORD OF HAWKFELL ISLAND • LORD OF RAVEN'S PEAK •
LORD OF FALCON RIDGE

"Coulter's characters quickly come alive and draw the reader into the story. You root for the good guys and hiss for the bad guys. When you have to put the book down for a while, you can hardly wait to get back and see what's going on." —*The Sunday Oklahoman*

THE LEGACY TRILOGY

THE WYNDHAM LEGACY • THE NIGHTINGALE LEGACY •
THE VALENTINE LEGACY

"Delightful . . . brimming with drama, sex and colorful characters . . . Her witty dialogue and bawdy, eccentric characters add up to an engaging, fan-pleasing story."

—*Publishers Weekly*

PENDRAGON

CATHERINE COULTER

JOVE BOOKS, NEW YORK

PENDRAGON

A Jove Book / published by arrangement with
the author

PRINTING HISTORY
Jove edition / January 2002

Visit our website at
www.penguinputnam.com

ISBN: 0-515-13225-X

A JOVE BOOK®
Jove Books are published by The Berkley Publishing Group,
a division of Penguin Putnam Inc.,
375 Hudson Street, New York, New York 10014.
JOVE and the ''J'' design
are trademarks belonging to Penguin Putnam Inc.

PRINTED IN THE UNITED STATES OF AMERICA

10 9 8 7 6 5 4 3 2 1

PENDRAGON

THE SHERBROOKE FAMILY

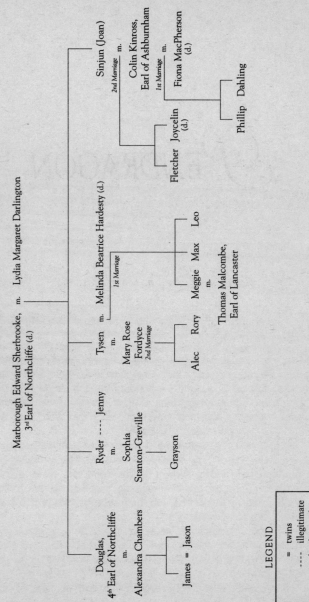

Marborough Edward Sherbrooke, m. Lydia Margaret Darlington
3rd Earl of Northcliffe (d.)

Douglas,
4th Earl of Northcliffe
m.
Alexandra Chambers

James = Jason

Ryder --- Jenny
m.
Sophia
Stanton-Greville

Grayson

Tysen m. Melinda Beatrice Hardesty (d.)
m.   1st Marriage
Mary Rose
Fordyce
2nd Marriage

Alec Rory   Meggie Max Leo

Thomas Malcombe,
Earl of Lancaster
m.

Sinjun (Joan)
2nd Marriage
m.
Colin Kinross,
Earl of Ashburnham
1st Marriage
m.
Fiona MacPherson
(d.)

Fletcher Joycelin
(d.)

Phillip Dahling

LEGEND

= twins
--- illegitimate
d. deceased

1

The Cat Races
The McCaulty Racetrack,
near Eastbourne, England
A bright Saturday afternoon, April 1823

"MR. RALEIGH, GET Tiny Tom out of Mr. Cork's way. Blessed Hell, he'll run right over him!"

Tiny Tom was jerked off the track just in the nick of time, not more than two seconds before Mr. Cork would have laid him flat. Tiny Tom was Mr. Raleigh's great hope, but he just wasn't yet ready for this level of competition. Tiny Tom, black as the devil's familiar with small white paws, was, after all, only one year old, not fully grown or as yet well trained.

But when the runners had scampered and darted past, Mr. Raleigh set Tiny Tom back on the track, swatting his hindquarters and growling in his little ear. That growl, evidently, promised chopped-up chicken livers. Tiny Tom, tasting those chicken livers going down his little gullet, shot forward.

Meggie Sherbrooke scanned the racers, cupped her mouth with her hands, and yelled again, "Blessed Hell, Mr. Cork! Run! Don't let Blinker II catch you! You can do it, run!"

Reverend Tysen Sherbrooke tended to ignore his

daughter's very occasional lapses into the favored Sherbrooke curse, since it really was quite fit for the racetrack, and yelled himself. "Run, Mr. Cork, run! Cleopatra, you can do it, sweet girl, go!"

Mr. Cork, who'd finally finished growing into his paws six months before, was a big tabby, all orange-striped on his back, the top of his head, and snow white all over his belly and legs, strong as Clancy, Mr. Harbor's prize bull. He ran only to the smell of a trout, about six pounds and thankfully always dead, baked with just a squeeze of fresh lemon, held by Max Sherbrooke at the finish line, who waved it back and forth like a metronome, keeping Mr. Cork's attention focused on that trout in front of him. When not in strict training, however, Mr. Cork many times spent his mornings beneath the dining table, his orange-striped tail waving lazily from beneath the tablecloth, announcing that he was ready to be served a nice strip of crispy bacon, or perhaps a small bowl of milk, or both, if the donor would exert himself a bit.

Strong and big, legs pumping with muscle—sheer power and poetry in motion—said Lady Dauntry of Mr. Cork in admiration. She'd been the mistress of ceremonies for the past fourteen years, always calling the race, even in inclement weather. Lady Dauntry deplored corruption on the racetrack, and even now, in 1823, it was rumored that there were still occasional attempts to fix races, and so there was always stringent oversight by all racing mews.

Mary Rose, Tysen's Scottish wife for eight years now, yelled in a very loud and lovely lilt, "Run, Cleo, my bonnie girl, run!" Then she ratcheted up her lungs and yelled, "You can keep up with her, Alec! Run, lad!"

Seven-year-old Alec Sherbrooke was actually trying to keep up with Leo, whom he worshipped. It was being said in the major racing mews that just perhaps Alec Sherbrooke was one of a very rare breed indeed—a cat whisperer. If he was, he would be extraordinarily special. It was said that Cleo would begin leaping whenever Alec was about and thus that was how she'd been trained so quickly to this new technique. Everyone marveled—a cat whisperer. If Alec Sherbrooke was so blessed, his was going to be a famous name in the racing world. Since Alec wasn't yet big enough to keep up with her, Leo, his older stepbrother, was Cleo's on-track trainer. Meggie privately wondered if Cleo ran because Leo ran beside her or because of what seven-year-old Alec whispered in her white ear before each race.

For those who preferred the more dainty racers, like Cleopatra, christened Clea Mia by a visiting Italian curate some months before, she was a natural leaper. Breath held, Mary Rose watched her run her very fast six steps, building up momentum, then like a dancer, she took off her hind paws, legs extended, leapt forward, stretching her long calico body in the air and landed directly ahead of Blinker II.

Everyone cheered. Lady Dauntry had announced that Cleopatra was grace in motion, and all agreed it was true.

In the beginning of the race, Cleo was content to run a good six lengths behind the leader, running alongside Leo, with seven-year-old Alec trying to keep up. Leo said her name over and over, just loud enough for her to hear, keeping pace with her, difficult when she leapt, but Leo was young and strong and he loved to see Cleopatra stretch and leap and land some three feet ahead of all the other racers. The Harker brothers, from the Mountvale mews, praised the technique as unique and ever so lovely to watch. Then they would speak of Alec and shake their heads and wonder how he would change the world of cat racing with his gift. A cat whisperer, just imagine.

Blinker II poked his head out, running all out, managed to pass Cleopatra again. He was running his paws off, staying right in the middle of the course, hearing his master's shout of encouragement, a shout that meant to Blinker that he would get all the fresh warm milk he could lap up as it was squeezed out of Trudy, the Grimsby cow. He didn't even veer away when another racing cat nearly ran over him. Mr. Grimsby hadn't overtrained him for this meet, heeding the Harker brothers' advice some six months before to keep laps at no more than ten per day. Blinker II was all gray, with bright green eyes. He always purred when he ran.

Meggie was getting hoarse, but it didn't matter. She yelled at the top of her lungs, "Come on, Mr. Cork! Move! You can run faster than Blinker II! Look at that delicious trout Leo is waving for you. Just you smell that tangy flavor!"

Mr. Cork was serious now, running so fast his legs were a blur, his golden paws barely skimming the dry dirt course. His green eyes were fastened on that gently swinging trout in Max's right hand, now in full sight, standing just over the finish line.

Cleopatra executed a major leap, landing her some three and a half feet ahead of Leo. He panted to catch up with her because when she couldn't see him out of her right eye, she would simply stop and wait for him. Or perhaps she waited for both Leo and Alec, no one could say for sure. It was the only drawback of this training method. Leo Sherbrooke, seventeen, trained as hard as any of the racing cats in the vicarage mews. In the early morning both Leo and Alec could be seen running across the fields toward the Channel.

Horatio Blummer's stark white racer, Candace, shaped much like a cannon, mean as could be, was all snarls and fangs when she got near another racer. Those racers who didn't move away from her quickly got bitten hard on the rump. Candace was running fairly well today, snarling with every step. Just plain mean, that was what Mr. Blummer said proudly of Candace. She didn't need any bribes to make her run hard.

Mr. Cork paused just an instant to snarl back at her before, tail stiff in the air, he sprinted past her.

Mr. Goodgame's Horace, ten years old now, but still game, a small joke, always repeated by Mr. Goodgame, was long and skinny and looked like a white-and-gray spotted arrow flying through the field of racers. Mr. Goodgame had attached a flag to Horace's fat white tail, and it waved madly in the breeze. It showed two cats standing on their hind legs, holding crossing swords, the words beneath:

Leve et reluis

Translated: *Arise and re-illumine*, a beautiful sentiment, surely, but not entirely understood by the locals.

They were nearly to the three-quarters mark. Only three cats had been seduced from the track by hooligans who hooted like owls to scare the cats into skidding off the track, or hollered like fishmongers, waving overripe fish or raw chicken legs. Training assistants from surrounding mews wrestled the hooligans away from the track.

Meggie shouted, "Mr. Cork, I'll give you three strips of bacon if you beat out old Lummley!"

Old Lummley was a champion. He knew his business, and needed only to see his mistress, Mrs. Foe, standing at the finish line, her arms crossed over her mighty bosom whistling the same tune over and over, to run straight and fast. He'd gotten a touch of arthritis over the last year and the experts predicted it would soon slow him down.

Four-year-old Rory Sherbrooke loved Cleopatra, although she twitched her tail and ran away from him whenever he was close enough to try to grab her. Rory waved frantically as he sat atop his father's shoulders, yelled until his father believed he would surely go deaf.

Meggie patted Rory's leg, then saw Mr. Cork suddenly pull away from Cleopatra, who'd just landed short on one of her leaps. There was a moan and a cheer from the crowd who lined the racetrack.

Cheering intensified. Five cats remained, running as hard as they could, all in splendid shape, all wanting to win. Four of them were grouped together—Cleopatra, Blinker II, Old Lummley, and Mr. Cork. They were moving fast, faster still. Candace, just behind them, her head down, was looking neither right nor left, just running hard out to catch the pack.

Suddenly, from the back came Tiny Tom, leaping over racers in front of him. His leap was a bit like Cleopatra's but with an added corkscrew flair just before he landed. The crowd held its breath as the small cat leapt over Horace, barely skimming the proud flag flying off that fat tail. Then, in the next moment, Tiny Tom landed, by awful accident, on Blinker II's back, causing the racer to twist about, bite Tiny Tom's ear, sending them both howling and spitting off the track and into Mrs. Blanchard, eighty years old and deaf, and tangle in her long skirts as she hit at them with her parasol.

Pandemonium broke out when Mr. Cork, in a final surge of power, flew over the finish line, beating Cleopatra by three whiskers. Old Lummley and Candace tumbled over each other vying for third place. Blinker II trotted back to the track, realized he'd lost and walked over the finish line, tail stiff, nose in the air. Horace followed behind him, his tail flag dragging in the dirt. There would be no re-illuminating this day. As for Tiny Tom, he was exhausted. He lay on his side at the edge of the track, licking his paws.

When Lady Dauntry, in a voice that carried all the way to Eastbourne, announced that Mr. Cork had won, Max hefted him up and carried him, draped over his shoulder, in state, to the winner's circle, Alec walking proudly beside him. Max was panting by the time he got there, as Mr. Cork wasn't a lightweight. When Mr. Cork saw Meggie, he automatically opened his mouth and let out a mighty MEOW. She dutifully pulled a piece of bacon wrapped in a pristine napkin from her pocket and fed it to him, telling him he was a beautiful boy and a splendid racer.

Mr. Cork consumed his bacon, licked Meggie's hand, and laid his head back on Max's shoulder. He looked very pleased with himself.

Cleopatra knew she'd lost. She wasn't happy about it. Unfortunately, good sportsmanship was something trainers couldn't seem to teach the racers, and so when Leo carried her too close to Mr. Cork, she reached out a paw and swiped his head. He opened one eye, tossed one hiss her way, then fell back to sleep, undisturbed by her bad manners.

"Next time, Cleo," Leo said, stroking his hand down

her sleek back, "you'll get the orange giant next time, you'll see. You need some more takeoff training, more power in your hind legs, and Alec and I have come up with just the way to do it."

Alec nuzzled her head even as his fingertips lightly touched her ears. Then he whispered something in her small ear, and everyone would swear that she was listening to him. He kissed the top of her head. She forgot her snit and purred madly.

Mr. Grimsby saw this, and nodded wisely. "A cat whisperer," he said to his wife, who looked profoundly awed. "Yes, Alec is a budding cat whisperer."

There was one more race that afternoon, this one just for the three-year-olds, no others, as this age was the most aggressive, the most untrainable. There always seemed to be cat free-for-alls, fur flying all over the track from yowling cat fights. Many times not a single racer crossed the finish line, and today was no exception.

"Kitters will be kitters," Ozzie Harker said, shaking his head as he carried off Monroe, a wicked three-year-old tabby with a mangled ear.

Meggie patted both Mr. Cork and Cleo, kissing their faces until they both drew back from her, wondering where the food was.

"An excellent day," Meggie said, and hugged her father. "Now that Alec is focusing on Cleo, I would wager she'll begin beating Mr. Cork."

"The boy is amazing, isn't he, Meggie?"

His daughter heard the love in her father's voice for his son, and hugged him. "Both he and Rory are wonderful. You and Mary Rose have done very well." She grinned. "And just as I promised, I have taught them what's what."

Tysen laughed, just couldn't help himself as he remembered that long-ago sermon that had ended in not only a good deal of laughter but profound acceptance.

Meggie said, "I wish Susannah and Rohan Carrington could have been here. I'm just glad they let the Harker brothers attend to scout out the competition. It's always more exciting when the Mountvale mews are represented."

Tysen said, "They'll be here in May. They're in Paris, Rohan wrote me, looking at all the new crop of beautiful gardens. You know Rohan and his gardens—he will return with a dozen new designs."

"It was a good day," Max said, still carrying Mr. Cork, no longer panting so heavily now.

"Yes," his father agreed, "it was."

"Papa, can I carry Mr. Cork?"

Tysen looked up at his four-year-old Rory, mentally added Mr. Cork's additional weight, and sighed. "Hand him up, Max."

2

Sherbrooke town house
Putnam Place, London
One week later

𝒯HE SHERBROOKE TOWN house, on the corner of Putnam Place, was a three-story Georgian mansion built in the middle of the last century by an earl of Northcliffe with far more money than good taste, or *bon gout*, as he was wont to shout out when he took his pleasure at Madame Orly's brothel. He was also the same earl who had filled the Northcliffe gardens with all the coupling Greek statuary. Sherbrooke children, adults, guests, servants, and the occasional tradesman had, for the past sixty-five years, spent hours staring at the naked marble men and women, all in the throes of physical endeavors. Meggie wished she could have met that earl. Neither Leo nor Max had ever let fall to their vicar father that their cousins, Uncle Douglas's boys, had quickly shown them the statues in the hidden part of the Northcliffe gardens, and how all four boys had gawked and made lewd remarks and studied the statues in great giggling detail for hours on end. None of them was stupid.

Meggie was just down the hall from her aunt Alex's bedchamber that adjoined to Uncle Douglas's in a lovely airy room that was all shades of peach and cream. She'd stayed in this same room since she'd been eight years old.

There came a light tap on the door.

"Enter," Meggie called out.

It was her aunt Alex, looking tussled and windblown and as happy as the spring sunshine because she'd been out riding early with Uncle Douglas in Hyde Park. They'd doubtless galloped to their heart's content because no one was about that early to see and remark upon such eccentric behavior. She was wearing a dark green riding habit that Uncle Douglas had presented her on her birthday. Her rich red hair had tumbled out of her stylish riding hat and was in curls and tangles down her back.

She looked flushed and happy and in high spirits. "I love to be back in London," she said as she stripped off her York tan riding gloves, the leather incredibly soft. "It's ever so when we first arrive. Everything is fresh and new again. Now, it's your first Season, Meggie, and I am so pleased that Tysen gave you over into our care. What fun we shall have. I've come to tell you that Douglas will be taking you to Madame Jordan's this morning."

"Who is Madame Jordan?"

"Why, she's my dressmaker, has been since Douglas and I married." Alex broke off a moment, a wicked memory breaking into a big smile. "Hmmm, oh yes, between the two of them, you will look like a princess. Trust whatever your uncle says. He has excellent style."

Both her uncles had had excellent style when it came to ladies' clothes, Meggie had been told all her life. Her own father did too, one assumed, since all Sherbrooke males had unconscionable portions of luck and style, but as a vicar, he normally didn't let his style out in full company.

Mary Rose, Meggie's stepmother, and Meggie, in a house full of males, had long ago pulled together and seen to their own shopping, enjoying it immensely. Because they weren't dolts, the four males in the Vicarage household, including Alec and Rory, knew that they were to instantly compliment any new garment, the greater the length of the compliment, the better treatment accorded them. Their father, hardly ever a dolt, roundly endorsed this.

"Now, Douglas wishes to leave as soon as he changes from his riding clothes. He has a meeting with the foreign office this afternoon. I do hope it's not yet another offer of a diplomatic post. The last one was to Rome. It was very hot when we were there. We spent a lot of time with cardinals and bishops, and that meant I was very well covered up."

"I would perhaps consider Paris," Meggie said.

"He turned that down two years ago," Alex said. Indeed, Lord Northcliffe had turned down several diplomatic offerings, and was frequently called in by the King, George IV, particularly on matters pertaining to the French, a people Douglas understood very well, and then he would snort.

An hour later Meggie and her uncle were discussing fashion with Madame Jordan in her elegant shop in the heart of Regent Street, at #14, on the east side.

It wasn't raining, a miracle, Meggie said to her uncle, since it had poured all the way to London, poured the entire previous evening, but beginning at dawn, April was strutting beautiful spring plumage. Flowers were bursting out and trees were turning green. Meggie couldn't breathe deeply enough.

There were only three ladies and their maids in the shop that morning because it was quite early. Madame Jordan took one look at Meggie's uncle, and flew to him, presenting her cheek to be kissed, which he did. After tea and gossip, Madame Jordan said to Uncle Douglas, considering Meggie irrelevant to the process, which she was, "Just fancy, a young lady for you to apply your excellent taste to, my lord. She will be a beauty, with my assistance. Hmmm, a nice waist, which is good since ladies are now allowed to have waistlines again, and her bosom is ample. Yes, nice skin, and that hair, the same rich color as Mr. Ryder Sherbrooke's and Lady Sinjun's, all blonds and browns and sunlight. And those blue eyes, I will make them sparkle with magnificence. Now, let me take her measurements, and we will see what is what." Meggie was stripped to her petticoat and chemise and stockings, stood upon a small dais, measured, large swatches of material draped over her, from the filmiest silks to the most brilliant and shimmery satins, all with Uncle Douglas looking on, making comments, stroking his jaw, looking like a man in charge of an army, and every soldier in that army was ready to do his bidding.

When she saw the ball gown Douglas picked out for her to wear the next evening, Madame Jordan nodding enthusiastically, her heart thrummed with excitement and pleasure. It was glorious, tulle over white satin with two lines of exquisite embroidery from the waist down the skirt to the hem, suggesting an open robe.

"Thank God you look very fine in white, Meggie," he said, looking her up and down and nodding. The sleeves were short and tight, the neckline square. There were very narrow flounces, one at the hem, the second nearly to the knees.

"It's not overdone," said Douglas, "and at last the waist is where it should be. You have a nice small waist, Meggie, and your bosom is particularly pleasant—ah, perhaps I shouldn't point that out in your hearing, but it's true, just as Madame said. Yes, this style will become you. No more schoolgirl gowns, my dear. You are now a young lady in her first Season."

Madame Jordan sighed. "Remember, my lord, when you first brought your young bride to me? What atrocious taste she had, and still has, for that matter, but she did understand the power of her magnificent bosom, and dug in her heels."

"Women always understand the power of the bosom," Douglas said, snorting. "As for my wife, she still wears her gowns cut nearly to her knees, and I don't like it any more now than I did then. Men ogle her, Nicolette. Three men could ogle her at the same time, she is so well endowed."

Madame Jordan laughed and poked his arm. "Ah, a jealous husband, isn't it delightful, my dear?"

Meggie looked from Nicolette to her uncle, getting her first glimpse of uncharted territory. "Yes, ma'am, now that I am thinking about it, why yes, it is quite delightful."

Then came a riding habit in royal blue that made Meggie want to weep it was so beautiful. "Oh goodness, Uncle Douglas, it is too fine," she whispered as she ran her fingers over the fabric that one of Madame's minions had delivered directly to Meggie's fingertips.

"We will come back tomorrow, Meggie, to order up more gowns for you and to have your ball gown fitted. This is just the beginning. Tomorrow evening you will look like a princess for the Ranleigh ball." He said to Madame, "Her coming-out ball will be in two weeks. I want something very special for her that night."

"I will find it," Madame said comfortably, and if Meggie wasn't mistaken—and she wasn't since she'd seen the same look many times in Mary Rose's eyes—there was a gleam of pure lust in Madame's fine dark eyes as she watched Uncle Douglas leave her shop.

"She, er, really appreciates you, Uncle Douglas."

A dark eyebrow went up. "You are eighteen, Meggie, a vicar's daughter. What do you know of men and women sorts of things?"

She laughed. "I live with my father and Mary Rose. Those two—they laugh and hug and sneak kisses when they think they're alone, which they never are in the vicarage. What's more, Rory came into my bedroom two weeks ago, afraid because he'd heard his mother yelling. I am not an idiot, Uncle Douglas."

"Your father is a very happy man," was all that Douglas would say to that revelation. Then, later, he laughed and said, "Ah, I would like to hear some day how you dealt with little Rory's concern. Now, Meggie, I have something to say to you. You will enjoy yourself here in London. You aren't hunting for a husband, just having fun. There is no pressure on you to attach some idiot gentleman. That's all your grandmother's idea, not ours. Your father is in complete agreement. Also, you are something of an heiress, so there will be some men drooling on your slippers in hopes of attaching you. You will be careful of any man who goes over the line. Do you understand?"

"Oh yes. Aunt Alex told me that she was thrown at you because her papa needed money desperately, but, she told me, since I'm not in that situation, I can just skip about and smile and flirt with whomever pleases me. Papa kept telling me that I was to waltz and learn how everything worked and remain reasonably modest. Mary Rose wants me to see all the plays. Now that I think about it, Uncle Douglas, I don't think Papa wants me to marry and leave the vicarage until I'm thirty."

"That's possible," Douglas said, and smiled, imagining that he wouldn't want a man near his daughter, if he and Alex had produced one, which they hadn't.

"Grandmother Lydia tells me I must be vigilant or I will end up on the shelf like Aunt Sinjun nearly did. She kept insisting that eighteen was the perfect age to marry."

Douglas laughed. "Bless my mother, at least she will never change. You will have fun, Meggie, that's what it's all about."

The evening of the Ranleigh ball, Alex said as she smoothed her hands over the soft silk of her deep rose ball gown, "I am so pleased that my waistline is finally down to where my waist actually is."

"On the other hand," Douglas said, looking over at his wife, "you always looked splendid in the empire style, with the focus on your endowments."

Meggie wasn't particularly surprised; it had always been so with her aunts and uncles. She saw her uncle's fingers creep toward her aunt's shoulder, pause, then fall back to his side.

After Douglas had seated his two ladies in the North-cliffe carriage, tapped his gloved fist against the roof, he said to Meggie as the carriage rolled forward, "You will be treated very nicely because, to be very honest about it, no one would ever dare to insult one of my family. On the other hand, both Alex and I are rather well liked in society, as is your uncle Ryder and aunt Sophie. You will be your charming self, and if you have a question about how to behave in any given situation, just ask either Alex or me."

"It's still rather scary," Meggie said. "I suspect the balls here are very different from ours in Glenclose-on-Rowan."

"People are the same," Alex said. "It's just the gowns and jewels that are more splendid."

"Some people are idiots," said Douglas.

"And some are not," Alex said. "Just like at home."

"However," Douglas said, "as I told you, if any man does anything that makes you uncomfortable, you will immediately tell him to take himself off. Then you will show me the clod and I will feed him a few choice words."

"Yes, Douglas is quite good at that, although he hasn't had much practice for a long time."

Douglas sighed, crossed his arms over his chest. "Just think, Alex. In a couple of years all the boys will be let loose on London. Can you begin to imagine the sorts of messes they will embroil us in?"

Alex groaned.

Meggie laughed. She thought of their twin boys, James and Jason—the most beautiful males she'd ever seen in her life. She rolled her eyes, thinking of the two of them strolling into a ballroom and hoards of wide-eyed ladies swooning in ecstasy.

Lord and Lady Ranleigh greeted their guests at the bottom of the grand staircase that led up to their pride and joy—a ballroom occupying the entire second floor.

"The first Sherbrooke offspring to appear in Society," Lady Ranleigh said, smiling at Meggie. "You are blessed with your family, my dear. There are many people eager to meet you. I trust you will enjoy yourself."

Meggie said, "Oh yes, ma'am, Aunt Alex says I am to dance holes in my slippers."

Meggie continued to smile, to laugh, to make jests with all sorts of people who were perfectly pleasant to her. Young gentlemen came by to meet her and stayed or asked her to dance. It was just before the midnight dinner that she saw a tall man she knew looked familiar. She cocked her head to one side as she stared at him.

Surely she'd met him before, but where? The tilt of his head, she knew she'd seen him somewhere before. But it wasn't just his air of familiarity that held her in place. It was the oddest thing. Meggie felt the impact of him to her toes, which, she was forced to admit, were on the sore side what with dancing every dance.

She recognized that impact in the deepest part of her. She hadn't forgotten it. It had simply lain dormant for a goodly number of years.

She was still looking toward him when she reached her aunt Alex. Her heart was beating, slow deep thuds. Why wouldn't he turn around? It had to be him, it just had to.

"You are enjoying yourself, love?"

Meggie managed to look away from him a moment. "Oh yes, I just danced with Viscount Glover. He speaks Spanish fluently and wants to enlarge his father's succession houses."

"Hmmm. He is an interesting young man. I believe he lost his wife in childbirth just last year."

Meggie nodded, but she wasn't paying attention. She was staring at that man. "Who is that man, Aunt Alex? The one who is speaking to the three gentlemen beneath that chandelier?"

Uncle Douglas came up behind his wife just then. "What man, Meggie?"

"That one," Meggie said, and watched her uncle turn to look at him. At that moment the man finally turned.

"Well," Douglas said slowly, "this is a pleasant surprise. I hadn't known he was in town."

Meggie was staring. No wonder she'd felt the familiarity, the impact that jarred her to her soul. It was Jeremy Stanton-Greville, Aunt Sophie's younger brother. She had fallen in love with him when she was thirteen years old and he was a wild young man of nearly twenty-four. She'd looked at him with a young girl's full heart and fallen at his feet, at least metaphorically speaking.

Douglas said to her, "I'm surprised you don't recognize him, Meggie, it's Jeremy Stanton-Greville. One of your numerous cousins."

"Oh no, he isn't really my cousin, Uncle Douglas," she said, and was so glad of that fact that she nearly shouted with the relief of it, with the wonder of it. He was finally back in her life, and now she was finally old enough for him. "He's my almost-cousin."

3

MEGGIE LOOKED AT him again, really looked, and she was so excited, she had to really pay attention or she knew she'd stutter herself right out of the ballroom and look like an idiot. "He looks a bit different. Of course it's been a very long time since I last saw him. Goodness, I don't remember him as being so very tall, and so stylish. Was that his laugh? Oh yes, I'm sure it's him laughing. It was a wonderful laugh, all deep and full, don't you think; and—" Meggie pulled back from the precipice and gulped because her aunt was looking at her with a good deal of appalled comprehension.

"Hmmm," said Uncle Douglas, all his attention focused on Meggie now. She'd been the cutest little girl, a benevolent tyrant to her brothers, the ruler of all the male cousins. But she wasn't a little girl any longer. Jeremy Stanton-Greville? There were a lot of years separating them—a good dozen—too many in Douglas's opinion. At least Jeremy wasn't yet married; Douglas would have been notified. "All right, then," he said slowly. "Why don't I fetch Jeremy and we can enjoy dinner together? Get reacquainted?"

"Yes," said Aunt Alex comfortably. "It's always interesting to reminisce, don't you think, Meggie? We haven't seen Jeremy in at least five years. He appears to have become a fine-looking man."

"Yes," Meggie said, never taking her eyes off him. "Do I look all right, Aunt Alex? My gown? My hair? Is my nose too shiny?"

"You look perfect." So much for flirting and just enjoying herself and not husband hunting, Alex thought, seeing her niece's heart in her beautiful Sherbrooke eyes as she stared at Jeremy Stanton-Greville, who had now turned and was speaking to Douglas. He was nearly Douglas's height, well formed, a big man, and his hair was a dark rich brown, his eyes dark as well. Then he smiled and nodded and walked beside Douglas toward them. Alex saw that he limped slightly and remembered that he'd been born with a club foot, but it hadn't slowed him down a bit, according to his brother-in-law, Ryder, who'd seen that he'd learned to fight dirty and ride like a centaur. He'd been a terror, Ryder had proudly said, during his years at Eton.

As Meggie watched him come closer and closer, her stomach pitched wildly. She felt like a fool, a dolt. She couldn't think of a word to say. All she wanted to do was hurl herself at him and beg him to marry her.

Well, perhaps not yet. That would be rushing things just a bit. Maybe tomorrow or even the next day. She cleared her throat. She had to say something, had to charm him, show off her wit, if she could manage to find it.

Oh dear. What would happen now?

At three o'clock in the morning Meggie crawled beneath the thick covers on her bed and turned onto her back. She smiled, an idiot's smile, but it didn't matter. She was thrumming with happiness, with anticipation. Giddiness washed through her veins, and she wanted to shout to the cherubs that adorned the ceiling of her bedchamber, she was so very happy.

Imagine, her very first week in London and she'd met her future husband.

Jeremy Stanton-Greville. Meggie Stanton-Greville. Lady Stanton-Greville. It sounded wonderful. It sounded perfect.

What a beautiful man he was. Just imagine, her almost-cousin, and she'd known him nearly all her life, and here he was in London at exactly the same time she was and surely a sign that he'd been sent here for a specific reason, namely to see a grown-up Meggie Sherbrooke through a man's eyes and throw himself at her feet. Oh yes, the last time he'd seen her, she'd been thirteen—bossy and loud, smacking her brothers and cousins whenever they deserved it, which was often. Not very appetizing memories for him. Her memories of Jeremy were, now that she thought of it, of a young man constantly in motion, constantly on horseback, always racing, windblown, laughing, white teeth. And he'd been full of himself. But it hadn't mattered. She'd loved him the moment he opened his mouth that last time she'd seen him when she was thirteen years old. He'd come with Aunt Sophie for a visit. She'd taken just one quick look and it had been all over for her. She'd not let him out of her sight. Then he'd left and time had passed. Five whole years. And, after all, she was young and there was so much to do, and she'd forgotten about him, about the impact of him. He'd had but to reappear and that impact was back, slamming her hard, right in the heart. Talk about heated blood, hers was boiling her from the inside out. It was entirely too wonderful.

No, evidently, tucked away deep inside her, she hadn't forgotten him entirely. She smiled up into the darkness.

And tonight, there he'd been and everything was different, everything had changed. When he'd taken her hand, when he'd smiled at her showing those lovely white teeth again, she'd wanted to throw herself in his arms. What would happen then—ah, kisses and more kisses. Nothing of that sort had happened, naturally, but to dance with him, she'd feel ready to burst with happiness.

After a few polite phrases had been exchanged, Jeremy had asked Uncle Douglas if he could pay a visit—today, in not more than eight hours from now.

He had another party to attend this night, a pity, but there it was. Just before he left them, he took Meggie's hand, smiled at her yet again from his superior height, and told her she'd become a beauty, and kissed her cheek.

"Young men will take one look at you and fall to their knees," he said.

"I used to line up Max, Leo, and Alec on their knees so Rory could walk over them," she said, and thought, *I only want you on your knees.*

Jeremy burst into laughter.

"Rory got so good at it, he'd beg them to line up for him, but farther apart, so he could leap from one back to the next. Then, of course, the boys lined up so that Cleopatra, one of our racing cats, could practice her leaping by jumping from one to the next."

"I had forgotten about the cat racing. I didn't know you were so involved."

"Oh yes. I'm Mr. Cork's official trainer. He's the current champion, at least until the next meet. We'll see. Cleo's leap gets longer and more timely with each race. I don't remember, do you like cat racing?"

He shook his head. "Not really. I love horses. You must admit that racing cats is rather ridiculous compared to racing horses."

She didn't agree at all, felt as if he'd smacked her, but just very lightly, and said only, "That is a pity. I'm sure you'll come about." She couldn't wait to see to it that he did. She would race cats and he would race his horses. It was a perfect match.

Jeremy said, "That is quite an image—of both the leaping cat and of Rory. How old is Rory now?"

When she fell asleep not five minutes later, Meggie dreamed that Cleo beat Mr. Cork in a race that lasted only three seconds. Cleo had pumped up her back legs, taken two long high leaps and landed over the finish line.

Another sign, Meggie thought when she woke up at nine o'clock the next morning, instantly awake, filled with so much excitement she thought she'd vomit. It was the sort of excitement and fear she'd never felt before in her life. If feeling sick to her stomach was the price, she'd endure it gladly. Yes, Cleo's dream performance was a sign. Two leaps, two graceful soaring leaps, and Meggie would have him.

• • •

Jeremy Stanton-Greville, Baron Greville, of Cardinal House in Fowey, arrived at the Sherbrooke town house at precisely eleven o'clock in the morning.

Darby, only fifty years old, had taken over his butler duties six months before, and he was still basking in his new responsibilities. And finally, the staff recognized his importance. He knew he was awe-inspiring, what with his measured walk, more of a smooth glide really, his dignified set of the shoulders and his incredibly well-pressed black knee pants and white linen.

He had known Jeremy Stanton-Greville since he was nine years old, newly arrived in England from Jamaica, and Mr. Ryder Sherbrooke's brother-in-law.

What a handsome man he'd become. Darby hadn't seen him since he was a carefree young man, wild and free and a new member of the Four Horse Club, wearing their colors, racing to the death.

For the first time since he'd assumed butlerdom, Darby smiled, showing a missing molar.

"It's Darby, isn't it?"

"Yes, my lord."

"Good God, I see you're now in charge of this place. Congratulations." And Jeremy shook Darby's hand, nearly sending the redheaded Darby into a swoon of pleasure.

"Ah, my lord, it's been too long, far too long. I haven't laid an eye on you since—what was it—September of 1815, yes, that was it, there were such celebrations because Napoleon was gone once and for all. How have you been?"

Jeremy smiled. "I have been just fine, Darby, traveling quite a bit, to Jamaica, you know, to my plantation there and then to Baltimore."

"You went to Baltimore? Why ever would you wish to go there?"

Jeremy turned at Meggie Sherbrooke's voice. He turned and smiled at her. "Hello, Meggie. Yes, I was just telling Darby that I spent several years in Jamaica at Camille

Hall, my sugar plantation there. Then I went to Baltimore to stay with James Wyndham and his family. They have a very famous stud and racehorses. I learned an immense amount."

"Surely you already knew an immense amount, Jeremy. After all, you were raised by my uncle Ryder."

He took the white hand she was offering him. "Would you believe it? I learned even more about horse racing and breeding. In addition to racing horses, I want to start a stud at my home in Fowey. I needed to learn everything I could before I began."

At the touch of his hand, Meggie nearly swallowed her tongue. Never in her eighteen years had she felt the slightest bit of anything at all when a boy or a man had touched her—admittedly most of the touching had been done by male relatives and the good Lord knew there was no titillation in that. Jeremy was a relative, but not really. They shared no blood. She couldn't remember his touching her when she was thirteen, except maybe to take her hand when he'd arrived or when he'd left. She could just remember standing about, staring at her god, perfectly willing to worship him from whatever distance was required.

"I suppose there is more money in horse racing than in cat racing," she said.

She looked down at his hand holding hers. She didn't want to release him. He'd stopped talking and was looking at her now, a dark eyebrow cocked up a good inch.

"Oh," Meggie said, and with the greatest reluctance, she let go of his hand.

His head was cocked to one side. "Is your father here?"

She shook her head, took a step closer, then drew up short. Where was her brain? It had shut down, it was that simple. Just looking at him, listening to him speak, watching how he used his hands when he talked, and her brain had moved out, vacated her head.

"No, Father and Mary Rose couldn't leave Glenclose-on-Rowan just yet. Perhaps in a fortnight they will visit London and see me all togged out in my new clothes.

Uncle Douglas and Aunt Alex are in the drawing room. I, ah, heard you speaking to Darby and came to fetch you to them."

Very weak, Meggie, she thought as she saw Darby blink at her, and hoped he would keep his mouth shut. Darby took his duties very seriously and here she was, interfering. Who cared? She took Jeremy's hand again and tugged him after her. "This way."

"You've grown up, Meggie," he said from behind her in a beautiful smooth voice. "You've grown up very fine."

That brought her to an immediate halt. She turned to look up at him. "Thank you. You've grown very tall and handsome. Although I remember you as tall and handsome. I think you were twenty-three or -four when I last saw you."

"Something like that, I guess." He had dark brown eyes. They were twinkling down at her as if he believed her to be flattering him—as a cousin would flatter another cousin.

Well, blessed hell.

"Jeremy, I'm glad you are here." *It almost seems like fate*, but she couldn't say that.

Uncle Douglas took over then, clapping Jeremy on the back, ushering him into to greet Aunt Alex. Meggie stood there a moment, until Darby cleared his throat.

"Miss Meggie, is there something amiss?"

She turned slowly to look at him. "Yes, Darby, there certainly is. I must figure out what to do about it."

"He has become a very nice man, hasn't he?"

Meggie nodded, thinking, *he has become a lot more than just nice. He was a lot more when I was thirteen. Now he's here and he's here for me. Thank you, God.*

Uncle Douglas called out, "Meggie, have Darby fetch us some tea and cakes, won't you?"

"Immediately, Miss Meggie," Darby said, gave her a slight bow, and took himself off to the nether regions of the big house.

The first thing Meggie heard when she stepped into the

drawing room was Aunt Alex saying, "You knew that Meggie was an exceptional horsewoman, didn't you, Jeremy? Ah, here you are, my love. Come and sit beside me and hear what Jeremy has been doing."

Jeremy said to her, "The last time I saw you, Meggie, you were thirteen years old, and you were carrying around little Alec, teaching him the names of all the flowers. I remember asking you the name of one particular pink blossom, and you said it was a lost cause, you couldn't remember, and you'd made up so many names that Alec couldn't remember either. Alec burped, if I remember correctly."

Meggie grinned. "I had promised my father and Mary Rose that if she had the babies I would teach them what was what. The names of flowers, however, defeated me. They still do. To me, a rose is a rose is a rose, all the rest is different smells. Alec is now seven years old, can you believe it? And Rory is four."

"I look forward to seeing your family."

Douglas said, "How long will you be in London, Jeremy?"

Jeremy said, "Well, Uncle Douglas, as it happens, I'm here for a very specific reason. Then I will be returning to my home in Fowey."

Meggie sat forward, words spilling out of her mouth because she couldn't dam them up. "Come, tell us, Jeremy. Spit it out. You're here for my first Season, aren't you?" *You came because you had to come, something powerful brought you here, and now that you've seen me, you know what it is.*

He looked perfectly blank, but just for an instant. "Not only your Season, Meggie." He paused a moment, then looked at his aunt and uncle, opened his mouth just as Darby said from the doorway, "My lord, Cook has sent you her favorite lemon tarts. She informed me that they were Lord Stanton-Greville's favorite."

"Yes, they are," Jeremy said. Conversation was desultory as Alex dispensed the tea and offered the cake plate around.

"They are delicious," Jeremy said. "How is Oliver doing at Kildrummy, Meggie? I haven't received a letter from him in nearly six months."

Meggie said, chuckling, "He is altogether too happy—you can just see him leaping over the sheep killers that haven't yet been filled in—you remember, Jeremy, the huge gouges in the earth that sheep, because they're stupid, have always fallen into? Anyway, he's filled in a number of them over the years. Oh yes, Oliver's very happy. You can just stand there and hear him whistling as he counts the sheep and cows and goats and directing any repairs on Kildrummy and the crofts, see that exuberant smile of his when he greets everyone in the village." She paused a moment, giving everyone a chance to laugh, then added, seeing everything so very clearly now, "Do you know what else—he has announced, just last month, that he is ready to marry."

"Good Lord," Jeremy said, choking on the lemon cake. "Oliver, married? I'd believed him quite content in his single state."

"He is thirty, I believe," said Douglas. "I was leg-shackled at twenty-eight. Oliver is behind schedule and so I have told him. He is ripe."

"Ah," said Jeremy, and grinned a fool's grin, "I am also ripe. Perhaps it is predestined."

"That's a nice thought," Meggie said, and wanted to leap on him.

"Douglas wasn't particularly ripe," Alex said and toasted him with her teacup.

"Just thinking about it makes me want a brandy. Jeremy, will you join me?"

"No, thank you, Uncle Douglas. I must be going. I very much wanted to see you, to see that everything was going well, and I see that it is. And here's little Meggie, all grown up now." He rose, hugged Alex, shook Douglas's hand, and walked to Meggie. She wanted to kiss him. She wanted to take him right down to the floor and kiss him until he was silly with it. She wanted him to moan, something she had heard her father and Mary Rose doing when they didn't think anyone was about. Jeremy took her hand, lingered just a moment—a bloody cousin's linger—nothing more. "I wish you the best during your Season, my dear."

Meggie realized in that moment that Jeremy wasn't even close to feeling about her as she did about him. Well, after all, the last time he had seen her she'd been only thirteen years old, and she shuddered at that thought. He'd already been a young man. And he'd only seen her for the first time in many years just fifteen hours before. She had to give him a bit more time, to build memories she already had of him, and that meant creating the opportunity for him to fall tip over arse. She said with a guileless smile, "Uncle Douglas and Aunt Alex aren't up as early as they used to be"—clearly a lie of the first order—"and I love to ride early in the morning before everyone is out and about. I would like to go riding with you tomorrow morning, Jeremy. Could you be here at seven o'clock? Is that too early?"

Jeremy said without hesitation, "I should like that very much. I would be delighted to observe an exceptional horsewoman in action. Tomorrow morning, Meggie."

He squeezed her hand. And then he was gone. She heard him say something to Darby, heard the front door close.

Meggie said to her aunt and uncle, "He was only here for fifteen minutes." Then she left the drawing room, humming.

"I don't like this, Alex," Douglas said and downed his brandy. "I don't like this at all. He is too old for her. Indeed, I don't think he even saw her—you know what I mean?"

"I wonder," Alex said, nodding, "what he was going to tell us before Darby came in."

"I don't know. Maybe I don't want to know. Hopefully it was something to do with his new stud. I heard he was dealing with Marcus Wyndham. Now, there is a man I would gladly drink with." A black brow suddenly shot up. "When did we become too old to ride in the morning?

All right, so we didn't ride this morning. On the other hand we didn't get to our bed until nearly three o'clock."

His wife rose and walked to him. She was wearing a lovely soft pink silk dress that was, he saw, cut far too low, displaying too much of a magnificent bosom. She touched her fingertips to his sleeve and said, eyes twinkling, "And then you were resolved to show me an excess of affection, Douglas."

Douglas looked at her barely covered breasts, grunted, and poured himself another snifter of brandy. His fingers still tingled at the thought of touching her. It was amazing.

4

$\mathcal{M}$EGGIE WORE HER new dark blue riding habit with
its beautifully worked lace spilling out over the bodice,
fitted at the waist with a narrow cloth belt. The skirts were
full and looked quite elegant spread around her as she sat
atop Eleanor's back, her black boots peeping out, waiting
for Jeremy Stanton-Greville. Stanton-Greville. She'd always thought two last names sounded rather absurd, but
realized that if everything came to pass as she wanted it
to, as she prayed it would, why, she herself would have
two names as well. She started, surprised at herself. *Meggie Stanton-Greville*. Yes, it sounded simply perfect. She
pulled in a deep breath and wanted to be sick, but she
wasn't about to deny it. She wanted to marry Jeremy
Stanton-Greville and she'd only known him as a man for
less than a day. It was madness.

No, no, it wasn't as if he were a stranger to her, he
wasn't. She'd known he was hers from that day when she
was only thirteen years old. So she had forgotten him for
five years. He'd probably forgotten her as well.

Now that she thought about it, deeply, she decided that
two names had become, overnight, quite distinguished.

She yearned for two names.

It was exactly seven-thirty in the morning, a dreary cold
morning, with fat gray rain clouds hanging low overhead.
To Meggie, the gray clouds were lovely, the morning was

perfect, holding more promise than the day before, more delight than just an hour before.

Yes, it would rain, but not for several hours, that was what Old Hamish had told her. He was the head stable lad, all of sixty years old, gnarly as an old oak and very smart about the weather. Surely she would have Jeremy out of the park, off his horse, and under a lovely romantic shelter before it started raining. All she needed was two hours, maybe less. She was committed; she was focused. She just had to set Jeremy thinking on a straight line, one that led directly to her. She just had to assist him to truly understand why he was really here in London. A distant boom of thunder sounded.

Ah, let it rain, she didn't care. But her riding habit, her beautiful new hat. No, only Jeremy mattered, and how he would feel when she poured out her heart to him. Not immediately, no, it would surprise him, perhaps make him wary of a girl who professed to have fallen in love with him when she was thirteen. No, she would hold back until the time was right, until he looked at her and simply *knew* she was his mate.

She looked up to see two people riding toward her.

She looked away, lips pursing. Well, blessed hell, she didn't want two strangers anywhere near her. She just wanted Jeremy, and she wanted him alone.

The two horses kept coming straight at her.

Meggie cocked her head to one side and looked now, really looked.

It was a man and a woman. The man, who looked like a bloody centaur riding a magnificent black barb, was Jeremy Stanton-Greville. As for the woman, curse her eyes, she was young. She was riding very close to Jeremy.

Meggie felt her heart begin to pound, slow thumping strokes. Her breath suddenly *whooshed* out when she realized she'd forgotten to breathe. She waited, sitting very still atop Eleanor.

Jeremy waved to her. In just another short moment he and the young woman were directly in front of her, not more than three feet from Eleanor's nose.

"Meggie," Jeremy said, riding his horse just a bit closer, extending his hand to take hers briefly, "I am so glad you're here. I wasn't sure that you would be here this morning. It's on the chilly side, you know."

"Yes," Meggie said, "I know. I wanted to see you." But she wasn't looking at him in that moment, she was staring at the most beautiful young lady she'd ever seen in her life, who had also ridden a big closer. Her glossy black hair was arranged in artful tight curls around her face with the rest of it pulled up atop her head into an Adonis knot. So much black hair, thicker than a female deserved, just barely covered by a clever little riding hat with a curling feather that caressed her white cheek. Ah, and such lovely white skin. She was more beautiful than a woman should be. Meggie wouldn't be surprised if her bloody name were Helen.

The goddess smiled, a quite lovely smile that reached those incredible blue eyes of hers.

Jeremy said, "Charlotte, I would like you to meet one of my favorite cousins, Meggie Sherbrooke. Meggie, this is Charlotte Beresford, my betrothed."

Betrothed. In that moment everything in Meggie closed down. She'd heard the term *coup de foudre*—struck by lightning, to signify falling in love upon first seeing someone. This was a different sort of lightning. This *coup de foudre* sliced right to her heart and split it apart, shattering it into a million pieces.

"How do you do," Meggie said in another's voice as the real Meggie lay there beneath Eleanor's hooves, mortally wounded. Both parts of her wished the heavens would burst open, right this instant, and every fat cloud would dump every ounce of rain until she drowned in it. No, until that damnable young lady named Charlotte drowned in it.

"I am very fine, thank you, Miss Sherbrooke," said the young lady. She grinned toward Jeremy and lightly tapped her riding crop to his sleeve. "I have told Jeremy that he comes from such a distinguished family. His uncle Douglas is known by simply everyone, you know. I believe your father is the vicar who is also Baron Barthwick of Kildrummy, is that right, Miss Sherbrooke?"

"Yes," Meggie said, and hated Charlotte Beresford all the way to the soles of her lovely pale gray boots, that perfectly matched her riding gown and that damned artful little hat she wore.

"I have been told that your other uncle, Mr. Ryder Sherbrooke, Jeremy's brother-in-law, has even taken a seat in the House of Commons. So quaint for a younger son, don't you think?"

"Not quaint at all," Meggie said.

Jeremy, who was looking a bit puzzled, hastened to say in the abrupt silence, "My brother-in-law hates to see children abused. He works tirelessly to abolish child labor."

Charlotte said, "I am eager to meet him. You and I haven't spoken of it, but I must say that I feel the same way. It makes one want to weep to think of the poor little ones forced to work at looms for untold hours on end." She nodded to Jeremy but continued to Meggie, "Jeremy is taking me to Chadwyck House next week to meet his sister and his brother-in-law. And also to Brandon House to meet all the Beloved Ones."

Meggie wished Charlotte would shut her lovely pink-lipped mouth, particularly since everything that had emerged was filled with kindness and charm.

Damn the woman.

She was Jeremy's betrothed.

"Meggie," Jeremy said now, pulling his gelding in beside Eleanor and motioning Charlotte to pull into the other side of her, "Shall we ride now? You and I can talk about your wild and fractious childhood tonight." He paused, patted her hand. "I wanted you so much to meet Charlotte."

"How very thoughtful of you, Jeremy," Meggie said, that distant Meggie, not the Meggie who lay in pieces on the ground. When it began to rain a few minutes later, she didn't even blink, just smiled at Jeremy, at Charlotte, and said, "It is too inclement to ride. Goodbye."

"Until this evening," Jeremy called after her. She didn't

look back. Her beautiful new riding habit was wet, her riding hat quite ruined, when she finally walked into the Sherbrooke town house. Darby took one look at her and shouted, "My lady!"

When Alex came out of the library to see Meggie standing there, dripping on the beautiful marble entrance hall, she knew something very bad had happened. Not being a dolt, she knew it had to do with Jeremy Stanton-Greville.

Meggie didn't want to see either Jeremy or Charlotte again, actually, for the rest of her life. No, just Charlotte.

She'd loved him for so long. It didn't matter that she hadn't particularly thought about him for years at a time, all the feelings she'd birthed for him so long ago, had just remained dormant, waiting for her to grow up, waiting to burst into bloom when she was ready to take a husband. And there he'd been. As if Fate had plunked him right down in front of her.

Only he hadn't waited for her.

At that moment she decided she would never again look at a man with anything resembling liking. She would become the premier cat trainer in the entire sport. She would devote her life to the cats and to her parents and brothers. That gave her a bit of a pause. No, it would work. It would be fine. Perhaps when Lady Dauntry retired, she would mount the dais at the McCaulty racetrack and shout, "Free the Cats!"

She dressed beautifully for dinner. She knew even before she stood in front of her dressing table, ready for company, that she couldn't possibly look finer than she did at this moment. She gave herself a ghastly smile in her mirror. Timma, Aunt Alex's maid, said from behind her, "The pale pink, it is delightful on you, Miss Sherbrooke."

"Thank you, Timma."

"And your lovely hair, I have done an excellent job arranging it, just so." Timma snapped her fingers.

Meggie tried for a smile, but couldn't find one. "Thank you, Timma."

When she went downstairs, Darby was there, as if he'd been waiting specifically for her, she thought, which he had, and allowed him to lead her into the drawing room.

Jeremy Stanton-Greville and Miss Charlotte Beresford were there. Uncle Douglas, unbeknownst to her, had invited him to dinner. Jeremy saw her and immediately jumped to his feet. He said as he walked quickly to her, "You are not thirteen years old any longer, Meggie." He kissed her hand, hugged her, then stepped back. "You look quite beautiful."

"Thank you, Jeremy."

But she saw that his eyes couldn't even remain on her face for more than an instant, perhaps two, before swinging back to Charlotte, who looked like a princess, sitting there, her lovely dark blue silk skirts fanned out around her, her décolletage not comparing to Aunt Alex's, but still, all that young very white flesh on display would make a man bite his tongue before swallowing it.

She nodded toward Charlotte. "Good evening, Miss Beresford."

Charlotte trilled a laugh. "Come now, we will soon be related. Do call me Charlotte."

Meggie couldn't say, *"No, you miserable hussy with your big breasts, I would like to shoot an arrow through your heart."* So she merely smiled and nodded. "No, we won't be related. Jeremy is not a blood cousin," she said and turned her full and complete attention to her aunt and uncle.

Meggie didn't remember much of the evening when she rode Eleanor the following morning with her aunt and uncle. She wasn't remembering much of this, either. She kept her head down close to Eleanor's sleek brown neck and let the wind rip through her hair.

She wanted to go home but knew she couldn't. It would distress her father and Mary Rose, and Uncle Douglas and Aunt Alex, particularly since they'd been so delighted to present her. They'd gone to so much trouble, smoothing her way, ensuring that she would have a grand time during her first Season. And the very worst was that they would also know what had happened and Meggie didn't think she would ever live that down. So she would remain and she would enjoy her Season. Blessed hell, she would enjoy every moment of the next two months.

She bit her lip to keep from crying. She would never cry for any man again.

She didn't believe her aunt and uncle realized her feelings for Jeremy, which made her profoundly grateful that she hadn't said anything. She had to be merry, laugh, tell them how very much fun she was having. Meggie wanted to howl to the ever-present bloated gray clouds overhead.

Meggie Sherbrooke was declared an *original* that Season of 1823. She was the most sought-after young lady in all that crop of debutantes, and feted until she should have been heady from her success, and become quite conceited. Her admirers were legion—that was the ridiculous word Meggie had heard Lady Ranleigh say about the gentlemen who never gave her peace, and she would have laughed, if she'd cared one little bit, but she didn't.

Uncle Douglas received four offers of marriage, each of them from excellent gentlemen, and each he discussed with Meggie. If any had interested her, then he would have sent the young man she'd selected to go see Tysen, but Meggie just shook her head when he presented them to her.

"Lord Marcham's son, Lancelot, is quite unexceptionable, Meggie, and appears quite taken with you. He really cannot help his unfortunate name."

"No, thank you, Uncle Douglas," she said, and that was that, similar words used to decline each of the other offers.

Douglas wrote to Tysen and Mary Rose at least once a week, his early letters filled with Meggie's successes, then they were filled with Meggie's disinterest in any of the gentlemen who praised her very nice Sherbrooke blue eyes, her lovely Sherbrooke hair, her somewhat distracted wit.

Reverend Tysen and Mary Rose arrived in London the final week of May, both of them very worried.

Meggie leaned against her father, felt his hands lightly stroking her back, up and down, and it felt so very comforting, and she whispered against his neck, "Please, Papa, I want to go home."

He loosed his hold and held her in the circle of his arms. "You met a man who did not return your affections. I'm very sorry about that." That was all he said, nothing more, and Meggie wondered how he could know. She prayed he wouldn't ever find out which man she'd wanted who didn't want her.

"Perhaps so," she said. "Papa, I want to go home."

"All right, love. Let us show Mary Rose some of the sights, just a week—she loves the theatre, you know—and then we will go home."

On June second the Sherbrookes returned to Glenclose-on-Rowan to the vicarage.

In October every Sherbrooke in England traveled to Eagle's Chase, in Somerset, the Beresfords' country estate, to attend the wedding of Charlotte Beresford and Jeremy Stanton-Greville.

It was carried off in grand style. Every Beloved One was there, and to everyone's amusement, all fifteen of the children applauded when the vicar said Jeremy could kiss his bride.

5

March 1824
Glenclose-on-Rowen

MEGGIE SHERBROOKE WALKED out of the church in the wake of her stepmother, Mary Rose Sherbrooke, Alec on her left side and Rory on her right side, holding her hand. She pulled him back so they could take their place in the vicar's receiving line. Rory's little arm was dry, his face flushed with joy and health, thank God. Just his hands were sticky.

It was a difficult time for the town. Three children had died of a fever during the past week, the cause unknown, and all three funerals had taken place at the same time, three days before. Tysen had spent a great deal of his time with the grieving parents. And today, Sunday morning, every parent was worried sick. They'd all come to church today because they needed reassurance. Her father's sermon had been both moving and practical, which had brought every parent in the congregation a measure of peace and a sense of control, which was desperately needed.

He'd said in his deep, reaching voice, "I know that all of you are afraid that your own children will be struck down. I know that I look at my own boys and pray devoutly that God will spare them. Then I realized that I am not helpless in this, that God has given me a brain and good measure of common sense and the determination to face what I must. Naturally I, as well as you, want to guard my children as best I can. I have spoken at length with Dr. Dreyfus. He believes that we must all be vigilant, that the fever could strike again. He wants us all to keep our children at home during this next week, keep them warm and calm and quiet. They will probably grow bored and you will want to strangle them, but you must endure." He smiled as there was a bit of laughter from his congregation. "I would only add that we must pray to God that it will be enough.

"God has given us all the strength, the fortitude, the ability to face illness, to face death, when need be. None of us are alone in this. Dr. Dreyfus will be visiting each family beginning this afternoon, to examine each child. As a congregation, as a town, we will survive this."

His closing prayer had made Meggie's heart ache and gave her a measure of hope.

The congregation spoke in low voices as they passed the vicar and his family, who stood in a line, shaking everyone's hand as they passed, and patted each child.

Leo was home for several days, down from Oxford to visit with his family for the first time in over two months. He was still horse mad and he had plans to join his cousin Jeremy Stanton-Greville at his racing stud in Fowey, to learn the business, which, Jeremy had written, put them in a somewhat unusual situation, since he was still learning the business as well. Leo had also told them that Jeremy's wife, Charlotte, was expecting Jeremy's heir.

Meggie had said nothing upon hearing that. Nor did she say anything about her brother's plans, not that Leo had asked her for her opinion.

As for Max Sherbrooke, their Latin scholar, who had finally surpassed his stepmother in his knowledge of everyday Latin, he'd announced that he planned to become a man of the cloth, like his father. There was, Tysen said, and blessedly so, a very big difference between father and son—Max brought laughter into the room with him, just like his uncle Ryder, and laughter was a wonderful thing, only discovered by Tysen after he'd met Mary Rose. Tysen was very pleased, knowing his son would bring joy to his future congregation from his very first sermon.

Meggie looked up at the sound of a stranger's voice, a man's voice that she'd never before heard, and she saw that indeed, she had never seen him before either. He was young, perhaps in his mid-twenties, and he was tall, taller than her father, possibly as tall as Uncle Douglas, and he was dark as a bandit on a midnight raid, dark hair, dark eyes, his complexion swarthy. There was no question that he'd spent a lot of his recent time at sea.

He was also taller and darker than Jeremy, whose wife was going to have a baby. No, no, put away that lump full of pain.

Rory tugged on her skirt. She looked down to see him holding the remains of a stick of candy Mary Rose had given him to keep him quiet during his father's sermon in his left hand, no longer in his right, as was always the instruction from his mother. His left hand was now as sticky as his right hand and now so was the skirt of her beautiful new gown.

"Oh, no. Rory, just look at my skirt. How could you?"

Rory shook his head, big eyes ready to weep. He whispered that he didn't know how he could have done that. He began frantically sucking his fingers, saying between his fingers and licks, "I'm sorry, Meggie," then he gripped her skirt and brought it to his mouth. He began sucking hard on the sticky material.

Meggie couldn't help herself. Her irritation with him evaporated. She burst into laughter, swung Rory up in her arms, and said, "You little sweetheart, how can I ever be upset with you when you are so cute?"

"I wonder," the man said slowly, his voice pensive, looking at her directly now, "if my mother ever held me like that and told me I was a sweetheart and cute. Somehow, I doubt it."

Meggie turned, still laughing, and said, "I'm not his mother and that, I believe, saves his adorable self from a hiding."

Tysen said easily, "Lord Lancaster, this is my daughter, Meggie, and one of my sons, Rory. The candy does work to keep him quiet during the service, but occasionally he forgets, and this is the result. Meggie, my dear, this is Lord Lancaster. He has just returned to England to assume his responsibilities and see to his property."

"Oh," Meggie said, "Lord Lancaster—how odd that sounds. Your father was an old man, you see, and quite deaf toward the end of his life. I am sorry that your father died, my lord." She paused a moment, and added as she hugged Rory closer, "However, he died some seven months ago, and you weren't here then."

"No, I was not."

And no explanation forthcoming, she thought, because it was none of her business. He'd put her very nicely in her place. But it was strange nonetheless. She'd never even heard Lord Lancaster himself mention that he had a son, although she remembered now that there had been an occasional mention of an heir by a servant. To the best of her knowledge, the new Lord Lancaster had never even lived with his father at Bowden Close. It was a pity that such things happened in families.

"Welcome home, my lord," she said, gave him an absent nod, and carried Rory away, back to the vicarage, Rory's mother on his other side, wiping his hands with a handkerchief dampened from the well that stood on the edge of the cemetery. When Old Lord Lancaster had finally shucked off his mortal coil, a heart seizure Dr. Dreyfus had said, Meggie had mourned him perfunctorily since she'd known him all her life. Why, she wondered, had the son never visited his father?

She turned her attention back to Rory, whose mother was playing hide-and-seek between his now clean fingers. She chanced to turn around some twenty steps later to see Lord Lancaster standing quite still, his arms folded over his chest, staring after her.

He was tall, she thought again, and darker than a moon-less night, and there was an edge to that darkness of his. It was as if he were seeing all them clearly but he himself was masked, hiding in the shadows. She was succumbing to fancies, not a very appealing thing for a lady who would doubtless become the village spinster.

Meggie saw Thomas Malcombe, Lord Lancaster, again the following Friday evening when the Strapthorpes held a small musical soir-ée—pronounced quite in the French way—the name Mrs. Sturbridge stubbornly held to de-spite her spouse's contempt.

Mrs. Strapthorpe, far more voluble now that her daugh-ter, Glenda, had married and left home, immediately pulled Mary Rose and Meggie aside and said in a rush, bristling with complacency and pride, "*He* doesn't accept invitations, Mrs. Bittley told me, a recluse he is, she as-sured me, possibly he's now ashamed he never visited his dear father in a good twenty years. Some folk remember a little boy and Lady Lancaster, but they were both gone very quickly." She lowered her voice. "I heard it said that the earl divorced his wife. What do you think of that? But now this splendid young man—an earl—is here, at my invitation, because, and so I told Mr. Strapthorpe, I wrote an ever-so-elegant note to him and he accepted my invi-tation with an ever-so-elegant note of his own—ah, his hand is quite refined, let me assure you—and now Lord Lancaster is coming, can you imagine? Yes, I snagged him. He is ever so handsome and obviously quite proud. No, don't mistake me, he isn't at all standoffish, he simply knows his own worth and expects others to know it, too. Yes, he is coming and I believe it is because of my elegant invitation and my brilliant idea to hold a musical soir-ée. A gentleman of his distinction would most assuredly be drawn to an elegant offering. Yes, this evening is tailor-made for his tastes. I have brought in a soprano, all the way from Bath—she last performed at Lord Laver's mag-nificent town house on the Royal Crescent—and she strikes a high C with great regularity and astounding verve. Such a pity Glenda is wed and far away, and only to a viscount, more's the pity, but she wouldn't wait, particularly since our dear Reverend Sherbrooke was gobbled right up by dear Mary Rose, so there it is. Of course she couldn't have waited for Lord Lancaster since she is nearly his own age, because, for a lady, unmarried at such an advanced age would announce to the world that there were serious problems with either her father's purse or her face."

Mrs. Strapthorpe, after this outpouring, took a long overdue breath, shook out her purple satin skirts, and marched to the punch bowl, to guard it from her spouse, who was fat, sported three chins, and loved to drink until he was snoring too loudly in his chair. "So distracting for guests," Mrs. Strapthorpe was wont to say.

"She has always amazed me," Meggie said, staring after their hostess. Then she giggled. "She spoke nearly a complete chapter in a book, Mary Rose, and she never lost herself between commas. Remember when you and Papa were first married and he brought you here for a visit?"

Mary Rose shuddered.

"And Glenda ordered him to take her to the conservatory—that miserably hot smelly room—and demanded to know how it had happened that he had wed you and not her?"

"I wanted, actually, to dance at her wedding," Mary Rose said, smiling now at the memory. "At last she would no longer send her sloe-eyed looks at your father. Do you know that she has three children now?"

"These things happen," Meggie said, grinning. "After all, you and Papa have given me Alec and Rory." She remembered that Jeremy would be a father soon. But not the father of her child. No, she wasn't about to think about that, she wasn't.

"Ah, the musical soirée begins. There is your poor papa, trapped by Squire Bittley, whose wife didn't manage to snag his lordship for her very refined dinner party last week."

Meggie said, "Smart man. Now, Mrs. Bittley—that old

battle-axe—has, thank the good Lord, quite come around where you are concerned."

"Yes, she is even pleasant to me most of the time now, unlike my own dear mother-in-law, your blessed grandmother, who still roundly tells Tysen he is wedded to a savage with vulgar hair. And then she looks at Alec, whose hair is also red." Mary Rose was still grinning as she lightly touched her fingertips to her husband's sleeve. Tysen turned immediately to take her hand.

Meggie sat beside her stepmother, in an aisle chair. She hated it when a singer pumped her lungs up to blast out a high C. If need be, if the high notes rattled her too much, she would simply slip out and walk in the gardens.

She did slip out after the sixth high C nearly burst her eardrums and made her toes cramp from quivering so much. She knew the Strapthorpe house very well and walked down the main corridor into the conservatory, Mr. Strapthorpe's pride and joy, the only room that everyone avoided because of the heat and the overpowering scent of the wildly blooming flowers. She imagined the garden was nearly full of escapees by now.

She was totally taken aback when he said from behind her, "I assume this is your sanctuary?"

Meggie turned so quickly she nearly tripped over her gown. She grabbed hold of a rose stem to steady herself, then yipped when a thorn punctured the pad of her finger.

"What a clever way of putting it, my lord. Oh dear, I have stabbed myself."

"The soprano drove me away as well. I'm sorry to startle you. Let me see what you did to yourself."

Lord Lancaster pulled a white handkerchief from his pocket, but he didn't hand it to her, he just picked up her hand, saw a fat drop of blood welling up, and lifted the finger to his mouth. He sucked away the blood.

Meggie didn't move, didn't breathe. He'd actually sucked the blood off her finger? Then licked her finger? How very odd that was. It felt very strange. Not bad, just very strange.

She stared up at him, still silent, as he then wrapped

his handkerchief tightly around her finger, and pressed his thumb against the wound. She was very tall for a woman, but still, she had to look up, a very goodly distance. Was he as handsome as Mrs. Strapthorpe had said? He could have been, she supposed, but the point was that he wasn't Jeremy.

She said, frowning slightly, "I have read that vampires suck blood. Usually, in the novels I have read, it's fangs sunk in a person's neck at midnight and there is a good deal of drama involved."

He laughed, a warm deep sound that sounded dark as his midnight hair. "Yes, I have read about vampires as well. However, since you met me at a church during the day, then you know that I cannot be one." He gave her a big grin. "See, no fangs either. There, that should do it. I'm sorry I startled you, Miss Sherbrooke."

Lovely white teeth, just like Jeremy's. No, she had to stop thinking about him. She shook her head as she said, "I will be fine. I did manage to hold on until that final high C nearly knocked me out of my chair."

"Such impressive lungs are fashionable, I'm told."

"Where?"

He laughed again, then paused, as if surprised that he'd laughed. "Why, do you know that I'm not really sure? I haven't lived much in England in the past five years. I suppose I believed that the ninnies in London lauded such performances."

"I spent just one Season in London, my lord. As far as I could see, there were very few true devotées of Italian sopranos. Most people I saw on those evenings were polite enough to endure in stoic silence. Ah, but Mrs. Strapthorpe believed that her musical soirée was just the thing to induce you to attend, that and her elegant invitation to you. She is very pleased with herself."

"Good Lord. Actually, though, I wished to attend."

"But not for the wailing soprano?"

"No, I didn't attend because of the music."

Meggie hoisted up an eyebrow.

"My name is Thomas Malcombe."

The eyebrow remained hoisted.

He laughed, couldn't help himself. She appeared to be utterly uninterested in him. Without conceit, he realized she was the first female to be indifferent to him since he'd come to manhood. It was a rather appalling realization, this unconscious conceit, and one that made him want to laugh at himself.

"All right. I came because I wanted to meet my neighbors, people who had known my father."

"I'm Meggie Sherbrooke," she said finally, and hoisted her left eyebrow again. "You aren't telling the truth, my lord. If I may risk offending you, I daresay you don't care a fig about anyone in Glenclose-on-Rowan."

"Meggie, it's a nice name. You're quite wrong."

"It's short for Margaret. No one has ever called me Margaret, thank goodness. That's a Mother Superior's name. I would have preferred something exotic, like Maigret, but it was not to be. No, I really don't think I'm wrong. If I am wrong, then I have offended you, and I apologize."

"You really are a Meggie, never a Margaret. I accept your apology, for it is merited. I understand you train racing cats."

"Yes." She saw a glass sitting beside an orchid that looked overwatered. Its leaves were suddenly trembling. Probably the soprano had hit more high notes. "Actually, my little brother Alec is a cat whisperer."

"I have never known of a cat whisperer."

"It is a very rare occurrence, and all agree that Alec is blessed. It still remains to be seen if the gift will mature with him. But ever since he was a very small boy, the cats in our mews would gather around him, very happy to just sit and listen to him talk, which he did, all the time. He is at present assisting my brother Leo train our calico racer, Cleopatra, to improve her leaps. Alec believes she doesn't yet have the proper motivation. As a cat whisperer, he will determine what it is she wants and provide it, if possible."

"I should like to see him in action. How old is he?"

"Alec is seven now."

"Cat racing is an amazing thing, really unknown outside of England. I understand that some French devotees of the sport introduced cat races there, but the French were, evidently, too emotional, too uncontrolled, and so the cats never could get the hang of what was expected of them."

Meggie laughed, then shrugged her shoulders as if to say, what can you expect? He smiled again. She said, "At the McCaulty racetrack, all the cats would desert their owners in a moment if Alec called to them. He must be very careful not to unwittingly seduce them."

"When are the cat races held? Surely now it is too cold."

"They begin again in April and run through October."

"And you are a trainer."

"Oh yes, for a long time now. You can call me the boss."

"Ah, you're the one who makes all final decisions, decides which techniques are the most efficacious, the overlord trainer?"

"I like the sound of that. I will tell my brothers that my new title is overlord. They can drop the trainer part. I will demand that they use my new title or I will make them very sorry." He looked very interested, and so Meggie added, "As a matter of fact, I did spend one entire summer at Lord Mountvale's racing mews being tutored by the Harker brothers." She lowered her voice into a confidence. "They are the ones who developed the technique of the Flying Feather."

"I have heard of the Harker brothers. I understand they have a special intuition when it comes to selecting champion racers. What is the Flying Feather technique?"

"Curled feathers are tied to the end of a three-foot pole. It is waved in a clockwise motion—it must always be clockwise, at no less than a six-foot distance. It evidently has a mesmerizing effect. Goodness, I hadn't intended to tell you all about the Flying Feather technique; it is still supposed to be a secret. I am considering adopting it when I have a proper candidate. Ah, listen, I don't hear anything. It is a good sign," she added, pointing to the orchid, "its leaves are no longer quivering from the vibrations of her voice."

He laughed, just couldn't help himself. He couldn't recall having laughed so much with one single human being. Life had always been rather difficult.

And Meggie thought it was as if he laughed only when he planned to and surely that was rather calculated and cold-blooded. She watched him closely as he said, "Actually, I set that glass there beside the orchid so I would know when it was safe to return to the drawing room. It isn't trembling either now." He smiled down at her. "Let's see if your finger has stopped bleeding yet."

He unwound the handkerchief and lifted her hand to inspect the finger. "Yes, it has."

Meggie said, "Thank you, my lord. Perhaps I don't know all the ways of the world, but I have never before had anyone suck my blood. Or lick my finger."

He felt a lurch in his gut; it was lust and it hit him hard. He looked at her closely, realizing that she didn't understand the teasing promise of her guileless words, didn't realize that they promised, on the surface at least, a woman's very pleasurable skills. No, she was outspoken, a vicar's daughter, just turned nineteen. "No?" he said slowly, then added, "Then I have added to your education."

She said abruptly, "My father will wonder where I am," and she turned to go. "Sharing sanctuary was pleasant, my lord."

She was just going to leave him? Another blow to his manhood. "Miss Sherbrooke, a moment please. Will you ride with me tomorrow morning?"

That got her attention, but she didn't hesitate, just said pleasantly, "I thank you for the invitation, my lord, but no, I don't want to ride with you tomorrow morning."

He looked as she'd slapped him, as if he simply couldn't believe her gall in turning him down. He looked, quite simply, flummoxed. She wanted to smile at his obvious male conceit, but she didn't. She just wanted to leave. She realized now that she shouldn't have remained in here, alone with him. He had gotten the wrong idea about her. She didn't want any attention from him, she didn't want any attention from any man. She wouldn't have stayed in here with him if she'd been in London, but this was her home. No matter, she'd been wrong.

He saw her withdraw completely from him. He didn't understand it. She'd been so confiding, so natural. But no longer. Despite her lack of enthusiasm, he persevered. "I understand from my steward, a very old man with fingers that tap by themselves when the weather is going to turn bad, that it will be unseasonably warm tomorrow morning, a fine morning for a ride."

"Mr. Hengis is famed for his weather predictions in these parts. I did not know about the tapping fingers. I hope it will be a fine morning and you will enjoy yourself. As for me, no thank you, my lord. I must go now."

He said as she turned to leave the conservatory, "I understand you enjoyed your first Season in London last spring. Do you intend to return to London in April?"

"No," she said, not turning to face him. She could feel his frustration, pouring off him in waves, and something else. Why did he wish to be with her so badly? It made no sense. "Goodbye, my lord."

"My name is Thomas." She would swear she heard a *damn you* under his breath.

"Yes," she said, "I know," and left the Strapthorpe conservatory with its dizzying smells and hair-wilting heat.

He stood there, watching the back of her head as she walked quickly out of the overly warm room. Lovely hair, he thought, blondish brownish hair with every color in-between thrown in, the same hair as the vicar's, her father. Their eyes were the same light blue as well. He sighed, then left the conservatory some minutes after her. Truth be told, he was getting nauseated from the overpowering mix of all the flowers.

He met several guests in the large entrance hall. Meggie Sherbrooke wasn't among them. Damn her. He wasn't a troll. What was wrong with her? He was polite and charming to everyone before he took his leave.

Perhaps she didn't ride. Yes, perhaps that was it and she was ashamed to admit it. He would think of something else. She was nineteen years old; for a girl she could have been long married by now, well, at least a year or so. As for himself, he was rich and young and healthy and now he even sported a title. What more could a girl possibly want?

She was a vicar's daughter, for God's sake.

And she trained racing cats.

6

$\mathcal{M}$EGGIE WAS PLAYING with Rory, telling him stories about famous cat champions from years past. The most famous of all the cat racers in this century was Gilly of Mountvale mews, who had died of extreme old age some two years before.

"No one had much of a chance when Gilly was racing," she was saying as she handed Rory a small cat carved in cherry, painted in Gilly's distinctive black, gray, and white colors. "See how high his tail is? Racers always carry their tails high. I'm told it means they're very proud, that they know their own worth, and they are very pleased with the world and their place in it."

"Meggie?"

"Yes, love?"

"I don't feel very good."

Meggie felt fear so strong that she couldn't breathe for a moment. Automatically she laid the flat of her palm against his forehead. He was roasting. The fever. Somehow he'd gotten the fever. They'd all been so careful, kept both Alec and Rory home, entertained them endlessly, taken such care, and still he'd gotten ill.

She lifted him in her arms, no mean feat because Rory was quite good-sized for his age. "Let's go see your mama."

He didn't try to pull away, as was his wont, for he was

a very independent little boy, no, he became boneless in her arms, his cheek resting on her shoulder. It scared Meggie spitless.

Meggie was praying frantically as she quickly walked from the nursery downstairs to the drawing room. Both her father and Mary Rose were there with his curate, Mr. Samuel Pritchert.

"Mary Rose," she said quietly from the door. Mary Rose looked up. The smile on her face froze because she knew, oh yes, she knew immediately that something was very wrong, wrong with Rory. Rory was ill, he had the fever. She said blankly, "Oh no, not Rory. Oh no, Tysen."

Tysen immediately went to Meggie and lifted Rory off her shoulder. "What's this, my boy? You are feeling a bit pecked?" Tysen felt his cheeks, his forehead, and felt fear cramp his guts. "All right," he said, all calm and easy, "I'm going to give you to your mother and be right back. You just rest, Rory."

"Yes, Papa. I don't feel good."

"I know. But you will be pulling on Meggie's hair again in no time at all." He hugged his son against him, then laid his palm against his cheek.

Tysen then lightly touched his palm to Mary Rose's cheek. Much cooler than his son's. "It will be all right. I'm going to fetch Dr. Dreyfus. I'll be back as soon as I can."

Tysen had never moved so fast in his life. He didn't realize that Meggie was trotting beside him he was so locked into himself, so frightened he wanted to curse loud and long to keep the awful fear at bay.

"He will be all right, Papa, you'll see." Meggie was panting, running now, and everyone got out of their way. They arrived at Dr. Dreyfus's cottage in just under seven minutes, out of breath, nearly beside themselves.

Dr. Dreyfus, Mrs. Midderd told them, was seeing to the Clay boy, no, not the fever, none of those this week, thank the good Lord, and thank you, Vicar, for all your prayers. No, the Clay boy had broken his leg, something very very serious.

"How long as he been gone, Mrs. Midderd?"

"At least three hours, Vicar. What is the matter?"

"It is my son, Rory. He has the fever."

Mrs. Midderd, a former Catholic, converted to the Anglican church upon her marriage to Mr. Midderd some thirty years before, crossed herself.

"I will send him to you immediately upon his return, Vicar."

Back at the Vicarage, both Tysen and Meggie stood at the end of Rory's bed watching Mary Rose bathe his small face. He was flushed, he whispered to his mother that his bones ached as he clutched her hand.

It was nearly another hour before Dr. Dreyfus walked into Rory's small bedroom, the longest hour of Tysen's life. Meggie hadn't moved from the other side of Rory's bed, holding the little boy's hand, speaking quietly to him. As for Tysen, he'd sent Alec with Leo to Northcliffe Hall. Why hadn't he sent both of them? No, he as the vicar, couldn't very well send his own children out of harm's way when no one else had that luxury. Because of his idiotic sense of what was proper, he might lose his son. He was a fool.

Dr. Dreyfus's large hand was on Rory's forehead, then he was sitting beside him, his ear to his chest.

When he looked up, he saw the corrosive fear on the vicar's face, and slowly nodded. "I have some laudanum for him. It will keep him comfortable. But the fever, Vicar, it will climb and climb, so we must keep it down as best we can." He rose and took both Mary Rose's and Tysen's hands. "Listen to me. We can pull him through. The Dixon girl survived it, so can Rory. Now, first things first. Let's give him the laudanum, then begin wiping him down."

It was near dawn; Meggie was sitting beside Rory, having taken over from her father an hour earlier. Mary Rose was asleep on a small cot that Tysen had brought into Rory's room. She looked frightened even in sleep, all stiff, her hands clenching and unclenching.

There had been other illnesses in Rory's young life, but none so frightening as this one.

Meggie felt Rory's cheeks. He was not quite so hot to the touch, she was sure of it. Then he was trembling, jerking about, shoving his covers off. "No, no, baby, don't do that." His teeth were chattering. "Oh goodness, you're freezing now, aren't you? Don't worry, baby, I'm here and I'll take care of you."

Meggie shrugged out of her soft warm velvet dressing gown and wrapped Rory in it. Then she got into his small bed and pulled him close. She whispered to him even as she stroked her hands up and down his small back. Suddenly he stiffened, moaned, and became perfectly still.

Oh God.

Meggie very nearly yelled, then, suddenly, she felt him jerk, heave in on himself, and he was breathing once again, shallow spiking breaths. She was crying now, holding him so close to her heart, so afraid, so very afraid. She was rubbing his back as she said over and over, "No, Rory, hang on, I know you can do it. Breathe, baby, breathe."

He was fighting for every breath now, wheezing. Oh, God, no. No.

"Meggie, what is it?"

Meggie didn't know how she managed it, but she said very quietly, "Mary Rose, get Papa. It's bad, really bad. Go, hurry. Send someone for Dr. Dreyfus."

Mary Rose stuffed her fist in her mouth and ran from the small room. When they returned, Tysen eased down and gently pulled Rory into his arms.

"He just stops breathing, Papa. Then when you think it's over, he manages to draw in a bit more air. He can't go on like this."

Tysen didn't look up. He just held his precious boy against him and willed him to breathe. Then he rose and carried him to the rocking chair that he himself had made for Mary Rose when Alec was born. Meggie and Mary Rose sat on the bed, watching the father and the vicar hold his child. Tysen rubbed the palm of his hand over his son's chest, pressing in, then out, trying to help him breathe. He knew he should send for Dr. Dreyfus. He also knew that he couldn't do anything for Rory that hadn't already been done. Rory would either survive this or he wouldn't. Tysen pressed and massaged his son's chest, over and over, and spoke to him, encouraging him, and he prayed; he, the vicar, was making agreements with God. If he could have, he would have freely offered his soul if the Devil had but come to bargain.

Mary Rose took Meggie's hand. "He can't die, Meggie, he just can't."

Meggie nodded, words beyond her. She didn't want to cry, it would gain naught. They sat together until the sun came up, until shafts of soft pink slipped beneath the pale cream draperies to bathe the room in dim light.

Samuel Pritchert came to tell them that Dr. Dreyfus's carriage had been thrown on its side and the doctor was in bed, his back wrenched. He couldn't move. He said there was nothing more he could do in any case. He was praying for them, Samuel assured them.

Some minutes later Meggie heard Mrs. Priddle moving about downstairs. Then, quite suddenly, she head a knock on the vicarage door.

Mrs. Priddle was breathless when she stuck her head in Rory's room. "Forgive me, Miss Meggie, it's Lord Lancaster. He says it's very important."

Thomas Malcombe? What could that man possibly want at dawn, for God's sake? She didn't want to hear him again ask her to go riding.

She simply nodded to her father and to Mary Rose and quietly left the room. She stopped by her own bedchamber, pulled on another dressing gown, this one so old the elbows were nearly worn through. She hurried down the stairs. No candle was needed, there was nearly full light now.

He was there, standing in the entrance hall, wearing riding clothes, boots.

Meggie felt no Christian kindness in her heart. "What do you want?"

He merely nodded to her, then walked swiftly to where she stood on the bottom stair. She saw then that he was carrying a small package. He pressed it into her hand. "I have spoken to Dr. Dreyfus. He said to bring this over and give it to Rory, that it couldn't hurt. It's a medicine, one of many that my shipping partner sent me from Genoa, Italy. It's for the fever. Is Rory better?"

"No," Meggie said flatly, and she knew, knew to her heart, "No, I don't think he will get better. What is this?"

She was ripping away the paper. There was a long thin bottle filled to the corked top with a dark brown liquid.

"It's a medicinal root called the maringo. It grows near a river on a lava plateau on the western slopes of Mt. Etna in Sicily. Perhaps it will help Rory. The letter from my man says that this particular root is effective for virulent fevers. Here, Meggie, give it to the boy, quickly, a small drink, that's all that's needed. Then another drink every hour, until—well, until he's better."

Tysen and Mary Rose believed the medicine was from Dr. Dreyfus. Meggie didn't correct them. She managed to get Rory's little mouth open and poured a bit of the brown liquid down his throat, then lightly rubbed his neck with her fingers. He wheezed and coughed even as his teeth chattered and his small body clenched with the violent spasms that were killing him. But he was breathing, little gasps of breath.

They said nothing at all, just watched the little boy continue to labor for each breath. Suddenly, without warning, he went into convulsions.

Tysen held him firmly while Meggie tried to keep him from swallowing or biting his tongue. Mary Rose rubbed his arms, his legs, to keep him still and warm. After an eternity, the convulsions passed. Rory became utterly still.

Mary Rose fell back on her heels. "Oh God, no! Tysen, no, he can't be dead, he can't!"

"No, just wait, just wait."

Meggie was praying harder than she'd ever prayed in her life. She couldn't hear him breathe, couldn't hear him do anything. He was dying. Oh, please God, no, not this wonderful little boy. She watched her father squeeze Rory's chest, then massage it, again and again as he whispered, "Breathe, Rory, breathe."

Meggie looked up then to see Lord Lancaster standing in the doorway, saying nothing, just standing there quietly, watching the tableau in front of him, his face pale, his dark eyes hooded.

"Thank God," Tysen said then, unutterable relief mixed with tears in his voice, "he's breathing." He grabbed Mary Rose to him and held both Rory and her close. "Thank the good Lord, our boy is breathing again."

He lifted Mary Rose onto his lap and on her lap she held Rory, her white hands shaking even as she stroked them up and down his small back, steady circular motions while Tysen still massaged his small chest. Finally, Mary Rose laid her head against his neck. He kissed her hair even as his arms tightened around the two of them. Meggie knew she would never forget that moment her whole life. Rory was breathing, not just the stingy little gasps, but full breaths that sounded more and more normal. His cheeks were flushed, but now it wasn't with fever. She took a blanket off the bed and wrapped it over all three of them.

"Another one, Meggie. He isn't shivering now, but I want to make all of us sweat."

"He's all limp now, no more shudders or convulsions," Mary Rose whispered, hope brimming in her voice. "Oh, Tysen, do you think he—"

"I don't know, love, let's just keep holding him and holding each other. Let's keep rubbing him and massaging him. It can't hurt. That medicine, Meggie—when you see Dr. Dreyfus, tell him it worked. Tell him I knew he would think of something more."

"It isn't from Dr. Dreyfus, Papa, it's from Lord Lancaster."

Tysen was silent a moment, confused, really, then he said, "Thank him for us and tell him it seems to have had something of an immediate effect. Tell him we are very grateful."

"Yes, I will tell him," she said, not mentioning that Thomas Malcombe was standing in the doorway watching them. She loaded them all down with all the blankets in the room. She lightly laid her palm against Rory's cheek. He was cooler, she would swear that he was cooler.

"Papa, I think he's truly asleep now, and his breathing is easy, regular."

Her father smiled up at her. She smiled back at him, then leaned down quickly to kiss his cheek. "I will bring you some tea. Ah, good, Mary Rose is finally asleep, too."

In truth, her stepmother looked like an exhausted Madonna holding her sick child close, her brilliant curly red hair all over her head, tickling her husband's chin, framing her pale face.

Tysen whispered, "I had prayed until I was out of words, until there wasn't another plea in my mind, Meggie. I think perhaps God heard me and sent Lord Lancaster here with that medicine."

"Perhaps," Meggie said, "I do think that Lord Lancaster felt some urgency to come here. Was it God nudging him? It is a comforting thought."

"Now, I want you to take the medicine to Dr. Dreyfus, tell him that it appears to have worked with Rory. If another child falls ill, then we can see that—"

"Yes, Papa, I will. I will ask if Lord Lancaster has more of it. We are to give Rory another swallow in about twenty minutes or so. Then, if he remains like this, no more is necessary." Meggie smiled, straightened, turned, and walked to where Thomas Malcombe stood, watching her come toward him, her old dressing gown flapping around her bare ankles, her lovely hair braided down her back, much of it come loose and now tangled around her face.

She nodded to him and he quietly backed away from the open doorway. He waited at the head of the stairs, his face in shadows now because the sun had slipped momentarily behind some clouds. She stopped right in front of him. She lifted his left hand in both of hers and clasped it strongly. "I thank you, my lord. Was it God who made you feel the urgency to come to us?"

"Perhaps it was," Thomas said slowly, looking down at his large brown hand held between her two smaller ones, not fine soft white hands. Meggie Sherbrooke's hands helped raise her brothers, trained racing cats, did countless tasks as the vicar's daughter. And he found himself wondering: *Why had he come so quickly?* He didn't know. He just knew that he'd had to. Was it God nudging him?

He said matter-of-factly, "The package of medicines arrived just a few moments before dawn along with other supplies. The fellow bringing it said he had this feeling that I would be needing it and thus pushed on from Eastbourne to my home. I heard that little Rory was ill and so I came here immediately. I think the messenger was the one whom God nudged."

"Is there more of the medicine?"

"Oh yes. My man will take it to Dr. Dreyfus now, and he can hold it for any children who become ill."

"Oh goodness. Look at me, I'm not dressed. Ah, Mrs. Priddle, please take His Lordship to the drawing room, then give him some breakfast. I will be down very soon."

Twenty minutes later Meggie walked into the drawing room. Lord Lancaster was standing beside the fireplace, now lit and warm, drinking some tea.

She said without hesitation, her hands outstretched to him, "My family is in your debt, my lord."

He raised a dark eyebrow. He wanted to assure her that she wasn't in his debt, that any decent human being would have brought that medicine to the vicarage without delay, but he wanted her in his debt, if that was what it would take. Just her.

He let her hold his hands yet again as he said, his voice deep, "You are exhausted, Meggie. I want you to rest today. If it doesn't rain on the morrow, why then, will you go riding with me?"

"Yes," she said, "I will go riding with you, my lord."

7

THEY WEREN'T ABLE to ride for two more days. It rained so hard everyone said that the skies wept. And wept. On the morning of the third day, it was cool and overcast. However, Mr. Hengis has claimed it wouldn't rain anymore, so no one was particularly concerned. The sun would burst from behind those rather gray clouds, and all would be well.

To Meggie, it was a fine day. She loved to ride, to feel the wind, strong off the Channel, tugging at her very eyebrows, flinging many a riding hat to the ground and under her mare's hooves, and the man riding next to her had saved her little brother's life. He'd even come every morning and afternoon to the vicarage to check on Rory's progress since he'd brought the medicine, even in all that dreadful rain.

Meggie was riding Survivor, a lovely bay mare whose name, she told Thomas Malcombe, had been changed early on from Petunia.

"Why was the name changed?" he asked.

Meggie laughed, couldn't help it. "Well, you see, Petunia just happened to be the first mount for all three of my brothers and me. That's four children she's survived. When Rory is just a bit older, then he will learn to ride on her as well. She's still happy and running, so we all thought Survivor fit her much better."

"A noble horse," he said, one of those black eyebrows of his arched, "with a great deal of stamina. Rory will mount her as well? Surely she has earned retirement by now. That is asking a lot of any of God's creatures, don't you think?"

"Survivor is a natural with children, so don't waste your pity on her," Meggie said, and laughing again, leaned forward to pat the glossy neck. Survivor slewed her great head around and whinnied softly. Meggie reached into her pocket and pulled out a carrot for her. The mare snagged the carrot and ate it without ever breaking stride.

"She is nearly twelve years old. I believe my cousin Jeremy wanted more than anything to breed her, but she is too old now."

He heard the slight change in her voice. Something sad or perhaps it was more wistful, he couldn't be certain. He didn't like it. "Jeremy?" he said carefully. "Which cousin is he?"

Meggie shrugged, stretched, looked all indifferent as she stared at a maple tree to her left, and said, voice all thin and watery, and that just made him all the more on edge, "Oh, Jeremy isn't really one of my dratted cousins. He's an almost dratted cousin. There is no blood tie. He's the brother-in-law of my uncle Ryder Sherbrooke."

She was obviously discomfited. He would let it go for the moment. He said, "I have heard many tales about your uncle. Is it true that he has sired more bastards than the sheiks in Arabia?"

Meggie reached out and smacked his shoulder. "That is your punishment for listening to gossip, my lord. Although, you know, there are certainly many wicked stories put out about him, my other uncle as well. However, the bastard story—that's nonsense. My uncle Ryder is one of the most moral men in the entire world."

"Forgive me," Thomas said, "he is your uncle. I shouldn't have said that so starkly. It is as you said—there are many wicked stories told about him. You're saying that he doesn't have a house for his bastards?"

Meggie realized the mistake. She patted Survivor's

neck, fed her another carrot as she said, "I haven't heard that in a long time now. You really don't know about my uncle Ryder, my lord?"

"My name is Thomas, and I thought I did."

"Obviously you don't. My uncle, from a very young age, began saving children he found in back allies, in servitude to cruel masters, beaten and starved by parents, even sold by gin-sodden mothers or fathers, it didn't matter. They are called his Beloved Ones. At my last visit there were at least fifteen children living at Brandon House in the Cotswalds, very close to Chadwyck House where my uncle, my aunt Sophie, and Grayson, one of my dratted cousins, live, although Grayson is now at Oxford. The bastard business—that was all started by one of my uncle's political foes. Because people are people, they wanted to believe it until they realized how silly such a thing would be. Just imagine, installing your bastards in a grand house next to the one where your own family lives. That would require a great deal of gall, don't you think?"

"Yes, a great deal. Beloved Ones?"

"Yes, that is the name my aunt Sinjun gave them when she discovered his secret many years ago. I believe she was around fifteen years old at the time."

"If this is all true, then why isn't it well known?"

Meggie smiled. "Because my uncle Ryder is extraordinarily reticent about what he does. He considers it his private business. He gets irritated if anyone tries to praise him for his good deeds. He claims that he takes in the children because they give him great pleasure, and 'it is no one else's bloody damned business.' That was a quote."

"Who was this political foe? The one who claimed he had his bastards right there under his wife's nose?"

"A Mr. Redfern, the incumbent, spread that ridiculous rumor because he knew he would lose if he didn't. His was not a moral character, and next to my uncle Ryder, he was very paltry indeed. It was quite a brouhaha at the time." Meggie paused a moment, felt a drop of rain hit the tip of her nose, and said, "Oh dear. Mr. Hengis must have had a falling out with the weather gods. His fingers must have been tapping incorrectly. It's raining. Again. We will all begin to grow mold if this keeps up."

"Yes," he said and raised his face. He had loved the rain since he'd been a small boy, even the grand sheets of rain that had dampened the earth to its core for the past two days. "No," he said, frowning after a moment, "no rain. I'm told that Mr. Hengis is never wrong. It must have been an errant drop, nothing more."

"Another errant drop just hit me on the chin."

"Keep your head down."

She laughed. "All right, but you see, I don't want to ruin my beautiful riding hat. Oh yes, Uncle Ryder's multitudinous bastards. Actually, he does have one natural child, Jenny, whose mother died birthing her. They love each other very much. Jenny is Oliver's wife, they married this past Christmas. He manages my father's estate, Kildrummy Castle, in Scotland. Oliver was, if I remember correctly, one of the first children my uncle rescued. If you remain in Glenclose-on-Rowan you will meet them, my lord. Oliver usually comes for a visit in the fall. Hopefully, this fall, both he and Jenny will come."

"Thomas. That's my name."

"Yes, I know, it's just that I am an unmarried young lady. You know as well as I do that I really shouldn't use your first name, much less be riding alone with you down country lanes." She looked up to get some rain in her mouth. "I shall have to tell Mr. Hengis that he must forego his potato sticks since he has blundered. Let's go to the Martins' barn that lies just beyond that rise. It's not much, but it will keep the rain off, if we're careful where we stand."

Meggie didn't wait, just *click-clicked* Survivor in her sides and said, "Another carrot if you get me inside before all this increasing number of errant drops make my feather collapse under their weight."

She thought she heard Thomas Malcombe's laughter from behind her, but she didn't turn, just smiled as she gave Survivor her head and hugged close to her neck. He had a very nice laugh.

When they reached the barn, Thomas realized that whoever the Martins were who had owned this barn had departed this earth many many years before, probably long before Thomas had been born. Long abandoned, it was small, utterly dilapidated, collapsing in on itself, boards hanging loose, part of the roof caved in—he hoped there would be enough roof overhead for all four of them. The rain was starting to pick up now. He would have a few words for the now-fallible Mr. Hengis.

He watched Meggie dismount, pull Survivor's reins over her head, and lead the mare into the barn. He eyed it again, hoping the wreck wouldn't collapse on them.

"I will try to save you, Pen, if something bad happens," he said to his big black gelding.

Pen whinnied. He was smart. He didn't want to go into that barn. Thomas couldn't blame him. It took him a good three minutes to convince the horse that the bloody roof wouldn't fall in on him. Thomas got a good soaking in the meantime.

Finally, inside the barn, he saw Meggie Sherbrooke and her mare in the one dry corner. Thomas shrugged out of his coat, shook himself like a mongrel, and plowed his fingers through his wet hair. It was a tight fit, but all four of them managed to be covered.

"What are potato sticks?"

"Why, they are Mrs. Bartholomew's specialty. She, my lord, is your cook."

"Oh, yes. I call her Morgana."

"Morgana? She was King Arthur's sister. Why would you call her that? Mrs. Bartholomew's name is Agnes, I believe."

"I call her that because she's a witch, a witch who, I'm convinced, is trying to poison me. Now, these potato sticks, the ones that Mr. Hengis really likes. If I deprive him of them will it be a fitting punishment for his weather blunder?"

"Oh yes, I promise. He nearly whimpers when he

smells Mrs. Bartholomew baking the sticks. Why does she want to poison you?"

"I believe it is my father she wants to poison, but he is dead, so I am the only one available."

Meggie had been rubbing her arms, but now, she was hugging herself she was laughing so hard. "You're right. Mrs. Bartholomew did dislike your sire profoundly. How did you know?"

"I heard her in the kitchen one morning when I wanted my tea replenished and Torrent was no where to be found, which happens more often than not. The downstairs maid, Tansie, wasn't about. I understand she is smitten with Tobin, the butcher's son. When I got to the kitchen, Morgana was slamming pots around and muttering about the crooked ways of the Devil, the dreadful thickness of demons on the ground. She had a truly amazing litany."

"I would say she sounds rather upset. Did she say anything else? How do you know she was talking about your father?"

"Well, a number of times she said Old Lord L—that's what she calls him—then followed that with miserable old bounder, blackguard, stingy coot who deserved to be drawn and quartered. Also, there was something about the hideous fate of the wicked."

"Hmmm. I wonder what that was all about. Your father was rather clutch-fisted, at least that was his reputation, but he did pay the local tradesmen within the same six months as a purchase. As for your butler Torrent, he is getting old, my lord, and he naps at least a half dozen times a day, just behind the stairs, in a small alcove in his own special chair with three pillows. As for Tansie, she makes quilts, every chance she gets, beautiful quilts from scraps of material. She is very talented. You should look into having her start up a shop of her own. She hides in the small nursery at the top of the house whenever she can to sew. To the best of my knowledge Tobin doesn't stand a chance with her."

He could but stare at her. "Do you know everything about everyone in this town?"

"Naturally. I was born and raised here. Now, of course, for the past ten years we go to Scotland for the summer, to Kildrummy Castle. We all love it there. It is wild and barren and then, just half a dozen steps later, you see clumps of white heather, then purple, ah, so many colors, all of them so very brilliant that you want to weep. Have you been to Scotland, my lord?"

"Call me Thomas. Yes, I have been many times to Scotland, to Glasgow for business and up to Inverness to visit friends and to hunt."

Meggie leaned down to pick up some ancient hay that had probably moldered in the same spot for at least twenty years. She began to rub it over Survivor's back. Thomas did the same with Pen.

Without warning, Survivor whipped her head around and tried to bite Meggie's shoulder. Meggie jumped back just in time, tripped on the hem of her riding skirt and went down on her bottom. She was laughing. "Oh, I see the problem now. The straw is too stiff and it is irritating her. Beware, Thomas, Pen might not like it either."

Pen neighed loudly but didn't move.

Meggie grinned as she brushed some dirt and straw off her skirt. "Survivor tries to bite you only if you're grown up, never children."

Thomas leaned down and clasped her hand. He pulled too hard, and both of them knew it was on purpose. She slammed against him. She'd never before slammed against a man. It was heady, that slamming.

It was too soon, he thought, then just couldn't help himself. He leaned down his head and kissed her. Not much of a kiss, just a light touching of mouths. She didn't move, didn't do anything at all. It took him a moment to realize this must be her first kiss.

Good. No Jeremy. He must have been mistaken about him, which was a relief.

Her first kiss and he'd been the one to give it to her. Slowly he raised his head. She was staring up at him straight on, not blinking. She touched her fingertips to her mouth. Then, finally, she frowned and stepped back.

"How very odd," she said, as she shook out her damp skirts. "Of course you should not have done that, but no matter. I am only a bit damp now. It is still raining quite hard."

She watched him plow his fingers through his dark hair, nice and thick that hair, a bit shaggy for popular tastes. "Meggie, you're right, I shouldn't have done that, but it was just a kiss, after all, not a mauling or a serious attempt at seduction. I apologize for taking advantage of our situation." His voice softened and deepened. He couldn't help the dollop of masculine pride that crept in. "It was your first kiss. I gave you your first kiss."

"Ha," Meggie said. "Ha ha. You are mistaken, my lord. I have been kissed many times."

"Thomas," he said. "My name is Thomas."

"Yes, I know your name. Let me tell you, I have kissed so many boys I can scare remember all of them."

"This was all during your Season last year?"

"Well, no, to be honest about this, and I suppose that I must be honest since my father is the vicar and this business of honesty is quite important to him, all the boys were my dratted cousins. I asked them, you see, when I was thirteen years old, to kiss me. I didn't ask any of the older ones, only the dratted cousins who were my age or younger."

"Jeremy was older?"

"Yes, he was much older," and she thought, no, not Jeremy, never Jeremy. She'd wanted to, more than anything, but she'd known she'd probably sink into a puddle at his feet if he'd kissed her, and her father would have been appalled. Doubtless Jeremy would have been appalled as well. She said, "The older male cousins thought it a great jest, but I ignored them." Jeremy, she recalled, had laughed his head off. Why had he asked specifically about Jeremy?

"What did you do?"

"I lined up all the dratted boy cousins. Each stepped forward when I called his name and puckered his lips and did it."

8

$\mathcal{H}$E COULD ONLY stare down at her. She was without guile. She also had an outrageous streak that was a good mile wide. She'd lined up her cousins? "You simply wished to experiment?"

"Well, yes. You see, Max and Leo, my brothers, absolutely refused to kiss me, so they announced that they would judge which cousin kissed the best. But as I think about it now, I think I should have been the judge, not two boys who knew nothing about anything."

"It makes sense to me. What criteria did Max and Leo use to choose the winner?"

Meggie thought back to that splendid day, at the line of dratted cousins, all of them nervous, afraid, knowing there was a lot on the line here, but each eager. "Hmm. They picked Grayson, my uncle Ryder's son. But the criteria—they claimed they awarded Grayson on form. But come to think of it, they might have picked Grayson no matter what the contest. You know, Grayson tells marvelous stories—ghost stories, adventure stories, really scary gnarly stories—and he'd told them a hair-raising ghost story just the night before about midnight. It was about this old man whose wife shoved him into a well and left him there to die, but his ghost came after her, did all sorts of gruesome things, and Max and Leo were so scared, so happy, wanting so badly to hear Grayson tell another story, that they didn't even hesitate. Do you know, they announced Grayson the winner before poor James was barely finished."

"This is an amazing story," he said slowly. He tried to remember a single evening in his growing-up years that could possibly have been as delightful as this one. He couldn't dredge a single one up. Then he remembered Nathan had taught him how to dive into the ocean from the cliff that summer of his tenth year. Nathan, who'd left, joined the army, and died in Spain so many years ago.

He shook this off. "Who is James?" he asked.

"He is my uncle Douglas's oldest son. He and Jason are twins, born only about thirty minutes apart. James will be the earl of Northcliffe someday. Did you know that they are quite the most beautiful young men in the world?"

"No, I didn't know. They weren't beautiful then? You weren't infatuated with one of them when you were younger?"

"Oh no. Both of them have very bad habits. I was always trying to make them better. Now it will be up to their wives to improve upon them, if they ever marry, that is. My uncle Douglas always despaired for their characters since they are so beautiful. In all fairness to other males, though, it's really unfortunate that today they are quite unspoiled—only male sorts of bad habits that one simply cannot eradicate—but in their hearts, they are not rotten at all."

"Not rotten at all?"

"No more rotten now than any of their contemporaries. You know, they curse and brag and steal their father's brandy, run races at midnight and nearly break their necks, lay wagers on who can spit the farthest, that sort of thing. They don't gamble or get sent down from Oxford or seduce local girls."

Thomas doubted that last sincerely. They were young men. That was what young men did, rotten or not. Hopefully, they really had outgrown the worst of it. "May I kiss you again?"

"Whyever for?"

He said slowly, even as he lowered his head, "I want to see if you compare me favorably to your cousins."

"But that was a long time ago and we were all children and—"

He kissed her. This time it wasn't just touching mouth to mouth. This time there was a bit of pressure, a bit more coaxing, and lots of warmth. His hands were on her arms, slowly bringing her closer. Then he opened his mouth.

He actually opened his mouth, Meggie thought, appalled, like he was going to speak or eat his dinner or butcher a high note like that Milanese soprano.

She felt his tongue lightly pressing against her lips, but she kept her mouth shut. Meggie blinked up at him. His eyes weren't closed. When he saw the shock in her eyes, he drew back.

She didn't jump back or slap him. She simply stood there, looking thoughtful, staring up at him. Finally she said, "That was very strange. Since you have lived outside England for a very long time, perhaps you have forgotten English customs, my lord. That, I am quite certain, cannot be one of them. You opened your mouth, you touched your tongue to my lower lip, my upper lip as well, and you sort of licked me. Surely that isn't done here in England, only in some foreign country where there is permission to explore shameless sorts of things."

He had to smile. "Actually, Meggie, I swear to you it is the done thing."

He saw that she wasn't quite ready to accept that. She said, "So it is the done thing where you have lived all these years? Did someone instruct you to do this where you were brought up? Where you grew into manhood?"

"Oh yes, but instruction really isn't necessary. Well, perhaps some instruction would be helpful to some young men. What is necessary is practice, a great deal of it, although by its very nature, there is a lot of built-in practice involved in the process."

"What process?"

"The lovemaking process. Kissing simply sets the whole business off."

"Oh."

"Yes, it is done all the time. It is even done in China." He was lightly stroking his hands up and down her arms. The velvet riding habit was still a bit damp. "Actually, Meggie, there is something that you need to know since you are now a woman."

"What is that?"

"It is even done here in England."

"You are certain about this? This tongue business?"

"Oh yes."

"Really in China as well as in England?"

"Oh yes."

And she realized: *Then Jeremy must do this to Charlotte. He opens his mouth when he kisses her. Does she open her mouth as well? No, no, don't think about that.*

"Did you find it distasteful?"

Meggie thought about that a moment, considered it. Her forehead was furrowed, and she chewed on her bottom lip. He wanted to touch his fingertip to her bottom lip, perhaps stroke her bottom lip with his tongue.

"No, it wasn't distasteful, just very curious. Goodness, I wonder if my father and Mary Rose do that."

She looked utterly appalled as she said the words, looked as though she'd give anything to take the words back, to take back the fact that she'd even thought of it. Again, he held back a laugh, and said, "I am not so deranged to comment on the marital habits of a vicar and his wife."

"You're right. I shouldn't either." Meggie sighed. "Is that a sliver of weak sun?"

"It is. And look, it is no longer raining."

She didn't know whether to be pleased or disappointed. This had been a very strange morning.

"I wonder," she said, "if Max and Leo would judge you to be the kissing winner now."

"Yes," he said, "they most certainly would."

She laughed, but it wasn't full and delighted, it was reedy and wary because she was thinking about his mouth against hers, about feeling him against her as well, his big hands stroking her, and it was as frightening as it was fascinating.

He looked at her upturned face and thought, *Well, I've taught you something and it both worries and interests you. It's a good start.*

He said easily, "You see, to ensure that they would select me the winner, I would tell them an excellent story about scaly fire-breathing dragons and the witless knights who had nothing better to do than track them to their caves."

"I fear Max and Leo are no longer bribed with good stories. Actually, I'm not sure what would sway them now. They are young men and I simply no longer know. The problem is the male brain—it is wholly mysterious and unpredictable. It's rather like a mass of confusion in your head." She sighed then. "I really did my best raising them. Max is going to be a vicar, like Papa, so he can't be too wicked, can he?"

"Oh no. So you're telling me that you raised your brothers?"

"Oh yes, at least until my father married Mary Rose. I was ten and a good-sized girl, lots bigger and stronger than they were. I could pound them whenever they needed it, which was quite often, being that they were boys, and had no sense at all. Yes, they required a great deal of discipline, and a vigilant eye. Leo was the prankster. I'll never forget the time he cut a strip out of the back of my gown. I threw him in the bushes for that stunt."

He laughed. He realized he'd laughed more since he'd met her than in a very long time.

They led their horses out of the barn. Pen whinnied, delighted to have escaped, hide intact. Leaves dripped water, the ground was spongy. He gave her a leg up, saying as she smoothed her skirts over her legs, "I hear from Dr. Dreyfus that Rory will be up to all sorts of mischief by the end of the week."

"Oh yes. Let me thank you again, my lord."

"You can thank me by calling me Thomas."

"If you put it that way. All right. Thomas. It is a good name, a solid name. I will use it. Since you've kissed me, using your tongue, I suppose I know you well enough."

"Yes, I believe you do, at last. Dr. Dreyfus also wants to analyze all the medicines my partner in Italy sent me. He has asked me to have that maringo root sent here to see if it can be grown in England. He is very excited about it."

Meggie wasn't really listening. Thomas Malcombe wasn't a cousin. She'd known him such a short time, and he'd opened his mouth when he'd kissed her that second time.

He wasn't Jeremy.

She managed to bring herself back to the point. "There was another case of the virulent fever, and Dr. Dreyfus immediately administered your drug. Little Melissa perked up very quickly."

"Yes, everyone in the village told me about it."

"Everyone in the village is also singing your praises. The men are toasting you in the taproom. The ladies are so fulsome in their praise that your ears should be burning. You are rapidly working up to local hero."

"I like that," he said, and lightly laid his hands over hers. "I would like to see the Channel."

Meggie raised her face to the watery sun, and smiled. "I should like that as well," she said.

She wondered if perhaps she should kiss him again. Was the female supposed to open her mouth as well? Perhaps touch his mouth with her tongue?

She shivered. This was new ground, probably unsafe ground. She wasn't at all certain that she wanted to walk here. She thought of Jeremy kissing her, knowing it would spin her off her feet, and felt a deep shaft of pain. He said, "Perhaps you could be specific about what the ladies are saying about me and my magnificence. I would like my ears to burn a bit. They never have before."

"I'm not sure that is such a good idea," Meggie said. "I think you could grow far too used to being worshipped," and nudged her boot heels into Survivor's sides.

9

"*That is quite* the longest leap Cleo has ever made," Meggie said, reading the distance stick again. "Yes, that's right—three feet and about four inches. Just excellent, my sweet girl."

"It's that new training method, Meggie," Alec said, humming under his breath. He stroked the cat's back, long light strokes. Cleo began to purr and arch her back.

Like what Thomas Malcombe did to me. At least I had the sense not to purr and squirm.

Oh dear, better concentrate on training methods. She wrapped the long length of pale yellow ribbon around her hand. A good foot of it was shredded by Cleo catching it, her claws seaming it, so that it was now five skinny strings of ribbon.

Alec said, "She might just beat Mr. Cork on Saturday."

"I have worked with Mr. Cork as well, and you know he has more endurance. He is very taken with smells, as you know. I tried a new one on him—mackerel. I chopped it up, added a dash of garlic, and dried it. Then I wrapped it in a netted bag. He nearly ran his legs off trying to get close enough to get a really strong whiff of it. It must replace the dead trout."

"Meggie, you will surely beat out the Harker brothers in the creativity of your training methods. They're entering three cats in this race."

"Never underestimate their ingenuity, Alec. I hear that Jamie, the head stable lad at the Mountvale mews, has come up with a new limerick to sing to the Black Rocket. It's so effective—all Jamie has to do is stand at the finish line and sing his heart out, and the Black Rocket will spead toward him like a bullet."

"The Black Rocket has very mean eyes," Alec said thoughtfully. "I think Mr. Cork needs to bring him down a peg. I need to think about this."

Thomas Malcombe listened to brother and sister discuss the Black Rocket—whatever sort of racing cat that was. He liked that name, it was quite menacing. He'd seen Mr. Cork, his gold and white body stretched out, all muscled and long in the sun, with just a bit of shade over one leg from one of Mrs. Sherbrooke's rosebushes.

He'd never had a cat, even when he'd been a boy. There were the barn cats, feral, all of them good mousers.

"Lord Lancaster, how nice to see you. Do you like thin ham slices? They're Cook's specialty. Do join us for luncheon."

He turned to see Mrs. Sherbrooke coming around the side of the vicarage. "Good day, Mrs. Sherbrooke. I merely came to see if Rory was well enough yet to train with the racing cats. I have no wish to intrude."

Mary Rose took his hand. "You saved my son's life, my lord. I want you to intrude until you are quite tired of all of us. Do call me Mary Rose."

Meggie overheard this and nodded vigorously as she joined the two of them. "Thomas, welcome. I'm delighted you could visit. The last time I saw Rory, he was climbing the trellis that divides Mary Rose's hydrangeas from her daffodils, the one with the red climbing roses on it."

Mary Rose's eyes nearly crossed. "Oh no, tell me you made that up, Meggie! Oh goodness, he can't. That trellis isn't all that sturdy. I swear that as of right now, I will no longer look at him and thank God endlessly. No, I will pull my resolve together and swat his bottom. Well, perhaps if he is more than two feet from the ground I will swat him. My lord, I will see you in the dining room in no more than five minutes. Rory! Get down off that trellis!"

And Mary Rose was gone, holding her skirt up to her knees and running toward the east side of the vicarage.

Meggie grinned after her. "This is a good sign. She's been hovering over him, so afraid he will stop breathing again."

"Being hovered over doesn't sound like a bad thing," Thomas said.

Meggie grinned. "Hovering in this case means she's always petting him, kissing him, squeezing him, stuffing food down his gullet, driving the little boy quite distracted, a very independent little boy, let me add."

"You mean you made that trellis story up to get your mother back on an even keel?"

"I wouldn't call it precisely a lie," Meggie said. "Perhaps Rory was looking longingly at the trellis. Now, I am delighted you came to visit. Cook's ham slices are so thin you can see yourself through them. No one knows how she manages it and everyone is always lurking about to watch when she slices the ham. Come along now. You needn't worry that she will try to poison you. The only person she ever mutters about is Mr. Samuel Pritchert, my father's curate."

"The very dour man who never smiles even when he eats a bite of apple tart?"

"That's the one."

"He's in a bad way."

"Yes. But do you know, he has but to look at someone, and that someone will spill his innards to Samuel. My father thinks it's amazing."

"I don't believe you."

She just laughed, took his hand, and pulled him toward the vicarage door. They heard Mary Rose yelling at Rory, who had, evidently, climbed the trellis, because she was telling him that she was going to swat him but good when she got him down from that great height. Goodness, he'd climbed at least eighteen inches and he deserved a good swat.

"That," Meggie said, "makes you wonder about the nature of deception, doesn't it?"

Jeremy's visit the following Wednesday was unannounced, thank God, or Meggie would have been an incoherent bundle of nerves. As it was, all she felt was longing and an immense pain at what couldn't be.

Jeremy Stanton-Greville was so happy. So incredibly, blessedly happy. He gushed; he grinned like a fool. He oozed contentment and smugness. He rubbed his hands together, so proud of himself, so pleased with life, so uncaring, so blind, to the one person who would have gladly played Sir Walter Raleigh to his Queen Elizabeth and thrown every cloak she owned at his feet. Thus, just seeing him, knowing he wasn't ever to belong to her, made her want to hide under the stairs and weep, but naturally, she couldn't. She was stoic. She endured, even managed, when a jest nearly punched her in the nose, to dutifully smile.

After an hour, however, Meggie was feeling less and less like bursting into tears when she looked at him. Actually, she wanted less and less for him to stare at her, just her, with regret and nameless hunger in his beautiful eyes. She wanted less and less for him to realize his tragic mistake that would keep them apart forever.

No, after an hour, Meggie was ready to smash him. She began to drum her fingers against the arm of her chair as he talked on and on about his dearest Charlotte, his beautiful, elegant Charlotte, so sweet, so clever—the embodiment of perfection, a flawless example of womanhood. Then he went on to his stud at Fowey. After a while, both the stud and Charlotte sported the same attributes.

Jeremy never stopped talking about either Charlotte and the stud, even after dinner when the adults were finally having tea in the drawing room.

Hour upon hour of his braying went on. Meggie knew it would never end unless someone shot him. She was ready.

His endless braying had become the fifth circle of Hell.

He was still beautiful, of course, no change there, and he still made her heart sigh and ache, but enough was enough. To keep her mouth shut, Meggie moved to the piano and played vigorously, to drown out his endless praise of himself and what he himself had found and fashioned. But he just didn't stop. Her father looked mildly amused, and to Meggie's eye a bit distracted, and she knew he was likely composing next Sunday's sermon while he was the perfect host. Mary Rose was constantly patting Jeremy's hand, as if to congratulate him on his brilliance, perhaps to keep herself from slapping him silly.

Meggie's limber fingers ran the last Scarlatti arpeggio, hit the last cord, perhaps too *forte*, since she used quite a bit of muscle, but it didn't matter. She waited just a moment to see if perhaps the conversation had shifted to someone besides perfect Charlotte or the perfect stud.

It hadn't.

Meggie said finally, in a very loud voice as she rose from the piano stool, "How are Uncle Ryder and Aunt Sophie?"

Jeremy, who been detailing every improvement he'd made on the stud—in only three months, mind you—and the plans he had for Leo, said, startled, "What? Oh, they are just fine, Meggie." He grinned, and Meggie felt her heart lurch. Well, blessed hell. "Yes, Ryder tells me the Sherbrooke boys have quite taken over Oxford. He says that when a letter arrives from Grayson, he's loathe to open it, fearing the worst." Now his grin turned fatuous. "I know you love to ride, Meggie. Did I tell you how much Charlotte adores this one mare I bought for her, a beautiful bay mare with a white blaze on her nose and white fetlocks. She is as lovely a mare as Charlotte is a woman. I will breed her, naturally. Her name is Dido, so fitting, don't you think?"

"No," Meggie said. "To escape her husband, Dido built a funeral pyre, stabbed herself, and threw herself on it."

He paused a moment, frowning. "I thought she founded Carthage, something both the mare and Charlotte will do, that is, they will both found a dynasty."

"She did, then she stabbed herself."

"Hmm," said Jeremy, "now that I think about it, I'm not certain that I should allow Charlotte to ride all that much now, since she is carrying my child."

"It is her child too," Meggie said, her voice rising an octave. "She's the one doing all the work."

"Well, yes, but she tells me over and over that she is having this child for me and that it will be a boy because that is what I want." He gave her a brainless self-satisfied grin.

This was nauseating. Her heart wasn't lurching in pain and regret now. Meggie said, her fingers tapping on the lovely cherrywood piano case, "I would only care if my child were healthy and that it managed to survive its first year on this blessed earth. I wouldn't care whether or not it was a boy or girl." She added, her voice even louder now, "Perhaps Charlotte can decide for herself when she should stop riding her beautiful mare that you bought her, whose namesake stabbed herself."

Jeremy gave her what she'd thought only four hours before was the most seductive smile in all of Christendom. Now it looked superior and smug. He said, all patient and condescending, "Meggie, as is proper, since I am Charlotte's husband, she looks to me to guide her, to tell her what is best for her."

"What a wonderful parent you will be, Jeremy," Meggie said, her own smile as false as Mr. McCardle's leg, "just look at all the practice you're gaining since you married Charlotte. But you know, I simply can't imagine what is proper about treating your wife like a child and a nitwit."

"Charlotte a nitwit? A child? That is absurd, Meggie. Oh, I see, you're jesting."

To keep the nausea at bay, Meggie played another song. She was quite aware that Mary Rose had cocked her head to one side, sending her glorious mass of curly red hair halfway down her arm, no doubt wondering why Meggie had lost her manners.

Meggie stopped playing in time to hear Jeremy say to her father, ignoring both her and Mary Rose, "Since you have approved, Uncle Tysen, Leo will be coming to me at the end of his term at Oxford. He is a natural with horses. He and I will do very well together. He writes me with new ideas. He is studying the science of horse breeding, he tells me." This was said with an indulgent grin.

"Leo knows more about horses than you do," Meggie said.

Tysen said easily, "Now, Meggie, Leo knows quite a lot, that's true, but he doesn't yet have Jeremy's years of experience."

"Does Charlotte think Leo will do well too?" Meggie asked.

Jeremy leaned back against the sofa back, smiling. "My dearest Charlotte has no idea what Leo will do since she is a woman and can't really understand the needs and requirements for someone to succeed at building a successful stud."

More nausea. How could he be so utterly obtuse? She couldn't believe the nonsense flowing from his mouth. Why hadn't Uncle Ryder beaten that out of him? Surely after four hours of it, he would have realized a good blow would do the trick.

Meggie nodded ever so pleasantly and said, "Oh yes indeed. How true. I, myself, have often wondered how God could have been so remiss as to have made women, when they are so very useless. He wasted his time."

"But Charlotte is pregnant," Jeremy said, looking at her, blinking, confused.

Meggie said, "Surely God could have found an *easier* way to provide boy children for men rather than forcing them to have to deal with women, don't you think? Imagine, Charlotte hasn't the brains to even understand how horses mate. Imagine, you have to tell her even when she should no longer ride a horse. Imagine, she will welcome Leo with no idea what he will do."

"Meggie." This from her father, who knew from her

tone of voice that she'd gone too far. "Jeremy didn't mean that. You are misunderstanding him."

Of course her father doubtless wondered why she was quite ready to clout Jeremy in the head. Oh goodness, she had to stop being such a shrew. Her feelings for Jeremy—this was something Meggie never wanted either him or Mary Rose to know. It was too humiliating.

But something she couldn't control made her ignore her father and say, "I believe he said that Charlotte is stupid, unlike him or Leo since they are men and seem to know what's what." She looked at Jeremy straight in the face. "When I met Charlotte, I never thought she was stupid. Indeed, if I'd had the opportunity, I would have asked her if she had any ideas about training racing cats."

Jeremy looked like a calm, reasoned man who suddenly had an eccentric cousin on his hands. He said easily, "Meggie, you played a lovely song. Why don't you play another?"

"It was a Scarlatti sonata, not a song. It has no words. Oh goodness, how foolish of me. You, a man, would know that even without being told, wouldn't you?"

"Scarlatti was a man, dammit!"

"Wouldn't you say that perhaps dear Scarlatti had ample time to do his composing since he didn't have to birth children, wash clothes, scrub floors, or pander endlessly to all the males around him?"

"Hmmm," Mary Rose said, leaping to her feet. "Do you know, I have a headache. It started a good while ago. Meggie, would you please press a rosewater cloth to my forehead? You do it so very well. Come along."

Mary Rose held out her hand. Meggie had no choice. She said as she walked to her stepmother, "Shouldn't you ask Papa how it is best done? Or is that one of the very simplest of tasks to accomplish—like birthing children—so that I have a chance of learning to do it?"

"Meggie, my headache is going to split my brow apart."

"Good night, Mary Rose, Meggie," said Tysen. "Ah, my dearest daughter, I hope you will apologize to Jeremy before you bid us a pleasant good night."

"I apologize, Jeremy. Surely you can forgive me. I am much too stupid to understand my own insults."

Mary Rose had hauled her out of the drawing room, even pausing to shut the door behind her.

Tysen said to Jeremy, "Although Meggie was rude to you, my boy, your opinion of women would raise most female's hackles. I believe you should think about this."

Jeremy, however, was grinning, a thoroughly wicked grin. He said, very quietly, because Meggie was known to eavesdrop, "Do you think I baited her too much, Uncle Tysen?"

"You were acting like a jackass to make her lose her head, which she, naturally, did. It was well done."

"Not at first, but then she was so appalled, so furious at me, I couldn't help myself."

Suddenly Meggie appeared in the doorway. Jeremy said without pause, "I don't understand, Uncle Tysen. I am a man and Charlotte is a woman. We each have our own roles, our own responsibilities. Is Meggie feeling ill? Perhaps in her head?"

Meggie, no matter how important her reason for coming back, now turned on her heel, cursed under her breath, but not under enough for the two gentlemen, one of them her father and a vicar, and ran up the stairs.

Tysen just shook his head. "Do tell me more about this Arabian stallion you wish to buy from Spain."

Jeremy said, "Meggie is growing up fast."

"No. Actually, she's already well grown. She has very firm ideas about things."

"She always has. What a joy to tease her until the smoke came out of her ears." And he grinned again. "Now, about that Arabian. The fellow's nasty as a cock who's been kicked out of the hen yard. He's also as fast as the fox who managed to break in just last week and eat one of our best setters. He made a big mistake, however." Jeremy laughed.

Tysen arched an eyebrow.

"He tried to bite Charlotte, and she smacked the toe of her boot against his nose."

10

ℐT WAS TOO soon. Thomas knew he made her laugh, perhaps she'd even found his two kisses more than interesting, not that he could know for sure. Dammit. He forced himself back to the task at hand, making himself finish writing the letter to his steward.

He didn't know what made him look up, but he did, and there she was, striding like a long-legged boy into his garden. He slowly rose, rounded his desk, and opened the French door. She was flushed, breathing hard, her breasts pumping up and down, a rather nice sight.

What the devil had happened? He opened the door wide.

"Mistress Sherbrooke," he said formally, giving her a small bow, "do come into my humble estate room. I didn't realize that small private gate still opened."

"I forced it," Meggie said. "Good afternoon, Thomas. It isn't raining. Have you finally allowed Mr. Hengis some potato sticks?"

"No. Morgana informed me that Mr. Hengis—Benjie—was a poltroon, that you, little sweetling that you are, got a soaking because he misread his nose and you could have easily succumbed to an inflammation of the lungs."

He watched her calm, even smile at his jest, regain her bearings. He said then, "Come in and sit down."

She did, saying nothing more. She eased down in the

leather chair across from the big mahogany desk.

He sat on the edge of his desk and swung his leg, content to watch her for a few moments. She was really quite upset.

"All right, tell me what happened before you spit nails on my carpet."

"Nothing, dammit."

He very nearly laughed. "You, the vicar's daughter, shouldn't tell lies, Meggie. You probably shouldn't curse either. Something bad is bound to happen, like your tongue might rot off."

"Why would you care? What is my tongue to you?" The instant the words were out of her mouth, she remembered all too well that kiss in Martins' barn. "Never mind, don't you dare say anything. All that tongue business was very improper. I am so angry, Thomas, I could kick something."

"That moldering old hassock is at your disposal."

Meggie leapt to her feet, gave the hassock a hard kick, so hard she nearly knocked herself backward. She turned and smiled at him. "Thank you."

"A person should never allow ire to build to high levels. It clogs the body's pathways and leads many times to bad things, such as cursing."

"Blessed hell, surely that is nonsense."

"Oh no. I once knew a man who worried all the time, even worried when he discovered that his watch was several minutes slow and how many people he'd offended by being late. He never said much, just walked about with a frown on his face and bucketfuls of worry in his heart. Finally, one day when he was worrying about how his hog would ever find enough mud to wallow in since there hadn't been much rain, he just fell over dead, his pathways all clogged. So the moral to this tale is to spit it out when you're upset about something and kick something. Now, would you like a bit of brandy?"

"Brandy? Goodness, I haven't tasted brandy since Leo, Max, and I once stole Papa's bottle, hid behind one of the big tombstones in the cemetery, and drank it empty. All three of us were vilely sick. Papa, as I remember, didn't give us a hiding, just said that we now knew firsthand what stupidity tasted like."

Thomas laughed. "A taste does not stupidity make."

"Who said that?"

"Some long ago brilliant fellow."

"You're lying, but all right, I will try my first taste of brandy as a grown-up person."

He poured her a bit and himself a bit more. He clicked his snifter to hers. "Here's to the demise of the obnoxious person who made you angry enough to spit."

She choked, spewing the mouthful of brandy all over the front of his white shirt. She dropped the snifter, and stared at the darkening stain on that pristine white shirt. "Oh no, I don't believe I did that. This is awful, just look at that stain. It's such a beautiful shirt and I've ruined it. I spit on you. I've never done that before. I'm so sorry, Thomas."

He set down his own snifter and took her hands between his. "It's all right. It's just a shirt. No, Meggie, please don't try to suck it clean like little Rory tried to do to your skirt that morning at the church." She looked as if she would burst into tears and laughter, both at the same time.

He didn't think, just leaned down and kissed her. He tasted brandy and that sweet scent of her that had tantalized him when he'd kissed her before, a scent he'd never before tasted on another woman.

He touched his tongue to her mouth, urging hers to open, and she did, just a bit. When he eased his tongue into her mouth, she jumped, pushed away from him, backed up three fast steps, tripped over the hassock she'd kicked and landed on her bottom not on the soft Axminster carpet, but onto the oak floor.

"Meggie! Are you all right?"

She blinked up at him. "I think I've jarred my innards," she said, "but nothing that will kill me."

"Your bottom is well padded. Your innards should be safe."

She shook her head, came up to her knees, and stayed there a moment, looking fixedly into the corner of the estate room.

"Why did you jump away from me?"

"This time I just happened to leave my mouth open and you slid in your tongue. It's very strange, well—very personal—you know what I mean?"

"If you will just hold still and give it a chance, just maybe you will like it. Meggie, why are you staring off across the room?"

"There's a dead mouse in the corner."

He laughed, the latest laugh in the long line of laughs that had come from deep within him since he'd come here and met this woman. He said, "That must mean that Tansie was making another quilt rather than cleaning properly. I will tell Morgana and she will either forbid Tansie potato sticks or have her go eat mushrooms in the forest."

Meggie laughed. She just couldn't help it. "I do wish you would stop that."

"Stop what? Making you forget that you want to be angry and miserable and that your bottom hurts?"

"Yes, all of that." She sighed and pulled herself up. He watched her rub her bottom, even as she chewed on her bottom lip and stared at one of his shirt buttons.

"The brandy has already stained your lovely shirt. I am so sorry. If anyone sees you they will believe you a drunkard. I will have to defend you, but alas, here is your shirt as a silent witness, and thus no one will believe me. So, may I take it back to Mrs. Priddle? She can remove any stain in Christendom."

"If it means that much to you, and to save my reputation," he said, and begun to unfasten his shirt.

Meggie grabbed his hands. "You can't do that! What is wrong with you? You can't take off your clothes in your estate room, particularly since I'm standing right in front of you. My father is the damned vicar!"

And he doubled over with laughter, and the feel of that laughter was deep and full and he was growing quite used to it. He said, knowing he shouldn't, knew it was too soon, but unable to prevent the words from bursting out of his mouth, "Meggie, will you do me the honor of becoming my wife?"

Meggie gaped at him. He wanted her to marry him? This was quite the strangest day—kicking a hassock, falling on her rump, and a marriage proposal. And then Meggie thought of Jeremy, thought of kicking him off the back of his prized Arabian stud, perhaps even kicking him off the edge of the earth. At least Jeremy had taught her a very important lesson. Ignorance of a man's opinions could bring a woman low. She said, "I'm sorry, Thomas, but before I give this consideration I must question you first."

"Question me? Oh, I see. No, Meggie, I'm not a wife beater. I would never strike a woman."

"Neither is Jeremy and neither would he."

Naturally he knew exactly who this Jeremy was, and he felt cold all the way to his toes as he said mildly, "This is your almost dratted cousin?"

"Yes, he is visiting. I wanted to smack him silly last night."

"Ah, so he's the one who caused your ire to rise to dangerous levels. He's the one responsible for making you boot the stuffing in my hassock?"

"He's the one. He's also a man. I couldn't believe what came out of his mouth, Thomas, and he's only been married six months or so. I know my father isn't at all like that, but I just don't know about you, and so I must ask you. You see, if I married you and you turned into Jeremy, then I would have to shoot you. A vicar's daughter isn't allowed to do things like that."

"I understand perfectly. Ask away."

"Do you believe women are stupid?"

"No more stupid than men."

"I personally believe we are far less stupid than men. I came to this belief quite objectively after raising Max and Leo. All right, so you claim to be even-handed. Now, do you believe it is a husband's right to tell his wife she may not ride her mare when she becomes with child?"

He could but stare at her, her voice so very serious, so intense, and he remembered the anger that made her face red to her eyebrows. He said slowly, "If I had a wife and she was carrying a child, why then I would trust that she had the good sense not to do anything to endanger either herself or the babe. I would not want a wife who is a twit. I would not want a wife who needed instruction on something as obvious as that."

"Excellent, just excellent," Meggie said. "I knew you weren't an idiot. Now, do you wish God hadn't made women so that you wouldn't have to deal with them when you wanted a child? You wish that He'd devised another way for men to acquire boy children?"

"No. Don't tell me Jeremy could have intimated anything that ridiculous? Surely you mustn't have heard correctly."

"That was a very long question and your answer was very short. Would you care to elaborate?"

"No, Meggie, I wouldn't. Have I passed your test?"

She stroked her jaw, frowned at the hassock that had laid her low, and said, sighing, "Actually, to be honest, I'm not sure that Jeremy really believes that. It's just what I accused him of believing. Do you believe that husbands have the right to give orders to their wives?"

He said slowly, "I've never been married, Meggie. Would I ever give you orders? Yes, if you were in danger and I wanted to protect you."

"That's all right," she said, staring again at the dead mouse in the far corner. "I would give you orders as well if I believed you were in danger. Also, you're bigger than I am. If we ever were in any danger, surely your size would be useful."

"I hope so."

"I know all about horses, Thomas. I don't know much about studs and how to manage them, but I know I'm smart enough to learn. If you had a stud, would you consider me too stupid to be useful, all of this based solely on the fact that I'm not a man?"

"You, the premier racing cat trainer, not useful? That's ridiculous, Meggie. No man, not even an idiot, could say that."

"He believes women are too stupid to know man sorts of things."

"A moron," Thomas said. "The man who said that is a moron. Jeremy, I take it? Would you like me to pound him, perhaps kick him off the cliffs into the Channel?"

She shook her head sadly. "No. If you did that, he would hit on the beach, not wash out at all, and his body would be quickly discovered and you would be hanged." She sighed. "Anyway, if I'm not allowed to pound him, then it wouldn't be fair to have you do it. Do you like women, Thomas?"

"Immensely."

"Do you really wish to marry me?"

"Yes."

"Why? You've known me no more than a month."

"How odd. It seems like I've known you all my life." He paused a moment, looked down at the floor, then out the window. Finally, he said, surprise in his voice, "The thing is, Meggie, you make me laugh."

She walked up to him, hugged her arms around his back, and leaned her head back. "I can't think of a better reason. All right, I'll marry you."

He nearly shook he was so relieved. He slowly closed his arms around his back. He didn't kiss her, just held her. He would have to accustom himself to being a husband.

"Thomas?"

"Yes, Meggie."

"If we were blessed, and I conceived, would you expect me to present you with a boy?"

Children, he thought, children, something he'd assumed were simply a part of married life, but he hadn't thought of them, not as a reality, not as a natural result of making love to Meggie. "I could probably expect all I wanted. I don't think one can predict these things." He held her closer, closed his eyes, and tried not to think of anything outside of right now and the both of them standing very close in this room with a dead mouse in the corner.

He said against her left ear, "Perhaps I will set Tansie up in a quilt business."

She laughed and lightly bit his collarbone, even as she groaned at the taste of the sticky brandy on the front of his shirt.

Jeremy Stanton-Greville left at nine o'clock the following morning, feeling just a bit guilty because Meggie was obviously still angry at him. He'd wanted to hug her and punch her arm, tell her that soon she would learn that men could be led about like pigs with rings in their noses. No, not a good image. Well, maybe some day he would tell her that he'd just been jesting. She'd been so defensive, so ready to tear his throat out at his steady stream of insults.

Fact was, he had insulted her and her sex quite thoroughly, but not when he'd said that a wife's well-being should be the husband's responsibility. When Meggie was married, she would learn that was one of the main uses for a husband. That and sex. He grinned vacuously and began whistling between his thoroughbred's ears.

Not seven minutes later, Thomas Malcombe, seventh earl of Lancaster, knocked on the vicarage door.

Mary Rose, who was devoutly grateful that Jeremy had taken his leave, fearing that Meggie would go over the edge and try to stuff him up the chimney, blinked at the sight of Thomas Malcombe, beautifully garbed in riding clothes, so grateful that it was he and not Jeremy returning for some reason, that she nearly threw her arms around him and squeezed hard. He was carrying a riding crop in his right hand, his hat in his left. His dark hair was immaculate and she suspected that he hadn't set that hat on his head at all this morning. He was, she realized, a very handsome man.

She gave him her hand. "Good morning, Thomas. What a delightful surprise. Meggie is visiting with Mrs. Beach, who suffers from asthma and was wheezing quite dreadfully all last night."

"I am sorry about Mrs. Beach. However, I am here to see the vicar, Mary Rose."

"Ah. May I ask why? You see, Tysen is dreadfully busy right now, or at least he's trying to be busy. Every time he looks at Rory, he still must pick him up and toss him over his head just to hear him shriek with laughter. That's why the sermon is lagging behind."

"I don't plan to keep him from either Rory or his sermon for very long. I just want to ask him if I can marry his daughter."

Mary Rose didn't hesitate, gave him a big smile, and said, "Oh, I am so very pleased, Thomas, so very pleased indeed. Meggie has been so unhappy, although you wouldn't readily see it, but her father and I know her very well, and we've worried so much about her since we didn't know what was wrong. Then you came and wooed her, and just look what has happened. Oh my, both Rory and Tysen will be delighted to see you. Come this way, Thomas."

Thomas set his hands on her shoulders before she turned to dance away down the corridor. "I hope the vicar will accept me. He is a fine man. I think you would make a magnificent mother-in-law."

"Now that's a frightening thought," Mary Rose said. "I will try not to become a shrew and a tyrant, like my own mother-in-law, who, I am convinced, will outlive even her grandchildren. Tysen! Come here, Thomas Malcombe wishes to speak to you."

When Tysen asked her to come in a few minutes later, Mary Rose said, "We will have champagne, in just a moment. How delightful that Meggie will live here. We had always feared the day she wed that she would move to a faraway land and we would scarce see her."

"Well," Thomas said, "we won't be living here all the time, Mary Rose. I have other homes."

When Meggie followed the commotion into her father's study, she realized that Thomas had already done the deed.

"Well," she said from the doorway, dangling her straw bonnet by its ribbons, "will my father allow this business to proceed, Thomas?"

"Oh yes," Mary Rose said, and rushed to enfold her stepdaughter in her arms.

The champagne was quite delicious. Rory, who'd never left the study, and who hadn't really cared that he would gain his first and only brother-in-law, was allowed a small sip.

Tysen drank the champagne, smiled, said all the right things, but worried. He worried that he didn't know a damned thing about Thomas Malcombe. He worried that Meggie was marrying the first acceptable man to ask her when she still loved Jeremy Stanton-Greville, something he wasn't about to tell Mary Rose.

As for Thomas Malcombe, Tysen would find out everything about the damned man—down to his birthmark—before he allowed his precious daughter to walk to the altar. But Meggie was smiling, grinning like a fool, actually. She'd always had excellent instincts. He'd always trusted her, but this was for life, no reprieves if the man turned out to be a gambler or a womanizer. And what about her feelings for Jeremy? Had he put the nail in her feelings before he'd left? Were they gone now? Was this a sign of it? He wished he knew.

When he thought about it later, Tysen knew he would be very surprised if indeed he found a skeleton lurking in the back of one of Lord Lancaster's closets. He was an excellent young man.

Still, he would look.

11

WHEN TYSEN FINALLY managed to snag his daughter away from the rest of the family, particularly Alec, who wanted to show her a new racing cat training technique that involved a bucket, he led her through the vicarage garden, to the gate, and down the path to the cemetery, where few parishioners chose to spend any time when not absolutely necessary. He needed privacy. He unlatched the very old black wrought-iron gate, slowly pulling it open for her to step onto the path that led into the depths of the cemetery.

The air was different here. Still and soft, as quiet as fingers stroking a racing cat's back. Meggie stopped, breathed in deeply, and said over her shoulder, "You come here when you wish to think, Papa. I remember you sitting on that one particular bench from my youngest years. I used to wonder why you so admired Sir Vincent D'Egle, a medieval warrior who likely wasn't an overly religious man. I picture him in battle, yelling and swinging his sword and finally being cleaved in two himself at far too young an age."

"Cleaved in two? Actually, I also rather fancy that might have happened to him. However, no matter how he died, there is something about his grave that draws me back," he said, smiling down at her as he took her hand. "I don't know why this should be so, but I know that when I sit there, and I hear Mr. Peters ring the church bells, I feel peace and calm seep into my very bones. You still bring flowers to his grave."

Meggie nodded, and said, "It will rain soon. Can you feel how heavy the air has suddenly become? How it is already wrapping itself about your head, wanting to soak you? I've decided that it rains too much in England. Everyone is so tired of feeling damp to their toes and—"

"Meggie, I must speak to you."

"I know, Papa. You're being very gentle with me. When you do that, I know there is something you're dreading to tell me. I can take it. Has Leo done something awful at Oxford? Will I need to go there and fix things? Try to teach him what's what?"

"I devoutly hope not. No, it's something else, Meggie."

She looked at him steadily. "This is about me, isn't it? And about Thomas."

"Oh Meggie, my sweet girl, let's sit here beside Sir Vincent on his bench. Yes, this is about Thomas. I am your father and you know down to your bones that I will always want what is the very best for you."

She didn't say a word, just looked at him and waited for the ax to fall.

He realized in that moment that she just wasn't ready to be blighted. He was willing to wait, and when he paused, she quickly said, her hand lightly closing over one of his, all forced smiles and enthusiasm, "I was listening to Mary Rose read Rory the story of *Renard the Fox*."

"It is his favorite," Tysen said, running his fingers over the smooth worn gray stone. "But Mary Rose must read it to him only in Latin." He shook his head, looking a bit bewildered. "How very strange it is. We live in the modern world, yet two of my sons and my wife speak Latin. Latin. It boggles the mind, Meggie. Now, my dear—"

Meggie said quickly, "I meant to leave, but then she started reading him *Chanticleer the Cock*. Mary Rose can even cock-a-doodle-doo in Latin."

"Rory is only four years old, Meggie. At least he doesn't announce his age yet in Latin."

Meggie laughed. "He will. Give him a couple more years. You know that Mary Rose is very smart, Papa. I believe she was learning Latin at Rory's age." Tysen looked at his daughter while she spoke, so Sherbrooke in her looks—blondish brownish hair with all the shades in between, and clear light blue eyes the color of the summer sky. In short, she looked like him, only her features were more finely drawn. Her chin, he thought, was very possibly more stubborn. As for her temperament, his daughter saw something that needed to be done, and she did it, no shilly-shallying about, no excuses, never procrastinating. She felt strongly about things, many times too strongly. No middle ground for her. He remembered she'd been three years old when she saw old Mrs. McGilly struggling with several packages on High Street and had immediately tried to help her. But she wasn't strong enough, and so had fetched two men from the tavern to tote the bundles. One of them, Tysen remembered, had been very tipsy and proceeded to drop the packages. Meggie had scolded him.

He grinned with the memory. Yes, his Meggie knew only one direction—forward. In this, she was just like her aunt Sinjun. And, he knew, she wanted to move smartly forward with Thomas Malcombe, Lord Lancaster.

Meggie was saying now, "Did you know that Alec wants to be the Prussian Gebhard Leberecht von Blucher when he grows up? He can even say the whole name. And spell it. He's had me play Napoleon more times than I can count. He's chased me all over the graveyard and into the bell tower. Then he finds me and claims he's not going to send me back to Elba. No, he's going to send me some place where I will rot. In perpetuity. He actually says perpetuity."

Tysen felt the tug in his heart, let it blossom a moment, flooding him with sweet memories of Meggie as a little girl, her finger in every village pie, her ear against every door, her opinion offered on every sermon. And that little girl had adored him since she'd come from her mother's womb and smiled up at him. He said easily, "He always chases me and Mary Rose too. I have yet to be graced with perpetuity." He took her hand in his, competent hands, beautiful long fingers. He said, "Meggie, you are only nineteen years old. You spent only one Season in London. You have lived all your life in Glenclose-in-Rowan."

"I live in Scotland every year too, Papa."

"Yes, well, that's true."

She turned to him then, took one of his hands between hers. "All right. I'm ready for whatever you have to tell me. Come, spit it out, Papa. What is wrong? What have you learned about Thomas?"

"I don't wish you to misunderstand me," Tysen said slowly. "I like Thomas Malcombe. He saved Rory's life, I am quite convinced of that, as is Dr. Dreyfus. He is a charming young man. He seems intelligent, witty, responsible. From what I have heard from your uncle Douglas's man in London, he was no pauper even before his father died and left him his holdings. Thomas's business interests are evidently primarily in Italy, where he has grown rich in shipping, in a very short time. I could find out nothing about him that would make me worry.

"He wanted to pay me a dowry for you. Naturally I refused. You will not go to your husband empty-handed. You are not quite the heiress your aunt Sinjun was, but your dowry is really quite satisfactory. Lord Lancaster is assuredly not a fortune hunter."

"Then what is Lord Lancaster?"

"Meggie, your dowry aside, you and I have known Lord Lancaster for only two months, maybe not even that long. I knew his father, didn't particularly dislike the man. He was secretive, Meggie, very tight-fisted, didn't speak well of anyone. He was not a man I would have easily trusted. Now, I don't believe you know this. The old earl divorced his wife and kicked both her and her young son out of Bowden Close. Neither of them ever came back. I have heard rumors about a second wife, perhaps another child, but I don't know if any of that is true."

"None of that in any way redounds on Thomas."

"No."

"Thomas told me that there had been a falling out between his father and his mother, and she took Thomas and left. He didn't mention a divorce. I didn't press him. He doesn't like to speak of it. I believe he's been very hurt by it."

"I asked Thomas as well. He told me much of the same thing, all said in a voice so emotionless that it smote me."

"Poor Thomas. He finally told me that he remembered terrible fights between his parents. He did see his father a few times over the years, but never here, never at Bowden Close. It is all very sad. I believe he came to hate his father. His father never visited him at school, where he spent most of his growing-up years, only in London, at one of his father's clubs. I know that Thomas doesn't trust easily, certainly understandable. And I know that he was very hurt by his parents, not physically, mind you, but his soul. Naturally he will not admit to any of this. He merely pretends that he doesn't care. Perhaps when we have been married for a while, he will grow to trust me more, to share his concerns, to share old secrets that have hurt him. He feels things deeply, that I do know. You did not see his face when he believed Rory would die. But there is this well of distrust that is very deep in him. These things take time, Papa.

"I do know that Thomas Malcombe is a principled man, a decent man. He told me he wants to marry me because I make him laugh. I cannot think of a better reason."

Tysen lifted an eyebrow. "Actually, he could have told you he loved you."

"Somehow," Meggie said slowly, looking up at the beautiful old church tower, wishing Mr. Peters would ring the bell at this very moment, "I cannot imagine him saying those words, at least not now. Actually, I didn't say them to him either." Meggie paused a moment, looking down at her clasped hands, and Tysen knew all the way to his boots that Jeremy was still in her head, perhaps even in her heart. Damnation.

"Yes, Thomas laughs easily now, a smile nearly always near his mouth. I'll never forget that first time when he laughed with me. I thought he sounded rusty, as if he were somehow surprised that such a sound could come from him. I've made great strides with him, Papa."

"Meggie, you are not marrying him out of some sort of misguided sense of gratitude, are you?"

"For saving Rory's life? No, Papa, but I was very grateful, and the result was that I spent more time with him initially than I normally would have. And I came to like him a great deal. He is an honorable man, I am quite sure about that."

"You won't be living here, Meggie. Thomas was evasive. He said he has two other houses, both outside of England."

"One is in Genoa, Italy. He was living in Italy, making his fortune. He came back to England only to take over his father's holdings. Can you imagine sailing to Italy, Papa? I should love to travel, to see other places, how other people do things, how they think. I wonder where his other house is."

At least Thomas Malcombe hadn't told him one thing, then told his daughter something else. There were no inconsistencies that meant a lie. But it wasn't the point. Tysen kissed his child's forehead, rose, and crossed his arms over his chest, the father now, the authority figure.

"Meggie, I am very sorry, but I must be blunt. I didn't want you to find out about this, but now there is no choice. You have to know. I cannot believe that Thomas Malcombe is honorable, and therefore I cannot trust his word on anything of import and I certainly cannot trust him with you."

"He saved your son's life."

"For that I owe him a debt that will never be repaid. However, I do not owe him my daughter."

Meggie knew something bad was coming, she just knew it. She drew herself up. "I'm ready, Papa. Tell me."

"As you know, Melissa Winters left last Thursday for an extended visit with her grandmother in Bury St. Ed-

monds. You know that, but not the reason for her leaving.
I didn't want to tell you this, I didn't want to tell anyone
this, and it is a confidence. I ask that you not betray it to
anyone, even Mary Rose. Evidently Thomas Malcombe
was in London before he came here. He met Melissa
there. She was staying with her aunt and attending parties
and such, sort of an informal come-out for her. There's
no easy way to say this, Meggie—he seduced her and got
her with child. You and I and Melissa's parents are now
the only ones to know. And Lord Lancaster, of course."

Meggie said slowly, "Thomas didn't tell me he was in
London before he came here."

"He was. I asked. Because he wants to marry you, it
was my responsibility to ask, to find out everything I
could about him. Mr. Winters heard, of course, that you
were to wed Thomas Malcombe. He searched me out. He
told me about this, in confidence, just this morning. It was
obvious he didn't want to tell me, Meggie, but he has
great liking for you and didn't want you to be hurt."

There was fire in her eyes as she said the fateful words
he would have given anything not to hear, ever, "I don't
believe it. Melissa is lying. She wanted him. I know that
Thomas must have rejected her, and thus this is her revenge. I know that Melissa—to punish Thomas—was intimate with another man, to make him jealous, perhaps,
and this is the result. I am sorry for it, but Thomas is
innocent. Papa, if Melissa were truly pregnant with his
child, then why wouldn't Thomas marry her?"

"You are not naïve, Meggie. You must know that Melissa's birth isn't high enough to tempt a man like Lord
Lancaster, nor is her dowry an incentive to overlook her
birth. Even though her mother is the daughter of a baron,
her father is in trade. In short, there is nothing to induce
Thomas Malcombe to tie himself forever to the Winters
family."

She was shaking her head, back and forth. "I am convinced that Thomas wouldn't behave dishonorably, Papa.
Truly, he is all that is kind and honest and—"

"Thomas Malcombe paid Melissa's parents for the care

of the child. Her father, although he was reluctant to do so, told me this. I have no reason to disbelieve Mr. Winters, Meggie. His pain over this was palpable. He tried his best to convince Thomas Malcombe to marry his daughter, but he wouldn't do it."

He watched her face pale, the light of battle fade from her eyes. He hated it, but now it was done.

"Oh dear," Meggie whispered, "Oh dear."

"I believe," her father said, lightly touching her fingertips to her smooth check, "that now is an appropriate time for you to say blessed hell."

Meggie just shook her head, pulled off her bonnet, and dashed her fingers through her hair, shining more blond than brown beneath the morning sun. There had been Jeremy, and she'd been sure her heart would never recover from that stomping. Then, thankfully, she'd seen Jeremy as a fatuous, self-aggrandizing clod, so superior to womankind, who would likely make Charlotte's life miserable, something she probably richly deserved, unless she was a doormat and she'd met the ideal mate for her.

And then Thomas had come along, and she'd realized that here was indeed a man she could admire, a man who admired her, who didn't denigrate her, who teased her and made her happy. The soul-eating melancholia that had pulled her down for nearly a year had vanished. She'd felt so very blessed for nearly a week. Six full days, no black clouds in the vicinity. And now this. She was cursed.

"Mary Rose and I would like you to visit Aunt Sinjun and Uncle Colin in Scotland."

She turned on him, bitterness overflowing. "Won't everyone think I'm pregnant?"

He hated the hurt in her, knew that rage would come, and he wished with all his heart that it didn't have to be like this. "I'm sorry, Meggie, but there are men in this world who are simply not worthy. I am so very sorry that you had to meet one of them, trust one of them."

Meggie felt pounded, felt the words hollowing her out, leaving her empty with only the bowing pain to fill her. She said as she slowly rose and shook out her skirts, "You know I must speak to Thomas, Papa. I must hear this from him."

"Yes, Meggie, I know you must."

"I will know the truth when I hear him speak."

"I hope that you will."

Meggie had turned away when he felt a sudden shaft of alarm, and called after her, "Do not go to a private spot with him, Meggie. I wish you wouldn't go to Bowden Close without a chaperone, but I know that you feel you must. So be mindful. Do you promise me?"

"Yes," Meggie said. "I promise." She wasn't about to tell him that she'd visited Thomas at his home alone before. She walked away, her head down, deep in thought. She wasn't aware that her father was watching her, pain in his eyes for the pain he'd had to give her.

Tysen rose from the bench, stared down at Sir Vincent's tombstone, and wondered what Sir Vincent D'Egle, that medieval warrior, would have done to Thomas Malcombe if Meggie had been his daughter. Probably lop off his head.

All Meggie could think about as she strode to Bowden Close was that she'd been wrong about him, that Thomas had fathered a child, that he'd professed to care for her when just a couple of months before he'd been intimate with another girl and fathered a child. That, Meggie knew, meant intimacy and that meant they'd caressed and kissed each other. Meggie stopped short. She touched her fingertips to the velvet of a blooming rose that climbed the wrought-iron fence that surrounded the cemetery. She knew in that moment that there was an explanation that would absolve him. She wanted that explanation and she wanted it pure and clean and straightforward, with no questions, no doubts, left behind.

12

Bowden Close

THOMAS WAS SMILING even before Meggie slipped into his library. It wasn't at all proper that she came in through that old garden gate, but they would soon be married. Soon he would no longer have to concern himself with the vicar's daughter bending society's rules. It wouldn't matter. That thought pleased him mightily.

Her hair was mussed, as if she'd been fretting about something and had yanked on it, her cheeks were flushed, and her eyes, so expressive, bright and vivid, so filled with what she felt— oh God, something was wrong. It was like a punch to the gut.

He was around his desk in an instant, his hands around her arms but a moment later, and he was actually shaking her. "What the devil is wrong? What happened? Did someone hurt you?"

She looked up at him and said, without preamble, "My father told me about Melissa Winters."

A dark eyebrow went up, making him look like a satyr, emphasizing the arrogant tilt of his head, the go-to-the-devil look. His hands dropped away, his voice was suddenly colder than the Channel waters in February. "Your father, my dear, shouldn't meddle."

Meggie sent her fist as hard as she could into his belly. He'd had an instant to tighten his stomach muscles before her fist landed hard and his breath *whooshed* out. At least the punch didn't bowl him over. He grabbed her wrist before she could hit him again.

"That hurt," he said.

Meggie tried to pull away, but he held her wrist tightly. She was panting even as she shouted at him, "I'm glad it hurt. Let me go and I'll do it again!"

He grabbed her other wrist and shook her. "Dammit, Meggie, what the devil is wrong with you?"

"Thomas Malcombe, don't you dare pretend that you're bored by all this, that you're indifferent to it, that you have no idea what I'm talking about, what I'm enraged about. Lower that supercilious eyebrow. Listen to me, Thomas, my father is the vicar. It is my father's duty to meddle, particularly since you wish to be his son-in-law. He wants to protect me."

"All right, now it's my turn to be angry. No, don't try to get away from me. I'm going to hold you awhile longer, there's still too much blood in your eyes. Now, your damned father should not have sullied your ears with this. It has nothing at all to do with you, Meggie, nothing at all. Melissa was a mistake, a very bad one, admittedly, but your father should not have told you about it."

"The mistake, as you so indifferently call it, has cost Melissa dearly. Now there will be a child to live with the consequences of that mistake."

He released her, walked over to the sideboard, and poured himself some brandy. She'd seen his indifferent act, then seen the anger gushing out, and now he was the controlled gentleman again. She watched him sip the brandy before he turned back to her. "I am sorry for it," he said, all calm and smooth, "but it happened and I couldn't prevent it from happening. If I'd known, I would have stopped it, but I didn't know."

All his male beauty disappeared in that instant, all his charm with it. Jeremy was an insufferable moron, but Thomas was worse by far. He was treacherous. She was appalled both at herself for her lack of wisdom, and at him, for his indifference, his utter lack of remorse for what he'd done. Her own anger, her outrage at what he'd done, was fast drowning out her pain at his betrayal. "You couldn't prevent it from happening? If you had known what? Are you mad?"

"No, I'm not in the least mad. Won't you sit down, Meggie?" His hand was shaking. He hated that. Even as he waved her toward a chair, he moved quickly behind his desk.

"I don't want to sit down," she said, strode to his desk, leaned toward him, splaying her hands flat. "I want you to tell me why you couldn't prevent this mess from occurring. Surely you aren't going to blame Melissa for all of it? She seduced you? She, woman of the world that she is, forced you to be intimate with her? Blessed hell, Thomas, please don't tell me that."

He remained standing behind his desk, leaned forward as well, his own palms flat on the desktop, his face not six inches from hers. He said slowly, "No, I won't tell you that. You haven't known me long, Meggie, but I had believed that you'd come to trust me. I gather your father told you that I am paying for the upbringing of Melissa's child."

"Yes."

"I told you I had no control. I meant it. You see, I didn't know what William had done until it was far too late. Hell, I didn't even know he was in town."

Meggie drew back, now standing ramrod straight. "William? Who the devil is William?"

"My younger brother, my half brother, actually. He is at Oxford. However, four months ago, he was in London, as I said, unbeknownst to me at the time. He and several of his friends decided to experiment with sin—whores and gaming hells. He did, unfortunately, attend one party, met Melissa, and things progressed rapidly from there." He frowned at her, then the frown deepened as he stared beyond her to the enclosed garden. "You believed I was the one to impregnate Melissa Winters."

"Yes, I did. That is what my father told me."

"I did not. She is a child, a silly foolish girl."

"We are the same age."

"Only in years, Meggie, only in years. William didn't admit it to me until Melissa's father arrived here at Bowden Close to call me a philandering bastard. Of course, then I managed to figure out what must have happened."

William. It was William, his half brother, and she hadn't even known he'd existed.

It wasn't Thomas.

Meggie felt the sun break over her head. The explanation—it had burst forth and it was clean and pure with no murky gray to muck things up. She felt such relief, such profound joy, she wanted to shout. She said, "How old is William?"

"He's twenty-one, much younger for a male than it is for a female. Using myself as a measuring stick, I have determined that youth tends to encourage stupid behavior. Haven't you done foolish things, Meggie?"

"Yes," she said without hesitation, "but I have never searched out a boy to seduce him."

This effortless charm of hers. It washed over him, whether he wanted it to or no. "No," he said, "you wouldn't."

"Why did you let Mr. and Mrs. Winters believe you were the one?"

He shrugged. "Evidently Melissa was afraid to tell her parents the truth, so she told them it was me. Since I am now head of this family, I am responsible for William, and he knows it. He made a mistake. I have taken care of it. Hopefully, both he and Melissa are now a bit wiser."

"My father always says that one must be accountable for one's own mistakes."

"Perhaps, but it is done and I cannot now change it. I will say, though, that William is on a much shorter leash now."

"He should have married her."

"He refused. However, I made it perfectly clear to him that if the child survived, then he would be its father. I told him I would cut him off if he did not agree to this. He agreed."

"Well, that's something. I am sorry, Thomas, but I am not going to much like William."

"Perhaps not. I am hopeful that he will improve as he adds a few more years." He paused a moment, then said, his voice every bit as austere as her father's when faced with wickedness, "I am disappointed in you for not trusting me."

"Don't put on that righteous act with me, Thomas. Actually the evidence would have hanged you."

She hadn't apologized, just smacked him in the jaw with the unvarnished truth. "All right, I accept that. Now, would you like me to go reassure your father?"

Meggie gave him a brilliant smile. "Yes, please do, sir. Oh, Thomas, will we live in Italy?"

He said slowly, "Perhaps, Meggie. Perhaps. Would you like that?"

"Immensely." She ran around his desk, went up on her tiptoes, kissed his check, then stared at him a moment, kissed his mouth, hers tightly seamed, and it didn't matter a bit. He watched her rush out into the enclosed garden, her skirts rustling, her bonnet dangling from her fingertips nearly to the ground. He knew she would snag it on a rosebush, and she did, but again, it didn't matter.

Glenclose-on-Rowan
April 1824

The wedding of Thomas Malcombe, earl of Lancaster, to Margaret Beatrice Lydia Sherbrooke, spinster, was attended by four hundred people, another hundred or so milling about outside the church for word of what was happening. The men who'd managed to beg off were in the tavern, drinking ale, listening to Mr. Mortimer Fulsome's advice on married life, something none of them paid the least attention to since he'd buried four wives, none of them lasting more than two years, and he was eighty years old now and could barely be heard above the toasts.

Tysen led his daughter down the aisle to where Lord Lancaster and Bishop Arlington of Brighton waited, a twinkle in the bishop's eye. He had known Tysen since he'd been born, Meggie as well. He was completely bald and the sunlight pouring through the stained-glass window above him sent a wash of colors across his head.

"He looks like God wearing a rainbow," Meggie said out of the side of her mouth.

"He's nearly blind," Tysen said to his daughter as they walked past people who had known her all her life. "Stand as close as possible to him. Tell Thomas to do the same. And don't stare at his head."

It was a glorious Friday morning in mid-April, the air was fresh from a rain that had dutifully stopped at midnight the evening before. Clouds were strewn in a very blue sky.

Every Sherbrooke was present, including the earl of Ashburnham and his family come all the way from Scotland. And, of course, Oliver and Jenny from Kildrummy.

There was no one from Thomas Malcombe's family, but if anyone remarked upon it, it didn't get to Meggie's ears. She, herself, believed it for the best. If William had shown up, she just might have kicked him. As for Thomas's mother, he'd simply said she was ill and left it at that. He was so very alone, she thought that morning as all her aunts helped her dress in her wedding finery. But that would change.

The Vicarage was filled to capacity. Had there been ladders to the rafters, Thomas thought, there would be folk hanging off those as well. All of the boy cousins were staying with him at Bowden Close.

The Sherbrookes were a very popular family. No, it was more than that. Meggie was the daughter of the town, beloved by its denizens. He thought, as he watched her come closer and closer, that he'd never seen a more beautiful woman in his life. He smiled when she chanced to look at him.

Meggie didn't look again at Bishop Arlington. She was staring at the man who would be her husband in not more than fifteen minutes from now.

Organ music swelled, so loud the windows rattled a bit. The air was still, fragrant with flowers, many from the Northcliffe Hall greenhouses, brought to Glenclose-on-Rowan by Uncle Douglas and Aunt Alex. So many people, all of them here to wish her well. She passed by the Winters family and felt a stab of concern. There were no smiles on their faces. Even though her father had told her they accepted that William Malcombe was the father of Melissa's child, they still couldn't bring themselves to like Thomas Malcombe.

All her boy cousins were seated in one row; Grayson, she knew, was memorizing everything, later to embroider a rousing tale, probably replete with a congregation that were really demons from some pit in Hell and the demons had sprung open the pit just recently, just for Meggie's wedding. Leo and Max, both looking faintly worried, and she understood that. Everything was different now that they were all grown up. Now they realized just how many years separated all of them from childhood—her marriage underscored this. She wished she could have stopped a moment and hugged them, reassured them. She wanted to tell them that being a grown-up meant change, something to be desired not feared.

There were James and Jason, looking more beautiful than she did, both of them striving to look as austere and distinguished as their father, who, seated in the row ahead of them, looked every inch the powerful earl. Meggie gave him a big grin, which was returned, and which the twins didn't see. They might have relaxed a bit if they'd seen that smile. Her aunt Alex gave her a small wave with her gloved hand.

Aunt Sophie and Uncle Ryder were to her left, and what with ten of the Beloved Ones coming to Glenclose-on-Rowan, they occupied an entire row, very tightly. Her uncle Ryder's brilliant Sherbrooke eyes were still wicked, still so startling a blue, that ladies stopped in the middle of the street and stared at him and grinned like idiots. This behavior Aunt Sophie normally ignored, or poked her oblivious spouse in his ribs to make him stop being so damned delicious to the opposite sex. As for Aunt Sophie, she was solid as a rock, always calm no matter the trouble, no matter the pain.

And her godmother, Aunt Sinjun, sitting beside Uncle Colin, Fletcher and Dahling beside them, Dahling a young matron, married to a Scottish baron from the Highlands near Glen Coe way. Phillip was far away in Greece with the Royal Navy, Uncle Colin had told everyone. Phillip, it seemed, was a cartographer, something most all the male cousins had had to look up in the dictionary. Fletcher was now twelve, as magic with horses as Alec was with racing cats. She remembered so long ago how he had renamed her father's horse. He spoke to horses and they spoke to him. What would he do when he grew up? Meggie wondered. She thought with a pang of his little sister, Jocelyn, who had died while still very young. Thank God Rory had survived.

Jeremy and Charlotte were there, Charlotte well into her pregnancy, smiling, looking utterly beautiful, glowing, Jeremy, so proud, so possessive of her, standing close by her, always. Meggie had greeted them warmly, so very warmly. As for Jeremy, he'd had time to say to her, "I need to speak to you sometime, Meggie."

She'd nodded, having no intention whatsoever of listening to him lecture her on something, probably on copying dear Charlotte, the perfect obedient subservient wife.

Mary Rose sat between Alec and Rory on the very front row. She was trying to hold Rory still since he was bouncing up and down, wanting, Meggie knew, to walk along beside her. She'd seen him just the day before practicing how to walk. Meggie saw her father try to frown his son down, but then she realized he just couldn't. It would be like scolding a racing kitten. When Tysen smiled at his son, Rory managed to pull away from his mother and dash to his father and Meggie. Laughter erupted from the congregation. Tysen swooped down and grabbed up his son, even as Rory tried to climb over him to get to Meggie.

Meggie took the little boy's face between her gloved hands and kissed him, then said, "Rory, will you and our papa both give me away?"

And Rory beamed and said loud enough for everyone in the church to hear, "Oh yes, Meggie, let me, let me. Meggie, is that really you under that white sack?"

Meggie lifted a corner of her beautiful veil and winked at Rory.

There was laughter until finally Bishop Arlington raised his hands.

Rory stood proudly by Tysen until the bishop asked who was giving Meggie away, to which both males replied, "I do."

More laughter. Meggie looked up to see that her groom was smiling, a relief since he was very pale, probably as scared as she was.

Bishop Arlington had a booming voice that probably reached even the folk down at the tavern. He spoke of all sorts of expectations for Meggie, all blessed and approved by God, which made Meggie want to roll her eyes. She peeked up at Thomas, saw that he was looking quite severe, and so didn't make a sound.

The marriage service barely lasted fifteen minutes. Now, she, Meggie Sherbrooke, was a countess and Thomas, at Bishop Arlington's kind direction, was pulling back her veil, kissing her, smiling, looking immensely relieved as he said close to her ear, "You're mine now, Meggie. Mine."

"And you are mine, Thomas. Forever."

And something deep moved in his eyes as he stared down at her, something deep and thick and veiled. He kissed her again, a quick light kiss because there were many people avidly watching. They turned toward the congregation, both smiling so big some feared their jaws would crack.

Meggie said out of the corner of her mouth, "This is so very exciting. Do you think you will drink champagne out of my slipper?"

13

It WASN'T UNTIL nearly six o'clock that evening when Mary Rose was fastening the small buttons of her traveling gown up Meggie's back.

"Has Thomas told you where you are spending tonight?"

"No, the man has refused to tell me a thing. Not even a single hint. I have wheedled and promised all sorts of wicked favors if he would just give me one sentence, but he refused. I even offered to put my tongue in his mouth, but he refused to speak a word about it. Oh, forgive me, Mary Rose, I didn't mean to embarrass you. It's just that this tongue business—I think I like it. Ah, I do hope we're on a packet to Calais, then to Paris. I should love to go to Paris again, Mary Rose. Remember when we went last time? I was thirteen and we walked in the Luxemburg Gardens and visited Versailles and Notre Dame, how magnificent that was, and—"

Mary Rose interrupted her, laughing, "Yes, love, I remember it well." She sighed then. "I believe I would have preferred to have your father to myself, but I endured having my interfering stepdaughter along." For just an instant Meggie didn't laugh at her jest. Mary Rose took Meggie's face between her hands and kissed her. "I loved you from the moment you rescued me and sneaked me into your bedchamber at Kildrummy. I loved you even more when I heard you try to convince your father that you were innocent as a shorn lamb, that you weren't hiding a thing from him. And I loved all the excuses your father had to invent to keep you out of our bedchamber at night.

"You have grown into a splendid woman. I want you to be happy with Thomas. I also want a letter from you, but I will give you a week before you have to write it."

She kissed her again, only to have Meggie's arms go around her and hug her tight. "Oh goodness, now you will have your own bedchamber with your own husband. Time has gone so quickly, Meggie, so quickly. Savor every moment. Be happy, love."

And Meggie said, "I knew I would adore you forever when I saw Papa carrying you over his shoulder back into the castle. I was trying desperately to pull your valise back inside, but it was so heavy because of the iron candlesticks."

Mary Rose laughed. "They weren't iron, Meggie!"

"I know, but they were very heavy, and I was only ten years old. I will miss you and Papa, Mary Rose. Oh goodness, what about Alec and Rory? Will you be able to manage them? Will—"

"Everything will be all right. They will miss you dreadfully and ask me every day when you are coming for a visit. Don't worry, love. You are a married lady now and that is a very different thing. Er, Meggie, is there anything you wish perhaps to ask me?"

"About what? Has either of the boys done something you're not sure about?"

"No, not today. When they are monsters I will simply lock them in the closet beneath the stairs. Now, Meggie—" She paused a moment, pumping herself up. "Would you like to ask me about marital sorts of things? I promised your father I would, er, inquire."

"Oh. Oh my, Mary Rose, you're embarrassed!" Meggie laughed, hugged her again as she said, "You know, I think it is rather exciting not knowing much of anything. Thomas does kiss very well. I assume he can continue this lovemaking business efficiently."

"Yes," Mary Rose said, her voice dry as the cherry-wood armoire in the corner, "I believe that he will as well."

Meggie said, suddenly appalled, "I cannot imagine speaking to Papa about those sorts of things." Then she looked thoughtful. "But perhaps you could tell me. Is this tongue in each other's mouths—is it the done thing? Do you and Papa do it?"

Mary Rose managed not to swallow her own tongue. "Well, as a matter of fact, if you are truly interested, and I suppose that you are since you have such an inquiring mind, well, I imagine that I would have to say yes, it is very much the done thing." Mary Rose then smiled, flushed, looked at the ceiling, then at the floor, patted Meggie's back, and picked up her traveling cloak, a rich burgundy velvet Thomas had given her for a wedding gift.

Thomas was waiting for her at the foot of the stairs. He wasn't smiling. He was, obviously, anxious to be off. She saw all her relatives spread out behind them, all of them speaking and laughing, the dratted boy cousins being idiots, as always. So many beloved faces.

She hugged her father, and it seemed to everyone there that she didn't want to let him go. Tysen saw that Thomas was looking utterly emotionless, but he'd known the young man long enough to realize that he wanted his new wife and he wanted her five minutes ago. He wanted her to himself, and that, Tysen thought, was something he would simply have to accustom himself to. He also saw Thomas looking several times at Jeremy, and again, there was no expression at all on his face. Tysen wondered, but he couldn't do anything else. He kissed Meggie once, twice more, then patted her shoulder, and placed her hand on her husband's arm.

"Be happy, sweetheart," he said.

Meggie looked down to see Rory tugging on her skirt. She lifted him up high, gave him two smacking loud kisses, and said, "Say hello to your new brother-in-law, Rory."

Rory looked over at Thomas, studied him for a very long time, and said finally, "You are the man who saved my life with that volcano medicine."

"Yes, I suppose I am," Thomas said.

"You will give Meggie everything she wants," Rory said.

"I will," Thomas said, and bowed his head.

Rory patted him on the shoulder. Meggie kissed the little boy one more time and handed him back to their father.

Her ribs sore from so many hugs, Thomas's hand firm in the small of her back, Meggie was lifted into the carriage. She leaned out the window, waving, smiling until she was sure her mouth would break.

Glenclose-on Rowan was gone from her view in the next minute because Thomas had turned her around to face him, pulled her to him, and kissed her.

He released her even before she'd had a chance to think about that kiss and what she should do. She said, staring at his mouth, her fingertips on her lower lip, "You didn't open your mouth. You didn't give me time to do anything at all. Perhaps I would have liked to open my mouth a bit."

"I never wish to begin something that I would be unable to finish."

"I suppose you're talking about lovemaking."

He didn't smile at her, just untied the bow beneath her jaw and pulled off her stylish bonnet. He laid it carefully on the opposite seat. "You have lovely hair, Meggie."

"Thank you. So do you, Thomas, all dark as ancient sins, nearly as black as your eyes. At least they look black in this dim light. You and I are very different, Thomas, and I like it very much. I will thank God every day for fashioning you just as you are. Now, will you please tell me where we are going on our wedding trip?"

"No, not yet. You will see. All right, a small bit of a hint. I am taking you to one of my homes."

She was nearly speechless with excitement. "We are sailing to Italy?"

"No. Not this time. You will see. Don't fret. It will be dark soon. We will spend the night in Exeter."

"We are traveling west."

"Yes."

She poked him very gently in his belly. He obligingly grunted for her. "I am your wife, sir. It isn't healthy for you to keep secrets from me."

He said nothing to that, and she leaned back as he pulled up the window against the chill evening air. "Are we going to Cornwall?"

"Yes, but it is not our final destination."

"I saw you speaking to Uncle Ryder. Do you approve of him now?"

"I believe him an estimable man. I have also determined that it is wrong to listen to gossip, to lap it up as fast as a racing kitten with a bowl of milk."

"That was well said." Meggie took one of his hands between hers. "You are my husband now, Thomas. Isn't that amazing?"

"I wanted you," he said simply. "And now you are mine."

"You make that sound like I was a prize that you somehow managed to win."

"Yes. I would say that a wife is a prize."

"Bosh. You also make it sound like I'm now some sort of possession. I don't know if I like the sound of that."

"You are chattel, though the word doesn't bring particularly pleasant things to mind. Chattel is owned and so is a wife."

She laughed, full rich, that laugh of hers, and he felt the tug of it. "That sounds just a bit like something Jeremy—the Jeremy who was the obnoxious superior one—would say. I pray you, Thomas, never treat me like I have a hollow room between my ears."

He gave her a look that, she thought, was far too serious and said slowly, "I've never believed that."

"Good. I'm sorry that William was unable to come. I

promised myself that I would try to be polite to him even though I would have probably smacked him in the head."

"I asked him not to come. It would have been awkward, particularly with the Winters family there. I did not wish to have today marred."

"I am glad my father told them the truth."

"I suppose it had to be done, else Mr. Winters might have shot me during our wedding."

"Mr. Winters is a very fine shot."

"Then your father saved my life."

Meggie laughed. "Will I meet William soon? You know, since your mother and father didn't live together, how was William conceived? He is five years younger than you?"

"Just four years. He is twenty-one. When he was born his father sent him and his mother away as well."

"It is a dreadful thing, Thomas. I am so very sorry."

He shrugged, said nothing.

"Will William be coming to the one of your houses where we're going?"

"We will see," Thomas said, folded his arms over his chest, and smiled at her. "You look quite beautiful, Meggie. I remarked upon it when you walked down the aisle toward me, when I was not remarking upon Rory, that is."

She laughed. "As for Rory, isn't he a little scamp?"

"Yes, he is. I'm very glad he survived that fever."

"I cannot imagine what it would have been like if he had not. But enough of that. Rory is well and speaking Latin again. Now, you are the beautiful one, Thomas. I am ordinary compared to you."

That made him laugh. He lightly ran his fingertip along her jaw. "A man is nothing more than a solid creature, Meggie, whose size allows him both to build and to bash heads together."

"And to laugh and to eat peeled grapes like the Romans did."

"At least to laugh. I haven't seen many grapes where we're going."

"That reminds me. I'm very hungry. Mrs. Priddle packed us a basket. Should you like a bit of champagne? Some of our wedding cake? Or scones that she made for my uncle Colin? He's the Scottish earl, you remember."

"Yes, some champagne would be just the thing." He raised a dark brow. "Should I drink some out of your slipper now?"

"No," she said, looking at him straight in his eyes. "I would like you to sip it out of my mouth."

Thomas refused to open the champagne.

Thomas had booked them the very best room in The Tipsy Nun's Inn, a corner room with a lovely view of the English Channel. It was long dark when they finally arrived, but there was a full moon, and it shone down on the Channel water, making it glisten like the brilliant sapphire on Meggie's third finger. The town was spread out behind them, silent and still.

"So beautiful," Meggie said over her shoulder as she pulled back the lace curtain to peer out over the still water. Gentle waves curled onto the sand, then sprawled out like a coquette's fan.

"Yes," Thomas said.

She turned then, for he was still standing by the closed door, his arms crossed over his chest, just looking at her.

"Mary Rose asked me if I had any questions about marital sorts of things."

If he felt any surprise, he didn't show it, merely remarked, "Did she tell you what you wished to know?"

"Oh no. I told her that since you kissed very well, I imagined that you would do the rest of it quite adequately. I did ask her about this tongue business. After much skidding around the question, she finally admitted that it was the done thing."

"Since she is your mother, I can well imagine that speaking of such intimate things would make her uncomfortable."

"Do you know that she and my father are always touching and kissing, particularly when they don't think any of the children is around?"

He really didn't want to smile, but he did.

Meggie said, her voice all off-hand, "Perhaps, if we are blessed, we would also have to pay attention when we kiss so as not to embarrass our children."

"It is much too soon to think about those sorts of things, Meggie." He paused a moment, then said, his voice very deliberate, "You are mine now. No matter what happens, you are completely and irrevocably mine."

She cocked her head at him. "You have said that several times now, Thomas." Perhaps she shouldn't have, but Meggie was never one to falter. She took one of his big hands between hers. "Listen to me. I am your wife. I am not like your father. I will not leave you. Since I am not a rug to be tread upon, I'm sure we will have fights and enough shouting to bring the roof down. If you haven't noticed, we are both stubborn and have our own ideas about things, but no matter how much we yell at each other, or how loudly, I won't go haring off in a snit, ever. Goodness, even my papa the vicar and Mary Rose occasionally yell at each other, but that's nothing, Thomas, nothing at all. We will be together and hopefully life will dish us up more laughter than tears."

He said, his voice cold, withdrawn, "That was very eloquent."

She said slowly, "Was it?"

"And naïve."

"It is true in my family."

He merely shrugged, and kept his back against the door, his arms crossed over his chest. He said, "My father and mother—they are none of your concern. I do not need assurances from you to calm my disordered brain. You seem to think I'm suffering from long-ago pain dished out freely by my parents. I am not. About my parents—I only said what I did because you seemed to need to know, and, indeed, your father demanded to know. It really wasn't his right to know."

"Yes, it was. He is my father. It is his responsibility to protect me."

"Your father wanted to refuse me your hand in marriage."

"Of course he did. He believed you were a lecher. But it was William. I believe my father was very relieved when he learned the truth of the matter. He wants me to be happy, you see."

Thomas said nothing. He looked as if he wasn't certain what he should do now, as if he was nervous, undecided about something, and Meggie found it utterly appealing. She skipped to him, wrapped her arms around his back, and pressed her cheek to his shoulder. "Kiss me, Thomas. That is something I like very much."

She raised her face, came up on her tiptoes, but for a moment, he hesitated, touched his fingertips to her cheek, so soft her skin, flushed now in excitement.

It was, after all, her wedding night.

She'd never done anything to harm him, he was thinking, and she was his wife. Slowly he brought his arms around her, holding her tightly against him. He didn't kiss her, just held her. Actually, it was he who was holding on to her. She was half his size and he was burrowing onto her.

He lifted his head to look down at her. "You're a virgin, Meggie."

She lifted her face and gave him a very small smile, a nervous smile, and he knew it. "Well, yes. I'm supposed to be."

In an austere voice he said, "Many women are not pure when they come to their husbands."

"I had never thought of it. Are you certain? No, that's all right. No one else has anything to do with us. Ah, Thomas, kiss me now."

He was rubbing his hands up and down her arms. "Do you like your cloak?"

"It's lovely. Do you like the onyx pen I gave you?"

"Yes."

"Mary Rose believed it to be very masculine."

"It is."

"It is solid, like a man is supposed to be."

"Yes."

"Thomas, are you uncertain what to do? No, it's all right, truly, you don't have to say anything. I rather like that the two of us can begin everything together. I'm sure that we will be able to figure this business out."

"You think I'm hesitating because I'm lacking in experience? That I just might also be a virgin?"

"It's all right, Thomas." She grabbed his face between her hands and kissed him, a girl's kiss that made him laugh. Another damned laugh, and he'd even come to like the feel of it, alive and snaking warmth all the way to his gut, and that was alien to him.

"I'll admit it, I'm nervous, yes, just a bit nervous," she said between light nipping kisses, "but we are married now, and you belong to me, and I wish to see what all these marital things are about. Oh goodness, does that sound terribly loose?"

"A man doesn't belong to a woman," he said slowly, his voice suddenly remote, all laughter dried up. "A man is his own being."

For an instant, Meggie was blank-brained. Whatever had happened? Had a woman hurt him badly in the past? He wasn't old enough to have been hurt all that often, surely. "Thomas, how old are you, exactly?"

"I am twenty-five. I will be twenty-six in December. I was born the day after Christmas. I don't think my mother ever forgave me for ruining her Christmas."

He was making light of it. Well, no matter. If a woman had hurt him, had made him cynical, someday he would tell her and she would fix it. She kissed him again, this time a line of kisses all along his jaw. She said, all the feeling that was in her vibrant in her voice, "I will make you want to belong to me."

And she kissed him again.

This time he kissed her back, hard, telling her to open her mouth, and she did and she felt his tongue sliding over her bottom lip, then inside. It was different, this kiss, urgent, on the wild side. He raised his head just a moment, and said, his hand suddenly cupping her breast, "Meggie, I'm not a virgin."

14

MEGGIE, OVERWHELMED BY that kiss, that surprise attack that had ambushed her and made her want more, exactly of what she wasn't certain, but she was eager to find out, managed to get herself together since this was obviously the way things were done, and said, "It's all right that you're not a virgin. I am not blind, Thomas. I believe that boys are somehow supposed to become experienced, that it is expected, that they aren't viewed by other men as being manly unless they do this, perhaps quite frequently.

"I have also seen how boys do not seem to be able to control themselves when it comes to the fairer sex. They step near a girl and begin to stutter, their hands shake, and they say the stupidest things. Just look at what William did."

"Men can control themselves. It is a matter of will, and a matter of character."

"I know that you would never take advantage of a female, for yours is an excellent character. Are you also strong-willed when it comes to matters of the flesh, Thomas?"

"Yes, but that doesn't matter. I must consummate our marriage or it isn't really a marriage."

"A good idea." She saw him looking at her so sternly, as if he weren't certain about something, and just couldn't help herself. She kissed him again, his shirt fisted in her hands, and she was pulling him down toward her, kissing whatever part of him she could reach.

He said against her mouth, "I will take your virginity, make you bleed, and only then will you be safely wedded, not before. Then there is no going back, Meggie. You're mine."

That brought her kisses to a stop and a frown to her forehead. "I don't know why you are worried about this, Thomas. I don't want to go back. Wait, I don't like the sound of this bleeding business. What bleeding business? What does that mean?"

"Oh God, Meggie, I wish you had asked your mother to explain this to you. Don't you know anything at all?"

"I now know all about tongues, although it's still a bit difficult for me to speak in them just yet."

Speaking in tongues. He tried to smile at that, but couldn't, and said, "But you don't know what we are going to do?"

"Well, not in any sort of elaborate detail, no."

"How about in a vague general sort of way?"

"I believe you must take your clothes off. I was swimming once when I was very young with my dratted boy cousins, and they took off their clothes. They were certainly different from me, but I don't know how it all would work to make a baby."

"I did ask, didn't I?"

"Are you jesting with me, Thomas? Perhaps laughing at me?"

He seemed to think about this for a goodly number of seconds. He said more to himself than to her, "No, I wouldn't jest about this, not at all. Now, it must be done, it must." It was almost as if he was angry with her, Meggie thought, suddenly panicked. He said nothing more, didn't kiss her, just picked her up in his arms and walked to the large tester bed. "I'll be your maid," he said, sat her down on the edge of the bed, realized the buttons on her dress were in the back and pulled her to her feet again. Thomas saw that she was pale, his exuberant Meggie looking a bit on the ragged edge, particularly since they were this close to the bed and his hands on her. He kissed her hard and fast, didn't try to part her lips with his tongue because he thought she just might bite him in her nervousness, then turned her around. He unfastened the long line of buttons down her back.

She was looking over her shoulder at him. "Thomas, perhaps I could have a glass of water?"

"No, Meggie. Hush. Don't worry about any of this. Let me do the worrying. It will be all right. Trust me."

"You certainly are very efficient with all those buttons."

He smiled, couldn't help it. "Yes. Some men believe it to be a calling. Other must practice assiduously to be competent at it. Be quiet."

"Thomas, is this going to be a nice thing? Despite the blood?"

At the sound of her quavery thin voice, his fingers stopped, three buttons from the bottom. He looked at her back, at the soft batiste chemise, the lace straps, all of it so feminine, so unlike him, alien from him, this soft creature who now belonged to him. Not to anyone else. To him. No, nothing hard about Meggie at all, particularly not her heart, and he knew it, but he didn't want to let it matter. He had to be strong about it, couldn't let her know. He couldn't. A man had to have his pride. He said, "I will try to make it a nice thing."

"All right, then I will try not to worry overly about this."

Slowly he turned her to face him. He pulled the gown down until her arms were trapped against her sides. He lightly stroked his fingers over her jaw, her throat, came to rest lightly on her bare shoulders. She was so bloody soft. "Meggie?"

"This isn't quite what I had expected, Thomas."

"What did you expect?"

She shrugged, but he saw that she was embarrassed.

"Come, tell me."

"Perhaps a small dinner by the fire, though it's quite warm, isn't it, so a fire might make us uncomfortable. All right then. We could leave the table by the window. We could speak quietly to each other, perhaps watch the moonlight play over the water, and comment on the feelings it brings to our souls."

"That is a bit sentimental for my tastes."

"I thought it might be. All right, some champagne then. You didn't want any in the carriage. Were you afraid that I would become ill? Were you afraid I'd really force you to sip it out of my mouth?"

He just smiled down at her. So young, he thought, too young. She didn't deserve that he maul her. He leaned down, pressed his forehead against hers. "You array yourself in your nightgown and I will go downstairs and order up a bit of food and champagne from Mrs. Miggs. I believe she is quite pleased that I chose her inn for our wedding night."

"Maybe she was, but Mr. Miggs just grunted at me and stared down at his shoes."

"It is Mrs. Miggs who deals with the patrons. Now, do you need a maid to help you?"

"No. I can reach the rest of the buttons."

He turned to go.

"Thank you, Thomas."

He paused a moment, and she wondered what he was thinking. At the moment she was afraid to ask.

Thirty minutes later they were seated opposite each other at a small table next to the window, Meggie wearing a very lovely peach silk peignoir that her aunt Sinjun had brought her from Edinburgh. Thomas, however, was still dressed in his very nice trousers and jacket and his beautifully polished boots. His cravat looked as fresh as it had in the church that morning. So many changes on this one single day. Tomorrow she wouldn't wake up the same Meggie as she had just this morning. So few hours had passed, and yet her life had changed irrevocably. She wondered if Thomas felt the same way. Surely he must. Men couldn't be that different from women.

"It's strange," she said, nibbling on a piece of bread, "to be sitting in my nightclothes across from a man who isn't either my father or one of my brothers, or one of my dratted boy cousins, for that matter."

"Come, Meggie, I cannot imagine you ever wearing that delicious confection to bed in the vicarage."

"Well, you're right about that, but still, you're still dressed, Thomas, and I'm not."

Thomas just smiled and held up a glass. "To our wedding night," he said.

Meggie was slow, but at last she did tap her glass lightly against his.

He'd given her too much time to fret. He said, "After we have eaten and drunk just a bit more, what were you thinking would happen?"

"Since I don't know anything specific beyond kissing, as you well know, I admit things get a bit muddled. All right, really muddled, perhaps even incoherent. Right now I know I'm happy and that you're smiling. Do you think maybe that could be enough for you to go on?"

"There will be a lot more than just smiling, Meggie."

"Like what?"

"You are endlessly curious, aren't you?"

"Since this will involve me very personally, I don't think it all that strange."

"What will happen is pleasure, hopefully for both of us."

"I have already felt pleasure when you kissed me."

"Different, stronger pleasure."

She looked very skeptical about that.

He didn't move from the table until she'd drunk a half glass of champagne. He sat back, his hands laced over his lean belly. "Why don't you get in bed, Meggie. I will blow out the candles."

"Do you really wish to?"

"To what?"

"To blow out the candles."

"Ah, a dollop of interest in me?"

"Well, yes, to be honest about it. It's difficult to think about this, but since Mary Rose and my father are married and they do sleep in the same bed, I suppose they do see each other without their clothes. That is difficult for a daughter to imagine."

"A son as well. Does this mean that you wish to see me naked?"

She met his dark eyes and very slowly she nodded. "I have been thinking some more about what I want to have happen. I want to add you to my fantasy. I want you to be my main character." She gave him a nervous smile.

He didn't say a word.

"All right, you force me to be blunt, Thomas. I want you to take all your clothes off."

"And will you undress for me as well?"

She rose from her chair and walked over to the bed. She paused a moment, and said over her shoulder, trying to smile a siren's smile, not all that successful, but she tried, "Well, this is my fantasy, not yours. However, to be fair, perhaps I can think about that later, much later. You are the one who knows what is going to happen. Let me at least decide how we will begin it." She sat on the bed and let her feet dangle over the side.

He too rose and walked to the bed, stopping not three feet from her. He stood in front of her for a moment, then pulled off his beautiful buff jacket. "You say I'm beautiful, Meggie, but I'm about to prove you wrong. I'm a big hairy man."

"I think since it is you, I shall quite like big and hairy. Show me."

She watched him remove each and every item of clothing, fold each and every item and lay it neatly on a chair, watched him so closely that when he straightened, naked, he was already hard as the oak floorboards beneath his bare feet, and surely that would alarm any virgin.

She stared at him as he stood there, his arms at his sides. He wanted to ask her if she believed him to be as well-looking as Jeremy, but he couldn't, of course, he wouldn't.

"I was wrong," she whispered, her eyes never looking away from his sex.

He was shaking, getting even harder, something he

wished didn't have to happen, but there was no hope for it, not with her staring at him like she wanted to—no, he wouldn't think about her in front of him, her mouth on him. For God's sake, she was a vicar's daughter. But to the best of his memory no woman had ever looked at him like that. Now that he thought about it, neither had he ever before stripped off his clothes in front of a woman in order to advance her education. He cleared his throat. "What were you wrong about?"

"You aren't beautiful, Thomas."

"You see, I told you I was just a big hairy creature, and that—"

"You are magnificent. I did not know what a man really looked like. But I do know, all the way to my toes, that no man could be as fine as you." And, really without thinking, she reached out her hand to touch him.

He closed his eyes, so tense he couldn't breathe. He wanted to spring, jump right on her, but he held himself perfectly still. He felt her fingers lightly touch his belly, just stay there, not moving, her fingers warm, until he thought he'd yell with it, then she stroked her fingers down the line of black hair over his belly, lower and lower, tangling her fingers in the hair at his groin, moving, still moving until she touched him, so lightly, as if she didn't know what to expect, but she didn't stop. When her fingers went around him and he felt the warmth of her hand, his breath *whooshed* out, nearly bowing him to his knees. All things being equal, he didn't want this ever to end. Yes, maybe her mouth as well as her fingers, oh God, this was too much, just too much.

He could stand it—a man could stand this sort of exquisite torture forever—maybe even beyond forever—but then, of course, he knew he couldn't, and it nearly killed him when he gritted his teeth and whispered, in obvious pain, "Meggie, please remove your fingers. Back away. Get to safety. I simply cannot bear that."

"I don't want to, Thomas. You feel so very different from me. Your belly is all hard and hairy and it makes me feel very strange to touch you."

That gave him a moment's respite. "It does?"

"Yes, so let me keep—" Her grip tightened, moved up and down a bit.

He nearly lost control of himself. He couldn't allow himself to spill his seed in her hands, he wasn't that great of a clod. He groaned in despair, in utter misery, as he forced himself to pull away from those hands of hers, drew a very deep breath, knew it was going to be close. He couldn't help himself, he had to be inside her, and it had to be now. He came down over her, nearly knocking the breath out of her. He was flat on top of her, pressed against her closed thighs, aware that she was stiff and so soft he just couldn't stand it. He tried to smile. He knew she was worried about all this. And now he was naked and on top of her, and he was big and hairy, so much physically stronger than she was, and his control had gone into hiding, far away, on the other side of the planet.

"Oh God."

She tried to rear up at the pain in his voice, but he was holding her down. "Thomas, whatever is the matter?"

"You're still wearing your nightgown, Meggie. That will never do."

"Perhaps I could leave it on for a little while longer?" She was afraid now, he heard it, but it just didn't matter.

He pressed his forehead to hers, his breath hard and fast, his body pulsing with lust. "I'm in a bad way. Give me a moment, and I'll give you a moment as well and then we'll proceed."

It wasn't even a moment before all he felt was his climax building, building, overwhelming him, and he reared up, slid his hand between her legs and came down on his knees between them. "Sit up."

"Well, I—"

He pulled her up, raised her hips off the bed, lifted her nightgown off her, and threw it over his shoulder. "Oh dear," Meggie said, but he was kissing her, not looking at her, just kissing her and kissing her, her neck and her breasts, kissing each rib, going down her stomach and then he was actually between her legs and she felt his mouth touch her—no, surely that couldn't be right—and he groaned, and then his breathing was sharp and he was looking down at her while his fingers were touching her, pressing against her, and she was staring up at him as he eased one of his fingers inside her. Actually inside her. She'd never imagined such a thing. It wasn't nice at all. It hurt.

She tried to push him off, but she couldn't. "Meggie, Meggie, just lie still, relax, trust me."

"No, no," she said, trying frantically to scramble away from him, to get his finger out of her, "it's far too late for any trust. This isn't going to be nice, it's going to be bad. That's just your finger, Thomas. I held you between my hands. You are much more than just one of your fingers, and that's what you're going to do, isn't it? You're going to stick yourself inside me."

He managed a "yes." It was bad? What he was going to do to her was bad? He eased his finger a bit deeper, then stopped. Oh God, he wanted her so much he ached to his feet, and she was claiming his damned finger was bad? He wanted her this very instant, and by God, he wasn't going to wait. He just couldn't. He came over her, his eyes on himself and on her, and came slowly inside her. Slowly, he moved forward. She was stiffer than a board. Her hands were fisted at her sides. Well, damn. He went just a bit more, felt her maidenhead.

"Meggie."

He looked down at her, really looked at her despite feeling like he would explode inside her at any instant, and this time he looked into those bright blue eyes of hers. Seemingly so guileless, those blue eyes of hers, filled with openness, no shadows lurking about anywhere at all in the depths of those eyes, but he knew it for a lie, a lie that had cut him to his knees, just hours before, but there was no going back. He hated her at that moment because of her goodness, because of her damned sense of honor, because of her betrayal. He hated the man she obviously still adored, hated that she adored him, and not her husband. She shouldn't have led him on, shouldn't have made him want her so quickly, so effortlessly, made him want to marry her. The fact was, she was betraying him in her heart and it was their wedding night. Was she thinking of him even as he pushed into her? He saw Jeremy's face, heard Meggie's voice. It all mixed with his lust and he butted her maidenhead. She yelled, struggling beneath him, trying to throw him off, but unable to. He paused for just an instant when he butted against her maidenhead.

"Thomas, no!"

She'd forced him into a life of lies. He looked into her eyes as he yelled his pain, his fury, his lust, and pushed through her maidenhead.

Meggie didn't have the breath to yell again or to curse or the will to move. It was very simple, really. She knew he'd killed her, a body couldn't continue after what he'd done. She realized that she'd been told a very big lie. Surely a man didn't treat a woman like this if he loved her, surely. But then again Thomas had never said he loved her.

He suddenly stopped cold, and he was staring down at her again, looking right into her eyes, and he seemed to be fighting with himself about something she couldn't begin to understand. He said, "No, I can't do this. Not with you feeling the way you do. I can't, just can't." And he moaned, deep in his throat even as he jerked out of her, came to his knees, stiffened, and climaxed. Then he hung there, his head bowed.

Meggie hurt inside, he'd made her bleed, she just knew it, and then he'd left her, rejected her. She yelled now, but not with pain, it wasn't all that bad now, truth be told, but she yelled at the top of her lungs with resentment, with rage that she'd actually been excited, actually anticipated this lovemaking business, and just look what he'd done—he'd hurt her, then left her. A man wasn't supposed to do that, was he?

He was breathing hard, his head bowed, and he'd not wanted to stay with her. And now she'd bleed. She should have demanded to know about the bleeding business before she'd even let him unfasten all those nice safe buttons on her gown. But no, she was an idiot, she'd trusted him, and now he was on his knees between her legs, heaving, looking at if he were dying. It was as if a sort of cataclysm had racked him all the way to the soles of his wretched feet.

He looked up at her then, and she saw that his jaw was locked, his eyes glazed, and all of him was pulsing madly. His seed was on himself, on the sheet, on her belly. It was an overwhelming upheaval that she couldn't begin to understand, really didn't want to understand, but she did know one thing for certain—he was a liar. It was obvious he knew very little about this lovemaking business.

She hurt really badly. She hated what he'd done to her and wanted to hurl him out of the window. And what had he meant that he couldn't do it? Do what? Stay inside her? What was he talking about?

She didn't care. Then he stopped his quivering, his shuddering, and just hung there over her, not breathing quite so hard now, his eyes closed, saying nothing, doing nothing.

She said loudly, right up into his face, "You shouldn't have done what you did. It wasn't right. You hurt me and then you just came out of me. I am going to kill you."

15

THOMAS COULDN'T THINK, just couldn't gather his wits together. He'd managed to come out of her, he'd actually managed to make his body obey his will, and he hated it.

Suddenly Meggie lurched up and bit his shoulder as hard as she could. She hoped she'd make him bleed.

That brought him back to his brain and miserable body. He managed to straighten. He blinked at her. "My God," he said slowly, disbelieving, "you bit me."

"Yes, you hurt me."

"It happened." She'd actually bit him. He'd come out of her, not his fault, he'd simply had to. Well, for the moment, he didn't give a damn about her feelings, about that damnable Jeremy. He wanted to punish her for what she'd done to him. He came down hard over her and went inside her again just as she yelled, "Don't you dare have the nerve to hurt me more, you bastard."

Then she shuddered.

He felt her muscles clenching around him, he was deep inside her, it was driving him mad, and this time, the rage banked, the desire to punish, to gain revenge on her both for what she'd done and hadn't done, fell to his own need, his own wild urgency and that was more powerful than anything else. He pushed again. "Oh God," he said, panting until he thought his heart would burst from his chest, "I don't want this. Damnation. This will kill me."

"Probably not, you clod. Get off me, damn you!"

He fell forward, flattened her, kissed her and shoved hard again and again. It was over again in less than a minute. He was heaving and panting, nearly crying because his body felt so very fine—nothing but soul-deep satisfaction and the overwhelming urge to sleep, to forget what he'd just done. Damn him and damn her. At least no one could take her from him now. Damn her honor. He'd been rough with her. He was sorry he'd hurt her, but in the end, she would have to learn that whatever he did, she had no say in it.

He thought about that life-changing conversation between father and daughter he'd overheard in the vicarage gardens not three hours after she'd become his wife. His wife whom he'd wanted to pull behind a shrubbery and kiss her silly, but that hadn't happened. He'd seen her father, taken a step forward to ask if he'd seen Meggie, but then he'd heard her say in a voice stumbling with pain, "I truly didn't want him to speak to me, Papa, but Jeremy believed that since I'd married Thomas, he could now redeem himself because obviously I didn't love him anymore and it bothered him that I believed he was an idiot. Papa, Jeremy is honorable. I should never have believed that wretched act of his. He did it to make me stop loving him, oh God—so noble and I hated him, scorned him."

Her father had held her close and whispered against her hair, "It will be all right. You've got a fine husband. You will come to love him, dearest. You will see."

And Meggie cried against her father's shoulder, and Thomas Malcombe's life, as he'd known it, as he'd anticipated it would be with his new wife, fell into pieces at his feet.

The candle was nearly gutted when he rolled off her onto his back. She was up in an instant, ready to clout him when, her fist hard and ready, ready to strike, he snored.

Meggie couldn't believe it, just couldn't. She wanted to kill him for what he had done, damn him a million times more than she'd already damned him.

She looked down at him, waved her fist not an inch from his nose, and whispered, "Blessed hell."

Slowly she got off the other side of the bed and managed to stand straight. Every part of her hurt, but nothing compared to the pain deep inside her, where he'd poked and pushed and shoved, and no, she still wanted to kill him, very badly. She felt wet and sticky and her legs were shaking. She could barely stand up.

She'd trusted him.

She'd been an idiot.

Was this the way things were always done? First a man left a woman's body and the second time he didn't? Was it some sort of strange ritual? Did her father do this to Mary Rose? Her brain shied away from that. What about Jeremy? Had he done that to his precious Charlotte their wedding night? Meggie had been eaten up with jealousy at the thought of Jeremy kissing Charlotte, not her, but if it had led to this utter humiliation, then her jealousy was ridiculous. Meggie walked over to the small table that held a basin of clean water and washed herself. She winced at the pain and saw that the water was red with her blood. He'd done that to her the first time just before he'd jerked away from her.

Then she headed straight to the table where the remains of their meal still were, and immediately picked up the champagne bottle. Thank the good lord it wasn't empty.

She downed the rest of it. Warm or not, bubbles or not, it was quickly down her throat. She didn't stop drinking until the bottle was empty. Then she stood there, staring out over the English Channel, at the magnificent moonlight that was a wide swatch across the water, making it glitter. Hah, glitter. Here she was admiring the beauty of nature when that man who was her husband was lying on his back, naked, snoring, on that wretched bed where he'd behaved so strangely. Surely a husband wasn't supposed to do that to his wife. She wouldn't believe that Jeremy had done that to Charlotte, that that was simply the way men behaved. Very well, if men weren't all like this, then why had Thomas done it to her? Because he didn't love her and thus didn't care if he hurt her or not? That just made no sense. He'd laughed with her, saved Rory's life, wanted to marry her. Meggie just stood there looking out over the moon shining onto the water, and wondered what to do.

She tipped the champagne bottle again, but the wretched thing was empty. She wondered what the innkeeper would think if she ordered another bottle, and then she just didn't care. She pulled on Thomas's dressing gown that he'd tossed over the end of the bed, an old burgundy velvet, its elbows nearly worn through, and tied it tightly around her waist. She left the room, walked barefoot down the hall and down the stairs. Mrs. Miggs was the only person in the taproom. Her hair was coming out of the tight knot at the back of her head, her apron was spotted, but she was humming as she wiped a wet cloth over the wooden tabletops.

"Hello, Mrs. Miggs."

"Oh my," Mrs. Miggs said, startled, her hand holding the wet cloth, clutched over her breast. "Lady Lancaster? Goodness, it is nearly midnight. What is the problem?"

"I would like another bottle of champagne."

Mrs. Miggs nearly dropped the cloth she was so surprised. Then she really looked at the tousled girl in front of her, barefoot, wearing a man's dressing gown that dragged the floor, very pale in the dim candlelight, and said slowly, "It's very late, my lady. I do not see your husband. You are obviously alone. Thank heavens I sent the rest of the men on their way a few minutes ago."

"I'm glad, too. I wouldn't have come in if there had been men. They're dreadful, men are. May I have another bottle of champagne."

"Why?"

Meggie looked down at her toes and said with no hesitation at all, "It's my wedding night and I don't feel very good about things at all. After I've drunk the champagne I'm wondering if I should bash my new husband over the head with the bottle. I finished the bottle upstairs, gripped it about its neck, tested its weight, but decided rather than

killing him right at that moment, I wanted to drink some
more champagne. To consider it more at length. What do
you think?"

"What does your new husband have to say?"

"The clod is sleeping in the middle of the bed, snoring."

"Let me get you the champagne."

Meggie didn't realize she was weaving about a bit
when Mrs. Miggs returned with a very cold bottle, but
Mrs. Miggs did. The young lady had been shocked to her
bare toes, and her new husband obviously hadn't behaved
well. She was too pale, and that worried Mrs. Miggs. She
said, "You just sit yourself down on that bench, that's
right, just slide right on in and I'll open the bottle for
you." She popped the cork out efficiently, then put two
glasses on a table. "Come, let us talk about this new marriage of yours. Shall, ah, we toast it?"

Meggie grumbled even as she slid across the wooden
bench, but she quickly accepted a glass from Mrs. Miggs.
"I don't want to toast my marriage. There is nothing to
toast. Please don't call me 'my lady.' My name is Meggie
and this is my wedding night. It was awful. I wasn't expecting any of it. He ambushed me."

Mrs. Miggs, thick in the middle now from birthing five
children and her own excellent cooking, said, "Wedding
nights can be bad sometimes for the woman."

"He left me the first time and then the second time—
goodness, it was only a minute or so later—he turned into
an animal. I wasn't expecting any of that. The kissing was
nice, but that didn't last for long. He kissed me before we
were married and I really liked it. He put his tongue in
my mouth. That was odd, but I knew I could get used to
it."

"Kissing usually is nice. Tongues, too."

"Ah, but the rest of it—I was hopeful, I actually trusted
him, and what happened? You truly do not want to know,
Mrs. Miggs."

Meggie clicked her glass to Mrs. Miggs's. She said,
"Here's to this bottle of champagne and to the witching

hour that will chime in not more than four minutes from now."

"Hear, hear," said Mrs. Miggs.

Meggie said, frowning at the bubbles in her glass, "Are men all like that lout upstairs snoring to the rafters? They get you all interested, and then they do as they please? They leave you and just hunch over you, gone from you, and shudder and shake and moan?"

"I don't know what you mean about him being gone, my lady—Meggie."

"He left me before he did anything."

Mrs. Miggs frowned. "A man does that when he doesn't wish to impregnate a woman."

Meggie hadn't thought of that. She shook her head as she said, "That can't be right, Mrs. Miggs. We're married. Why would he do that on our wedding night? It doesn't make sense because then he did it, I mean he went all the way to the end with the business. I didn't like it either time, not at all. It was like he was someone else, not Thomas."

Mrs. Miggs drank, and said slowly, "Men are not a patient lot, so aye, just maybe many men are too rough and maybe too they change their minds, just can't help themselves. After all, they're really a weak lot, now aren't they?"

Meggie didn't know about that. He changed his mind? About her? About their marriage and he didn't care if she liked this lovemaking business or not? "What about your wedding night, Mrs. Miggs?"

Mrs. Miggs poured each of them another glass. They clicked their glasses together again and drank.

"Well, let me see if I can remember that far back. A full long number of years ago that was. Hmmm, well, my Mr. Miggs, he was a big 'un, all full of fire and hops— because he always liked his ale—even when he was just a young man. We got hitched and the neighbors and our folks gave us a fine party and then Mr. Miggs lifted me up into the cart and off we went, to spend several days at my aunt's house over in Fowey. Ah, but Mr. Miggs, he just couldn't wait to get us to Fowey and to a bed. No, he—"

Meggie, mesmerized, held up her empty glass. Mrs. Miggs filled it to the top, then her own. She looked thoughtful.

"Come, tell me. What happened, Mrs. Miggs?"

"Mr. Miggs stopped the cart, patted that big mare on her rump, then jerked me over his shoulder and carried me into a field of wildflowers."

"That sounds terribly romantic."

"It was February."

"Oh."

"Aye, it was so cold I can't believe now that Mr. Miggs managed to get himself upright, if you know what I mean."

Meggie didn't, but nodded just the same. She drank more champagne; so did Mrs. Miggs.

"Aye, he hauled me into that field, then yanked off his coat and laid me on it. Of course the coat wasn't big enough and my lower parts were on the bare ground. It was over in under a half a minute and I was just lying there on my back, looking up into that cold gray sky and wanting to kick him. He looked like a blissful ass, just lying there on his back, maybe he was even whistling, I forget. I didn't say a word to him. Instead, I got up, walked back to the cart, leaving him there panting and grinning like an idiot, so happy and pleased with himself. I yelled to him that he was a selfish pig, and then I drove away."

Meggie was vastly impressed. She applauded after she'd carefully set her champagne glass down on the wooden table. She sighed, then said, "He might have been too rough, but he did get it done, didn't he? That first time?"

"Aye, he got it done, all right."

"Unfortunately I can't leave my husband. I can't imagine that our driver would be willing to leave his master here. We're in a carriage pulled by two horses, and unfortunately I don't know how to drive two horses."

Mrs. Miggs nodded. "Have some more champagne."

"Then what happened, Mrs. Miggs?"

"Mr. Miggs had to run after me even as he was pulling up his pants, hobbling about, looking like a fool until finally I slowed down that big old mare so's he could climb in. The dear man never tried to do that again."

"Was it better in Fowey?"

"Oh yes. You see, Mr. Miggs had learned his lesson."

"So you're saying that I must tell Thomas what's what?"

"Aye. And you must ask him why he behaved as he did. Perhaps it's some sort of tradition for the men in his family—well, I've never heard of it and that's a fact, but men being men, it's difficult to know what they hold dear and necessary."

"I will ask him, but you know, I would rather do something like you did, Mrs. Miggs. You took action, and that was well done of you. You taught Mr. Miggs what was what right then and there. You didn't give him the time to roll over and snore."

"I doubt he could have slept, it was powerful cold in that open field."

"That doesn't matter, it's a mere detail. Here's to you, Mrs. Miggs," Meggie said, and both women drank deeply. "What should I do to my new husband? I must show him that what he did was reprehensible, after I've gotten all his manly reasoning from him." Meggie rested her chin on her hands, thinking hard. She said after a moment, "I mean, perhaps it wouldn't be wise to hit him over the head with the champagne bottle. I might kill him. I really don't want to hang. Also, my father is a vicar and that wouldn't look good to his bishop or to his congregation. Ah, Bishop Arlington even conducted my wedding ceremony. He would be profoundly distressed."

"A bishop, you say? My, that's something. No, don't take a chance of killing him, dearie. I don't want you dumping cold water on him either, it would ruin my good bed."

Meggie agreed and drank until her glass was empty.

She looked at Mrs. Miggs. "Nothing feels bad now," she said and burped and smiled at the same time. "As a matter of fact, I rather think I would like to dance."

"Drink yourself one more glass, then go back upstairs to that husband of yours."

"But what can I do besides ask him questions?"

"Hmmm. Let me think about this, Meggie. Are you leaving in the morning?"

"I think so. He won't tell me anything, curse his eyes. He has really quite lovely eyes, you know, all dark and brooding, but then he'll laugh and his eyes change and dance and lighten up and flash. I don't think he wets his finger and dampens his eyelashes to make them look longer and thicker. Many girls do that, you know. No, his are naturally thick and long. Did you remark upon his beautiful eyes when we arrived? No, well, you can remark upon them in the morning. Ah, perhaps I could take a mail coach and just go back home. I wonder if he would run after me, tugging on his trousers." Meggie frowned. "Somehow I cannot imagine Thomas running after anything, particularly if his trousers are down."

"No, Meggie, forget about mail coaches. They aren't for you."

Meggie was forced to agree. But she really didn't feel at all bad now, didn't feel like Thomas would be better off dead. "I can play the fiddle a bit, Mrs. Miggs. If you have one I will play for you and we could both dance."

"I'm sorry, no fiddle, Meggie. Do you play well?"

"No, but it is at least music. I thought I loved my dratted almost cousin Jeremy just last year. Actually, I would have sworn I would love him to my deathbed just three months ago, but then he opened his mouth and out came such obnoxious condescension. I saw the real him and it wasn't a pretty sight."

"Cousins can get under your skin, that's true."

"Then he spoke to me right after the ceremony. I didn't want him to, but he insisted. He told me it was all a ruse, a performance he'd given just for me, and he apologized and said he didn't want me to feel badly about him anymore, that he really wasn't a pig. He was noble, Mrs. Miggs, and for a time this afternoon, I just couldn't bear it. I'd loved him so very much, then despised him while loving him, and then he has to tell me he was noble all along. It gave me a headache. And now Thomas is upstairs, snoring, and I'm not particularly pleased about anything right now."

"I know, but things will change. You will learn how to manage him, Meggie. A taste of the whip, a lick of honey, and you can have a man at your knees, his tongue out, ready to evict your mother-in-law. Now, here's a last glass for you, dearie. Then you need to get yourself to bed. You're slurring your words, which is a sure sign that you will wake up wanting to die yourself. You just send your new husband downstairs first thing and I'll give him something that will set you to rights again."

Meggie said to the now-empty champagne bottle, "He makes me bleed, leaves me, then finishes the business, and now that I'm feeling really quite fine, she tells me I'm going to feel awful again."

"It's the wages of drink, my dear."

16

MRS. MIGGS WAS wrong. Meggie awoke alert, full of energy—no pounding head, no queasy stomach, not a single fuzzy residual thought in her brain. She felt strong and fit except for the ache between her legs and just a slight feeling of silliness. Actually, she believed she could still dance a bit. Had she really said she could play the fiddle for her and Mrs. Miggs?

Oh, dear.

Blessed hell. She'd forgotten—she was married. She had a husband, a husband who had behaved very peculiarly last night.

Meggie turned slowly, fully expecting to see Thomas lying beside her, on his back, still snoring, but Thomas was gone, none of him anywhere to be seen. And he'd been gone for a while. His pillow wasn't even warm.

She looked at the small clock on the mantel. It was only seven o'clock in the morning. He'd left her very early indeed.

When she'd eased into bed long after midnight, her husband of one day—and one half of one night—had been sprawled on his belly, arms flung wide, taking up much more than half the bed. A single cover was to his waist, leaving him bare the rest of the way up. There was a lot of the rest of the way up to see. She'd seen the front of him and now she was seeing the back. Without considering what she was doing, Meggie raised her candle higher. He was a big man, long and smooth, not hairy on the back like he was on the front, very nicely made—she'd give him that—but nothing else. For a moment, no, just for the quickest of an instant, she wanted to pull the cover down, but she got her brain back, and backed away. She finally doused the candle, made herself into a ball, and hugged the side of the bed until her fuzzy brain became so vague, so empty of anything save visions of swimming in the sea, only she wasn't really wet or even swimming, just there somehow in the water and it was cradling her, making her feel just fine. When she fell asleep, she slept deeply, not a single disagreeable dream to wake her in the night.

She sat up when she saw the door slowly opening, and there he was, her husband, just standing there, one booted foot inside the room, looking toward the bed, looking at her. A man had just opened the door to her chamber, hadn't even bothered to knock and now he was in the same bedchamber as she was and he was looking at her. It was astounding, this husband business. The power it gave men over women and the most private parts of their lives. Actually, she'd had some power as well when he'd taken off his clothes for her to see him the previous night. Now that she thought about that, her skin turned warm, particularly the skin on her face.

"Meggie," he said, not moving from the doorway.

He was smart, she thought, not to come any closer. "Shall I pack your dressing gown in my valise?"

"What?"

"Shall I pack—"

"Yes, I see that you're wearing it. Shall I ask you why?"

"I couldn't very well go downstairs to get more champagne wearing my nightgown, one, I might add, that didn't make it past the bed and to safety and is thus spotted with my blood and with you as well."

He appeared flummoxed for a moment at this stark talk, then said, "I see. You know, a girl shouldn't speak so openly about intimate matters, particularly her virginal blood and her husband's seed."

He would swear he saw her lips form a word, and he knew that word was *moron*.

"Why did you go downstairs for more champagne?"

"You haven't seen Mrs. Miggs this morning?"

He shook his head.

"I finished the champagne you ordered up for my fantasy dinner—actually my lovely fantasy dinner spun out of a stupid girl's head. It turned into quite something else, didn't it?"

"As to that, I don't wish to speak of it. I, ah, washed out your nightgown when I awoke this morning and hung it over the back of the chair. It should be completely dry shortly."

"Thank you. You have erased the evidence—very wise of you."

"The champagne left on the table wasn't enough for you?"

Meggie began swinging her legs over the side of the bed. Her toes were a good six inches off the floor. She said in a chatty voice, "How very odd. You sound all stiff and disapproving, like a father whose child has sadly disappointed him. Surely that is an absurdity after what you did." He would swear again that her mouth formed the word *moron*. He also realized that she was on the edge of saying it, and knew he couldn't allow it. Maybe he deserved it, but that wasn't for her to decide.

He said, very quickly, "You are not my child. However, as my wife, you are my responsibility. Naturally I am distressed. It cannot be wise of you to drink so very much."

"You are," she said quite clearly, "a buffoon."

He wondered if a buffoon was better or worse than a moron and said, "You shouldn't insult your husband," and knew it was pathetic. At that moment he wanted more than anything to yell at her, curse at her, demand why she'd married him when she loved her damned almost cousin Jeremy Stanton-Greville, who was already married, his wife pregnant. And then, of course, that was exactly the reason Meggie had married him. She couldn't have Jeremy, so why not take a man who obviously wanted her? But he didn't yell, didn't curse her. He didn't say anything at all. If a man didn't have his pride, he didn't have much of anything at all.

Meggie whistled, a nice fresh spring tune about a boy and a girl and a field full of violets.

"No," he said slowly, "now that I've listened to your song, now that I see the blood in your eye, I suppose that the champagne wasn't enough. You went downstairs to drink more champagne?"

"That's right. Mrs. Miggs and I shared a bottle."

She wished he would leave, maybe lend her the carriage and let Tim McCulver drive her back to Glenclose-on-Rowan. She was, she realized, succumbing again to melancholia, something she recognized very well ever since that fateful morning when Jeremy had met her in the park with perfect Charlotte at his side, a sinking of spirits made only more profound after Jeremy had confessed that his loud and obnoxious act had been for her benefit to ease her pain, damn him and damn her father for knowing of her pain in the first place. And Charlotte, of course, really was a goddess, blast her.

Was Thomas that different from Jeremy? Was he in fact the real ass while Jeremy was only the pretend ass? Had he hidden his true colors until he'd gotten her to the altar? Her spirits fell lower, if that were possible.

However, when he said, cold outrage in his voice, "May I ask how many men were in the taproom to see you swilling champagne, wearing nothing but my dressing gown?" Meggie immediately perked up.

She said in a voice more serious than her father the vicar's when confronted with an unrepentant sinner as she tapped her fingertips against her chin, "Let me think. Oh, I don't think there were more than ten men drinking in the taproom. Were there?" She tapped, tapped, tapped, all thoughtful. "You know, it was very late. Surely most men had gone to their homes, mauled their wives, sprawled out on their bellies, taking up most of the bed, happy as clams, snoring to the ceiling."

"If they were on their bellies, then they would be snoring to the mattress." He held up his hand knowing a fine display of wit was ready to burst from her mouth, "No, you don't have to tell me—you were speaking metaphorically. Now, you're telling me that you went downstairs wearing only my damned dressing gown, your damned feet bare—and you drank champagne with ten damned men looking on?"

"Ah, I can see from your spate of curses, repetitive but nonetheless curses just the same, that you're winding yourself up to really blast me now. I pray you won't forget that Mrs. Miggs was there."

She was sneering at him, playing him for the fool, and doing it quite well. No hope for it and so he climbed down from his high horse and sighed. "No, you're lying to me and you don't do it well, Meggie. So there were no men there, then."

"To be certain I'm not lying to you, you will have to ask Mrs. Miggs, won't you?"

"No, I don't think so. You're not a very good liar. You will stop mocking me, Meggie. A wife shouldn't be disrespectful to her husband."

"Well, then, should a man be allowed to do whatever pleases him to do to his new wife?"

He wanted to yell out that damned Jeremy's name to her, but he didn't, said only, "I don't wish to speak about that."

"I see. You said a wife shouldn't be disrespectful to her husband. Perhaps you could prepare a list for me for all these pesky things a wife shouldn't do that would irritate her husband. Do you think that would assist you into whipping me into shape?"

"It isn't a very long list."

"A list for the goose. How about a list for the gander as well? Yes, a list is a very good idea. I shall prepare it for you immediately. Then we can trade lists. I certainly know what will be the very top item on the list. Enough respect for your wife so that you don't maul her."

He had mauled her. It hadn't begun that way, but that's the way it had ended. Didn't she remember what she'd done, what she'd bleated out to her father? Damnation. He said, "As for mauling, that is quite absurd. I was merely overeager, that's all, perhaps a bit over the edge, a bit out of control. As for the second time, perhaps that also was a bit too much, but it happened, it's over, and you will forget about it." He held up his hand. "No, don't say anything. You are quite good at forgetting things, it seems, so you may forget this as well."

"What have I ever forgotten? Come, tell me. Ah, you can't. The truth is that I'm a veritable elephant, I simply never forget a single thing. You must fish in another stream, Thomas."

"Stop your damned wit, Meggie. Listen to me, I was rough but I really didn't mean to be. Everything was just too much, nothing more, just too much."

"What reason could you possibly have to maul your bride on her wedding night?"

"I told you, I don't wish to speak of it again. I didn't mean to hurt you. I am sorry for that. Now, you will forget it."

"Gone? Just like that? Very well." Meggie snapped her fingers.

He stared at her, wondering what was in that frighteningly active brain of hers now.

She said, "Actually I would like to ask you a question, Thomas."

A question? He didn't want a question, but he couldn't very well clap his hand over her mouth and leave it there. He nodded, unwillingly.

Meggie opened her mouth, then closed it. No, now wasn't the time. She'd told him how she felt. It was enough. She said, "Still, I was wondering if perhaps all men fly out of control on their wedding nights. You know, they've been forced to contain themselves for such a very long time, controlling all their base desires, that when they finally have the right to open the door, so to speak, they can't help themselves? They just fly right through, not pausing to perhaps even turn the doorknob?"

"That makes no sense."

She sighed. "Of course it does. You just don't like to see yourself in this light."

"I don't wish to speak of it. No more."

And she snapped her fingers again. She said, "It is odd. Mrs. Miggs told me I wouldn't feel at all well this morning, what with all the champagne, but she was wrong. Will you please leave, my lord? I wish to bathe and dress. Oh my, I should have respectfully inquired about your plans, which must, perforce, be mine as well since I am the adjunct here. Do you intend that we leave this morning?"

"Yes, as soon as you are able."

"Ah, do you also have plans that aren't any of my business?"

"We are on our wedding trip. Now, you will cease your ridiculous anger. A wife should not be angry with her husband."

"That is on the list?"

"Among other things."

"Go away, my lord. Go take a strap to one of the horses."

"How much champagne did you drink?"

"Enough to want to play a fiddle and perhaps dance a bit with Mrs. Miggs. Enough to forget that I wanted to kill you. In any case, even drunk, I realized I would be hanged if I did you in, and that would be distressing to my father. Hmmm. Since I can't ask my father about this, perhaps the next time I see Jeremy, I can inquire about this door business and a husband blasting through it on his wedding night."

He went pale, then red to his hairline with rage. "You will not speak of him further, do you understand me? Oh yes, I would be more distressed than your father if you killed me."

"No, you would be dead and not feel a thing."

She simply didn't know that he'd overheard her and

her father, so how could she possibly know why he was so damned angry? Maybe that was a good thing. He said, "You honestly feel fine now?"

"I feel ready to take on the world. I feel more than ready to take you on, my lord."

"I am your husband. My name is Thomas. A wife doesn't take on a husband, if you mean by that to start an argument with him."

She realized they'd done nothing but argue since he'd shown himself in the doorway. She said slowly, "Actually, I was thinking about hitting you in the nose."

He said nothing to that, very wise of him to keep quiet, she thought. He believed in some self-preservation.

She looked at him a moment, wrapped his dressing gown more closely about her, then said slowly, "Actually, I feel very sore between my legs. Does a man regard that as an accomplishment, something he's expected to do on his wedding night?"

"Since you are not riding, you will be fine by evening. It is nothing. There is no accomplishment here. Last night simply happened. Don't speak of it again."

"You are an expert then. You have done this particular business many times, at least enough times to know that my pain was and is a mere bagatelle. I don't suppose you experienced any distress from your splendid performance last night?"

He shook his head, but he was lying, of course. When he had broken her maidenhead, he'd wanted to scream at her and howl from the intense pleasure that filled him.

"I see. So you didn't realize what you were doing? Neither the first time nor the second time? You didn't hurt me either time on purpose?"

"Be quiet, Meggie. It's over."

She looked up at the ceiling. "God is letting me down here."

"Sometimes God forgives actions when they are justified."

"Whatever that means. Would you care to clarify that a bit?"

"I don't wish to discuss it further."

"Yes, yes, don't mention anything a husband might find thorny. I must relieve myself. Go away."

He looked as if he would say more, but he didn't, just turned and closed the door quietly behind him.

"Thomas."

At the sound of his name, he turned slowly.

She'd poked her head out the door. "Here." She threw his dressing gown to him.

She closed the door, leaned against it, covering her bare breasts with her hands, and sighed. She saw that he had indeed washed most the blood out of her nightgown. She folded the nightgown into a small square and stuffed it into her valise. She planned to look at it quite often, a reminder that expectations were quite different from reality.

She was downstairs within the hour, her bonnet ribbons tied beside her left ear, her pale green muslin morning dress, freshly pressed by Ann, one of Mrs. Miggs's daughters, and Mrs. Miggs herself assisted Meggie to dress, marveling over and over how splendidly hard Meggie's head was when the good Lord knew she should be moaning this morning, still in bed, the covers pulled over her head.

Meggie assured Mrs. Miggs that she felt dandy. As a matter of fact, she looked young and fresh and very innocent. She smiled when she said good-bye to Mrs. Miggs and heard the lady say into her ear as she hugged her, "Do not kill him. You would hang and I would be unhappy. If I were unhappy, then Mr. Miggs would be unhappy as well because I would see that he was. Not as unhappy as your family, but still, there would be some active discomfort."

"No, I won't kill him, even though he refused to answer any questions. No, I have other plans for the clod," Meggie said, gave her another quick hug, saw her new husband's dark eyebrow raised at this affection between his wife and the innkeeper, and helped her into the carriage.

17

$\mathcal{S}$PRING WAS SERIOUSLY in doubt on the northern coast of Cornwall. As they traveled to the northwest, it became more cold and blustery. The wind blew hard, making the tree branches moan and rustle in the darkness. The air off the Irish Sea tasted of brine and the smell of seaweed was strong.

Thomas didn't call a halt until nearly eight-thirty in the evening. For the entire day he had ridden some fifty feet in front of the carriage, leaving her to stew alone. She'd been so bored, and finally so desperate to relieve herself, that she'd finally opened the carriage door, leaned out as far as she could, and shouted up to Tim McCulver, "Stop the bloody carriage or I'll jump!"

The carriage stopped in under six seconds.

"Thank you," Meggie said, climbed down, and walked into the stand of oak trees beside the road.

When she came out some minutes later, her new husband was sitting astride his horse, looking intently at her. "Are you all right?"

"As in was I careful not to attach any poison ivy to myself?"

"No, but were you careful about that as well?"

She nodded, paid him no more attention, and climbed back into the carriage. If he didn't want to be lover-like, perhaps beg her pardon a dozen times, then she would do her part and ignore him.

Exactly two hours later Tim McCulver pulled the carriage to a stop, opened the carriage door, and said, "His Lordship asked me to see if you wished to stop for a moment and perhaps commune with nature."

"Yes," Meggie said. "Thank you."

They didn't stop for dinner. It was nearly twilight. Meggie was so bored, she couldn't stand herself anymore. She didn't think, just climbed out of the carriage window. Tim McCulver didn't see her until she swung onto the top of the carriage, crawled over the low railing and slipped down onto the seat beside him. He was so startled, he dropped the reins and let out a yell.

"It's all right, Tim. Goodness, the reins. Here, let me get them."

Before Meggie could reach down for the horses' reins, Tim squeaked, threw himself forward, nearly falling between the two horses, managed to snag the reins, and as Meggie nearly lifted him back into his seat, he was moaning.

"Are you all right?"

"It ain't the done thing, milady, it jest ain't the done thing. Ye're here wi' me, and his lordship will twist me ears off me head. Oh Lord, listen to me, yer favorite sinner needs yer good graces."

"His lordship will do nothing of the kind. If there is any twisting to be done, let him just try it on my ears."

And she laughed, feeling the wind tear at her bonnet.

It wasn't until they drove into St. Agnes, a very small village one mile inland from the Irish Sea, that Thomas rode back to the carriage to see his wife seated beside Tim McCulver, who'd driven his mother since Thomas was five years old.

He couldn't think of a thing to say. He saw Tim's anguish, saw the grin on his wife's face, not a sweet confiding grin, but rather a grin that dared him to make a scene. He wasn't without sense. He kept his mouth shut. Later, he thought, later, he would take her apart. He pictured her hauling herself out of the carriage window and blanched.

There was some moon, but it was hidden behind dark bloated clouds.

Tim said, "It will rain before midnight, milord. I'm glad we didn't get caught in it."

"I just hope it will clear by tomorrow."

"Why?" Meggie asked as she stuffed her windblown hair back under her bonnet and retied it.

Thomas said, "Traveling by boat is more difficult in bad weather. Women tend to moan and complain and puke their guts over the side."

"What a perfectly happy thought," Meggie said and climbed down without waiting for anyone to assist her. Her skirt snagged on the brake, and she very nearly went crashing to the ground. She said a small prayer of thanksgiving that she didn't fall. She could just see him standing over her, legs spread, hands on hips, sneering at her, treating her like a nincompoop. She said, "How nice it must be for men not to get seasick. Do you think it is due to a man's natural superiority? Or to a female's frailty, her inherent weakness?"

"Dammit, some men get seasick."

She said slowly, tapping her fingers to her chin, "Why did you admit that to me?"

"Because Tim is one of them and you would find out soon enough and point it out to me in a perfectly snide voice."

"What a fine example of logic. You saved yourself from my ill manners. Goodness, it's very cold here," she said as she shook out her skirts.

"Yes, a bit," Thomas said, then gave Tim instructions while he handed Pen's reins to a stable boy who was staring at the big black horse. "He won't hurt you. Just be firm and gentle with him. Tim, go along with the boy, see that everything is taken care of."

"Pen is a very big horse," she said, then sighed. "I will miss Survivor, but Rory and Alec need her."

For the first time since they'd arrived, Meggie turned to look at the inn that was set behind some oak trees. She didn't see much, just a flapping wooden sign that said The Hangman's Noose beneath a lantern that hung over the inn door.

Meggie looked from the inn to Thomas. "This is very strange. We haven't seen a soul except for the stable lad. This place looks utterly deserted. There is only the lantern over the front door and look, it seems there is just a single candle shining out that one front window."

"This isn't right at all," Thomas said, and she heard the alarm in his voice. "No, usually, Bernard's inn is very busy. Why didn't the stable boy say anything? Good Lord, I wonder what has happened. I want you to stay here, Meggie." She didn't want to, but she saw him pull a pistol from inside his jacket. An eyebrow went up. There was no one else about in the inn yard.

What was going on here?

The sky was filled with rolling black clouds, obscuring any hint of light. She fastened her eyes on that single lone candle set in the window.

Then she knew something was very wrong when she saw Thomas break into a run to the inn, the pistol gripped firmly in his right hand.

She was just behind him in seconds. "I don't like this."

He stopped, turned. "I don't want you here, Meggie. Go back there where it's safe."

"Safe with the stable lad? How do you know he's safe? Where is he, by the way? You don't think he's hurt Tim, do you?"

"Don't be absurd, but you're right, surely he must know if there is something wrong. Why didn't he say anything? Stay here. I will see to this. Obey me."

"No," she said and fell into step beside him. "This is a very important item on my wife's list: *Keep your husband from harm.*"

A black eyebrow went up, but he didn't say anything,

just tried to get in front of her when they reached the inn door. Later he'd be inordinately pleased about what she'd said, but not now. Slowly he opened the door, shoving it slowly, inexorably inward. It creaked loudly, making Meggie's hair stand up on the back of her neck, making her suck in her breath.

"I don't like this at all," she whispered against his shoulder.

"I don't either. Dammit, stay behind me at least."

"I'm scared."

"I am too. Be quiet."

Thomas walked into the small beam-ceilinged private parlor where the single candle was flickering in the window. It looked like it was a signal, but to whom?

Other than the candle, the room was empty. Thomas picked up the candle, saw that it was nearly burned all the way down. How long had it been lighted, and set in that particular spot? An hour? More?

Meggie moved to within two inches of her husband, came up onto her toes, and whispered in his ear, "Is there smuggling on the northern coast of Cornwell? Between Cornwall and Ireland?"

He shook his head, placed his fingers over his mouth.

He checked every inch of the room, then said, "I want you to remain in here, Meggie. I must check the rest of the inn."

Meggie walked to the fireplace and lifted a poker from beside the mantel. It was big and soot-covered. "No," she said. "Let's go. The Hangman's Noose. I don't like the sound of that name. Who owns it?"

"Bernard Leach." He said nothing more until they were across the hall and through the open door of the taproom. It was perfectly dark and smelled of years upon years of ale. "Keep your voice down. Bernard is a Cornishman I've known all my life. We need a light, I can't see a damned thing. Stay put. I'm going to get the candle."

He was back in a moment, the candlelight shining upward, setting his face in relief, making him look like the devil himself.

"I wouldn't have married you if it were dark like this and you were holding a candle. You look evil, Thomas."

"You hold it then," he said, and then laughed low when he saw her pale face lighted by the candle flame. "You have the look of a succubus."

"Not a good thing," Meggie said and shuddered even as she walked toward the long bar and raised the candle to look behind it. "If I have a child, he or she will be a demon or a witch. Did you know that Merlin was supposedly spawned by an incubus? That's a male succubus."

"No, I didn't know that," he said.

"Where could everyone have gone? Perhaps there was an accident in the village."

"It's possible. St. Agnes village is still a half mile to the west. Bernard's grandfather built the inn in an oak forest because he liked his privacy."

They went through the entire downstairs, ending up in the small cramped kitchen. That was where they found Bernard Leach lying unconscious in the middle of a pile of flour, blood from his head seeping into the white flour.

Thomas went down beside him and felt for a pulse in his neck. "Bernard, wake up. Dammit, man, come on, wake up now!"

The man, older, grizzled gray hair, thin as a broom handle, a huge white apron wrapped around his middle, moaned, then opened his eyes. "Oh God, be it you, Thomas?"

"Aye, you old buzzard. You just gave me a mighty scare. Where is everyone? What the hell has happened?"

Bernard clutched at Thomas's shirt. "Oh my lord, Thomas, it was the Grakers. You know about the Grakers, don't you?"

"I think I've heard the name but now, I don't know. Who are the Grakers?"

"Not who, Thomas. They're not people. They're not of this world. They come and they destroy and then they leave again."

"All right, what are the Grakers? Where are they?"

"They're like your English pixies, they live under rocks

and in caves and only come out at night. But they're not like pixies, they're vicious, attacking if they're displeased with you."

"You're telling me that some sort of evil pixie came to your inn, took you in dislike, and smashed you on the head?"

"It weren't quite that simple," Bernard said, and struggled to sit up. He moaned, gently rubbed his head.

Meggie said, "Let me get you some water, sir. How do you feel?"

"Is that a girl I hear? She shouldn't be here, Thomas. God only knows what the Grakers left upstairs. They scared off all the guests, but I have this very bad feeling that they did something she's not going to want to see. Aye, they're mightily displeased with me. I kilt one of them. It was an accident, I swear it, but they don't believe me. They came for their revenge."

Thomas shook his head. "First things first." Thomas took a wet cloth from Meggie, motioned for her to hold the candle closer, and examined the wound. "It isn't bad, just a single blow. After I take care of you, Bernard, I'll go upstairs and see if there's anyone else here. Where's Marie?"

"Marie?" Bernard frowned.

"Your wife, Bernard."

"Oh my lord, I'm in a bad way here, my boy. Marie—I don't know, I just don't know. What if the Grakers hurt her, Thomas?"

"I will go search the rest of the inn. You will stay here and rest."

"But who is this girl?"

"This is my wife."

"Ah, your wife. Ain't she a pretty one? Look at all the lovely hair, can't make up its mind what color it wants to be."

"That's enough, Bernard. Your head should hurt too much for you to flirt with her. All right, I'm going to help you to that chair and you will rest until I see what's going on here. Do you have a lantern?"

Once the lantern was lit, Thomas said, "Meggie, you will remain with Bernard to, er, protect him."

"No, he's not my husband. His head isn't bleeding anymore. Mr. Leach, you don't move. Thomas and I will find your wife. Don't worry. Let's go, Thomas."

He could tie her down, he supposed, then just shrugged, raised the lantern high, and left the kitchen, Meggie on his heels.

Thirty minutes later, after looking into every bedchamber on the second floor, they went to the attic rooms where the servants stayed. There were no servants anywhere.

But they found Marie Leach hanging by the neck from a thick rope wrapped and knotted about a high beam in the far attic room. Meggie didn't pause, just ran to the woman and lifted her up, trying to relieve the pressure of the rope around her neck. "Hurry, Thomas, hurry. I can't hold on much longer."

"I'm sorry, Meggie. It's too late. She's dead."

She was holding a dead woman. Meggie gulped, slowly released her, and stepped back. She didn't want to look, didn't want to accept that she was seeing a dead woman, and such a horrible way to die, but she forced herself. She wouldn't faint, she wouldn't moan and groan, she wouldn't be useless.

She might have weaved a bit, but managed to say in a fairly firm voice, "Tell me what to do, Thomas."

"Please hold her up again, Meggie. I need to get the rope off her."

Thomas managed to untie the rope around her neck. "The knot wasn't well tied," he said as he eased Marie down onto the single narrow cot in the small bedchamber. He paused a moment, lightly touched his fingers to the dead woman's cheek, then drew the cover over her. He was silent for a moment.

"You knew her. Well."

Thomas raised his head. "Yes, this is Bernard's wife, Marie. I've known her since I was a small boy. This shouldn't have happened, Meggie. Now, there's nothing more we can do for her. Let's go downstairs. I have to tell Bernard, and then we must fetch a magistrate."

18

It was nearly midnight when the housekeeper led Thomas and Meggie into a newly aired bedchamber at Squire Billings's house at the head of Morgan Cove, just south of St. Agnes Head, a fine property some three miles distant from The Hangman's Noose.

Once the housekeeper had left them, Thomas said, "Go to bed, Meggie. Squire Billings and I must speak about this further."

She nodded, saying not a word. She'd not said a word, but she'd hurt and cried deep inside and let the shock burrow deeper than the tears, and now she was exhausted. Within five minutes she was stretched out on her back beneath a marvelous goose-down comforter.

Thomas came into the bedchamber to see that she was all right before going back down to Squire Billings's library. He held the candle high and looked down at his wife. She was already asleep, her hair spread out about her head on the pristine white pillowcase. She looked so very young, untouched, but that wasn't true. And now she was no longer innocent—she'd seen a woman hanging by the neck.

He didn't like this at all. He turned on his heel and went back downstairs.

• • •

Meggie awoke the next morning, still alone. No sign of Thomas. She wondered if he'd even come to bed at all. Then she remembered what had happened.

She closed her eyes and tried not to think about Marie Leach. She looked about the bedchamber and didn't like it. It was dark, the furnishings heavy, Spanish in flavor, she believed, having visited a Señor Alvarez in his home in London during her Season the past spring.

She looked toward the windows, not seeing the heavy draperies, but rather Marie Leach, and she was dead and it was perfectly horrible.

Thomas knocked lightly then quietly opened the door to see his wife sitting on the side of the bed, her face in her hands, sobbing, great ugly sobs that seemed to bow her utterly.

He strode to the bed, picked her up, and carried her to the large winged chair beside the fireplace. He sat down and settled her on his lap. He held her for a very long time.

She felt in those moments that she was once again with the man she'd enjoyed so very much before they'd married, the man who'd never hesitated to comfort her, to laugh with her, to simply appreciate what and who she was.

"Thank you," she said, and straightened up. She was knuckling her eyes with her fists, and it made him smile.

"You're welcome. It's morning. A maid is waiting in the hall to assist you. We will spend the day here. This business with Bernard and his wife, it's a mystery and Mr. Billings hasn't a notion where to begin."

"And you do?"

"Yes. I wish to speak at great length with Bernard. I will ask the local physician to look at Mrs. Leach."

"But why? Didn't she die by strangulation?"

"Perhaps not."

"I will speak to the stable lad."

A thorny problem, Thomas thought, and cleared his throat. He said, "That won't be possible."

"Why not?" She was off his lap in an instant, standing

there in front of him, frowning, her hands on her hips, that white nightgown of hers flowing from the throat down to her toes. "I could question him as well as you could. I will even have Tim there with me."

"The stable lad is gone. Tim is looking after Pen and the carriage horses. Tim said he must have left while he was asleep, probably fearing he'd be blamed."

"Oh."

"Sorry to take the wind out of your sails."

"You have surprised me, true enough. Do you believe the stable lad knew what had happened even while he was leading your horse to the stables?"

"If he did, then it would mean that he must have been involved. I will ask Bernard about the lad's family—"

"Ah, and then I will go speak to them, find out where he is."

"Perhaps. Now, I will meet you downstairs for breakfast."

Life had turned very strange, Meggie was thinking as the maid, Tossa—a Spanish name, she told Meggie when asked, handed down from an ancestor who'd been flung up on the southern Cornish coast during the wreck of the great Spanish Armada during the reign of Good Queen Bess—helped her bathe, arranged her hair and her clothes. Tossa told her Squire Billings was all bluff and no brain, but a good man even so. When Meggie emerged nearly an hour later, she looked like a lady, and it was a good feeling.

She heard Mr. Billings's voice as she eased into the dining room.

"I say, my lord, I know all about the Grakers, they're bad, there's no question about that. I didn't know that Bernard had killed one of them. However did he manage it? It's rare to see one. I've never heard of actually catching one."

"I will find out," said Thomas. "Bernard told me it was an accident."

"Ah, here's some more eggs for you, my lord."

"Thank you. This is my wife, Squire, Lady Lancaster.

We appreciate your hospitality." Thomas rose from his chair, followed by Squire Billings, who gave her a brief bow and a fat smile.

"Good morning," Meggie said as she eased into the chair opposite her husband, held out for her by a butler with trembling hands, who was so pale he looked nearly dead. Squire Billings said matter-of-factly, seeing the countess's alarm, "Elroy is distraught. He finds death, particularly violent unexpected death, very upsetting to his innards. Fetch her ladyship some eggs and toast, Elroy. Try not to think of Mrs. Leach, and whatever you do, don't drop the tray anywhere close to her ladyship."

"It were a bad thing, sir," Elroy said, hands trembling even more, "a more terrible thing than I could imagine," and left to fetch the food.

"You are newly wedded," Squire Billings said between mouthfuls of kippers. "A miserable thing to have happen. Ah well, at least you had your first night together in relative peace and calm, eh?" Squire Billings actually leered, most of it, thankfully, behind his napkin, but Thomas still wanted to kick him.

Meggie realized what he'd said, fastened her eyes on the scrambled eggs, and said, "Ha." She spent a good minute buttering her toast and decorating it with some gooseberry jam.

Thomas said, "I was taking my wife home this morning, but given what has happened, we will remain here at least for today."

"I would indeed appreciate your assistance in this dreadful matter, my lord. Nothing like this has ever happened before."

Thomas nodded, took a final drink of coffee, neatly folded his napkin, and laid it beside his plate. He rose, saying, "Meggie I don't know how long this will take. You will amuse yourself."

She wanted to shoot him, but she merely smiled, tossed her own napkin down, and rose as well. "I have decided to accompany you, Thomas." And the look she gave him dared him to order her to stay, like a damned dog.

She turned to their host. "Thank you very much for your hospitality, Squire Billings. Do you wish to accompany my husband and me on our inquiries? There are so many people to speak to who might know about what happened last night at the Hangman's Noose."

Squire Billings sputtered his coffee onto his necktie. "Well, as for that, I'm not a young man, you know, my lady, and who's to say what—"

"If it is not too difficult for you, I would ask that you speak to your staff, sir," Thomas said as smooth as the butter he'd spread on his toast. "This evening we will all compare what we have learned. Meggie, fetch your cloak and bonnet."

That evening at eight o'clock, Squire Billings knew nothing more than what he'd known at breakfast. He'd had to hunt, he told Lord and Lady Lancaster, looking not a whit apologetic, aye, a full day of it, and he'd been desperately fatigued upon his return and had to nap before dinner. He had asked Elroy to conduct interviews with the staff, but the butler was still too overcome, and besides, what would his staff know?

Everything, Meggie wanted to say, but wisely kept quiet.

As for Thomas and Meggie, they'd found out two things: the local doctor had told them that Marie Leach was unconscious from a blow to the head before she was hung, maybe even already dead, and Bernard Leach had packed up and left the Hangman's Noose suddenly, and no one knew where he'd gone. Nothing more. Even the stable lad had gone missing.

"Did Bernard go missing because he murdered his wife or because he was too scared to stay?"

It was an excellent question, the only one Thomas had ever heard from Squire Billing, and there was no answer.

It was late when Thomas came into the bedchamber. Meggie was sitting up in the big heavy bed, three pillows behind her back, a candle burning on a small table at her elbow. She appeared to be reading.

She looked up when he came into the room, watched him close the door quietly behind him, watched him set his candle down on the dressing table, then straighten and turn to face her.

She cocked her head to one side and said, "Hello, my lord. What do you want?"

"What are you reading?"

"John Locke. He isn't very amusing."

"No."

"What do you want?" she asked again.

"You," he said. "I want you, Meggie. Take off your nightgown."

"I believe some specifics are in order here, my lord."

"My name is Thomas." He said again, his voice cold and remote this time, "I said that I wanted you. That is quite specific enough."

"Do you mean that you want to maul me again?"

His hands stilled on the top button of his trousers. It was a good question. He had mauled her, rutting bastard that he was, but it wasn't really his fault. If she hadn't said those things, hadn't rubbed his nose in the fact that she didn't love him— no, that was a lie if he'd ever told himself one, which, of course he had. He'd known she hadn't loved him and he'd believed it wouldn't matter, that he would make her love him soon enough.

Damnation.

He stripped off his clothes, knowing she was watching, looking at him, pointedly. Surely that could be seen as a good thing, perhaps.

When he was naked, he walked to the bed and sat beside her. He looked into those Sherbrooke eyes of hers, beautiful light blue eyes, vivid as the summer sky—and said, "I will not hurt you tonight. I will come into you and you will like it. I'm going to teach you pleasure, Meggie." *I will be the teacher, the lover, not that bastard Jeremy, and you'll learn to love my hands and mouth, and stop your dreams about him.*

"That's very hard to believe that it can actually be nice."

"I'm going to make you grin like a loon, make your eyes go vague. Eventually I'll even let you go to sleep." He said nothing more, just drew her against him. "Kiss me, Meggie."

"All right." When his tongue was in her mouth, when she'd eased, when he knew she was becoming interested in what he was doing, he threw the pillows on the floor and came down beside her. "You're beautiful," he said into her mouth. "And you're mine, Meggie. You will never forget that. No one else's, mine."

She gave him a clear look and said, "Of course I'm yours, Thomas, and you are mine. I pray you will not forget that either."

That warmed him to his toes, then made him cold again, on the outside. Meggie might not love him, but she was loyal. He wanted her loyalty true enough, but he wanted her to love him too, it was just that simple. He wanted everything. Well, damnation.

When her nightgown was on the floor and he was on top of her, kissing his way down the length of her, he knew it would be difficult to keep himself in check, but he wouldn't allow a repeat of their wedding.

Thomas's heart was racing, the blood was pumping through him, hot and heavy, and he hurt with urgency. Then he kissed her white belly, feeling her muscles tense, knowing she was excited, knowing that she was ignorant as a post, but was beginning to enjoy herself and wanted to yell with it. He would make her love him, make her want him above all men, above that damned Jeremy, make her yield her soul to him, whisper his name in her dreams. He smiled when he came between her legs, wanting her, wanting her, lifted her in his hands, and gave her his mouth.

Meggie's brain shut down. Yes, he was actually touching her there, with his mouth, his teeth, his tongue. Then she lifted off the bed, so embarrassed when she tried to yell at him, she could only stutter. She tried to jerk away from him, shoving at his shoulders, yanking on his hair, but he just raised his mouth a bit, looked at her straight in her Sherbrooke eyes, and said, his breath hot against her flesh, "Lie down, Meggie. Close your eyes and let yourself enjoy what I'm doing to you. It's the done thing, just like the tongues. Relax. I'm your husband. This gives me great pleasure. Don't deny me my pleasure, Meggie."

"Oh no, oh goodness, but, Thomas—"

"Be quiet," he said and blew his hot breath against her. Meggie lurched up and yelled.

He eased a finger inside her and she yelled again, only this time, he knew she'd shoot him if he stopped. Good, he had her now. He pushed her until— "Come now, Meggie. Just let go. Come along, come to me—"

Meggie didn't understand what was happening to her, but she knew she'd simply shatter into pieces if anything or anyone tried to stop it happening, whatever it was. She was quaking, stuttering she was so frantic, so maddened by the feelings building and building until—she arched her back, fisted her hands in his hair, and screamed to the beamed ceiling.

He pushed her and pushed her until he felt every bit of tension, every frantic need from deep inside her finally quiet, leaving her utterly limp, utterly his. He gave a shout of satisfaction as he came into her hard, deep and deeper still, and she raised her hips, something that nearly sent him right over the edge. No, he wouldn't leave her this quickly, it wasn't fair to either of them. Where had she gotten the energy to want him more? Then he looked down at them, saw himself going deeper inside her, and trembled like a tree branch in a high wind.

Those long legs of hers went around his flanks, and she moaned, and he tried, he truly tried to slow himself, to come out of her a bit until he managed to grab on to just a bit of control, but then he just couldn't, couldn't do anything but go forward and he did, touching her womb. Her womb, he was part of her. Oh God. Even then he gritted his teeth, trying desperately to hold himself still, not to move even a small little bit, but it did no good. He went right over the edge when she bit his shoulder, then licked where she'd bitten.

He yelled louder than his wife had, then collapsed on top of her.

Meggie, flattened by a very big sweaty male body, didn't mind a bit. So this was pleasure. She bit his shoulder again, licked it, and grinned. She was astounded. She'd wanted to sing and dance with the champagne, but it was nothing compared to this. Now she wanted to whirl about in a fast waltz, she wanted to stomp her feet to some wild music that the gypsies played. She was filled with energy, with power, and all because of him, because of Thomas, her husband.

"Thank you," she whispered against his ear, and squeezed her arms around his back.

He was breathing hard, his face beside hers, and she'd brought him to this.

"I was very good, wasn't I?" she said, and bit his earlobe this time. "Just look at you, my lord, felled like a tree, breathing so hard I fear an attack of apoplexy, and all because I'm me and I did it to you."

"I'm going to die," he said finally, tried to bring himself up on his elbow but failing. He fell on her again.

"Perhaps I should give lessons, do you think?"

"Meggie, aren't you at all tired? Utterly relaxed? Your limbs weak and useless? Your brain ready to nap?"

"I want to dance, Thomas. Waltz with me. Then may we do this again?"

He groaned, and managed to pull himself up on his elbows. He was still inside her, and when he moved, he felt himself harden again. It was amazing. He didn't want to waltz, oh no. "Meggie, I don't think we are quite finished yet. Do you mind if we dance a bit later?"

She stared up at him, her head cocked to the side. "I must be truly amazing," she said, and lifted her hips. She felt him hard now, as hard as he'd been before he'd reached his climax. It felt wonderful. "All right. We will waltz after. Do something, Thomas, please."

And he did, grinning even as he kissed her mouth, the underside of her breast, her hipbone, the inside of her left knee. He kissed her until she moaned in his mouth, and he thought, *You're mine, not his, just mine.* It didn't take long since he was already far gone. He shuddered and quaked and threw his head back and moaned long and deep. Then when he managed to focus on her face again, he saw that she wasn't unconscious from pleasure as she should be. He didn't pause, pulled out of her, took her with his mouth, and sent her right over the edge, again. She didn't manage a moan or a yell, but just heaved and jerked about like a puppet, then sighed deeply, and reached for him. Before Thomas fell asleep, he brought her close against him, felt her breath against his flesh, knew the instant she was asleep, and he thought, *I am really excellent at this. Perhaps even better than my bride.* He smiled, knew that Jeremy hadn't intruded this time, and closed his eyes. He was gone in just under two seconds.

19

Off the coast of southwestern Ireland
Between Cork Harbour and Kinsale

MEGGIE DECIDED SHE loved the Celtic Sea. This morning it looked like the English Channel on a very bad day, a gray raucous day, water whipped up by the wind, tearing and whipping about the boat. Today the sea was as rough and pure and wild as the frigid North Sea that slammed into the rocks near her home Kildrummy Castle in Scotland.

Then, suddenly, a gleaming sliver of sun slid through a sky full of fat gray clouds, knifing into the high waves just ahead of their boat. As for the boat—The *Kelpie*—it rocked madly, lifted to the top of a wave, then slammed down hard into a deep trough. It was like slicing a knife into bread, fast and deep. Then holding steady, a long pause, as if the boat were holding its breath, then up again, towering on top of the cresting waves.

She'd never experienced anything like this. It was magnificent, exciting, and she loved every instant of it. She thought she'd even go so far as to say that she loved it as much as she'd loved the pleasure she'd wallowed in the previous night. Then, of course, morning had come as it always did, and even though one just wanted to lie there and smile and do nothing at all, except reach for her husband and begin it all again, it wasn't possible because her husband had been gone. Long gone and it was only six o'clock in the morning, a stormy morning that would have made staying in bed, sipping chocolate, and kissing until her mouth was numb, a very lovely thing indeed.

It was not to be, dammit. And then he was there beside her, looking up at the billowing storm clouds overhead, feeling the harsh sea wind whip his hair around his face.

He said, "We'll be landing soon in Cork Harbour."

She had her hand firmly on her bonnet. She turned to see her husband, his dark eyes watering from the sea winds whipping about his head. He looked immensely wonderful, but he had changed again. This wasn't the man who'd groaned and yelled and kissed her numb the previous night. What was wrong with men? Were they all like this—utterly unpredictable, without a single idea how nice it would be to smile and kiss?

"I hope it storms before we land. I love storms."

"The horses don't. They don't like this pitching about a bit. Add rain to the mix and they would want to stomp until they toppled into the sea."

"It is a pity that they don't have thumbs—then they could hang on to something."

He smiled, remembering how he'd hated to leave her, she'd been so warm and soft, a slight smile playing about her mouth. She'd opened her eyes then, looked at him and saw only him, he knew it, smiled at only him. He'd had to leave her, there was so much to be done.

He said, "Pendragon lies only two hours south, right on the coast, at the end of a short promontory. It was built four centuries ago, a sentinel at the edge of·the land to watch for enemies. It was burned by Cromwell because the Kavanaghs refused to surrender, then rebuilt by Charles II."

"The Kavanaghs?"

"My great-uncle, Rodney Malcombe, my grandfather's

younger brother, bought Pendragon with his inheritance when the Kavanaghs found themselves betrayed by the French toward the end of the last century."

"Napoleon betrayed them?"

Thomas nodded. "It was a question of turning on their neighbors. It was said that the Kavanaghs would butcher a neighbor's cattle without thinking twice about it, but they simply would not kill the neighbors' families. The French made them promises, then broke them. The Kavanaghs took what money my uncle paid for Pendragon and went to the Colonies, to a town called Boston, I believe. Pendragon is a grand old place, Meggie."

Her eyes were shining with excitement even as the wild whipped her bonnet off her head.

Thomas caught it before it whirled overboard and set it back onto her tangled hair. He lightly patted her cheek, leaned down, and kissed her. "I wish I could have stayed with you this morning," he said, and kissed her again.

Meggie leaned into him, licked his bottom lip, and he stepped back to tie her ribbons beneath her chin. "It simply won't do for the earl of Lancaster to make love to his bride on the deck of a pitching boat."

"Why not?"

"Be quiet, Meggie," he said, stroked his knuckles over her jaw, and grinned at her. He cleared his throat. "We have our own small harbour where our local fishermen moor their boats. We have a small village, Pendragon, that sports a few small shops for the hundred or so people who live around us. Mostly we ride to Kinsale for supplies, just to the south of us."

"Pendragon," she said. "It has taste, that word, the taste of adventure and secrets and old passages that no one knows about." She rolled the name around in her mouth, said it out loud again. "Pendragon. My cousin Jeremy's home in Fowey is called Dragon's Jaw. Isn't that a marvelous name as well? I so wanted to—well, that's silly, now isn't it? No, I wanted to visit Dragon's Jaw. There are these sharp rocks at the base of the cliff just below the house and thus, its name."

If Jeremy had magically appeared, Thomas would have hurled him overboard without a second thought. She was thinking about living at his home. He was so angry he wanted to curse the billowing sails down, but he knew he couldn't, and so he said, "Pendragon is very old. It was once very important. Now it is simply beautiful. Now it simply endures."

Meggie frowned up at him. "What's wrong, Thomas? You sound as cold and sharp as my grandmother Lady Lydia who can both slice ham and a witless neighbor with just a single glare. She lives at Northcliffe Hall with my uncle Douglas and aunt Alex. She couldn't come to our wedding because she was ill. However, given the letter she wrote me, she is very pleased that I married an earl who's an Englishman, not a dreaded Scot like my uncle Colin. Still, given five minutes she could still find something significant lacking in your character.

"And so don't you look down that very elegant nose of yours at me, just like she does. Don't forget, my lord, that I gave you remarkable pleasure last night if your grunts and groans are any measure of pleasure, which they are, I know that firsthand." She gave him a smile that made him want to jump on her and take her down to the deck.

She said, "One would think you would perhaps wish to reminisce a bit, perhaps smile a bit vacantly, but here you are, thin-lipped, and I have no idea why."

All right. He would forget Jeremy for a moment and his ridiculous house in Fowey. Dragon's Jaw, a really stupid name, so precious it was nauseating. He didn't want her to guess that he was beyond jealous. He looked at her, saw the wind had burned her cheeks bright red. He also saw that she was so proud of herself, and now that he thought about it, she had pushed him right over the edge, and he'd happily fallen and fallen yet again, until he wouldn't have cared if the bloody roof of Squire Billings's house had come crashing down on his back.

He took her mittened hand and looked toward the distant shore, listened to the wind howl and poor Tim McCulver vomiting over the side of the boat, thankfully downwind.

"Yes," Meggie said after a moment. "Pendragon—it is a vastly romantic name, just flows off the tongue and makes you shiver with the feel of it—so unlike our home in Scotland—Kildrummy Castle. That is utterly pragmatic and down-to-earth, feet firmly planted. Tell me about it."

"I much prefer it to Bowden Close. You will see it yourself this afternoon."

"Where did the name Pendragon come from? Is it named after an ancient Irish warrior?"

"No. My great-uncle changed the name from Belleek Castle to Pendragon. Uther Pendragon wasn't Irish, he was Celtic or early English, the father of King Arthur. My great-uncle was obsessed with King Arthur. I believe he dreamed of finding Arthur's burial site on Pendragon land. I heard rumors a couple of years back that North Nightingale, Lord Chilton, had found King Arthur's sword *Excalibur* when a cliff wall collapsed into an ancient cave. Probably nonsense, but I would like to meet him someday and ask about it.

"My great-uncle always used to say that Tintagal was nothing but a heap of rocks, that Arthur could have easily sailed to Ireland, to Pendragon, and spent his final days there. But I wonder."

"Oh, I remember that now. Pendragon." She grinned at him. "Let me roll it about on my tongue for a moment."

He watched her and her tongue rolling around, could practically feel her tongue rolling about on and in his own mouth, and got harder than the mast.

She said, "Do you plan to live most of the time at Pendragon?"

"I haven't yet decided. Bowden Close is now also my responsibility. Your family is there. We will visit often."

"That's good. I would miss my family."

"Yes, I know. As I said, I don't wish Bowden Close to be left only in a steward's hands."

"My uncle Douglas says that a man is a fool if he ignores what is his."

"I agree."

"My father agrees too, which is why he traveled to Kildrummy Castle when he inherited it. We couldn't live there, however, and we were very lucky. Oliver manages Kildrummy Castle. Actually now it is as much his home as it is ours. Did you know that Oliver was one of my uncle Ryder's first Beloved Ones?"

"Yes. Your uncle Ryder found him trying to pull himself out of an alley so he could beg for food. His leg was badly broken, you see, and he couldn't walk."

"My uncle took care of him until he was eighteen, and then he went to Oxford. He was going to be my uncle Douglas's steward, but the instant he saw Kildrummy Castle, he fell in love with it. Oliver is very smart and married my uncle's daughter, Jenny. You met Jenny and Oliver at the wedding. They are very happy."

Meggie shook his sleeve. "Now, my lord, when will you thank me for last night? When are you going to sing my praises? Tell me you have never experienced such a woman as I? Goodness, Thomas, I laid you lower than a slug."

"I don't like the sound of that. You do know that you're ignorant as a stick," he added, and lightly touched his palm to her the underside of her breast. "But I have high hopes."

Meggie didn't move, became still as a statue and looked up at him, not saying a word. Then she leaned forward, pressing her breast into his palm. Thomas's breath hitched. He saw one of the sailors coming and regretfully dropped his hand to his side. "Yes," he said, "lower than a slug. Now, let's think about the pleasure I gave you. Meggie, the look on your face when I kissed you."

"Well, I love to kiss you. You make my mouth tingle."

"No, not on the mouth, Meggie."

He laughed when she turned even redder, none of it from windburn.

He couldn't help himself. He smiled down at her, at the loose hair pulled from beneath her bonnet, whipping against her face. "If I hadn't pleasured you, would you have shot me after you felled me?"

She pursed her lips and he knew, knew all the way to his boots, that she was giving this due thought. Finally she said, "Well, that's a real possibility. Who knows what you would have demanded to do? Our wedding night was memorable, but I wouldn't precisely say that it was a memory that I will cherish when I am an old woman. Yes, I might have shot you."

She was so likable, so damned open and giving. Not a reticent bone in that ever so white body of hers. Her body. No, he wouldn't think about that, not now, not on board a wildly rocking boat.

He looked out over the billowing wave that would slap the side of the boat in another instant. He waited, put his arm on hers to keep her steady, and felt the taste of the water in his mouth from the wild spray.

He said after a moment, "My mother lives at Pendragon."

"I shouldn't be surprised," she said slowly, "but you hadn't told me where she was living. Remember I asked you if your mother would come to our wedding, and you just shook your head and said something about her being ill."

"That is true. She was ill, just like your grandmother. As a rule she dislikes leaving Pendragon. When I was five, she took me to her brother's home, to Pendragon. I was raised there."

"I look forward to meeting her," Meggie said.

Thomas said not another word.

They turned into Cork Harbour within the hour, where the water was much calmer because of the long curving mole that broke the storm's might.

A mother-in-law, Meggie was thinking. She hadn't given the actual flesh-and-blood lady much thought until now that she was going to meet her in a very short time. She thought of her grandmother Lady Lydia and spent a good five minutes praying hard.

20

Pendragon Castle

"So you are my son's new wife."

"Yes, ma'am." Meggie smiled as she stepped up to the older woman, who looked a great deal like Thomas, from her dark hair and eyes to her olive complexion. Her mother-in-law, something she'd never had before, someone who was now more a part of her life than her own parents. If Thomas's mother hadn't come to their wedding because of ill health, she certainly looked as fit as a top-form racing cat to Meggie.

Best to begin the way she meant to go on. Meggie gave her a big smile, oozing with respect and goodwill, and offered her a curtsy only a duchess deserved—a royal duchess.

Her mother-in-law said, after looking her up and down, "From my son's letter, I thought you would look much better. You are not presentable. You are wet. Perhaps even on the frowzy side. The feather on your bonnet is drooping badly."

"Mother, as you can see, both Meggie and I are soaked to the skin. Just before we managed to steer into the harbor, a big wave struck the port side of the boat. Even Pen got wet, and I can assure you that he wasn't happy about it. I will take Meggie to our bedchamber now so she may change."

"My son wrote that you have your family's eyes."

"Yes, my lady," Meggie said. "They're the Sherbrooke eyes."

"Blue as a summer sky," Thomas said, and Meggie, inordinately pleased with this remarkable male offering, turned to him and gave him a dazzling smile. "Thank you," she said.

"I'm not a 'my lady,' " Thomas's mother said, her voice all sharp, "not since Lord Lancaster divorced me. But now he's dead, so I suppose I can now be a dowager countess since my son is the new earl."

"I see nothing at all amiss with that," Meggie said, then just couldn't prevent herself asking, "Thomas really wrote to you about my Sherbrooke eyes?"

"Among other things, as, for instance, the amount of your dowry, which is quite adequate. A healthy dowry goes far in assuring a young bride's reception. He might have remarked upon things that aren't quite so adequate, I cannot remember."

Thomas rolled his eyes. She was his mother and he knew her well, and now he rather wished that—well, forget it. She would never change.

She continued after just a moment of the blank silence, "However, none of this is here nor there for the moment, young lady. Now, as to the other, you may continue to call me my lady."

"I'm sorry, my lady, that you were ill and could not come to our wedding."

"That is nonsense. I am never ill."

Thomas had known from the age of ten that a lie, one with meat on it that promised consequences if discovered, always came to light, and the perpetrator always came to a bad end.

"But why then didn't you come?"

"Meggie," Thomas said. "Let it go." He squeezed her hand. Deep water, she thought, and nodded.

"It is nearly teatime," the dowager countess said, and pulled out a monocle and placed it against her right eye.

It was a rather frightening sight. She said, "Bring her back then, Thomas."

Meggie thought that her mother-in-law could have spoken to her rather than through her. Not a very good beginning.

"I believe we will both be ready for some tea in a short time," Thomas said, and turned to Meggie.

She said, "Yes, my lady, I will be delighted to be brought back for tea."

Meggie said not another word as she trailed Thomas out of the large, cold, dismal drawing room with its tattered furnishings and thick heavy draperies that tightly covered all the windows.

What a dreadful room.

"My mother is perhaps a bit eccentric," Thomas said, not looking at her.

"Maybe she should meet my grandmother," Meggie said, not dropping a bit of her good cheer. "I will probably be able to tell you in a week who would win that battle. I was rather hoping that since she believed my dowry was adequate, I would be treated better."

"Perhaps it wasn't entirely ill health that kept her away from our wedding."

To his surprise and relief, Meggie giggled. "You were trying to save my feelings, and so you told me a very blameless lie." She sighed. "You did it well, but still, you were caught out. I always am as well. I don't suppose you'll tell me what those things you wrote to her about me that aren't so adequate?"

"I wrote only that you were a brilliant flower ready to be plucked."

"That's nauseating."

"Yes, I thought you'd like that. Truth is, she didn't want to come because she is the most perverse woman in England. I could have been marrying a princess, and she still would have sniffed and stuck her nose in the air."

"That's all right then. Perversity is interesting."

"I just hope you will still think that in a week from now." Thomas nodded to a desiccated old man who looked like he was in horrible pain. He was walking slowly toward them, his back terribly bent, an occasional moan slipping out of his mouth.

"My lord," the old man said, rolling the *lord* around on his tongue. "Aye, what a lovely sound that be."

Thomas said, "Barnacle, do see to our luggage."

"Aye, my lord, but it will be an awesome struggle, as ye well know, since ye have cracked my poor back for so many times for me over the years."

"I know, Barnacle. What I meant was, get Ennis to fetch the luggage and you will instruct him as to how to carry it and where to place it."

"It is good of ye to be more specific, my lord. Be she the new ladyship?"

"Aye," Meggie said. "That I be."

"Yer pretty, all that hair what can't make up its mind what color it is. Yer not all that big, leastwise not as big as his lordship has become. Mayhap ye'd walk on my back for me when it gets all knotted up?"

"I would be delighted to walk on your back, Barnacle."

The old man nodded, threw back his head, and yelled, "Ennis! Get yer skinny buttocks and yer strong back in here, lad."

Meggie was sure she saw one corner of Thomas's mouth turn up a bit, but he said nothing.

Barnacle made his way slowly back to the front door.

Meggie said, "Barnacle looks as if he's nearly dying with pain, Thomas. How bad is it?"

"Not at all bad."

"But he looks like he's ready to yowl in agony. I even heard him moaning. I've never seen anything like it."

"Few people have. Actually, I've seen him practicing his agony in front of the mirror. He nearly caught me because I laughed, I just couldn't help it. I was about fourteen at the time. I don't doubt that his back bothers him a bit, but most of it's a sham. He's done it since before I was born. The old bugger will doubtless outlive all of us, even with his back nearly bent like a horseshoe."

"That look of his does have a potent effect," Meggie said.

"You sound impressed."

"Oh, I am. He looks to be a splendid old man. Did you ever walk on his back for him?"

"When I was a boy. Now it's your turn. He will grunt and groan and enjoy himself immensely, and complain the whole time."

"He is an unusual butler, Thomas. Ah, I wonder what you will think when you meet Hollis, my uncle Douglas's butler. He's more distinguished than the king."

"It wouldn't require all that much."

She smiled and said, "Barnacle. That is a very strange name."

"You haven't begun to see all the strangeness at Pendragon yet, Meggie."

"Thomas, why didn't your mother wish to come to our wedding? Besides just being perverse?"

He looked her straight in the eye and said, "She didn't want me to marry."

"Me?"

"No, anyone. She believes I'm too young, but she'll come to love you, Meggie. How could she not?"

"Maybe she doesn't like the fact that my father is a vicar. Maybe she thinks I'm not well enough born for her son the earl."

"No," her son said with a goodly dose of cynicism, "she just doesn't want to relinquish the reins of control here at Pendragon."

"Well, I don't have to, you know, I—"

"Meggie, you are my wife, the countess of Lancaster, the mistress of Pendragon. Pendragon is your responsibility. Don't forget about what your uncle said about responsibility."

"No," Meggie said slowly, "I won't." She turned and looked around the entrance hall. It wasn't dreadful at all. It was cold and dismal, like the drawing room, but it had some majesty to it, soaring up three stories to the blackened beamed roof. There was a huge old chandelier hang-

ing down from that immense height. Meggie hoped the
rope holding it was very sturdy indeed and wondered
when it had last been checked and cleaned. Probably not
since it had been rebuilt after Cromwell had burned it
down. She looked down when her heels clicked on the
marble floor. Those black-and-white tiles were lovely. All
they needed was a good scrubbing, maybe three good
scrubbings. The filth didn't hide how impressive they still
were. Suits of armor lined one wall, one after the other,
and at least a half dozen sconces soldiered along in a
straight line above them. The sconces and the armor
looked like they hadn't been used or cleaned or polished
for at least a century, maybe two.

Thomas seemed to see nothing amiss. He said with a
negligent wave, "The armor—it's Flemish, for the most
part, fifteenth century. My uncle bought them from a viscount in Surrey who'd lost all his money, and had them
carted here."

Then he said as he pointed to the huge oak staircase
that could accommodate a near battalion marching side by
side, "The house is old. Since it was originally built in
the late fourteen hundreds by the Kavanaghs, it was added
to over the years, then destroyed, rebuilt, and ended up
looking like this. Both my great-uncle and my uncle did
very little. You will find it somewhat drafty. Now that I
have access to unexpected funds I will finish off all the
necessary repairs."

"Is that why you married me, Thomas? You needed my
dowry?"

"Yes, that's exactly the reason."

"Good. I hope there is enough for everything you wish
to do."

He said, "You amaze me, Meggie, the way your brain
works. No, I didn't marry you for your damned dowry.
You will forget that."

"I never thought that you did." She was looking at his
mouth. He started, then took a step back. He pointed to
the very old paintings climbing up the wall beside the

staircase. Meggie, engaged, said, "Are these your ancestors or Kavanaghs?"

"My uncle claimed they were all Malcombes. They are so old, no one, however, really cares. In the master's bedchamber there are portraits of Malcombes. A gloomy bunch. A couple of rogues, an out-and-out scoundrel, a womanizer, and a prominent member of the House of Lords."

"Now you are the earl. You will do something amazing, Thomas, I just know it. You have a strong sense of duty, your brain is quite fit, and you don't indulge yourself overly."

He appeared startled. "You really believe that?" he asked slowly, stopping on the stairs and looking down at her. *You believe that my brain is better than that damned Jeremy's? Is my sense of duty greater?*

"Oh yes, certainly. I'm your wife and I should know all your good points as well as your bad. Now, your uncle was, of course, your father's younger brother?"

"That's right. He made his money in trade, something my mother doesn't like to speak of, but his brain served him well. I happen to agree with him. Making money all on your own isn't a bad thing. In my case, it was necessary because there wasn't much."

Meggie looked down at the stair railing that needed polish very badly. "Actually, I've never really had to think about money or the lack of it. My uncle the earl manages vast estates and is very rich, but it all comes from old wealth, you understand. Uncle Douglas is an excellent caretaker and more, he has added to the coffers through his fine management. At least that's what I overheard his estate manager saying."

"However would you, a female, know of that?"

She said without guile, "I have told you, have I not, that I have been a great eavesdropper in my time? My father would sometimes come to me if he suspected something and needed it verified. I just wish I'd eavesdropped when Jeremy and my father—no, never mind that, it isn't at all important."

Thomas wished Jeremy were here right at this moment, standing on the stair next to him. He'd pick him up and hurl him to the marble floor, then stomp him. He wanted to hear his jaw snap when his fist hit him.

He said, "Whereever did you get this eavesdropping tendency?"

She said easily, thinking everything was just fine, "I inherited it from my aunt Sinjun. I fear it is a lifelong habit, my lord."

"I will keep that to myself. I will also be watchful of what I say when you don't appear to be around."

"Wise of you. Now, my uncle Ryder inherited a huge amount of money from my great-uncle Brandon as well as a sugar plantation in Jamaica. As for my father, thanks to Uncle Douglas, who has always tended his money, he is also rich. Then Kildrummy Castle came into our lives and that brought more money into my father's pockets. Not that he ever noticed or spoke of it." Meggie looked at him closely. "If you did marry me for my money, why then, I think you made a very wise investment."

"Thank you. I agree. It was actually far more that I'd expected."

"How much was it?"

He stopped again, looked down at her, and said slowly, "One doesn't speak of that to a lady, surely you know that."

"No, I don't know that at all. I was bought. Isn't it fair that I know my price?"

"You weren't bought."

"My father paid for me, thus I was bought. Come on, now. Spit it out. How much, Thomas?"

"Dammit. Ten thousand pounds."

He wanted to kick himself for just spitting that out. He arched a brow and tried to look supercilious. "Do you think you're worth ten thousand pounds?"

She sighed. "I've lived all my life never knowing hunger or want. If I saw a bolt of material that pleased me, I would order it. My father spent so much money on my Season in London and I never even thought about it." She sighed. "I didn't even find a husband. After Jeremy—" Her voice dropped like a stone off a cliff.

21

Ήe SAID, VERY carefully, unable to help himself, "What do you mean, 'after Jeremy'?"

"Forget Jeremy. He's just an almost dratted cousin, nothing more. The fact is that I'm pitiful, Thomas, and I never realized it until now. No, truth be told, I'm not worth anywhere near that many groats. I think you got a pig in a poke."

"No," he said, "I got a Sherbrooke with beautiful blue eyes that she'll pass along to our children."

"Yes, I will try. I'm sorry, Thomas."

Thomas stopped, looked at her, an eyebrow arched up. "Whyever are you sorry?"

"I'm very sorry if you were poor after your father divorced your mother."

"Never hunger or real want, Meggie. My uncle was at low ebb the last twenty years of his life, but he took my mother and me in, and he did it gladly, generously. He was a fine man. I will tell you something though. It's a sorry thing when there are people depending on you and you have to think and scheme and dicker with all sorts of very distasteful men to get together enough money to see to their needs. That was true for me until two years ago. That was when my first ship arrived back in Genoa from China." He took her arm and they continued up the stairs. The stairs creaked beneath their feet. There was a thread-worn Turkish carpet tacked down to the steps. Ancient, by the looks of it. "I wonder how many feet have walked on this rug?"

That got his attention. "I've wondered that myself. I think when I was about thirteen years old I decided that several armies had stayed here, bringing the feet up to at least five thousand."

"That sounds about right. Two armies?"

"Cromwell came twice. The first time he failed, but not the second time."

"Oh. I didn't tell you that my aunt Sinjun was an heiress. Actually she was one of the premiere heiresses in all of England. She married a Scottish earl who was so poor his castle was near to falling down about his ears. She saved him. Do you think perhaps that I am saving you just a bit? You could consider me another one of your ships sailing into port, all loaded with wonderful goods?"

"You're more than one ship, Meggie. When I think of your goods, my toes curl." He gave her the wickedest grin imaginable.

"I like the sound of that. Now, about your goods—"

He kissed her hard and fast, then straightened. "Also, my father was very well off, Meggie. Together, you have made me rich indeed. Generations to come will bless your dowry."

Down at the very end of a long, dim, very wide corridor that echoed and another threadbare Turkish carpet over oak planks that creaked, lay the master bedchamber. Actually, it was a suite of rooms, she heard Thomas say from behind her. The master bedchamber, she saw, was so dismal that she had to swallow and seam her lips together to keep back a moan of disappointment. She shouldn't have been surprised after that drawing room. But still, she was. The large room was filled with heavy old furniture, tattered draperies, miles and miles of bare oak plank floor leading to a mammoth bed that sat on a three-foot dais. If anything, it was more depressing than the drawing room. She said finally, her arms crossed over her chest,

"It is certainly a very big room, Thomas. There is an extraordinary amount of floor."

"There is a dressing room in there with a nice big copper tub, then another bedchamber beyond, which would be your bedchamber, I suppose."

The dressing room was small and dark and smelled of camphor balls. The bedchamber beyond surprised her. When she opened the door, she had to blink because the sun was flooding in so brightly. Where had the storm gone? She would have sworn it was still battering the area, given the dankness of every other room she'd seen in Pendragon, but not this room. It was white, pure white, no other color, and it made you want to fling your arms out and whirl about.

She walked to the middle of the room, standing on a thick white carpet that covered nearly all the floor in this airy room. "Oh my," she said.

"You weren't expecting this. It's called, originally enough, the White Room."

"No. I like it very much, Thomas." She paused a moment, not knowing exactly how one spoke of this, and Thomas said, "Just spit it out, Meggie."

"My father and Mary Rose share a bedchamber. So do my uncles and their wives. I've seen Uncle Colin carry Aunt Sinjun into his bedchamber over his shoulder. I've always believed that was the way things were done. Do you think we could do that as well?"

"You wish to share a bedchamber with me?" he asked slowly, and knew he was stupid to feel the leap of hope.

"Well, yes. How can I improve upon you if I don't have you with me?"

"It would be well nigh impossible. I need improvement?"

"Oh yes, but I will say that I truly believe in ten years you will become the perfect man."

"Only ten years?"

"I've always been an optimist."

He walked to her and cupped her face in his palm. "Yes, I knew you were the moment I met you."

Meggie went up on her tiptoes and looked right at his mouth.

"You want me to kiss you?"

"Yes," she said, nuzzling his chin. "If you have to ask me that, then I'm afraid that it will constitute an additional improvement. We're perhaps talking more than ten years here, Thomas."

He ducked his head down and kissed her. Her mouth was so bloody warm and soft, just like the rest of her—both inside and out—and that included her loyal heart, damn her. He lifted his head and continued to cup her cheek. "Your face is very expressive, Meggie. You hate my bedchamber, don't you?"

"It could be improved upon—"

"Just like me."

"No, I expect you'll be much easier. I propose that we use this lovely white bedchamber until I have managed to make the larger one more inhabitable."

He said even more slowly, his fingers lightly stroking her jaw, "I have never heard of husbands and wives sharing a bedchamber unless they were forced to. Certainly it is difficult for me to imagine that my father and mother ever shared the same bed. I mean, certain husbands and wives share a bed long enough to, well, perform intimacies, but not the entire night. Are you certain that all your male relatives share with their wives?"

"Oh yes."

He said slowly, "I think I need to think about this, Meggie."

"I don't think I snore," she said. "You do, though, at least you did that first night. However, that first night was undoubtedly a strain on you, so I should not be too swift with a conclusion here."

He dropped his hand from her face. "Perhaps snoring is one reason husbands and wives don't sleep together the entire night."

"I think Mary Rose just shoves my father over on his side when he snores. I heard her speaking of it once to him."

"I will think about it, Meggie."

Well, Thomas hadn't mentioned love, but still, she thought, two people who were not only married but also enjoyed the other's company, as she and Thomas did, except for their debacle of a wedding night, should surely wish to sleep together. She gave him a long thoughtful look, and said only, "Do that," and walked to the huge white-painted armoire. When she opened the doors, she saw a row of gowns. Shoes of all sorts lined the bottom of the armoire. Slowly she pulled out one of the dresses. It was high-waisted and looked to be rather old. She turned, holding the dress, her head cocked to the side in question.

"I suppose the gowns belonged to my uncle's wife, Aunt Sarah. She died back in 1810, in the winter. She was always cold, didn't matter if it was deep summer. My uncle painted this room white and built more windows so when there was bright sun, as there is now, she would feel it on her face and be warm."

"When did your uncle die?"

"Two years ago. I was living in Italy at the time, in Genoa, immersing myself in shipping. At least before he died, he knew that I was making enough money to assure that Pendragon would be revitalized, that all his dependents would be taken care of."

"Then your father died six months ago. You were in Italy at that time as well?"

"Yes. I'm in business with the earl of Clare, a man I much admire. His boys are your age and a bit younger."

"How many does he have?"

"Six."

Meggie's eyes widened at that. "Six boys? Goodness, Thomas, his poor wife."

"Lady Rayna rules all of them with an iron fist. He is also in business with his brother-in-law, Kamal, who is half European and half Muslim. He was at one time the Bey of Oran—a king in his own right, loaded down with a palace and a harem, master of all he surveyed. He married Arabella Welles, the earl's sister. She is one of the most beautiful women I have ever seen."

"Does she have six daughters?"

"No, two girls and two boys. All of them come to England once a year, in the early fall. You will meet them."

"And will we travel to Italy?"

Ah, she wanted to, he saw it on her face, heard it in her voice. It was something he could give her that Jeremy couldn't. "I don't see why not. It's quite beautiful in the early fall. Now, I will tell Ennis to put my valises in the master bedchamber for the time being. You may have this room. I can see that it pleases you."

"It pleases me," Meggie said in a perfectly pleasant voice, "because it isn't dark and dank and dismal, like that big room just yon that you really should let me fix before you move in there for just one day."

"I will think about it," he said yet again and left her standing there, staring at the empty doorway to the dressing room. He knew all the way to the soles of his big feet that if she were to whisper Jeremy's name in her dreams, and he was there beside her to hear it, he would be worth nothing much at all after that.

Thirty minutes later Meggie found her way back down the huge oak staircase, pausing a moment to admire the carving on the newel post on the top of the banister. She also wanted to admire the plastered ceiling, but it was dirty, in bad need of painting. She walked to the drawing room. She paused when she heard raised voices—the loudest one belonging to her mother-in-law. It was probably about her, since she was the only new specimen about. Meggie practiced her smile. Getting that smile all the way to her eyes, however, was another matter.

When she walked into the drawing room, it was to see not only her husband and her mother-in-law, but also another lady of indeterminate years, sitting on a faded brocade sofa opposite her mother-in-law. This lady was as plump as Thomas's mother was thin. Her hair, probably once richly blond, was now faded, threads of silver weaving in and out of the fat braids that sat atop her head, unlike Thomas's mother, whose hair was very dark, heavily laced with snowy white strands of hair. This lady was very fair, her skin as pale as a new snowfall, her eyes light blue, deep dimples in her cheeks. She was really quite pretty, and she was also yelling. "By God, Madeleine, this is nonsense! Tell me you do not mean that!"

So her mother-in-law's name was Madeleine. That was very pretty.

"I mean it all right, Libby, so you may shut your trap. I tell you, he's— Ah, here's my new daughter-in-law with her blue eyes, nice eyes, if one considers the size of her dowry. However, she smiles too much."

That really made Meggie feel low as a chunk of dirt. *I smile too much?* Meggie wiped the smile off her face and walked stiff as a soldier at attention to the center of the horrible drawing room and looked first to her husband, then to her mother-in-law, and finally to the plump Libby with her fat blond braids and very pretty smile.

"Hello," she said, then turned to her husband and nodded. "My lord."

Thomas said, "I would like a cup of tea, Meggie. Just a bit of lemon for me. Mother? Would you like Meggie to pour for you? Aunt Libby?"

Aunt Libby?

Madeleine puffed up, no other way to put it. She swelled inside her dark blue gown, pushed out her cheeks. "You want her to pour, Thomas? I am your mother. I was the first person ever to pour tea down your little gullet."

"Meggie is now the countess of Lancaster, Mother, and the mistress of Pendragon. It is her responsibility to pour the tea down both your gullets and now mine as well. Sit back and ease yourself into the cushions and let her serve you."

"She isn't smiling now, showing off all those white teeth of hers, so I suppose it would be all right." She gave a regal nod to Meggie. "I like sugar and milk."

Meggie merely nodded, not smiling, but looking as serious as Mary Rose when she was trying to outdo Max with a new Latin aphorism. She said toward Libby, "And you, ma'am? Would you like tea?"

"Certainly not. I wish to have sherry, as Madeleine knows very well. Thomas, fetch me sherry. I will pour it down my own gullet, thank you."

Thomas, looking immensely patient, walked to the sideboard and poured Aunt Libby a large dose of sherry.

Meggie poured and distributed the tea.

"It isn't sweet enough," said Madeleine after taking one tiny sip.

Meggie added another spoonful of sugar to the cup and watched her mother-in-law stir it until surely the tea was cold.

This wasn't at all promising. Meggie sipped her own tea, looking toward her husband, who was standing beside the fireplace, his back against the wall. He'd set his teacup on the mantel and crossed his arms over his chest.

Barnacle tottered into the drawing room, looking to be in agony, and gasped out, "Ennis has delivered yer luggage to yer rooms, my lord. He didn't do it well, even though I instructed him thoroughly all along the way. My lady, I will be ready for yer ministrations in an hour."

"Her what, Barnacle?" Libby asked, and poured the rest of her sherry down, holding out her empty glass even as she thrust it toward Thomas.

"Her ladyship, the one wot's married to our new lordship here," said Barnacle, screwing up his face into even more agony, "is going to walk on my back, since both ye and the dowager countess are too heavy and would surely break me in two."

No one said a word. Meggie was the only one who watched Barnacle totter out of the drawing room. The two women were arguing again, but low now, and Meggie couldn't make out what they were saying.

This was surely the strangest household Meggie had ever visited. No, not visited. She lived here. Blessed hell. Then she remembered Glenda Strapthorpe, who'd gone to great lengths to try to trap Meggie's father into marriage, and knew she'd have to think about this before making a judgment. Perhaps every household was strange in its own way. She thought of her grandmother Lydia and sighed. She kept her eyes on her teacup.

Not many minutes later Barnacle was standing again in the open doorway to the drawing room. He said in a very formal voice to Thomas, "Lord Kipper is here, my lord. Since ye are now an earl and he is only a baron, he isn't worthy enough to be shown into the drawing room unless ye expressly wish him to."

"You're right. He is only a baron. What do you think we should do with him?"

"Lock him in a bedchamber with a half dozen maids and see if he emerges alive."

"Hmmm. A creative idea, but just think of the maids, Barnacle. Bring him in and we will pretend he is worthy enough to be in my presence."

22

Madeleine and Libby were laughing even before Barnacle was out of the drawing room, and Barnacle knew it, bowing his shoulders and tottering even more.

When Barnacle and his back were out of sight, Thomas ignored the laughing women and said to his wife, "Lord Kipper is an old smuggler who was knighted by George way back in 1809 when he accidently managed to sink a French warship. He really believed it was a boat of English soldiers bent on taking him to Newgate."

"You're making that up," Meggie said.

"Young lady, my son never makes anything up," Madeleine said. "Lord Kipper is a very brave man, not like that wretched Lord Lancaster, who, thankfully, is finally six feet underground. Had I been there, I would not have worn mourning nor thrown a rose atop his casket. I would have spit."

"Meggie's father, the vicar of Glenclose-on-Rowan, gave the service. He surely wouldn't have appreciated that, Mother."

"My lord. Ladies."

Meggie looked up to see a man stride into the drawing room. He was as tall as Thomas and twice his age. He was very possibly one of the most beautiful men Meggie had ever seen in her life. He looked like a fallen angel, fair and blond, but the compelling strength in his face, the planes and shadows of the bones, the blueness of his eyes, the way all of him fit together was incredible. She imagined that Uncle Douglas's twin sons, James and Jason, would be as beautiful as Lord Kipper when they were his age, and that was saying something indeed since her dratted cousins had been so beautiful since early boyhood that her uncle Douglas and aunt Alex had been constantly bombarded with gifts from all the girls in the neighborhood, hoping to be noticed by the twins.

It was amazing, this male beauty. Lord Kipper looked toward her and smiled, an absolutely devastating smile, all white teeth and intimacy, and it made her toes curl in appreciation. Six maids with him in a locked bedchamber? Hmmm.

"I am Meggie Sherbrooke—"

"You are now a Malcombe. I am her husband, Niles."

"And he's an earl now, not just a mangy baron," Barnacle said from just on the other side of the still-open drawing room doors.

Lord Kipper laughed. "I was always too big to walk Barnacle's back," he said, "and he's never forgiven me." In that moment Meggie knew to her toes that he was as outrageous and as charming as both of her uncles. She wondered what her uncle Ryder would have to say about the six maids in a locked bedchamber.

As Lord Kipper walked across the wide expanse of dismal drawing room, Meggie noticed that he limped. When he reached her, he gave her an intimate smile again, devastating it was, took her hand and slowly raised it to his lips, never looking away from her face. "Meggie. What a lovely name, my dear."

"You will not try to seduce my wife, Niles," Thomas said, just the barest hint of menace showing through the amusement in his voice. "Drop her hand this instant."

Lord Kipper didn't drop her hand, rather, he very gently lowered it until it was nearly touching her breast. Then he eased free, pressing her fingers lightly downward until she was touching herself. He smiled. Meggie was so shocked, so utterly mesmerized by what he'd done, that she just stood there like an idiot, gaping at him.

"You are such a tease," Libby said, a wealth of knowledge and a touch of coyness in her voice, Meggie wasn't mistaken about that. And a dollop of jealousy perhaps because Lord Kipper hadn't done it to her?

"Do you have a wife, sir?" Meggie asked, pulling herself together by the simple act of taking three steps away from this dangerous man.

"Oh no, my dear. Well, there was Nell. She gave me my heir, then departed to her reward very shortly thereafter, bless her, and she did it quickly, with little fuss. Unfortunately my heir died at the age of six. I admit I worried about an heir for a while, but no longer. No, I decided I didn't want another wife. Far too confining, you know. Since I am English and I have money, why, I much enjoy keeping a mistress now and again. My nephew is my heir, a good boy, at Oxford now, and so he isn't around to sniff after them."

Meggie knew he was now looking at her bosom, and she was so disconcerted she said, "You are speaking of your mistress, sir, in polite company?"

"Ah, this group isn't at all polite," Lord Kipper said. "Just ask that husband of yours, one of the wickedest young men I've met in a long time."

He grinned over at Thomas, who'd taken a step away from the fireplace when he'd threatened to kill Lord Kipper, now moved back, relaxing again against the mantelpiece, his arms crossed over his chest.

"Thomas isn't wicked," Meggie said, frowned and paused, tilting her head to one side. "At least I don't think he is. We haven't known each other all that long, you see."

"Yes," Lord Kipper said, "I see."

"Niles hasn't ever changed his stripes," Thomas said to his wife. "He was a terror when he was a boy, sowed more wild oats than an entire class at Oxford, and decided he quite liked it. Meggie, I am not wicked at all. He is the master and he's always wanted a student to follow in his path, but it isn't me. I doubt not that Niles will go to his grave a terror."

"Praise the Lord," Libby said. "Thomas, you are teasing your bride. My dear, he is quite wicked enough. Now, Niles, who is your latest mistress?"

"Well," said Lord Kipper, "I just dismissed a young lady who returned last week to her home in St. Ives." He looked down at his hands for a moment, utterly distracted. Was he still thinking about her?

"Ah, yes, Melinda," he said. "I expect I shall miss her, particularly as the days grow longer and there is so much light to see and to enjoy and—well, perhaps with the addition of your wife, Thomas, the company is polite enough now to forego specificity."

Meggie looked frankly disappointed. Her husband grinned at her.

"Then why did you let her go?" Madeleine asked.

"Unfortunately my nephew paid me a surprise visit and nearly lost what few wits he possessed when he saw her. He refused to go back to England, read poor Melinda love poetry from below her window, standing in the rain. I was afraid he would catch an inflammation of the lung, so what was I to do?"

"Send the fool packing," Thomas said. "Not Melinda."

"Ah, well, such a pity I didn't think of that at the time. What's done is done. Now, I am on the lookout, you could say." He paused a moment, stroking his long fingers over his jaw. "I think I just might be in the market for an older, more experienced female person. Will you consider it, Libby?"

"Will I have to lose flesh?"

"I have decided that a bit of strategic padding on a woman's body isn't as distasteful as I have always believed. How could a man dislike such a lovely expanse of white flesh? No, my dearest Libby, you may continue eating to your heart's content. I will come back on the morrow and we will discuss how this is to be accomplished."

Libby nodded and bowed her head, a lovely smile on

her mouth. She was humming under her breath.

Meggie's uncles were outrageous, no doubt about that, even though they did try to keep their hands off their wives and keep all their drawing comments to a whisper when any of the children were near. But since she was the next generation eavesdropper after her aunt Sinjun, she'd heard quite a bit over the years, but never anything like this. She stared at her husband. He had no expression at all on his face. No, that wasn't right. He was looking a bit amused, maybe a touch of irony mirrored in those dark eyes of his. She wanted to go to the stable, find herself a stout horse, and ride back to Cork Harbour. Maybe there would be a boat headed back to England.

Thomas said abruptly, "Niles, you remember Bernard Leach, do you not? He and his wife own the Hangman's Noose near St. Agnes?"

"Oh yes, a tippler is Bernard, tried to cheat me once about ten years ago. I kicked him but good in his ribs, his wife holding him down for me, all the while cursing him from Cornwall to Scotland. Marie's a good woman. Why do you ask?"

"His wife, Marie, was murdered—hanged—and Bernard is missing. Before he disappeared, he told me the Grakers did it."

"Marie is dead? Murdered? Oh no." He sighed deeply and everyone in the room knew he was much affected. "How we enjoyed each other whenever I managed to sneak into the inn, usually right under Bernard's nose. Now, what is this about Grakers? Cornish pixies? Why, those little mites wouldn't harm a soul. Whenever I am in England I swear I can hear them singing in the yew bushes. Bernard is lying. He killed her, the bastard."

Lord Kipper had slept with Mr. Leach's wife? "Evidently Grakers can be vicious," Meggie said, knowing in that moment that she'd been thrown into Bedlam.

Niles shrugged. "That's a tale. You say that Bernard disappeared? Come now, Thomas, where could he possibly disappear to?"

"I don't know. I didn't join the search for him because

I needed to come home to Pendragon. Stay away from my wife, Niles, or I will break your leg, not your lame one, your very fit one."

Niles, Lord Kipper, sighed, and toasted Meggie with his teacup when she handed it to him and said, "I shall miss Marie. Lovely woman, although her tongue had grown sharper over the years. I hope they catch old Bernard and stretch his neck."

Alvy Shanahan, Meggie's fifteen-year-old maid, was small, pert, her hair was as black as Thomas's, and she had the most beautiful lilting accent Meggie had ever heard.

And she heard a lot of that lilt because Alvy didn't stop talking, not for a single moment, from handing Meggie her chemise to the final pat on her hair, Alvy talked. And she talked of only one person—Thomas Malcombe, how very handsome he was, and ah, so very big and manly, and all that lovely black hair, and those forearms of his, thick with muscle and brown from the sun with black hair on them, and don't forget those lovely dark eyes of his, that ye could just fall into.

Oh dear, Meggie thought, she didn't want her maid to be in love with her husband.

Just after nine o'clock that evening, Thomas led her into the White Room, dismissed Alvy, ignoring her look of abject adoration, and said, "I have decided to sleep with you, Meggie."

"Good. Then I can begin improvements on you immediately."

He laughed even as he unfastened the long march of buttons down her back. "Cook—Mrs. Mullins—came here to Pendragon with my mother. That's why you had English fare."

Another area needing improvement. "You liked the beef, Thomas?"

"Oh no, but no matter. She has been with us as long as I've been on the earth. When I am really hungry, I ride into Kinsale to visit a friend and beg my dinner. However, you will have a pleasant surprise at breakfast."

"Perhaps I can give her some new recipes that will improve upon the meals."

"Just go easy, that's all I ask, Meggie." He pulled her sleeves down to her elbows, trapping her arms to her sides. Slowly he turned her to face him. "I like the dark blue against all this white. A splash of color in the snow."

She raised her face and he kissed her.

"Oh my," she said when he finally raised his head some time later. "Oh my. That is so very nice, Thomas. Perhaps I was wrong. Perhaps you are wicked, in the very best of ways."

He was pleased with his wickedness when he brought her to orgasm some fifteen minutes later, had her shuddering with such deep pleasure that she looked ready to expire from it. She lay panting on the beautiful white bed with its white counterpane and white sheets with him still deep inside her, and she loved the feel of him, the sound of his voice as he said love words to her and sex words, many of which she didn't understand, for after all, she was a vicar's daughter. Many of them, however, she did understand because she was, after all, also her uncles' niece.

"Thomas," she whispered against his shoulder, then lightly bit him and licked his salty flesh.

"Ah, don't," he said, but it was already too late. He groaned, harsh and low that groan that bespoke his innards were being stomped on as he spilled his seed so wonderfully deep inside her.

When he was breathing again, his eyes focused on her face, she said, "That was very nice, too, Thomas, very nice indeed."

A vast understatement. He was too far gone to talk. How could she manage to speak coherently?

After some time, Thomas managed to lean over and douse the row of candles in the filthy silver holder. When it was dark, when she was lying on her back, staring up at the white ceiling which she now couldn't see, she said,

"I like children. I remember I was so pleased when Mary Rose birthed Alec and—"

"Go to sleep, Meggie."

"The ten years—perhaps I can accomplish it in nine years."

"What ten years? Nine years? What are you talking about?"

"To make you the perfect man."

He laughed and pulled her against him. He felt her warm breath on his flesh. He was asleep long before she was. He didn't snore.

The next morning when Meggie walked down to the small family dining room that Alvy told her about, in between more choice comments about the new earl, she heard a man's voice. It wasn't Thomas.

Barnacle said from behind her, "Ye didn't walk on me back, milady, now did ye? Ye forgot."

"I'm sorry, Barnacle. After breakfast I will meet you in the kitchen. I will walk on your back in there."

He gave her a nod, a small salute, and staggered back to the front door.

She should have asked him who was in the dining room. She walked in the small dark room. What a dreadful room, what with the curtains drawn tightly over the two bay windows that gave onto something, what, she had no clue, and she found herself staring at a young man who looked a great deal like Aunt Libby.

He saw her, rose slowly from his chair, and said, "You are Thomas's new wife."

She nodded, walked to the draperies and pulled them open, fastening them with the wide golden ropes. Light flooded into the room. It made it look even worse, but at least now she could see outdoors.

She looked at the fine-looking young man. He was blond and fresh-faced, tall, not as tall as Thomas, but very nearly, and he was giving her a fat smile. "Yes, I'm Meggie Malcombe. And who are you?"

"Oh, I'm William Malcombe, Thomas's half brother."

He was, Meggie realized in that moment, as she looked across the table, Aunt Libby's son. He was the young man who had impregnated Melissa Winters and let Thomas take the blame and the responsibility.

What was going on here?

23

"MY WILLIAM ARRIVED late last night," Aunt Libby said, and patted his arm. "Sit down, my love, and let me serve you some nice bacon that's just barely been waved over a flame, just as you like it. My, look at all the light in here. I had no idea there was even any sun to be had. Does it make me look wrinkled?"

"No, Mother, you look beautiful," William said, and took his seat again beside her. "You always do."

"What a sweet boy you are, William."

"No one else ever says that to me, Mother."

Meggie certainly believed that. She saw that Madeleine was eating at a fine clip, not paying any attention, and eased herself into the empty chair next to what she assumed was Thomas's chair.

She said, "Does anyone mind that I opened the draperies?"

"You are doubtless trying to show us all that you are the important one here now," Madeleine said, her mouth full of eggs.

"No, ma'am, I'm not, truly. It's just that I would like to see who is at the breakfast table this morning and what is on my plate."

Cook suddenly appeared out of the wall. No, it was a narrow door cut very cleverly into the wall, its seams fitted perfectly to the striped wallpaper, her arms filled with covered trays. "Och, the new countess. Hello, milady. It's a fine breakfast I've made for you, now isn't it?" And without another word, Cook broke into song as she served Meggie's plate, piling it high with scrambled eggs with four nutty buns arranged around the eggs.

"Hey Ho—it's a fine day for the nutty buns!
Hey Ho, Hey Ho—here come the Nutty Buns!
Hey Ho, Hey Ho, Hey Ho—NUTTY BUNS!"

A new experience for a Sherbrooke at a breakfast table, Meggie thought, wanting to laugh, but she only smiled, nodding toward Mrs. Mullins. "That was lovely. Thank you, Cook. May I have a cup of tea?"

Cook continued singing even as she poured the tea. Soon every nutty bun was in capital letters. Then, with a final hey ho, she disappeared back through the wall.

No one saw anything amiss with anything. Just another breakfast at Pendragon.

Meggie ate. The eggs were delicious, as were the nutty buns. So Cook made a perfectly wonderful breakfast, just as Thomas had told her, but why, then, was the dinner so abysmal? She would write to Mary Rose immediately for recipes. Wait, maybe she needed to have a song to accompany the dinner dishes she prepared. Hmmm. Meggie hadn't ever tried to write a song before, but now she would.

William Malcombe said, a limp piece of bacon draped over one finger, "You're a very pretty girl."

"Thank you, William. You are a very nice-looking boy. You look like your mother. Are you really sweet?"

Libby said, "A pretty compliment. Madeleine, did you hear that?"

"I heard. Where is Thomas, young lady? Did you exhaust him last night?"

Thomas said in a very loud voice from the doorway, "Mother, forgive me for being late. I wanted to see that Pen was all right after his soaking yesterday. He is. Meggie, you have met William, I see. He is visiting us from Oxford. A surprise visit."

"Yes, I have met William."

She said nothing while Cook served Thomas scrambled eggs and nutty buns. She wasn't singing now. Meggie continued to say nothing when Madeleine said, "What are your plans today, Thomas?"

"I am taking Meggie about the property. Would you like to introduce her to Mrs. Black?" He added to his bride, "She is our housekeeper."

"Here from before you were born?"

"That's right," he said, all pleasant and easy, and ate a nutty bun.

"I will need a horse," Meggie said.

"I have selected Aisling for you. That means 'dream' in Gaelic. She is a bay with one white stocking, and on a good day she can beat Pen in a race."

"Prepare, my lord, to eat dirt."

He laughed. "After Survivor, I couldn't very well provide you with a nag, now could I?"

Closer to two hours later, since Meggie had agreed to walk on Barnacle's back in the kitchen, she joined her husband at the Pendragon stables to meet her new mare, Aisling, and give her two carrots.

When they were riding down the long drive, the sun hot overhead, she said, "I met Mrs. Black in the kitchen. She is very nice. She is also nearly blind, Thomas."

"Yes."

"She can't see dirt."

"No, probably not much."

"Then why hasn't your mother seen to it that Pendragon is cleaned and the furniture waxed and the draperies replaced since Mrs. Black is blind?"

"I never asked. However, now you will see to it. At last I will have a clean house." She was so startled she nearly got knocked off Aisling's back when the mare swerved too close to an oak tree branch.

"Have a care, Meggie."

"Oh yes, I'm sorry, Aisling. Goodness, you have noticed that the place is a mess then?"

"Mrs. Black is nearly blind, not I. I was hoping that you would notice and wish to take a hand in fixing things. There is enough money to make any reparations you wish to. I have already done quite a bit of work on our tenant cottages and outbuildings. You have but to ask Paddy, my steward, and he will see to it. He will be about this afternoon. I ask only that you tread diplomatically around my mother and all the servants. Change is usually very difficult for people."

Meggie nodded. "Maybe your mother believed there wasn't enough money and that was why she didn't do anything."

Thomas raised an eyebrow to that. "You're kind to make that excuse, Meggie. However, as you know, cleaning really doesn't require much money. No, she merely doesn't care. She has always hated Pendragon. Her home was Bowden Close. I imagine that she might want to go live there now that it belongs to me. She spends all her time producing endless journals, recording all her woes in both English and French."

"You have read her journals?"

"No, that would be abusing her privacy. She speaks of them quite freely, reads them during tea. No matter she doesn't like you, she will still see you as fresh ears and insist upon reading to you in the evenings. If you wish to escape, you will wink at me or roll your eyes in a discreet manner. You understand?"

Meggie nodded.

"Why doesn't she like me, Thomas?"

"She truly believes I'm too young to be wed. She's afraid I've inherited some of my father's more dreadful propensities. She told me last night that she'd prayed I'd spend more time in Italy. There are mistresses to be had there, no need to take a wife to relieve my man's lust. Yes, my age is too tender, too easily hurt by a conscienceless woman. She will get over it, Meggie. Don't worry."

Easy for you to say, Meggie thought.

They came to the end of the promontory, and Meggie looked out, speechless, over the Irish Sea and the magnificent coastline, rugged hunks of land chipped inward or thrusting out like long fingers into the sea, the shore lined with scored and barren rocks.

She slipped off Aisling's back, shook out her riding skirts, and made her way to the edge. The water sparkled beneath the morning sun. It was very calm, low tide, the waves collapsing gently against the dirty sand, fanning out, then easing back again to be swallowed into the next wave. She became aware that Thomas was looking at her. She turned slowly, feeling him close to her, feeling the pull of him, the pull she'd felt when she'd first met him, even though her mind had been full of Jeremy. Jeremy, now at Dragon's Jaws with his pregnant wife. No, she wouldn't think about either of them.

"Thomas," she said.

He crossed the distance between them in an instant and pulled her up against him. The wind was mild, but still it plastered her riding skirts to her legs.

He didn't kiss her, just held her and looked down at her. "You're so bloody innocent."

"Well, yes. Could you expect much else given my father is a vicar?"

He kissed the tip of her nose and pulled her about so she leaned her back against him. She loved the feel of him, the strength, the heat. She'd never really thought about the heat of men, but now she did, and those wicked thoughts heated her as well.

She said slowly, feeling his arms cross over her chest, pulling her closer to him, "Can I trust you, Thomas?"

His arms tightened. He rested his chin on top of her head for a moment, said without hesitation, "Yes."

She said, her voice clear and calm, "You can trust me too, Thomas."

"Meggie—"

She turned then and lightly touched her fingertips to his jaw, to his lips. "It's all right. I made vows before God, as did you. I keep my promises, Thomas. You are my husband. I will be with you until the day I die. I will never leave you. I haven't made you laugh in a while. I will work on that. You have a beautiful smile. It pleases me to see it."

"A beautiful smile?" She wouldn't leave him and he had her loyalty. It wasn't enough, dammit.

"Oh yes."

He looked away, but not before she saw something flash in those eyes of his, something she couldn't begin to understand.

And, at the very bottom of things, she knew she didn't know him very well at all.

She pulled away and looked back toward Pendragon, a magnificent heap of gray stone fashioned into a lasting structure that was more a castle than not. It was big, over-powering, it would surely make an enemy pause, and they had held Cromwell off the first time. Yes, Pendragon dominated everything around it, including nature, and it was, she thought, watching a dark cloud chase across it, menacing. It had secrets, perhaps even secret passages. One could only hope. She shivered, but she was smiling.

Meggie lay in her bed, wide-awake. Thomas had loved her, then leaned over her and said, "I think I want to sleep in my own bed tonight. Good night."

And he'd kissed her mouth one last time and left her.

There was moonlight spilling in through the windows, and it was beautiful. It was also frightening, that moon-light. It cast strange shadows on all those white walls.

Why had he changed his mind? He'd made love with her, and she'd felt flooded with pleasure and with some-thing that was deeper, something that made her want to cry with the power of it. She'd thought he'd felt the same things. Evidently not.

She shivered beneath the thick covers. It was turning cold, a storm was coming, and very soon now, a big storm with lightning, pounding thunder and torrents of wild rain. But the moon was still so bright. She felt tears sting her eyes and swallowed. She wanted him beside her. What was wrong?

"Damn you, Thomas," she said, then willed herself to sleep. She'd written to her father and Mary Rose, telling them about Pendragon, the lovely stretch of coastline, asking for recipes, asking Alec and Rory to write a cooking song for her, praising, for example, a buttock of beef done in the French way. She'd sounded happy because she penned her words to make it seem that way, but she wasn't, not completely. So many strange people here at Pendragon.

Her mother-in-law had read from her journal, dated from the fall of 1808, for two hours, without pause. Unfortunately it was in French and Meggie understood perhaps one word in five. She'd finally rolled her eyes toward her husband, and he had stood up and taken her hand. "Meggie is very tired, Mother."

They'd left William, his mother and Madeleine, her journal still open, in the drawing room. Barnacle was hovering just outside. He said, shaking his head, "I remember it was five years ago now, she read those very same pages. It was 1808, was it not?"

"It was," Meggie said. "You've an excellent memory, Barnacle. Do you speak French?"

"One must when one's back hurts this much," and he screwed up his face into such agony, that Meggie automatically stepped forward.

"I'll walk on your back tomorrow, if you wish, Barnacle. Did today help?"

"A bit, milady, a meager bit. Naturally I speak French."

Meggie fell asleep. She didn't know what woke her, but it was something she hadn't heard before in this strange house. A mouse scurrying across the wooden floor? A moth trapped against the windowpane? Just the crackle and heaviness of thunder in the air, not quite ready to strike yet?

She was suddenly very afraid.

24

MEGGIE LAY THERE, eyes wide open, perfectly still, adjusting her hearing, her vision. Waiting, waiting for another sound. The moonlight no longer sliced into the white room. There were only clouds now cloaking the sky, thick, bloated, black as the bottom of a cauldron. It was nearly black inside the bedchamber. The storm was here, the wind coming hard through the partially open window, too cold now. Rain would begin any time now. She'd heard nothing, for how long now?

She'd been a fool. She started to get up to close the window when she heard it again. It wasn't a scurrying sound, it was quite something else. It was close, very close. Too close. She didn't see anything. But that didn't matter. She rolled to the side of the bed that gave onto the dressing room, and when she jumped up, she tangled in the covers. She staggered, fighting to get free of the covers, when suddenly lightning lit up the black sky, once, again, and then the thunder rolled and boomed, making Pendragon shudder as those huge hits shook it to the ground. She heard someone's intake of breath, and that someone was right behind her, she could hear the breathing, low and fast and something else, something— She yelled even as she whirled about to see who was there.

She saw something, it was black, a figure, and then something struck her hard on the side of her head. She slid down into the pile of covers that she'd pulled off the bed.

"Meggie!"

She thought she heard a man's voice, but she wasn't all that sure and what's more, she didn't really care. She felt warm and safe and there was nothing to touch her, nothing at all.

"Meggie! Damnation, wake up! What the hell's wrong? Wake up!"

The man slapped her face, and not light taps either, he really smacked her good, and it made her so mad that she reared right up and said in his face, "Don't hit me again or I'll clout you back."

Thomas said, "Good, that's better. Please don't clout me. Are you all right?"

"I must think about that."

"Jesus, Meggie, I heard you scream, thought the thunder and lightning frightened you. I'm sorry I slapped you so hard, but I was scared, you wouldn't wake up." He grabbed her against him. She felt his pounding heart beneath her cheek.

She said against his shoulder, "You really heard me scream? I didn't know if I managed to get it out before whoever it was hit me on the side of the head with something hard."

His breath caught in his throat and he coughed, and continued to cough until Meggie got herself together enough to hit him on the back.

"What did you say?" he finally got out, his voice a croak. "Oh God, you're bleeding." He stared at her blood, wetting two of his fingers. He was up in a flash, hauling her in his arms and gently laying her out on the bed, as if for burial. She expected him to fold her hands over her breast, but he didn't. "Don't move." And off he went, lit a candle, then searched every inch of the White Room. He closed the window, as rain was blowing into the room. A huge strike of lightning filled the room with light. He still saw nothing. He pulled the draperies closed over the battering rain. Then he opened the bedchamber door and went into the corridor. It was some minutes before he was back.

"No sign of anyone." He placed the candle on the small table just beside the bed, and leaned over to gently ease her hair away from the wound.

He cursed, fluently, with great variety, she thought, and she asked, "Did you make those things up?"

"Make what up? Are you all right, Meggie?"

"The curses, all those incredible uses of animal body parts, did you make them up?"

He grinned, just couldn't help himself. "No. All of those words have been around for a very very long time. Does this hurt?"

Meggie bit her bottom lip and yelped. "I'm sorry, just a bit, not bad—"

"All right. Be quiet, I'm going to get you cleaned up. Don't move, Meggie."

She didn't. Her head was starting to pound and truth be told, she felt light-headed. The wispy candlelight was wavering, the white walls were shimmying a bit, now leaning to the right.

"Oh dear," she said, and held up her hand in front of her face.

"Meggie, what are you doing?"

"I want to see if I can count my fingers."

"Damn," he said, then pulled the covers over her. "Whoever hit you, knocked you out, and that can be dangerous. Now, count my fingers. How many am I holding up?"

"I believe there are three fingers there. Do you know, Thomas, all of those fingers you're waving about have touched me very intimately?"

"Well, yes, I suppose that's true."

"Particularly that middle finger of yours—it's rather long—goodness, I remember just a couple of hours ago when you—"

"Yes, yes, Meggie, I remember everything about that finger. Now, do you hurt?"

She nodded, and that small movement nearly sent her

into oblivion. She managed to hold really still until the pain let up. She said then, "You shouldn't have left me. I was kissing you all over your face, and you told me you wanted to sleep in your own bed. Why did you do that, Thomas?"

"You want the truth? No, don't frown like that, you'll just scramble your brains. Lie still and relax. All right, I'll spit it out. I left because I'm afraid of storms, have been since I was a little boy. I didn't want you to see your strong manly husband cowering when lightning filled the sky and thunder sounded like cannon fire, in fear for his life."

"It's not all that bad. Whatever happened when you were a boy, I'll make you forget it. I'll hold you close. You can cower all you want."

"You'll pat my back?"

"Oh yes. I could even sing you to sleep. Just don't leave me again, Thomas."

"I won't. Now that you know about my weakness, there's no reason to go hide." He stood. "I'm going to get the physician."

"Will I have to walk on his back?"

"Dr. Pilchart? Why no, his back is in grand shape."

"Will I have to lose flesh?"

For a moment, he didn't know what she was talking about, then he remembered Aunt Libby saying that to Lord Kipper.

"Actually, you need to gain a bit of flesh, not much, mind you, I've always liked skinny girls. Meggie, when you're struck on the head you don't usually remember anything leading up to it. Do you remember more than you told me?"

"I'll tell you if you don't get Dr. Pilchart."

"But you might be seriously hurt."

"But what could he do? Would he break open my head and look inside? Even if he did, would he know what he was looking at?"

"I guess not. All right, for the moment, I'll stay right here with you. Now, do you remember anything more?"

"Oh yes," Meggie said, "I remember everything." She stopped every few moments, closing her eyes against those slashes of pain in her head. Finally she said, "It was the lightning, the thunder, I heard him draw in his breath, really sharp. It scared him. When I turned about, then he struck me."

"You know it was a man?"

"No. But whoever it was wasn't small. All in black, Thomas, he was all in black, his head, everything, covered." She cocked an eye open. "Please don't fetch Squire Billings to assist you in finding the culprit."

He smiled. "I won't. Actually, I'm the magistrate around here."

"I made you smile," she said, and brought up her fingertips to lightly touch his mouth, "but I didn't really mean to."

"Meggie, I want you to stay awake a bit longer. Head injuries are unpredictable."

"I'm really tired, Thomas."

"I know, but hold on." He took her hand and said, "I'll help you stay awake. Listen to me now. Let me tell you about my first ship, mostly financed by the earl of Clare, which went all the way to India. It was due back the first week of October. It didn't come. I tell you, I was down at the harbor in Genoa at dawn every single morning, scanning the horizon until I was cross-eyed, but no *Star of Genoa*. Every night I was there, until it was so dark I couldn't even see the water. Adam Welles—the earl of Clare—found me one night on my own private hill overlooking the Mediterranean, drinking brandy. I was so drunk, so despairing, I was ready to go down to the wharf in Genoa and bust heads together, a very stupid thing to consider because there are more miscreants down at the dock than you can imagine.

"Adam stood over me, hands on hips, and said, 'All right, you young fool, enough is enough. If the bloody ship has sunk, you will simply raise money to finance another. Get up or I'll knock you in the head.' "

"What happened?"

"I got up and jumped on him."

"You hit him?"

"I surely tried. I wanted to kill him, at least maim him. It was a very good fight, until he got me in the stomach and all that brandy—I thought I was going to die there for a while."

"What happened?"

"The *Star of Genoa* arrived in Genoa the following Tuesday afternoon. As I recall, I think I kissed her hull. There'd been a vicious storm just outside of Gibraltar, but she'd managed to survive it. I immediately financed another ship. I've lost only one ship in the past three years. I have three ships out right now and, thank God, excellent men in Genoa I trust to oversee things."

"What did the earl of Clare have to say about the one lost ship?"

"He bought me a case of brandy, said he didn't want to see a single bottle drunk for at least six months or he'd hit me in the belly again."

Meggie laughed, she just couldn't help it even though it made her sure her brains would rattle right out of her head.

"Did you wait six months?"

"Actually, the entire case is still intact. I haven't had any brandy since that night."

"Oh Thomas, that's a wonderful tale. Our children will enjoy it. Did you sail one of your ships here to England when you came back to Glenclose-on-Rowan?"

"Yes, she's in between trips right now. We decided some English goods bound for the West Indies would be an excellent thing. She's being fitted and goods bought as we speak."

"What is the name of your ship?"

"The *Hope*."

"I can't wait to see her. How much longer will she be here?"

"Another week, in Portsmouth."

"I am so very proud of you."

He flushed, just couldn't help it.

"You will see, everything will be all right. Oh dear, please find the person who struck me on the head."

"Yes," he said slowly, giving her some laudanum now in a glass of water, "I will."

25

"WHY IS WILLIAM here?"

Thomas said, "I asked him. He said he'd heard that I'd married and he wanted to meet you."

"What does he want to meet me for? Perhaps to seduce me?"

"Meggie—"

"He's a rotter, Thomas."

"He's young, Meggie, very young."

"So are you and so am I, and I know that neither of us would have never done something as dishonorable as what he did. Just imagine, he let you shoulder all the blame for getting Melissa Winters with child. He probably fully expected you to shoulder all the blame. I'm afraid it will be difficult for me ever to come to accept him, Thomas."

He looked bemused, and said slowly, going to what was the most important thing to him, "You really believe I'm honorable?"

"Well, of course. I wouldn't have married you otherwise. Would you ever, Thomas, let someone else accept the consequences for something you did?"

He said, his voice still deep and slow, "No, I don't believe I would ever do that."

"He doesn't know that I know what he did to you? To Melissa Winters?"

Thomas shook his head.

"Who hit me?"

He sighed. "I don't know. Everyone claims to have been sleeping until the storm started last night. Everyone also claims to have woken up when the lightning and thunder struck and the rain started coming down in torrents. It was so heavy, a couple of windowpanes were blown in. No one heard anything at all. What would you expect, Meggie?"

"Why would someone want to hurt me, Thomas?"

There it was, stark and clear, in the open, heavy and frightening, deadening the air between them.

Thomas rose from her bed and began pacing the White Room. He looked back to see his bride sitting up, white covers pulled to her waist, a white nightgown spilling lovely lace from her shoulders, and a white bandage around her head. And she was in the middle of a stark white room. He shook his head. "You look like a virgin who protesteth too much."

It took her an instant to understand him, and then she laughed, raising a hand to hold her head because laughing made it hurt. "Too much virginal white, I guess you mean. The good Lord knows I'm not a virgin anymore. Did I tell you that I'm pleased not being a virgin anymore, Thomas, in fact—" She paused a moment, and he knew, just knew all the way to his boots, that she was thinking about him kissing her, probably on top of her, going wild, and he shook with it.

"Don't look at me like that, Meggie. I don't want to hurt you."

"Oh, you mean my head."

"Yes." He was as hard as the heavy door latch, but he grinned, just couldn't help himself. "Yes, I mean your head." It seemed as every day passed, he had to simply think of her and he wanted her. It was unnerving, particularly now. And mixed with that lust he felt just thinking her name, just seeing that vivid hair of hers in his mind's eye, mixed with that was the fact that someone in the dark of night had sneaked into the White Room and hit her on the head.

And he had no idea who it was.

He said, wanting it to be true, willing it to be true just by saying the words, "It has to be someone from outside, Meggie. Someone who doesn't like me, someone who wants revenge, someone who's lived here and knows Pendragon, how to get in and how to get out again."

"Do you have any ideas about who it could be?"

"I've thought and thought about it, but no, I really can't think of anyone. But that's not saying much. Every old castle has shadows, mysteries, if you will, things hidden for a very long time, but—" He shrugged, then there was a fierce look in those dark eyes of his. "I won't let anything else happen to you, Meggie, I swear it."

"If you had slept with me, Thomas, maybe you would have been the one hurt, maybe the person who did this believed we did sleep in here together. Maybe you were the one he was after. Oh dear, I want you safe, Thomas. All right, here it is. I've decided that I want you to continue to sleep in your bedchamber and I will lock the door between our rooms. That way no one can get to you."

He felt intense pleasure flow through him as he said very matter-of-factly, "Don't be an idiot, Meggie. The person hit you, not me. It was your bedchamber, not mine. I dare say that that person now knows that you were quite alone. No, Meggie, we will sleep together, but we will make certain the doors are locked." He cocked his head to her, swallowed as he said, "I am considering sleeping on top of you to further protect you."

"Oh my."

He swallowed again, cleared his throat, mumbled under his breath, "Sorry, forget I said that. Now isn't the time."

That was a pity. "Maybe," Meggie said, wrapping her arms around her knees, unable to get that image out of her mind, "just maybe there are some secret passages in this wonderful old place. What do you think? Are there any you know about?"

Thomas plowed his fingers through his hair, making it

stand on end. For an instant she was sure he looked frightened. "No, no," he said at last. "There have been rumors about passages, my uncle occasionally whispered about them, but I've never actually seen one."

"Your mother doesn't particularly seem enthralled with me. You have my dowry and maybe she thinks I'm no longer necessary. Then there's William. Maybe he's found out that I know what he did to Melissa Winters, maybe—"

"My mother is eccentric, that's for certain, but to the best of my knowledge she wouldn't even kill my father, and she hated him more than one can imagine. As for William, I can't imagine he would care if all of Cork and Kinsale knew he was a little lecher. Why would he care if you knew or not?"

Meggie sighed. "I wish to get up now, Thomas. I'm bored and my head hurts only a bit. Also, someone could simply open the bedchamber door, take one step inside, and shoot me. I'm rather helpless here, amidst all this virginal white."

His eyes nearly crossed. God, he wanted her, right now, and he didn't want to leave her, he wanted to pump into her, deeper and deeper and yell his pleasure to the rafters of this drafty old castle and fill her with his seed. And lie on top of her, to protect her. He was in a bad way and he knew it. And she didn't. It was amazing. He said, "No one is going to come in here and shoot you, all this white or no." Then, because he just couldn't help himself, he said, "By God, you look delicious."

This was interesting and she gave him what she believed to be a very warm smile, one filled with the promise of wicked things.

He didn't move a muscle.

He was being noble, bless him. Truth be told, her particular place in the world didn't feel all that steady right now. She realized she was scared, but she wasn't about to say that out loud. She said, "I'm getting up now."

He looked like he would protest, then shook his head, at himself, not at her. "I'll send Alvy to you." And he was gone. Guilt had driven him away, of that she was certain. He didn't want to take a chance of hurting her head anymore. Yes, he wanted her and now that Meggie knew what this wanting was all about, she wished he would come back. He could leave her aching head to her. She smiled as she swung her legs over the side of that stark white bed. Yes, she was quite certain his eyes had become glazed, fixed on her face. She wondered if she were the first of all the cousins to make love, then frowned. All her dratted cousins were boys, and outrageous, just like their fathers, even her brothers, Max and Leo, seemed to know things, yes, even Max the Latin scholar. She'd seen him speaking to Leo just a couple of months ago, there had been this fixed smile on his face, really a rather stupid smile, and she hadn't understood then. Now she did. She'd worn that stupid smile a couple of times now; she'd seen it in the mirror.

Ah, marital sorts of things were all well and good, but when all was said and done, when everything was right there, ready to smack her in the face, what was important was that someone had hit her on her head. As he'd said, an old place like Pendragon was filled with secrets, with mysteries. It was up to her to discover if any of them had come out of hiding and didn't like seeing her as the countess sleeping in the White Room.

Meggie began pacing her bedchamber, her white nightgown disappearing amongst all the other white, the only thing keeping her set apart from the furnishings was the flapping gown at her ankles as she paced.

His mother, Meggie thought. She had to be the keeper of Pendragon secrets. Madeleine, who didn't like her and didn't bother to hide it. Madeleine, who wrote journals in both French and English. Why not beard the lioness in her den?

Was his mother mad?

She was becoming hysterical, just like Maude Freeberry, whose wails could be heard every third night throughout Glenclose-on-Rowan when her husband stumbled home drunk.

Well, if Madeleine wasn't mad, she certainly was un-
pleasant, and perhaps, just perhaps—

"Why," Meggie said aloud to the empty white room,
stripping off her virginal white nightgown, "is Aunt Libby
living here at Pendragon?"

Two hours later, after taking a very brief walk on Barnacle's back, each step accompanied by groans and com-
plaints and sighs, Meggie found Madeleine in her
bedchamber, penning in her journal. She wondered if she
was in a French mood or an English mood today.

"My lady," Meggie said from the door, then stepped
into the room. It wasn't like any other room she'd seen
at Pendragon. The room looked as fine as a London salon.
It was large and airy, furnished in the Egyptian style, out-
of-date, but distinctive and quite interesting, what with the
sphinx feet on the sofas and the bird claws on the arms.
Her mother-in-law sat behind a lovely antique ladies'
writing desk, perfectly positioned to get most of the sunlight coming through the very clean windows.

Madeleine was chewing on the end of her pen. She
said, "Oh? It's you, is it? Well, come in, don't dawdle.
You don't look at all ill. Thomas said someone hit you
on the head. I see no sign of it. I dare say that a real lady
who'd been struck would be lying in her bed, pale as
death."

"Sorry. If I'd realized you needed some proof, I
wouldn't have taken off the bandage."

"You've a very smart mouth, don't you? It's a pity.
Mrs. Black told me that you had six women hired from
Kinsale to come to Pendragon to clean. What is this all
about?"

"I would have told you myself, ma'am, but someone
hit me on the head last night and I was a bit fuzzy for a
while. I'm fine now."

"I think you're the sort of girl who demands attention,
and when she doesn't receive the attention she believes
she deserves, she enacts a scene."

Meggie struck a pose, said, "Now why didn't I think of that?"

"You might amuse my son on rare occasion, miss, but you don't amuse me."

"Actually, I'm a Mrs. Actually, I'm a countess. Come to think of it, I'm even a 'my lady.' Even more to think about—I would precede you at an official function. What do you think of that?"

"Not much."

Meggie sighed and said slowly, looking at her mother-in-law dead on, "You asked what this is all about. It's quite simple and straightforward. I want Pendragon to be clean. I want the foundation of the castle to shudder from all the cleanliness, the smell of lemon wax, the smell of plain soap. I want Pendragon to sparkle just like your room sparkles. I want all the windows so clean they squeak to the touch, just like I'm sure your windows do. I want to destroy all those dirty old draperies that are frayed and have moth holes in them and let the sun shine into all the rooms. I want that ancient chandelier in the entrance hall to glitter. I want no more dust flying around when one walks on the carpets."

"You want too much. It is absurd."

"Why, may I ask, ma'am, is your room so lovely and the rest of Pendragon sporting dirt from the last century?" Hmmm, she wasn't treating Thomas's mother with much solicitude, but blessed hell, this was beyond too much. The dollop of sarcasm tasted good. The woman seemed to hate her anyway, no matter if she snarled or smiled. It made no sense.

Madeleine said, holding the black pen in her hand as if she wished it were a stiletto, "I want Pendragon to remain just the way it is. Be quiet and stay in your room. Wrap the bandage around your head again. Take to your bed and stay there, perhaps a week should do it."

"Do what?"

Madeleine only shrugged.

Meggie said, "Pendragon is a beautiful old castle. It deserves to be cared for. I am now mistress here. It will be beautiful once again, just like your room."

"There is little sun. It won't matter."

"It seems to matter to you, at least in here. Please tell me, ma'am, what is going on here?"

Madeleine looked up for a moment, her eyes focused not on the present, but somewhere in the past, and they weren't good memories. She said at last, "I like the two heads of the coin—one light, the other dark. It is alternately satisfying and mysterious."

"Or perhaps you mean a Janis head?"

Madeleine merely cocked her head to one side. Her black hair with its rich white strands was very shiny today. She looked lovely. Hers was the cast from which Thomas's face was molded, except, Meggie believed, his face more pure, the lines more stark, more finely chiseled. There was no wildness in his dark eyes, except when he was kissing her.

"No," Madeleine said, shaking her head. "Not Janis. A Janis head has two faces—one evil, one good. But with light and darkness, there is both good and evil in both, don't you think?"

"Things are never that simple, ma'am."

"Naturally they are. No, I don't wish there to be evil at Pendragon, but evil comes in all shapes and forms, doesn't it? No, I wish to have both light and darkness and I have achieved it. Leave things alone."

Meggie sighed and sat down on a spindle-legged chair from early in this new century, one with what looked like lion's paws with long toenails filed to sharp points, and said slowly, "No, I will not leave things as they are. Pendragon is now my responsibility and I won't let it continue to molder. If you do not wish to help me, I pray you will keep still. I do not wish Thomas to be at odds with his mother."

"He would be at odds with you, not me."

"The women," Meggie said, looking out those crystal-clear windows onto lush gardens beyond that were badly in need of a gardener, "are working well. Men will come in to rehang the chandelier. All the draperies will be replaced as well as most of the furnishings. Pendragon will look like it did three hundred years ago right after it was rebuilt, only better. It will be done."

"I have but to tell Mrs. Black to send them back to the village"—Madeleine snapped her fingers—"and it will be done."

Just you try it, Meggie wanted to tell her, but instead, she said with all goodwill and exquisite calm, "Mrs. Black is very happy that Pendragon is being tidied up, those were her words. She may be almost blind, but I fancy she's smelled the neglect, felt it with her housekeeper's special touch. She has even given her own cleaning solutions to everyone. She's supervising all the help with a fine eye, albeit a blind one."

"Someone should stop you."

Meggie said, "Someone tried last night. Are you really certain it wasn't you, ma'am?"

"No, I was sleeping, dreaming beautiful dreams. Actually, Lord Kipper was in one of them."

Meggie wasn't about to touch that, at least not now. She said, "Your son wanted me to marry him. He didn't know my dowry was so magnificent until he actually spoke to my father when he asked for my hand."

"Men, including my son, always manage to sniff these things out. That's exactly what he did—married you to get his hands on all that lovely money of yours. And now he has it. What are you saying, Miss—Mrs.? You now want to accuse my son of hitting you on the head in the middle of the night so he can be rid of you since he now has your dowry?"

"Oh no. There is one thing I am very sure of. Thomas is as honorable as my father, as are my uncles. I would never have married him otherwise. No, ma'am. Your son will protect me. He cares for me." Not love, Meggie thought, he hadn't yet said a word about love. On the other hand, she hadn't either. She said, "I have come to realize that there is a lot going on here that I don't understand. Perhaps after you dreamed of Lord Kipper, you moved along to dream you struck me on the head last night? You perhaps dreamed it was you who tried to stop me?"

"I don't want you dead, you little idiot, either dreaming or awake. There weren't any dreams after Lord Kipper. You're a fool, Meggie Sherbrooke."

"My name is Meggie Malcombe. Goodness, I hadn't thought about the alliteration before. It sounds rather nice to say, doesn't it? Just imagine, I'm now Meggie Malcombe."

"No, it sounds ridiculous."

"Let's just say that you did indeed dream that you hit me. Tell me then, why would you want to hurt me? To make me less foolish?"

"If I had hit you, I would have done it right. I have no idea who struck you. It was probably Mrs. Black. I told you she wants things left the way they are. Aye, she's the one who wants to stop you in your tracks."

What did that mean, she would have done it right? Madeleine would have hit her hard enough to kill her?

"Go away. This is none of your affair."

"I don't wish to die, ma'am."

"Then keep your nose out of things that aren't your business. Are you with child yet?"

That made Meggie nearly fall out of her chair. "I have no idea. We've been married for a very short time."

"You knew my son for at least three months before your married him."

That was a shocker. Meggie said slowly, "Thomas is a gentleman. He would never seduce me before we were married."

"Well, my son needs an heir now that he is the earl of Lancaster. If he passes without an heir, why then, William would take his place. I cannot stomach that. Prove you are worth something, and see to it."

"William," Meggie said slowly, "Libby is his mother. I don't understand this, ma'am. Did the earl of Lancaster divorce both his wives?"

"Yes, the foul wretch. There was a terrifying sickness in his brain. He desperately wanted a wife who would be loyal to him. I was as loyal as a tick, but it didn't matter. This sickness ate at him, you see, and he became utterly convinced that I had deceived him. Then he married Libby and it began all over again." Madeleine snorted. "I suppose we are lucky—the old bastard might have married and divorced a third wife and all of us would be here, sharing tea."

"I have never heard of such a sickness."

"I was told that his mother deceived his father and no one was certain that he was indeed his father's son. It corroded his soul. I would have been strong enough to have overcome this, but he wasn't. You cannot imagine the thousands of pounds he spent—mainly bribes, you know—to secure both divorces. All those lords laughed at him behind his back as they stuffed his groats in their pockets. Now, you've seen William. Although I am quite fond of Libby, her son is quite paltry. He would make a very bad earl of Lancaster and master of Pendragon."

"Yes, I've seen William. I must admit that I was shocked to see the two wives living together. Both wives."

"Yes, of course. Why not? That wretched man left us with sons to raise and little money to do it. He was furious when his younger brother Edward took me and Thomas in. Naturally Libby came here when he booted her out, small William with her."

"And now Libby will have an *affaire* with Lord Kipper?"

Madeleine smiled at that. "Libby is the only woman in these parts he hasn't taken as a lover. At least I think that's true. With Niles one can never be certain of anything. Isn't he a delicious man? Of course you would like to have a liaison with him, but you aren't stupid. You will wait until you present my son with his heir."

Meggie only sighed. "Ma'am, like you, I will stick like a tick to Thomas. As for Lord Kipper, he is older than my father. Perhaps I would knit him a pair of socks for Christmas, but nothing beyond that."

"Ha," said Madeleine. "You're young. You see everything, yet you know nothing at all."

"This is all passing strange, ma'am."

"Mind your own business and stop thinking about it. Why did you ask about Libby and Niles? I know you want Lord Kipper for yourself."

"In only a few years I could call him Grandfather."

"What is your point? He is a glorious man."

"Well, yes, he is quite beautiful. You're right about that. However, I much prefer your son."

"Ah, go away now and send all those women back to the village. I wish you to be pregnant soon. See to it. Perhaps you will be so ill that you will leave the dust where it collects."

Meggie slowly rose from the chair and shook out her skirts. "As to my becoming with child, ma'am, both Thomas and I would like to have a child." Did he really? Actually, they hadn't spoken of children.

"I wouldn't put it past you to deny him."

Meggie's head began to ache. She stood a moment outside Madeleine's bedchamber, leaning against the wall. A picture frame caught her shoulder and she moved over a bit. She closed her eyes and thought, *How long have I been married now? Four days? And already I have a lump on my head. Surely marriage isn't supposed to begin like this.* She remembered stories of her aunt Sinjun's trials when she'd first gone to Vere Castle with Uncle Colin in Scotland. They'd sounded so romantic, so adventurous, and Meggie had dined on those stories for days and nights at a time. She realized now that she'd been a fool. There was nothing romantic about this; there was only fear of every sound she heard and every shadow she saw.

26

$\mathcal{M}$EGGIE WENT DOWNSTAIRS to the estate room, a small back room, that gave onto a small garden that would give her stepmother, Mary Rose, heart pains to see what bad shape it was in. She wanted to find the steward, Paddy. She had things to do.

Paddy walked in just as she was about to give up. He was shorter than she was, round as a cannonball, a head thick with riotous red hair, and blue, blue eyes, darker than hers. He had lovely white teeth and a ready smile. "My lady," he said, bowing to her. "At last I meet you. Is it really you now? What a pleasure, a vicar's daughter, the niece of a duke—"

"He's an earl, actually, just like Thomas."

"Aye, niece of an earl. Ah, his lordship—it has a fine sound to it, doesn't it now? He deserves the title and the money. A good man is Thomas Malcombe, albeit very young to wield such power."

"Yes," Meggie said. "He is a good man. I don't think age has anything to do with it."

"Well, he's your new husband, now, isn't he? I am to meet his lordship here in just a moment. We have more repairs to consider."

"I want that ancient chandelier to be rehung, Paddy, before it crashes down and mashes one of our heads. And there are stairs to be replaced. Also, I need a score of gardeners, not people who see a weed and step on it, but people who know their way about a garden and a lawn."

"I always go around that chandelier, don't you know?" Paddy said, shaking his head. "I'll do that, my lady, don't worry about it. And the gardens, I'll find the best men in the area. Mrs. Black is singing, so happy she is with the women we brought in from the village. Ah, here's his new lordship."

"Paddy, I must speak to my wife in private for a moment. Please come back in a half hour." The door no sooner closed on Paddy than Thomas said without preamble, "My mother trapped me in the corridor just beneath a portrait of my great-great-uncle Mortimer who went to Wales just after his elder brother came into the title, so furious that he went into a coal mine and the roof caved in on him and killed him."

"She's your mother. I suppose that she has a right to trap you whenever she wishes to."

"She did. She demanded to know if I was trying my best to get you pregnant."

Meggie gave him the wickedest smile. No daughter of a vicar should smile like that. "Are you, Thomas? Trying your very best?"

"Dammit," he said, and grabbed her. He moaned in her mouth, and that sweet sound, the taste of him, made her wild. Her hands were on his britches' buttons before he managed to pull away. He leaned his forehead against hers. He was breathing very hard, trying to get hold of himself. "Oh God," he whispered, leaned down to kiss her, cursed, and took four steps back.

"Why did you dismiss Paddy if you didn't want to kiss me until I jumped on you and carried you to the floor?"

He laughed, just couldn't help himself. "I dismissed Paddy because I wanted to know what you spoke to my mother about. Her eyes were nearly red, Meggie, so furious with you she was sputtering."

"So she's angry, is she?"

"Yes. You sound very pleased with yourself."

Meggie felt a jab of unworthiness. "Don't worry about

233

it, Thomas. She and I will learn to deal with each other. Ah, did she tell you exactly what she was angry about?"

"She just said you needed discipline and I was to beat you, that it was obvious I hadn't brought you to heel yet."

"Well," Meggie said, giving him a sunny smile. "Perhaps you can bring me to heel if we go riding."

"Your head, Meggie. You shouldn't ride until tomorrow at the earliest. You should lie down now and rest."

He was right and she said, "Blessed Hell, all right." Her hair was long and curling to the middle of her back, tied back with a length of black velvet ribbon. He knew, knew all the way to the oak floor beneath his feet, that she was distracted because she wanted him, and she wanted to hit him because he'd pulled away from her. She might not love him, but she wanted him and surely that was an excellent beginning. He would have her yet, or he didn't know what he'd do. He was an optimistic man. He had to hold to that. He heard her say, a bit of a sulk in her voice, "Yes, I will feed Aisling carrots and explore Pendragon grounds. I wish to plant more trees. I must see what sort grow well here."

"Meggie—"

When she turned, her eyebrow up, he looked at her closely for a very long moment, then slowly shook his head. Let her stew. "Please, be careful and don't walk too far from the castle." He didn't tell her that one of the smaller stable lads would be following her everywhere at a discreet distance.

"Ah, that person who struck me last night might be lurking about to do it again?"

"Everyone is accounted for," he said, lying easily. "No, I just don't want you to overdo." Actually, he knew the exact location of everyone in the castle, including Mrs. Black and Barnacle, who was currently lying on his back on the kitchen floor, arms flung out, groaning. Mrs. Black merely stepped over him.

She left him. She wanted to kiss him again, feel that moan of his in her mouth.

• • •

Lord Kipper found Meggie in the center of a maze that had fallen to ruin at least twenty years before. She was standing there, staring about at all the yew bushes, wondering how she could fix it, when she heard him say from behind her, "Ah, my beautiful young bride."

She raised an eyebrow up at that, knew he'd said it exactly that way on purpose, and said, "Thank you, Lord Kipper."

"I wish I had seen you first, but alas, I didn't."

"My father would have howled had you inquired about me, sir, since you are even his senior by many years."

"When it involves men and women, years don't matter."

"I shouldn't like to be a widow at twenty-one because my husband died of old age."

"How old are you now?"

"I am nineteen. That would give us two years of bliss before you croaked it."

He stared at her, as if she were, Meggie thought, some strange bird that had just dropped out of the sky, as if he didn't know whether to shoot her or stroke her feathers. Then he laughed, threw back his head and laughed and laughed.

Meggie just looked at this beautiful man, and now that he was laughing, he looked more than beautiful, he looked dazzling, surrounded by overgrown yew bushes, a watery sun shining down on his head.

"I understand that Libby isn't at all certain that you are serious about admiring her."

He was still grinning when he said, "That's true. But we will see, won't we?"

"You will, certainly. What do you want, Lord Kipper? You are certainly far afield from the castle as well as far afield from your own home."

"I heard that someone struck you on the head. You saw absolutely nothing at all?"

"I heard some harsh breathing when the thunder had just boomed and the lightning had just lit up the bedchamber, and I saw a shadow of someone, wearing black.

Nothing more. Why? Were you the one in my bedchamber, Lord Kipper?"

That remark sent one of his perfectly slanted eyebrows straight up. "I? No, my dear, I was sleeping, as I recall, in the arms of a very pleasant young woman in Cork."

"I did ask, didn't I?" Meggie looked heavenward.

"Yes, you did. You are not at all what I would expect from a vicar's daughter." He paused, his eyes darkened. "Thomas doesn't deserve to be a widower when he is so young."

Meggie laughed, just couldn't help herself. "Indeed he doesn't. You have been a terror, haven't you, sir?"

"Oh yes," he said, and looked around. "I am still able to, thank God." He looked about for a moment, then pointed. "There was a lovely old bench here at one time. It's quite a mess, isn't it?"

"Yes. Ah, there's the bench, but it's very dirty."

"No matter." Lord Kipper pulled a clean handkerchief from his pocket and wiped off the bench. "Do sit down, my lady."

Meggie sat.

"Does your head hurt?"

"Just a bit now. Do you know what is happening here at Pendragon, sir?"

"Call me Niles. No, I don't."

"Someone tried to kill me. I've only been here two days. Surely that's too short a time to make anyone hate me enough to crack open my head. I have been thinking about this. Someone knew I was coming and because I was me—Meggie Sherbrooke—I was hated enough for that someone to want to kill me. Does that make sense?"

"You mean," Lord Kipper said slowly, looking deeply into her Sherbrooke blue eyes, "that someone hated you before they even met you?"

"Or hated my family perhaps. Or the person believed Thomas would be with me, only he wasn't. I am very worried that this person is after Thomas, not me."

"I also heard that Madeleine wants you pregnant, by tomorrow if that's possible. She was even mumbling about putting an aphrodisiac in your tea. She even asked me to give you advice on how to seduce Thomas if he tired after only one or two encounters."

Meggie nearly fell off the bench she was so shocked. "I—sir, you can't speak like that, surely. An aphrodisiac? You're making that up just to make me turn red and stutter."

"Oh no. Thomas's mother, you know, she's always told me everything, asked my advice endlessly, even things I had no interest in. She is single-minded, is Madeleine."

"Have you been her lover, too?"

"Of course."

Meggie slowly got to her feet. Her head was pounding. She felt light-headed. The morning sun had disappeared behind a mass of soft gray clouds. It would rain soon.

He was beside her in an instant. "Meggie, lean against me. I can see you're not well."

She didn't want to. His hands were around her arms, pulling her closer, then she jerked away, fell to her knees, and vomited. There was little enough in her belly, so her body shook with dry heaves. She felt as though she were jerking apart, from the inside out. She just wanted to fall over and not move, maybe for the rest of the morning, or maybe for the entire day. The thought of her mother-in-law putting an aphrodisiac in her tea made her dry-heave some more.

She was aware that Lord Kipper was holding her hair back. "I'm sorry, but I don't have another clean handkerchief," he said. "Let me help you back to the castle."

Meggie didn't make it. They reached the entrance to the maze when she felt so dizzy she couldn't stand up. She was shaking, her teeth chattering. She heard him say her name, then she didn't hear anything at all.

Thomas was with William when he saw Lord Kipper striding toward them, Meggie in his arms. Thomas ran.

"I say, Thomas, what's—"

Thomas had her in his own arms in just a moment, so scared he thought he'd choke on it.

"She vomited, then fell over, Thomas," Lord Kipper

said. "Put her to bed, my boy. I'll fetch Dr. Pritchart."

When Meggie awoke, it was to see her husband not two inches from her nose. He looked very worried. No, it was more. She saw a thick veil of anger in his eyes.

She raised her hand to his cheek. "Thomas," she said, her voice as thin as gruel. "I'm all right."

He took her hand in his and held it. "Just rest, Meggie. Be quiet. Don't talk now. Damnation, what happened?"

"I nearly shook myself apart I got so sick, then I tottered beside Lord Kipper a bit, then just collapsed. I'm sorry, Thomas."

"Dr. Pritchart will be here soon. Just hang on."

"Thomas, I don't want to die."

His breathing hitched. He hated this, couldn't bear it anymore. "You won't die, Meggie, I swear it." The stable lad had been so scared, he'd nearly followed Thomas into the bedchamber.

She closed her eyes against the pain. He held her hand, spoke nonsense to her until Dr. Pritchart arrived.

"Go away, my lord," he said, and Thomas reluctantly left the White Room.

He heard voices coming from the drawing room. When he neared the open door, he heard his mother say, "What a weak-kneed chit. Just a small blow to the head and here she is whining and carrying on."

Then Aunt Libby said, "I wonder if perhaps she wasn't trying to flirt with Niles. Did she follow him into the maze? The foolish stable lad wouldn't say anything, just that Lord Kipper had seen him watching her ladyship."

Thomas said as he walked into the room, "This will stop right now. Enough from both of you." He paused a moment, then attacked. "Mother, I think you're the person who struck Meggie. You have yet to tell me why."

Madeleine slowly rose to her feet, her face pale, her eyes darkening. "No, Thomas, I didn't strike her."

"Is she going to die, Thomas?"

"No, William," he said, turning briefly to his half-brother, who'd just come into the room, "she isn't going to die."

Barnacle tottered into the dim drawing room. He had to yell over the sudden blast of thunder that made the crystals on the overhead chandelier shimmer and hit against each other. "My lord, Dr. Pritchart wants you upstairs for her ladyship. Oh dear, I do hope this doesn't send her underground. I only just found her. She's the perfect size to walk on my back."

Thomas, who dearly loved the old man, wanted at that moment to shoot him. He was back in the White Room in not more than forty seconds. Meggie was sitting up, leaning against a pillow, smiling at him. He nearly shouted he was so relieved.

Dr. Pritchart, seeing that His Lordship just might leap on his bride he was so thankful, moved to block him, saying, "I have told her to remain in bed the rest of the day. We will see tomorrow how her head feels."

Meggie jumped when more thunder rolled overhead. Rain slashed hard against the windows. "I'm all right, Thomas. Don't be frightened."

But he was. After he'd shown Dr. Pritchart out, he sat beside her on the bed and pulled her into his arms. He pressed his face into her hair. He kissed her temple, said low and deep into her ear, "You scared every ounce of wickedness out of me. I will become more reverent than your father. He will be so impressed with me he will ask me to give one of his sermons."

She turned her head slightly, moving very slowly, and kissed his neck. "I should like to see you in my father's pulpit. Please don't lose all the wickedness, Thomas. I do like it. I can't bear this either. Don't leave me, please don't."

He closed his eyes as he held her, kissed her hair, the tip of her nose, felt the softness of her through her muslin gown. "Let me get you into your nightgown."

27

Meggie watched Miss Crittenden run to the end of the long kitchen, come to an almost instant stop, then wheel about and race back toward her.

"By all that's wonderful," Meggie said in awe to Mrs. Black, "that was amazing."

"Demned Cat's been acting like that since the big tom, McGuffy, went to sea with the Midland's youngest boy, Davey," Mrs. Black said, narrowing her eyes to better see Miss Crittenden flashing by, but it didn't help much, and Meggie saw that it didn't. "Running everywhere to find him, but he's no where to be found. And now it's just habit with her."

"So she started all this marvelous running trying to find Davey. Hmmm. Maybe you've hit upon a new training technique. Mrs. Black, have you asked Dr. Pritchart about glasses?" she asked.

"Oh aye, my lady. Dr. Pritchart has tried everything. He says it's the cataracts that are like veils over my eyes, that they will just thicken and thicken until there won't even be shadows. He calls it white eyes."

"I'm very sorry."

"It's just that I would like to see Miss Crittenden race about Cook's jugs of flour and sugar. Many the times I've nearly tripped over her. So many changes you're bringing, my lady, and all of them exciting. Do you know I can smell how clean Pendragon is now? It's a blessed thing, it is. Now, why are you interested in Miss Crittenden and how she runs?"

"Have you ever heard of cat racing?"

Cook came into the huge kitchen and said, "Cat racing? Now, that's a loony thing, it is."

"Not at all, Mrs. Mullins," Meggie said, and since neither of them had heard of such a thing, for the next ten minutes, Meggie told them about the history of cat racing, begun at the Mountvale Mews in the last century, brought to its premiere place in the racing world by the Harker brothers, the major trainers for two decades now. "The McCaulty Racetrack is the major venue for cat racing," she said. "The meets are held from April to October. Mr. Cork is the current champion. He from the Vicarage Mews and I trained him."

"You really trained a cat to race?" Barnacle said, dragging himself into the kitchen, and one eyebrow arched up so high he looked like a bit of a demon, in agony, of course.

"I most certainly did. I think Miss Crittenden just might take to the sport. What do you think? Cat racing at Pendragon?"

"Oh, aye, that would be something, now wouldn't it?" Mrs. Black beamed.

Cook harrumphed. "It's loony, now isn't it?"

"There's nothing like seeing those sleek bodies flying by," Meggie said. "It makes your heart gallop."

"Meggie."

She turned to see Thomas striding into the kitchen. He was carrying a package under his arm. "Here you are." He didn't sound at all surprised. During the past week, once he'd let her out of bed, she'd been everywhere in Pendragon, overseeing everything and everyone, and that pleased him all the way to his gut.

"Oh, my lord," Barnacle said and creaked into a semblance of a bow, adding a little moan as he straightened, his face a hideous mask of pain. "Mrs. Black, it's his lordship."

Mrs. Black, instantly flustered that the master was in the kitchen, of all places, curtsied and knocked a teacup off the table.

"No harm done," Meggie said as she snagged the falling cup out of the air, and added to her husband, "Miss Crittenden just might be a racing cat. What do you think?"

Thomas looked over at the large calico, sitting in a slice of sunlight in a corner of the kitchen bathing herself. "She's huge."

"Well, I think most of it is muscle. I just watched her run. She's amazing, Thomas. She will lean down a bit during training."

"Cat races at Pendragon. Let me think about that, Meggie." He handed her the package. "This is from your family."

"Oh my," Meggie said, clutched the package to her bosom, and nearly ran from the kitchen.

"But I want to see what's in that package!" Barnacle yelled from behind her.

She just laughed and ran all the way to the White Room, Thomas on her heels.

"I took it out of the wooden packing box," Thomas said, standing against the wall watching her, his arms crossed over his chest. "You feel all right, Meggie?"

"I'm all right," she said, not looking up from the paper she was tearing. "Really, no headache at all now. Oh goodness, my father must have sent this right after we left. What could it be? I just realized, he didn't know where we were going, did he?"

"Well, yes, naturally I told him. I didn't want him or your stepmother to worry."

"But you wouldn't tell me anything."

"No, that's the way it's done."

She pulled away the last bit of paper and lifted out a beautifully carved wooden cat. It was a perfect likeness of Mr. Cork, even the size. There was a plaque at the bottom with Mr. Cork's name, his sire and dam, and the dates of his racing wins beautifully etched into the wood.

Meggie held it close, then burst into tears.

"Meggie! What's wrong? It's a statue of Mr. Cork. It's a very nice statue, but tears? What is this?"

"I miss him so much, and Cleopatra, too. All the cats, Thomas, they would run and jump, meow their heads off, or sit there and tell you, without words, that they weren't going to move a paw, no matter what you did."

"I think," he said slowly, watching her dance around the room clutching the wooden Mr. Cork to her chest, "that just maybe we should introduce cat racing to Pendragon. Did your father carve this exquisite piece?"

"No, Jeremy."

"I see," he said and wanted to howl. Couldn't the mangy bastard just leave her alone?

After Thomas left her to go downstairs to see Paddy, Meggie was humming as she dusted off Mr. Cork's fine statue. Suddenly she stopped cold. At least an hour had passed since she'd thought about the person who'd slammed whatever it had been down on her head. Just the thought of it now brought a flash of pain. Even when Thomas had mentioned it, she'd been too excited about her present and hadn't heeded it.

She winced, walked slowly to the window, and looked at the breezy spring day. It was cloudy, but at least right now it wasn't raining.

She picked up her father's letter and read it through again. "My dearest girl, Jeremy sent this wedding present to me since he didn't know where you would be. I am enclosing his letter."

Meggie didn't want to read Jeremy's letter, she really didn't, but nonetheless, now that Thomas was gone and she was alone, she slowly unfolded the single sheet of paper, pressed it out with her palm, and read, "Dear Almost Cousin Meggie, I wish you and your new husband the very best. Charlotte and I would welcome a visit from you. I hope you enjoy this rendition of Mr. Cork. It took me a while to carve it which is why it was late." And it was signed just Jeremy. His direction was written on a separate piece of foolscap. Jeremy. *Jeremy and Charlotte*.

She walked slowly to the fireplace and stood there, staring at the three stacked logs, bits of paper stuffed around them. She shredded the letter and tossed the pieces in amongst the kindling. Then she lit the fire and watched it burn. She heard Alvy moving about behind her, but didn't move.

"Dr. Pritchart is here to see you, my lady."

She frowned, not realizing at first why he would come to Pendragon. Oh, her head. She turned and smiled at Alvy. "I will see him shortly in the drawing room. Please let Barnacle know, Alvy."

Ten minutes later Meggie, Thomas beside her, greeted Dr. Pritchart, who was sipping at a cup of Cook's tea and scratching his ear.

"There is a rash on your ear, Dr. Pritchart," Meggie said, walking to him. "Is it all right?"

He paused and looked at her, for a very long time, didn't say anything, just looked. "You'll do," he said, snapped the cup into its saucer, and gave her a brief bow. He said to Thomas, "If she suffers a relapse, you will call me. Good day to you both. The rash comes twice a year, one of those times is right now, in April. It's nothing at all." And he was gone.

"Well," Meggie said. "I wonder how much his bill will be for that visit."

"He thinks you're fine. That's all I wanted to know. He's had that rash twice a year since for as long as I can remember." He crossed to her, pulled her against him, and kissed her.

Meggie was nothing loathe and kissed him back. She said into his mouth, "This is so much nicer than those dreadful things you did to me on our wedding night." She pulled back and looked up into his face. "I know, you don't want to talk about it."

"No," he said against her ear, then stroked his thumb along her jawline. His hands were on her hips when there was a clearing voice from the doorway. Thomas slowly raised his head. "Damnation."

He turned to see his mother standing there, and she didn't look at all happy.

"Yes, Mother?"

"Lord Kipper has decided to take Libby for a ride in his curricle. He told her he had a very lovely spot to show her and that she would truly appreciate it, especially since it wasn't raining. He told her how much he admired her. I told her he was lying, that he didn't like women with as much flesh as she has. He was just going to drive her to this nice spot and bed her on a blanket just because there was no one else about for the moment, no one with less flesh than she has. She was merely a temporary convenience, I told her, surely she realized that. She called me horrid nasty names and slammed out of the castle. It was unforgivable. I'm thinking of having her live elsewhere."

Thomas stared at his mother, then laughed.

Meggie, fascinated, said, "What did she call you, ma'am?"

"She had the absolute gall to call me a pernicious old tart. Can you imagine?"

"Well, no, I can't," Meggie said.

"Imagine calling me a tart. I never slept with any man other than your father and Lord Kipper, and who wouldn't bed him if they had a chance? He was beautiful twenty years ago and he's beautiful today, and ever so talented. I'll wager that little wife of yours would take him to her bed in an instant if he crooked his finger at her."

"Niles enjoys life too much to try that, Mother."

"You would shoot him if your wife here were unfaithful to you?"

"In an instant."

"And what, may I ask, would be her punishment?"

"Since this will never happen, then I really don't have to think of one, do I?"

"I saw her looking at Lord Kipper, Thomas, just like Miss Crittenden looked at that bit of sea bass Cook served for dinner before you arrived."

Thomas just smiled, but there was something in his

eyes, something dark and hidden from her. Meggie frowned.

"I didn't realize Libby knew such a deadly word as *pernicious*," he said.

Madeleine said, "I didn't either. *Pernicious*. I am here to look it up in that dictionary on your desk. I hope I have the spelling right. I ask you, what good is a dictionary if you don't already now how to spell the word? Stand aside."

Thomas took Meggie's hand and led her from the estate room. They were half a dozen steps beyond the room when they heard his mother squawk.

"Let's hurry," Thomas said.

"Thank you, Thomas."

He turned to smile down at her. "For what? Dragging you out of the room before she found *pernicious*?"

"For telling your mother that I wouldn't ever betray you."

"Yes," he said slowly, turning away from her to look out over the Irish Sea, "I did say that, didn't I?"

That night a storm blew in, rain slammed hard against the windows, and the black of the night was absolute.

"Oh God, Meggie," he said against her mouth, felt the world tilt and every muscle in his body scream, and managed to pull out of her just in time. He hung over her, panting, so beyond himself, that for many moments it was very close.

"Thomas? What's wrong?"

"You weren't with me," he said, low and harsh, and gave her his mouth.

When she arched her back and yelled to the ceiling, he came into her again, hard, deep and deeper still, and harder than he should have, but he just couldn't help himself.

Some time later Thomas was lying on his back, his breathing slow and calm now, his wife's breath warm against his bare chest. Suddenly he felt her jerk, and tightened his arm around her.

"Meggie," he said against her hair, kissing her. "You're dreaming. Come, wake up."

She moaned quietly, pressing closer to him, and her breath was hot against his flesh, wheezing in and out. Something bad was happening. She sucked in a deep breath, shuddered. He started to shake her awake when she moaned, *"Jeremy, no, no. Blessed Hell, no. Jeremy."*

He didn't shake her. He didn't do anything for a very long time, just let her thrash about and moan, deep in her throat.

When finally she was calm again, when she hadn't moaned his name again for at least five minutes, Thomas eased away from his wife, and rolled off the side of the bed. He came up to stand over her. He couldn't see her well because of the storm, the blanket of rain that obscured any outside light, the blackness of the room. But yet again he heard her moan his name; it wouldn't leave his brain. Over and over he heard her say that bastard's name: Jeremy. He wished he had the sod right here, right now. He wanted to choke the life out of him. He knew he wouldn't hesitate a minute to kill him.

And she'd said his name, damn her. Said it again and yet again. Just as she'd spoken of Jeremy to her father, and she'd been married to him not more than two hours.

It was as he'd told his mother—Meggie would never betray him. He knew it all the way to his gut. No, Meggie would never make an assignation with another man and break her marriage vows.

But the fact was he also knew that she already had— in her mind, in her heart, and he believed to his soul that betrayal in the heart was the worse. She'd married him under false pretenses. He'd forgiven her, knowing she liked him, perhaps admired him, knowing he could make her love him, want him as he'd wanted her since the first time he ever saw her. She certainly liked bedding him. He'd let himself grow complacent, secure in her. He'd let it all fade from his mind. Until now. She'd dreamed about the bloody sod. He didn't think he could bear it.

He didn't leave her, although he wanted to. He

couldn't. There was a madman out there who wanted her dead. He couldn't leave her alone.

But he wanted to. He wanted to hoard his misery, wallow in his misery by himself. He didn't want to hear her breathing beside him, feel her body pressed against him and know that he would be hard in an instant, and know too that she could be dreaming of that bastard.

Then something happened, something hard and vicious and he recognized it. It was rage and it was what he'd felt on his wedding night.

He wouldn't let his rage overwhelm him, he was a man who could control himself. He wouldn't ravage her again like he had on their wedding night. But he itched to punish her, to hurt her the way she'd hurt him.

He took one of the blankets, carried a chair to the windows and watched the dawn break through the gray rain.

28

Pendragon
Two weeks later

WILLIAM WAS ON his knees, trying to pet Miss Crittenden's head. She snarled and tried to bite him. "There now, nice kitty," he said, and stuck out his hand again. Meggie gave him a disgusted look.

"She is a racer, not some lazy creature to sit on your lap and take treats from you, William. Take care or she'll nip off the end of your finger. What are you doing here? I'm busy."

He rose and dusted off his hands on his tan riding pants. "You don't like me, Meggie."

"No," she said, not looking up from the brushing she was giving Miss Crittenden, a reward for her excellent leaping, this time a running start that kept her in the air for a good two seconds and an amazing distance of over four feet.

"Why? Whatever did I do to you?"

Meggie said, "Why haven't you left to go back to Oxford, William? Perhaps a serious bit of study would improve you."

"Well, I can't go back. You see, I didn't tell Thomas the precise truth. I was sent down, but just for this term. I will go back again, it's just a matter of time."

"Why were you sent down?"

He flushed, turned, and tried to pet Oscar DeGrasse, one of Lord Kipper's mousers, long, lean, short-haired, black as a moonless night, with a chewed-up left ear. Oscar arched his back and purred.

Meggie didn't have much hope for Oscar. True racing cats were born with a goodly amount of arrogance, a cold and snarling sense of self, and woe be to any other cat who challenged him. They were disdainful, they were tough. They would burst their hearts to win. Oscar was asking to be petted. It wasn't a good sign. She'd asked Lord Kipper why the name DeGrasse, and he'd said, quite in a straightforward way, that it was the last name of one of his long-ago mistresses who'd been an excellent mouser in her own right, very dedicated to catching her prey and consuming it. When Meggie had asked him what that meant, he'd just laughed, and lightly touched his fingertip to her mouth. "A roundabout allusion to something you should know about by now."

She'd jerked away. He was a dangerous man; it was stupid ever to be alone with him. Unfortunately he was undoubtedly one of the guards who, when he visited, stuck close to her. Too close for Meggie's comfort. There were always two guards, not just one. Meggie sighed. She wished William would go away. She wanted Thomas. She wanted him to smile at her, kiss her, tell her what had happened to make him go away from her.

She wondered where he was right now. During the day she was never alone, thus here was William. And, of course, Thomas slept with her every night. She would lie there on her side of the bed listening to his deep smooth breathing.

He hadn't touched her in two weeks. She'd tried only once to initiate lovemaking with him, and he'd pulled away, saying only, "I'm tired, Meggie. I'm also not interested. Go to sleep."

It was worse than a slap in the face. She wanted to scream, perhaps even yell right in his face, but in the end, she whispered, "What's wrong, Thomas? I don't understand."

And he'd said his favorite litany, "I don't wish to speak of it. Go to sleep."

She hadn't touched him since. He had fast become a stranger who stayed close to her at night, to protect her. At least he didn't want her dead. He just didn't want her for a wife either.

And now here was William hanging about her, and she knew that Thomas had set him to be another guard.

"Why were you sent down, William?" she asked again even as she thought of Ezra, big, fast, and gray with a white face, from Horton Manor. The squire's wife claimed he could fly faster and straighter than an arrow on the wing. What she'd seen of Ezra's talents the day Thomas took her to visit was him rolling across the floor with one of the squire's children. She decided that she would simply have to set up a competition of sorts to see how many country folk hereabouts were interested.

William was still stroking Oscar, now on his back, all four paws sticking into the air. "That's disgraceful," Meggie said, frowning at the cat. "That cat has no sense of self-worth. Why were you sent down?"

William cleared his throat when he saw her eyebrow arched at him.

"I, er, got a local girl pregnant, maybe, one really never knows, and her father wanted to kill me."

"Not an uncommon reaction, I should say. Was she prettier than Melissa Winters?"

William's jaw dropped. He tried to say something, then shut his mouth fast as a clam trap.

"You are a miserable human being, William," Meggie said, so furious with her half brother-in-law that if she wouldn't hang for it, she would have cheerfully stomped him into the ground. "You probably should have been strangled at birth. Saved everyone a lot of difficulties, particularly the female of the species."

"But it wasn't my fault," William said, and Meggie

knew a whine when she heard it, having four brothers and so many dratted boy cousins about. She was so furious with him that she jumped to her feet, her fists at the ready. She wanted to fight him, to sock him in the jaw.

"The girls just hold you down, William, and rip off your clothes?"

He looked shocked that she, a vicar's daughter, would speak so bluntly. She just stared him down until he said, shrugging, "Well, no, but they're the kind of girls who are with ever so many men, and I'm just the one who always gets caught. It wasn't my fault. But you didn't like me before you saw me, Meggie. Why?"

"Melissa Winters, you dolt. I know all about how you blamed Thomas for that. You're a dishonorable cretin, William."

"But it was Thomas who got her with child," William said. "At the time I was in Glasgow with Aunt Augusta."

Meggie couldn't help herself. She slammed her fist into his jaw, a really solid hit that sent him reeling backward, his flailing arms nearly hitting Oscar DeGrasse. Oscar screeched and leaped straight up and backward, an amazing feat that Meggie couldn't help but admire. William couldn't catch himself and went crashing down on his back. He didn't move, just stared up at her, trying to catch his breath.

"Thomas is honorable," she said between fiercely gritted teeth. "You ever say something like that again, and I will kick you in the ribs after I've knocked you down."

William whimpered and didn't move.

"Thank you."

Meggie whirled about to see her husband standing in the doorway to this big sparsely furnished room, his arms crossed over his chest, one of his favorite poses. The irony of that thank-you had hit her square in the nose. She raised her chin. "You are many things, Thomas, but dishonorable isn't one of them."

"No," he said. "I'm not." He walked over to William and held out his hand. William looked at that hand, and Meggie thought for a moment that William would whimper. She said, "Oh, for goodness' sake, William, be a man and take your brother's hand. He won't kill you. He is more civilized about things like that than I."

"But *you* still might."

"That is true. Go away. I'm trying to train these cats."

William dusted himself off, gave his brother a very uncertain look, and was out of the room very quickly.

Thomas said slowly, "You defended me."

"What would you expect me to do? Tell your dim-witted half brother that you ignore your new wife, that you treat her like she bores you silly, and thus he can say anything at all he likes about you?"

"No. You're not like that."

"Is it possible that another man did impregnate Melissa Winters?"

"No."

"William said he was in Glasgow with Aunt Augusta."

"He was. I sent him there after I beat him to within an inch of his life."

"Well, good." Meggie wiped her hands on her skirt, looked over at Oscar, who was now curled into a tight ball, sleeping in a corner. "He doesn't look like much of a winner, does he?"

"Niles says he's fast."

"Did you see him execute that backward leap?"

"I wasn't looking at him at the time."

"What's wrong, Thomas?"

"I came to get you for tea, Meggie. My mother, Libby, and Lord Kipper are in the drawing room. Cook has already brought the tea and cakes. You're the only one missing."

"And William."

"Undoubtedly Barnacle will nab him."

"I see. All right," Meggie said, then looked over to see Barnacle grimacing toward them, his face contorted in awful agony.

She just looked at him, an eyebrow arched. "You're supposed to nab William."

"I'll nab him all right, but this is more important. It's vital to set things in their proper order and his lordship—our lordship, that is, my lady—is the most important thing hereabouts in any order. He has told me to tell you that he wishes to see you at your convenience in the estate room. And here he is telling you all by himself—and here I am doing the telling as well, but no matter. Two times is better than a chance on none doing the telling."

"I am very afraid, Barnacle," Thomas said, "that I understood you."

Barnacle beamed at him before he remembered, and reset his face into a fearful grimace.

Meggie gave the old man a smile and a very light pat on the back. "Yes, he has told me himself, Barnacle, and now so have you. I surely haven't a chance of forgetting now. Thank you." When he hobbled out, moaning with each stiff step, Meggie turned again to her husband. "You said tea. Barnacle said you wanted to see me in the estate room. What's going on, Thomas?"

"I just wanted to tell you that there is another package from your family." He paused a moment, examined his fingernails, and said easily, "Perhaps it's another gift from your almost cousin."

"Jeremy? Another gift? Probably not."

Then Meggie paused. There'd been something different in his voice when he'd said that, something just out of her reach.

"Tea or the package first, my lord?"

"That would depend on how excited you are about receiving another present from your almost cousin."

This time it smacked her in the nose. Jeremy, he was jealous of Jeremy. Had he heard something? No, surely neither her father nor Mary Rose would have said anything. Goodness, Mary Rose didn't even know. She was shaking her head even as she knew that he couldn't know, just couldn't. Then what was going on?

"His name is Jeremy Stanton-Greville," she said. "You met him at our wedding. He is five years older than you. He is married, his wife expecting a child. It is no more likely to be a present from him than from any other cousin or uncle or aunt or brother."

"I see," he said, and she wanted to hit him for that snide tone.

"I must go now and straighten myself before presenting myself in the drawing room with your blessed mother. I will look at my package later."

"Take care, Meggie. Five minutes, no more. Otherwise I will send someone for you."

"I doubt someone will try to bash me on the head on my way to my bedchamber."

"Five minutes."

She merely nodded and stalked out of the room. How could he possibly be jealous of Jeremy? It made no sense at all. But his voice had been different. She sighed. She just didn't know, had no idea, and she'd thought and thought about what she could have done to alienate him so very much. All she could figure out was that her husband had gotten himself in a snit because Jeremy sent her a carving of Mr. Cork. It was ridiculous.

She nearly knocked over her mother-in-law she was so deeply immersed in her own thoughts.

"Watch your direction, Missy!"

"What? Oh, ma'am, sorry I nearly plowed you down. It would surely be different if I'd meant to, but I didn't."

"You are entirely too smart for your own good. Just look at that dreadful chandelier overhead with all that raw-looking rope holding it up. My ancestors are thumping in their graves."

"You don't have any ancestors to thump here, ma'am. It's the Kavanaughs, don't you remember?"

"A low lot, the Kavanaughs," Madeleine said, staring at that rope, "so low they don't deserve to have ancestors here. No matter. Now, as for you, Missy—"

"It's my lady."

"Bah. I can tell that my dearest son is already tired of you. He keeps his distance from you, just plain avoids you, everyone has noticed it. Didn't take him long, did it? You are boring, obviously, you no longer amuse him, and he bitterly regrets marrying you. At least he got a lovely big dowry out of it. Well, are you pregnant yet?"

"Ask your son, ma'am," Meggie said, and nearly knocked her mother-in-law down on purpose this time. She managed to hold her temper, and forced herself to breathe in the wonderful fresh lemon wax that had shined up every bit of furniture and armor in the castle. There wasn't a single cobweb in any corner. Everything shone. Even though Mrs. Black couldn't see into any corners, she claimed she could always hear spiders weaving their webs and she didn't hear a single thing now.

Meggie was smiling as she strode away from her mother-in-law, shoulders finely squared, her step light until she thought of Thomas and knew that his mother was right. He was bored with her, tired of her, whatever. What had happened? What had she done? Surely it couldn't have anything to do with Jeremy.

I'm not boring, she thought, and pulled an early blooming rose from a vase that sparkled with cleanliness and crushed it in her fist. I train champion cat racers. How can that be boring?

Madeleine called after her, "I will prove to you that I can train racing cats better than you can."

Meggie didn't even pause. But she did smile, just for a moment. Madeleine just didn't give up.

The package from home—it was a painting of her family. She wasn't aware that she was crying until Thomas said, all stiff and hard, "It is a fairly good painting. I do believe though that Mary Rose's hair is not quite as red as that rendered by the artist. Also, Max has a sharper chin. As for Leo, he looks ready to vault over a fence and race around the fields. All in all, it is excellent. Stop crying."

Meggie sniffed, then set the painting on a table against the wall, backed up, and stared at it. "It's just excellent. My father knew I would be terribly homesick. He's the best father in the world."

Thomas didn't say anything. "Shall we take it downstairs and show it to everyone? Too bad your uncle the earl isn't in it. My mother would surely appreciate you more if reminded of your high-ranking relatives. I forgot to tell her that your aunt is the daughter of a duke. Hmmm. Maybe you can salvage her yet."

"She still calls me Missy. I've corrected her twice, just a bit on the snide side. I don't think she'll ever stop."

Thomas nodded. "Probably not. Let's go." He carried the painting all the way to the drawing room, set it atop the mantel, and stepped back.

Libby said, "Goodness, Meggie, your father is a fine figure of a man. Does he truly have silver wings in his hair?"

"I believe so," Meggie said.

"She is too young to be your mother," Lord Kipper said, both his eyes on Mary Rose. "Wonderful features, interesting the way she is leaning toward your father, you can feel it, even though she appears to be sitting straight."

"You cannot seduce her, Niles," Madeleine said.

Lord Kipper turned and smiled. "Would you like to wager on that, my dear?"

"Mary Rose is Meggie's stepmother. She's Scottish," Thomas said, turned from the painting, and added toward his wife, "Would you be so kind as to serve us tea?"

And so she did. She knew everyone's taste in tea now and moved quickly. Cook had made scones for her, and they were really quite good. Cook now made, besides a brilliant breakfast, a very acceptable luncheon. She never sang except delivering the nutty buns to the breakfast table each morning. Dinner, however, still strained her abilities. She needed a song, Meggie knew, and felt guilty because she hadn't thought about it.

She said more to herself than to Thomas, "I should be receiving some more recipes from Mary Rose soon now."

"Cook will butcher them," William said, coming into the drawing room. "Give her a haunch of beef and she will turn it into a fence rail." So saying, he cast Meggie a wary look.

Meggie frowned at him and began rearranging the

scones on the platter. "Oh, stop looking like a whipped dog, William. Would you like tea?"

He nodded and managed to slink all the way across the huge room to stand behind a very old wing chair that Meggie planned to replace just as soon as— She frowned into her teacup. She had to go to Dublin to the Gibbs Furniture Warehouse. She wondered what her husband of three weeks would say when she asked him about that.

"I say, that's your father, Meggie. The vicar."

"That's right. You caused a very fine mess, William, and he was the one to resolve it, he and your brother."

"What is this?" Libby said. "What did you do this time, dearest?"

"Mother, I haven't done a single thing since I've gotten home. Lord Kipper, you promised you would show me your new hunter. I should very much like to see it, sir."

"Since your mother bought it off me for your birthday, I suppose you can see it."

"The new hunter, Mother?" At Libby's nod, William swooped down on her and nearly crushed her into the sofa, so exuberant was he with his hugs.

"You are a good boy, William," she said, kissing his cheek, "you always have been."

Meggie nearly turned blue she held her breath so long so that she wouldn't say anything.

Near midnight, when Thomas finally came into her bed, making his way quietly from his own bedchamber, Meggie said from the depths of the goose down, "Thomas, we must go to the furniture warehouse in Dublin."

He jumped a good foot.

To her delight, after he paced the room three times, he turned back toward the bed on his bare heel, frowned, and nodded. "All right. You'll probably be safer in Dublin than here. Make your lists, Meggie, and we will leave when you're ready."

"Would you like to come lie beside me and we can discuss it?"

He looked over at his wife. She was sitting up now and she wasn't wearing one of her usual white muslin nightgowns. She was wearing something that looked sinful, the color of a peach, and fit her so well he could clearly see her breasts. He was so hard he hurt. By the time he reached the bed, he was harder than Lord Kipper's pipe stem.

He stopped cold. "No."

"No what?"

"I want you, Meggie. You can look at me and I am incapable of hiding it from you."

"I am your wife. I want you as well. Please, Thomas, if you can't tell me what's bothering you, can't you at least come here and make love to me?"

He felt himself shaking, beginning at his feet, those shakes working their way up. "You're trying to seduce me," he said slowly, the shakes now to his knees.

"Well, yes," she said, and smiled at him. "If you won't talk to me about what's bothering you, why then, I might as well enjoy you in other ways."

She'd brushed her hair out and it was curling and falling down her back and over her right shoulder, framing her right breast, her hair and that wicked nightgown she was wearing that was now in danger of falling off her right shoulder.

He swallowed. "If a man doesn't have pride, he has very little."

"Pride? Whatever are you talking about?"

He said at nearly a shout because it had been festering inside him for so very long now, and he just couldn't hold it in anymore, it was corroding his innards, "Jeremy, that damned almost cousin of yours! That's what I'm talking about, as if you didn't know.

"You betrayed me in your heart, Meggie. You married me when you knew you loved him, and you still love that damned bastard, and here he is married and will have a child soon. You married me because you couldn't have him and thus it didn't matter to you. I knew you didn't love me, but I thought I could bring you around. But it had nothing to do with anything, did it?

"I was the fool who was ready to offer you everything. Did you even hesitate, Meggie? Did you feel the least bit guilty when you agreed to marry me? I don't think much of you for doing that, Meggie, I really don't."

29

MEGGIE SAID, HER voice dull and accepting, "I loved him beginning when I was thirteen years old."

"Why did you marry me, dammit, when you loved another man?"

"I liked you very much, Thomas, you pleased me, you made me laugh, better still, I made you laugh. I esteemed you. I admired you and knew you were honorable. I wanted to marry you."

"You loved another man."

Slowly she nodded. "You didn't love me either."

"How do you know?" He slashed his hand through the air. "Not that it matters. Is that your defense? Let me tell you, Meggie, I wasn't cherishing some other woman in my heart, which is balderdash, naturally, but that is the way one says it, I suppose. I didn't marry you under false pretenses."

Meggie felt her heart pounding slow deep strokes. Her mouth felt dry. "May I ask how you know about Jeremy?"

"Yes, I'll tell you. We had been married all of an hour when I happened to overhear you speaking to your father about how very noble Jeremy was, how you admired him, how you would have loved him forever, if only he hadn't met Charlotte."

Meggie squeezed her eyes closed, remembering each word, feeling the pain each one brought her, pain that just by saying them had flowed over her husband. "You remember so very much. I'm sorry, Thomas. You see, my father was very worried about me and about you as well. He didn't want either of us to be disappointed. When he asked, I admitted that I knew Jeremy had been playacting when he'd come to the vicarage, that he'd just told me he wasn't really obnoxious at all, that it had all been an act to help me get over my feelings for him. He was telling me then since it wasn't important any longer since I'd just married, and he didn't want me to dislike him anymore."

Thomas wanted to yell down the moon, which was bright overhead tonight, not a single cloud in the Irish sky, a perfect spring night, the air soft and fragrant with the scent of new flowers, but he didn't want her anymore now. His sense of betrayal was greater now that she'd admitted to it.

"Well, damn you, you didn't get over your feelings for the bastard. Then you married me."

"Yes, I did."

"But he was married and he didn't want you?"

"No, but he was betrothed, something I didn't know about until it was too late."

"I see. If Jeremy walked through that door this very instant, told you he wanted you, would you go with him?"

"No."

"Because you're a damned vicar's daughter."

"Because I don't break my promises."

He plowed his hand through his hair, making it stand straight up. Meggie smiled.

"So I am stuck with a wife who loves another man," he said finally, and hated the words as they poured out of his mouth, hated them to his gut. They were stark and ugly, those damnable words, sounded like nails in a coffin lid.

"Listen to me, Thomas. I have a very high regard for you. I very much like it when you kiss me, when you love me. You have given me great pleasure just as, I trust, I have given you. Jeremy isn't part of my life now. Only you are. I am your wife and I will protect you and honor you until I die."

"Wonderful," Thomas said, and began pacing, his dressing gown flapping at his ankles. "Just bloody wonderful. An honorable wife who's already betrayed me. Damnation." The fingers went through the hair again.

She said suddenly, "That is why you were so very rough with me on our wedding night, wasn't it? You were thinking about Jeremy and you wanted to punish me."

"I'm not proud of it, but yes. I heard you talking about him and I couldn't bear it. I hurt you." He paced again. She could feel anger radiating off him. She realized fully what she'd done to him.

"I'm very sorry, Thomas."

"Yes, naturally you are because you're so damned honorable and you recognize that you've done a very wrong thing."

"Yes, but you are my husband, Thomas, forever."

"Isn't that just dandy?"

"Why did you withdraw from me again? Two weeks ago."

"You dreamed about him. You said his name aloud." He slammed his fist against the wall. "Damn you, Meggie, I had just given you immense pleasure and you dreamed about that damned bastard! I wanted to kill him—I still do."

"What do you want to do to me?"

"I don't know. I've thought about it, but I just don't know. I don't want to hurt you again, not with sex. Never with sex again."

"I don't remember dreaming about Jeremy. To be perfectly honest here, Thomas, I don't think of him all that often anymore. You are my husband. Pendragon is my home. I want to be your wife, in all ways. I hate that you distrust me, that you blame me, that you don't want me anymore."

"Oh, God knows I want you, Meggie. I am a young man, young men are randier than goats, and I have grown up hearing that goats will bed anything that wags a tail or chews a boot."

"That's vulgar," Meggie said, and laughed. It dried up very quickly. She said slowly, looking at him intently, "Do you think perhaps that we can start over, Thomas?"

"Start over? Start over what? This sham of a marriage?"

She'd been wallowing in guilt, knowing she'd been profoundly wrong. She'd been trying to exert reason and logic, trying to make him see how hideously sorry she was, but now she felt anger filling her, coming right out of her mouth. "This isn't a sham marriage! Blessed Hell, Thomas, I wouldn't let a man do what you do to me, and I surely wouldn't let a man hear me scream in pleasure, if this were a damned sham marriage! I am your bloody wife. Do you hear me? I will grow old with you. Get used to it!"

She was breathing so hard that she was panting now. She realized in that instant that he was looking at her breasts, heaving and pressing against that wicked peach satin. She, the vicar's daughter, straightened her shoulders, stuck her chest out, and said, "So what are you going to do about it, Thomas?"

He slammed out of the White Room.

Meggie stared at the still vibrating door. This was not good. She knew she'd hurt him very badly. But she couldn't control her dreams. She tried and tried, but she simply couldn't remember even dreaming about Jeremy. Oh yes, it had been after he'd sent her the carved statue of Mr. Cork. What could it have been?

And then she remembered.

She bounded out of bed and burst through the adjoining door into his grand and massive and very gloomy bedchamber, which she'd had cleaned, but not really paid much attention to since Thomas spent so little time in here. He was standing by one of the long skinny windows, staring out over the sea.

"Thomas, I remember."

He turned slowly. "You follow me, even into my bedchamber, where I should have privacy if I wish it?"

"Climb down from your hobbyhorse, you ass. I remember the dream about Jeremy."

"You have had time to make something up, Meggie."

She ran straight across the room, right at him, and grabbed his dressing gown lapels. She stood on her tiptoes and said right into his face, "I haven't made up a single thing. Listen to me. I dreamed about him right after he sent me Mr. Cork. Naturally he was on my mind, but not in the way you think. I dreamed about a cat race."

"Ha."

"Shut your trap, curse you. I dreamed that Mr. Cork was running, he was way ahead of the other racing cats. Then he began changing—he turned black, his eyes were bright orange, and then, he was suddenly fat, his belly nearly hanging to the ground. I just couldn't believe it. And then Jeremy was saying that he would have to re-whittle him, make me a whole new statue and it would take him more time than he had, but he had to so he could be faithful to the real Mr. Cork. And I was begging him not to. I wanted my own Mr. Cork back, not this monstrous thing."

"Do you honestly want me to believe that, Meggie?" He spoke very quietly.

She backed away from him, a good two steps. She said slowly, "Have I ever lied to you?"

"You lied by omission."

"Ah, that's a grand sin, isn't it? Will you chew on that until your jaw locks? No, that was rhetorical. Have I ever lied to you, Thomas?"

He was silent. She opened her mouth, but he raised his hand. "No, be quiet. I'm thinking. We were together a goodly amount of time before we married. I'm trying to remember if you lied to me."

Now it was Meggie who began pacing that dismal gloomy room. It was filled with shadows and every step she took sent her into deeper gloom. She hated gloom, she knew too well how it felt inside her. He turned to look out the window again, at the beautiful moon that glistened over the water.

It was magic, a night like this.

"No," he said at last. "I don't remember you ever lying to me."

"Well, good," she said, nearly at a loss for words since she'd fully expected him to come up with something. She was only human, after all. "Then may we please try to begin again, Thomas?"

"Meggie," he said, staying where he was, which was very far away from her indeed, "what if I loved another woman and couldn't have her, then I married you, all without telling you a thing about her."

Meggie stopped cold. She was shaking her head, then she stopped that too. She stared across the gloom at him. "Oh dear," she whispered. "Oh dear."

"Yes," he said. "There is that, isn't there?"

"I would throttle you if I found out. I would stomp you into the mud. I would shave your head and blacken your eyes, both of them. Oh dear. I hadn't thought of the shoe on the other foot."

He was pleased, but he wasn't about to let her see it. "What I did to you was bad enough—forcing you on our wedding night."

"No, what was worse was the last time when you just went away from me and didn't say a single thing. That is horrid, Thomas. Please, don't do that again. If you want to stomp me, I will allow it."

She'd walked into the moonlight again, and that peach thing she was wearing shimmered all the way from her breasts to the floor. He could see too much of her.

"If I slam out of this room, I will be in the White Room again, your room."

"Please don't leave me," she said and came up to him. She didn't touch him, just stopped an inch short and looked up at him. "Thomas, why did you marry me?"

"Because I love you, you twit, because I believed you loved me as well."

"But you never said anything about love to me."

"No."

"Why?"

He said very slowly, "Because there was just something about you, Meggie, something that made me understand how very young you were, how very innocent, untouched. You weren't ready for that."

"All that young and innocent, yet you believed I loved you? That it wasn't some sort of schoolgirl infatuation?"

"I sometimes hate the way your brain works."

"So does my family." She sighed. "There is so much going on here at Pendragon. There is the someone who doesn't want me here, enough to try to kill me. Then there's you, Thomas. You don't know whether you want to strangle me or kiss me or just slam out of the room."

"If you are giving me a choice, then I would prefer to kiss you." He had to touch her breasts, had to mold his fingers around her through that satin, and so he did and he closed his eyes as he cupped her in his palms, as his fingers roved over her.

He felt her pushing against his hands, and he opened his eyes. He smiled down at her. "I believe you want me as badly as I want you."

"More," Meggie said. "You taught me, Thomas, and you taught me well." She went up on her tiptoes and kissed his mouth. "Please open to me," she whispered and he did, and all his heat, all the strength of him, all his passion and the immense hurt she'd dished out to him, it was all in that kiss, in the way he held her so tightly, she believed her ribs would crack, and then she just didn't care.

The huge old bed was only ten feet away. When he lay her on the Aubusson carpet that was so threadbare she felt pricks of cold air touching her shoulder blades, he forced himself to stop, just for a moment, and said, his voice thick and deep and guttural, "I want this to be hard and fast, Meggie."

Meggie couldn't think of a single word, she was thrumming, mewling like her racing cats she was so excited, she felt so very urgent, it was beyond anything she could begin to understand. She grabbed him around his neck and pulled him down to her. "Please, now, Thomas. Now."

He was a wild man, all over her, not a touch of gentleness, and Meggie hummed with power and urgency. She also hummed with something else, but she didn't know what it was.

Meggie would swear that the gloomy room lightened, that the air itself lifted and fluttered when she yelled to those beams in the darkened ceiling. But he wasn't through, bless him, and within a very short time, she was breathing hard again, beside herself, her hands all over him, pulling and caressing and hitting, and her cries heaved out of her mouth against his shoulder.

"I'm going to die now," she said, "a happy woman," and she didn't move a single muscle.

He grunted beside her.

"I felled you."

He grunted again, and she would swear she felt a smile on his mouth before he kissed her hair and collapsed again.

"Will you give me another chance, Thomas?"

"Your timing is excellent," he said, and was asleep, sprawled naked on the Aubusson carpet, a smile on his face.

Meggie's brain began to function again only when she realized she was shivering from cold. She came up on her elbow over her husband, looked down into his hard face, not so hard now in sleep, and said, "Thomas, how am I going to get you into bed?"

He grunted, then opened a dark eye and looked up into her shadowed face. "If I really concentrate on this, I can move."

"What will I do," she said, lightly caressing his shoulder, kissing his face, light nipping, sweet kisses, "when you are an old man and we end up on the carpet?"

"You will just roll me up in the carpet and leave me be."

She laughed even as he scooped her into his arms and carried her into the White Room. She kissed his shoulder, whispered against his neck, "Are you willing to let me perhaps kiss your belly the way you kiss mine?"

His breath *whooshed* out and he ran through the adjoining door, nearly knocked Meggie in the head when he ran too close to the wall. He was laughing until her hair cascaded over his belly and she touched him with her mouth. He nearly heaved himself off the bed. Nothing could be better than this, he thought, and nearly expired. Dear God, her mouth.

His last thought before he fell into a blessedly numb sleep was that his wife, the vicar's daughter, would come to love him. He was smart and he was persistent. He was also determined.

The following morning, however, Thomas wasn't smiling.

30

"*Y*OU DAMNED IDIOT, you've been home only a fort-night and you've already done this?"

William didn't feel well, he really didn't, and here was his too-sober half-brother, his voice black as the misery William was feeling, each word staccato, colder than an Irish winter morning, slamming right into his ear. He wanted to bolt behind the wainscoting. He wanted to seal up his ears until he knew his head wouldn't explode.

Thomas said, "Teddy MacGraff was here, fists at the ready, his face so red I was afraid he would fall over with apoplexy, that or come up here to your bedchamber and wring your damned neck."

"Let him," William said. "I want to die."

"Damn you, you're a man, get up and face this!"

Thomas jerked his half-brother from his bed and dragged him across his bedchamber to his dressing table, where there sat a pitcher filled of water, waiting for soap and his razor.

Thomas poured the water over William's head. William howled, flopped about, but it didn't matter.

Thomas let him slide to the floor, then called for his valet. "Wring the little sot out, Dickie. When you have poured enough coffee down his throat, bring him to me in the estate room. Oh, and don't let him out of your sight, he's liable to slink out of here and try to hide."

He heard Dickie say in a far-too-kind voice, "Come along, Master William. It's not a good thing you've done and you're in for it. Best face it like a man."

William moaned.

Thomas was shaking his head, wondering how he was going to handle this one, when he nearly ran into Meggie, who was dancing down the corridor, humming an arpeggio. He grabbed her arm to keep her upright. She squeaked in surprise, looked up at him, blushed—it was that blush that alerted him—then gave him a fat smile, and he knew, knew all the way to his belly, exactly what she was thinking, saw it clearly in his mind. She was kneeling over him and her mouth was on him. And her hands. And the feel of her hair on his belly. Oh God. He couldn't bear it. He was shaking.

"Good morning." He kissed her hard and fast, then straightened, took two steps away from her. When she reached for him, he said, "Don't, Meggie, I can do nothing about it, at least for the next couple of hours. William has gotten another girl pregnant. Her father came here, fully prepared to send William all the way to Botany Bay. In a boat without a paddle. Perhaps without a boat as well."

"That's it, Thomas. I'm going to kill the little sod, right now."

He managed to grab her before she ran around him. She was breathing hard.

"No, sweetheart, you can't."

"Of course I can. Just watch me."

"I mean, since I'm the magistrate and I would be a witness to the crime, I would have to take you to the gaol in Dublin."

But Meggie had already moved ahead. "But how can William have gotten another girl pregnant? He's only been here a matter of weeks."

Thomas sighed. "The little sod was home before."

"This is just too much, Thomas. Let me go. I will get a gun. I will shoot him in the feet, make him crawl away from Pendragon. You won't have to be a witness and arrest me."

"No, Meggie, keep away from William. If you would, please ask Aunt Libby to come to the drawing room. It is time that she faced what William is, what he has done, what he's obviously done every chance he'd gotten since he was old enough to figure out what to do."

"Aunt Libby doesn't know about any of the other girls? She doesn't know what he's like?"

He shook his head. "I don't see how she could. William certainly would never tell her, you can wager your last groat on that, and I've kept quiet, protecting her. But now this cannot continue. She needs to know. If she has any control, any influence over him, now's the time she used it."

"I'll fetch her, Thomas."

At least, Meggie thought, watching her husband stride down the corridor, head down, hopefully planning punishments for William, he wasn't thinking about Jeremy.

Jeremy. Meggie paused a moment, and blinked. It was strange. For the first time since she'd known him, Jeremy wasn't all that clear in her head. How odd that she could be so very fickle.

Odd but good. She had honestly believed he was her world, believed that when he had married Charlotte that her world had come to an end, at least all the fun part of it.

But no longer.

She found Aunt Libby in her bedchamber, humming as she carefully selected a sweetmeat and popped it into her mouth. She closed her eyes as she chewed. Meggie also saw that Libby was writing something. She quickly slid the piece of foolscap beneath several books—both of them, Meggie saw, were Lord Byron. Now, what was this all about?

Meggie hated this room. It was as dark and dismal as the rest of Pendragon, except, of course, for Madeleine's room.

Meggie looked around as she said, "Are you certain,

Aunt Libby, that you don't wish me to make your bed-chamber a bit more cheerful? Perhaps more light could come in if we took away those dark draperies. Thomas and I will be going to Dublin soon to visit the furniture warehouses. You could accompany us, if you would like to."

Libby just shook her head, her smile never faltering. "Isn't it a beautiful morning, Meggie? Would you care for a sweetmeat? The almond ones are exquisite. Niles tells me they have no substance to them at all so I can eat as many as I wish without gaining flesh. As for having more light in this room, goodness no. A woman of a certain age looks much fresher if there isn't too much ghastly sunlight showing all the imperfections, don't you agree?"

"Yes," Meggie said and stared at Libby. She knew to her toes that Libby had been with Lord Kipper. She recognized that very self-satisfied look, that air of utter complacency, that sparkle that came from somewhere in the inside that made one want to hum and smile and fold one's hands across one's lap and do nothing at all except enjoy the sweet flow of life. She'd seen it on her own face when she'd looked in the mirror that morning. If William weren't such a rotter, she'd still have that smile on her face, damn him.

"Thank you, but I'm not all that fond of almonds, Aunt Libby."

Libby stopped humming. She rose slowly, shook out her skirts. "What is wrong, Meggie?"

"It's William."

"Oh my God—my precious boy is hurt? Someone has harmed him? Oh no. Don't keep me waiting, Meggie, spit it out."

"No, your precious boy is just fine. However, he has done a very bad thing."

"Not just a simple bad thing? A very bad thing? That's impossible. He is delightful. He is perfect, or nearly so. Now, what is this all about?"

"Come downstairs with me and I will let Thomas tell you."

"Thomas is a man. Thus he will be rough and not at all conciliatory. You will tell me."

"William has evidently gotten a local girl pregnant. Her father was here and quite enraged. He wanted to kill William. Thomas told the father that he would see to things, and so he will."

"Oh, is that all?" Libby heaved a huge sigh of relief and sat herself down again. "Thomas can give the father a bit of money, tell him boys will be boys, and all will be well. You frightened me, Meggie. It wasn't well done of you. Do tell Mrs. Black to bring me a bit of tea. Thank you."

"But, ma'am—"

"Go away, Meggie."

Meggie went. Pendragon Castle—it sounded so very wonderfully gothic, so very mysterious, filled with romantic legend. It sounded as if ancient memories and perhaps a sprinkling of magic could make their way into your bones if you lived here.

Surely Pendragon Castle hadn't expected to have such a strange concatenation of people living in it, giving it not a whit of mystery, romance, or magic. What would future generations believe permeated the castle walls after this crew departed?

Thomas was pacing the estate room. He looked harassed. He looked to be talking to himself.

Meggie said from the doorway, "Aunt Libby doesn't care. She doesn't think it's anything at all. She says you'll just give the father a bit of money and that will be that."

Thomas looked heavenward in utter weariness and said, "Why am I not surprised?" He sighed, plowed his fingers through his hair, which made her smile even through the dark cloud of misery William had brought into the castle.

Meggie said thoughtfully, "I suppose you could have him gelded, like a horse."

"Now, there's a good thought. Who would we get to do it?"

"The girl's father," Meggie said without any hesitation at all.

Thomas walked over to her and pulled her against him. "This is a damnable situation," he said against her hair. Her hair—it smelled of some sort of flower, he didn't know which. He found himself rubbing his nose in her hair, realized what he was doing, and pulled back.

"I am going to tell William that he will marry the girl, if, that is, she and her father will have him. I will also give her a dowry. And I will tell William if he doesn't change his colors and become a decent husband, I will have him join the King's navy. What do you think? I will also cut him off without a cent. That will doubtless provide his biggest incentive to keep his male parts at home with his wife."

"William doesn't have any money? From his mother?"

"Oh no, my father kicked her out not long after William was born, didn't give her a sou. I have paid for Oxford, for tutors."

"That's a wonderful idea, Thomas. It should keep him in line." She went up on her tiptoes and kissed his mouth, running her fingertips over his black, black eyebrows. "If I were the girl's father, I'm not so sure I'd want William as a son-in-law."

"I think Teddy MacGraff will be quite pleased. He'll see William as being completely in his power, which he will be."

She thought about that a moment. "Is Teddy MacGraff big and tough?"

"Very."

"Let's do it. We can announce it this evening."

"Perhaps we can even tell Aunt Libby that she will shortly be a grandmother. It will rile her no end to have a grandchild before Madeleine." He laughed.

"Good heavens, why?"

"She is very vain, just like my mother. Only thing is, Libby is younger than my mother by two years. Yes, my mother is going to be delighted."

Lord Kipper came to dinner, as he did nearly every evening since he and Libby had become involved in an *affaire*. At the end of the meal that still wasn't very good, even though Cook swore she'd followed Mary Rose's recipe for the stewed mutton down to the dash of thyme, Thomas rose and tapped his fork on his wineglass to gain everyone's attention. "William," he said to his younger brother, "you look less dead this evening than you did this morning."

William raised hopeful eyes at the sound of his half-brother's jovial voice. "Yes, I am fine now, Thomas."

"You will be more than fine very shortly. Actually, very shortly you will be a married man. You will wed Jenny MacGraff right here next Sunday. You and Jenny will live here, of course. I will provide Jenny a dowry."

With surprising agility, Libby jumped to her feet, nearly knocking her chair over she came up so quickly. "You cannot mean this, Thomas. It is absurd. The idiot girl's pregnant, who cares? It happens all the time. Give Teddy MacGraff a couple of pounds, he'll go away happy."

Madeleine said, "Thomas, Libby's right. This can't be the best way to solve this problem. The MacGraffs are nothings—nobodies! Goodness, Teddy MacGraff is a merchant! Oh, wait a moment—goodness me, can you believe it? Libby, you will be a grandmother! Ah, what a terrible thing, just terrible."

"No, I will not be a bloody grandmother! I do not recognize this child as William's. Indeed, I imagine he isn't the father at all. She drew him in, seduced him. He is a boy, incapable of producing a child."

Thomas laughed, he just couldn't help himself. He looked over at William, who was pale as the tablecloth, his fingers clutched around his wineglass, his eyes glazed.

Thomas said, "Yes, you will indeed be a grandmother, Aunt Libby. And yes, Thomas is the father. The wedding will take place next Sunday right here at Pendragon or—please listen to me, William. Are you?"

William jerked his eyes up from the wine that was such a lovely red. "I am listening, Thomas."

"You will marry Jenny MacGraff. You will be a good husband to her and a good father—at least better than our own father, which isn't saying much at all—or you will never again be welcome here at Pendragon. I will also cut you off without a sou. That is your choice. William, it is your decision. What say you?"

William looked from his mother back down to his wineglass. He picked up his fork and played with it, then slumped down in his chair. He raised pitiful eyes to Thomas. "Perhaps it isn't my child, Thomas. Perhaps Jenny has bedded many men and—"

"Don't be a fool, William. She was a virgin. Or will you try to tell me that she wasn't?"

"Perhaps a girl can have many virginities, perhaps she can develop a new one to lure in young men—"

"Which will it be, William?" Thomas asked with great patience, his voice implacable. Thomas had said earlier to Meggie that he couldn't imagine why any girl would want William, but the girl did. As for her father, Teddy had rubbed his hands together and smiled. It hadn't been a nice smile. "I'll see to it the lad behaves himself," Teddy had said, and Thomas believed him. He then gave Thomas a ferocious smile and shook his hand to seal the bargain.

"Marriage," William said into his lower lip. "I choose marriage."

"And you swear you will do your best to be a good husband and a good father?"

"I swear."

"Good. Niles, will you attend William's wedding?"

Lord Kipper raised a sleek brow, smiled, and raised his wineglass. "It will be a very nice wedding," he said. "To William and—what's-her-name?"

"Jenny MacGraff."

"To William and Jenny."

Everyone drank except Libby and William, who both moaned into their glasses.

"It's done," Thomas said when he and Meggie were finally alone some two hours later in the White Room, the door closed and locked. "It's been a very long day. Now, at last, I can concentrate on you. I've been thinking about this since this morning."

"Yes, it's done. Let me tell you, Thomas, Mrs. Black

is thrilled about it. Your mother is chortling because Libby will have a low-born daughter-in-law and be a grandmother before she will. Really? Since this morning?"

"Remember when you were dancing down the corridor and I ran into you? Yes, since that moment when I saw exactly what you were thinking. Your eyes tell me everything, Meggie. Everything. Come here."

Meggie went, nearly skipping to him since she was so very eager. It was much a repeat of the previous night, but better, Meggie thought, grinning down at her husband, who looked nearly dead. She felt so good she wanted to sing, perhaps write a ditty for Mrs. Mullins about Mary Rose's stewed fish stew.

She whispered against her husband's ear, "Perhaps we could hold a cat race to celebrate the wedding."

Life, Thomas thought, would never be boring with Meggie in it. He kissed her temple and wondered what the future would bring. More lovemaking, that was what he wanted, much more.

"Should you like to go to Italy, Meggie?"

"I should love it above all things."

"Soon," he said. "Soon." He pressed his forehead against hers, breathed in her scent, unique to Meggie. "I was just wondering what life would bring us."

"Lots of good things, I hope," she said, and kissed his chin. "You know, Thomas, when I take you into my mouth like that and you—"

He jerked. He was hard that instant, something he'd sworn was beyond him for the next twelve hours. When she was moaning into his mouth, he was the one who wanted to sing with the pleasure of it.

31

MEGGIE WAS WALKING along the trail that led to the Pendragon cliffs, whistling, occasionally flinging a stick for Brutus to retrieve, which he did with great enthusiasm. "Too bad," she said, scrubbing behind his ears, "that there can't be dog racing, but it just isn't possible. Can you imagine racing, Brutus? No, you'd just sit there wagging your tail, wouldn't you, or rush to bring back sticks. Your brain just isn't fashioned for racing." And she'd throw the stick again. Brutus was one of Thomas's dogs, an exuberant terrier who looked more like a Clara, in truth, than a Brutus. One stick flew too close to the edge of the cliff. Brutus skidded at the edge and slunk down onto his haunches, whining softly. He would go no farther.

"What's the matter? Oh, I see, you're afraid the ground isn't steady and you'll go right over. You're right. I'm too strong in my throwing. Let me get this stick, Brutus, and I'll hurl it in the other direction." She leaned down to get the stick when she heard a snicker of sound right beside her. She turned, then there was another snicker of sound and this one landed in her shoulder, hurling her backward off the cliff.

She screamed, loud, wailing, and hit the water below. She struck the water flat on her back and sank like a stone. She was sure she'd broken her back. She hit the bottom, but thankfully not hard. Waves washed over her head, rocks and sand tore her clothes and scraped her skin. She swallowed water, gagged.

It was the gagging that brought her right back up. The water was just over her head, and even though her clothes were heavy, she managed to struggle to shore. She was wheezing, choking, gagging on the harsh salt water, trying to get her breath and ignore her back, which felt like a large sofa was sitting atop her from striking the water so hard. *Think about now, just about now.* She pulled herself out of the water and fell on her face onto the sand.

She vomited up all the seawater. She was shaking so badly that she could barely catch her breath. Then she realized that blood was dripping onto the wet sand.

She stared at the blood, at first not understanding. Blood, it was her blood. She hadn't seen her own blood since she'd gotten scratched by Tiny Tom. It was faded, all that blood, since is was mixed with water. It had turned the bodice of her blue muslin gown into a faint pink color, and now, it was oozing out of her, snaking downward. She swallowed, realizing now that the strange snicking sound—it had been a bullet and it had gone into her body, hurled her backward over the cliff and into the sea below.

Thank God it had been high tide, otherwise she would be dead now.

She didn't want to think about that.

She tried to straighten, to push herself back onto her knees, so she could stand up, but ferocious pain suddenly ripped through her shoulder, and she groaned with the shock of it, the unexpected clout of pain, and fell back onto her face. *I've got to move, got to move. Someone tried to kill me and he can do it again. I've got to get away.*

She heard Brutus barking his head off above her on the cliff edge.

She had to get up. She had to get back to Pendragon. She just couldn't remain here. Where was the person who should be close by protecting her?

Oh, God, the person who had shot her could simply

walk down the cliff walk and shoot her again. This time, dead. She wouldn't stand a chance.

She couldn't, wouldn't, do that to Thomas.

Get up, get up.

Slowly, her chest blazing with such pain she was gasping with it, Meggie managed to come up onto her hands and knees. She looked up. There was someone up there, she felt it. Then she heard Brutus growling, then barking loud and louder still.

She saw movement, then a shadow through the bright morning sunlight, saw a gun, a hand was raising it, raising it and pointing it downward, toward her. Meggie crawled toward a boulder, managed to fall flat behind it. A chip of the rock flew off.

Oh God, he was going to kill her. At least he was up there and not down here.

Was it really a he?

She didn't know.

She lay there, panting, trying to control the pain, listening to Brutus barking louder and louder, then heard the dog cry out.

The bastard had hit Brutus.

Silence.

Where was he? Was he coming down that path? She had to move, she had to do something, but there was nowhere to go, just miles of beach strewn with heavy boulders, seaweed drying on chunks of driftwood. No place, no cave, where she could hide. She could arm herself, yes, that was it. She looked around to find a rock. Too small. No, that one she couldn't begin to lift even if she hadn't been injured.

There was one. She managed to pull herself within reach of a round black rock, sitting just beyond her fingertips, all by itself, as if waiting for her. She pulled herself toward that rock, then got her hand around it. It felt nice and heavy. She gripped it against herself, then managed to get back up onto her knees. She pressed against the boulder, then slowly, carefully, eased her face around to look toward the cliff path.

She didn't see anything, didn't hear anyone climbing down.

She didn't hear Brutus.

Time passed. She blinked, cursed herself, tried to hum a song, anything to stay alert, but it was hard, her shoulder hurt so badly. She felt tears trail down her cheeks, couldn't stop them. She tasted her tears mixed with the salt water.

More time passed.

She hurt, but she kept her eyes on the cliff trail. She ripped a long strip of wet material off her skirt and wrapped it as tightly as she could around her shoulder. It wasn't a very good job since she had only one hand, but it was the best she could do.

Where was Brutus? She prayed he hadn't been shot.

Then she heard a man's voice yelling her name. She nearly shattered from fear until she realized it was Thomas. She tried to call back to him, but just a very thin whisper came out of her mouth. It didn't matter. He would come to her. She smiled even as she sank down to rest her cheek against the wet sand.

She saw his shadow over her, felt his hands on her, and opened her eyes. "Is Brutus all right?"

"Oh yes, the man just knocked him in the head, but he's all right. As for you—"

She heard him say her name, faintly, faintly, then she was gone, away from the pain, away from the fear. Everything would be all right now. Thomas was here.

Panic nearly sent Thomas over the edge. He pressed his hand against her chest, felt the smooth, slow beat of her heart. She was unconscious. He lifted his hand, covered with her blood. He gently tied the ripped material more tightly over her shoulder.

He prayed she would remain unconscious. He lifted her into his arms and began the long trek back up the narrow cliff path.

He was going to kill William.

• • •

"She'll live, but it's bad enough, my lord."

Thomas couldn't stand it. She was still unconscious, so pale she looked dead, her flesh so cold. He pulled another blanket over her. Every few moments he lightly laid his palm on her chest to feel her heart.

He stared up at Dr. Pritchart with haggard eyes. "You swear she will live?"

Dr. Pritchart rubbed his palm over his forehead. "I think so. The bullet went through her, high on her shoulder, which is a good thing, less chance of infection, which would most certainly kill her. Now, I must set in stitches, both in her shoulder and in her back."

Meggie moaned and opened her eyes.

Thomas cursed. Meggie frowned. "What's wrong? Oh, Blessed Hell, something hurts, Thomas, hurts really bad."

"I know, sweetheart. Just hold on."

"Give her some brandy, that will help. Then hold her down, my lord."

When Dr. Pritchart had finished setting the black stitches, Thomas stared down at her white flesh, the blood and black thread all mixed together, and he couldn't bear it.

Her eyes were closed. She'd said not a word while Dr. Pritchart was stitching her flesh together. Not made a sound, but she'd clutched his hands so tightly they hurt. He'd wished she'd pass out, but she hadn't. She said now, "I'm going to be all right, Thomas. Stop worrying. I heard you saying over and over that you were going to kill William. Why? Did he get another girl pregnant?"

"Not that I know of. No, Meggie, he was supposed to stay with you. Since he was worried you would try to stomp him into the ground if he stayed too close, he said he would keep his distance. Didn't you wonder?"

"Well, I saw Jem the stable boy walking just behind me, and I thought he was the one who was to make sure no one came close."

"Yes, Jem was to stay fairly close as well. However, he got sick to his stomach and had to come back to the stable. I had also told William to stick close to you."

"He wasn't there?"

Thomas shook his head, brought her hand to his mouth, kissed her fingers.

"Maybe he was the one who shot me."

"He could have, but why would he do it? He knows you dislike him, but why would he want you dead? That makes no sense, Meggie. Now, here's some more laudanum for you. Dr. Pritchart says just a few more drops of this will send you off into a very nice place where there isn't any more pain."

"That would be good," she said and drank down the barley water laced with laudanum.

"Will the girl live?"

"Yes," Thomas said to his mother, and walked to the sideboard to pour himself some brandy. "Her name is Meggie, not 'the girl,' and she is your daughter-in-law. Speak of her properly, Mother."

"You should hear what Libby calls her."

"And what would that be?"

"A little ingrate."

Thomas's eyebrow shot up. "Why would Aunt Libby call her that?"

"She believes it is Meggie who is forcing you to have William marry that worthless girl. All because she's a vicar's daughter and is very rigid in her morality, too rigid obviously. Libby also says she likely highly disapproves of her liaison with Lord Kipper, and she has no right."

"I will tell Aunt Libby otherwise," Thomas said. "Surely you corrected her, assured her that I am even more staid than my wife."

"No I did not. I don't wish you to be staid. A bit of wickedness from you wouldn't be amiss, Thomas."

"William has performed enough wickedness for the both of us."

"His is just a boy's wickedness."

"William is a man," he said, then just shrugged. His mother many times baffled him. He said, "Barnacle told me that Lord Kipper was here asking about Meggie."

"He doesn't think William should marry until your sweet wife is able to attend. He is afraid she will die and then poor William would be attending both a funeral and his own wedding, which will be, you must admit, like a second funeral."

Thomas sighed. There was so much to be done here at Pendragon, but none of it was important. The only thing that was important was Meggie. He had to find out who had shot her. He had a very bad feeling about a third attempt. He left his mother, went to the small estate room, and wrote a letter to Meggie's father. It was his right to know there was trouble. It was the hardest letter he'd had to write in his life.

"Open your mouth, Meggie."

Meggie obeyed, but she didn't open her eyes. It was potato soup and it was delicious. She kept eating until Thomas said, "You ate the entire bowl. I'm proud of you. Now, how does your shoulder feel?"

"Not as bad as yesterday."

"Good. There's no infection, no fever. You've got grit and guts, that's what Dr. Pritchart said. You're so strong, he doesn't believe he'll have to coddle you even when you birth our children."

The last was said with a good deal of satisfaction, and Meggie smiled, now opening her eyes to look up at him. She frowned. "You've lost weight, Thomas. You should have eaten some of that soup."

"Now that I know you're not going to heaven before your time, I will get food down my gullet again." He lightly traced his fingertips over her cheeks, her brows, smoothed her hair behind her ears, leaned down, and kissed her.

"You scared me out of a good year of life."

"I was afraid of that. I knew I couldn't die, knew it would flatten you. You feel things so very deeply."

A black brow shot up a good inch. He felt things deeply? "What do you mean?" he asked slowly.

"I mean that if something final happened to me, you

wouldn't recover. You would feel guilty and it would gnaw at you."

"It would be warranted. It's more than that, Meggie. Perhaps you finally realize how important you are to me."

"Oh yes. Possibly as important as you are to me."

She yawned even as those words of hers floated through the still air to his ears. He went still. He wanted to ask her what she meant, but he didn't. He watched as her eyes closed. He listened as her breathing evened into a light sleep. Her thanked God she'd survived.

"It must be luncheon potato soup."

He didn't have any idea what she was talking about. For a moment, he feared she was losing her wits. "What about Mrs. Mullins's soup?"

"It was delicious. Since she still can't manage a tasty dinner, this must be for luncheon. I'm very grateful. Please thank her for me, Thomas."

"I did hear her singing."

"That's it, then. She's come up with an ode to the potato."

32

TWO DAYS LATER Meggie was sitting up in her bed, smiling. A beautiful smile, Thomas thought, balancing a tray on his arms. On that tray were Cook's famous nutty buns, smelling like cinnamon and butter.

Meggie's mouth watered. She even began singing Cook's Nutty Bun song. She clutched the tray to her chest, had one of those nutty buns to her mouth within a second. While she ate, Thomas said, "The wedding will go forward. I have decided that no more time will be wasted. I will carry you downstairs. What do you think?"

"I agree. Get that miserable William on the straight and narrow. I'd do it now, today."

He laughed. "Dearest, if I could get the preacher here, I would, but upon inquiry, he was seeing to a very ill uncle in Cork. On Sunday it will happen, as planned. Now, this afternoon I have invited Jenny MacGraff to come for tea. You will wish to get to know her as she will be your sister-in-law. I think you will like her, Meggie. She's honest and straightforward, a pretty girl with a nice smile and a good heart. The only thing in question is her taste and her good sense, since she succumbed to William. Damn his eyes, if he would only realize it, he's a lucky man."

Meggie yawned, took another bite of the nutty bun. "I

look forward to it. Will you tell your mother and Aunt Libby to be kind to her?"

"I will make suitable threats to keep them reasonably civil."

"William came to see me," Meggie said as she swallowed the last of a nutty bun and reached for another. "He was all sorts of apologetic, told me he'd had to see about a wedding present for Jenny and had trusted Jcm to stay with me and that was why he hadn't been watching over me that day."

"Yes," Thomas said. "That is what he told me as well."

"You don't believe him?"

Thomas rose and began his familiar pacing. Meggie looked forward to the day when he wouldn't have to pace more often than, say, once a month.

"I don't know," he said over his shoulder. "He could have shot you, just like you said to me, but again, why?"

"My lord."

It was Barnacle. For once, there was no look of agony on his face. For once, he was standing straight, his shoulders squared.

Thomas was over to him in an instant. "Oh God, something dreadful has happened. Out with it, Barnacle. I can take it."

"I'm very sorry, my lord, but Teddy MacGraff is here. His daughter is missing."

Thomas just stared down at him blankly. "Jenny is missing? What is this?"

"That is all Mr. MacGraff said, my lord. His daughter is simply missing. This is a conundrum that will unsettle us all. Mrs. Black has done away into one of her silences, something she has not done in a very long time. Everyone knows there is something very wrong here, and now this. Jenny is much liked, my lord."

Thomas merely nodded. "Thank you, Barnacle. Tell Teddy that I will be down shortly and we will immediately start a search."

"Yes, my lord." Barnacle turned toward Meggie, saw

that she was pale, and said, "You just ate some nutty buns and that is good. You must be certain my lady, that you must keep enough heft so it will help me when you walk on my back."

"I will have her walk on your back when she is carrying my child, Barnacle. Then we'll hear you yell."

"Aye, my lord, that you will. I will go stay with Teddy MacGraff."

Thomas nodded, then turned back to his wife. "I want you to remain here in bed, Meggie. I don't want you to rest, I want you to think about this. I am going to find William."

William was standing by the far wall in the drawing room, at least twenty feet between him and his future father-in-law.

Teddy MacGraff yelled so loud a crystal shepherdess nearly shook herself off the mantel. "Where is she, you little puke?"

"I don't know, sir, I swear it on my late father's grave."

"That old blighter? From everything I've heard about him, he was a rank one, the old lord. Kicked you and your mother right out, he did, his lordship and his mother before you. Aye, obviously the old earl was a grand one, he was, and you're his spawn, now aren't you? If I were you I would certainly swear at his bloody grave, but never on it." Teddy wanted to spit, but knew he couldn't, not in the drawing room of Pendragon. He was scared, more scared than he'd been when his wife had struggled so hard to birth Jenny. She hadn't made it the second time, curse him for his lust. Jenny, his pride and joy, now missing. Where? Someone took her, he knew it.

William took a very small step farther away. "Perhaps, sir, she didn't want to marry me, sir. Perhaps she's run away to Dublin."

"I don't think so, William," Thomas said from the doorway. "When did you realize she was gone, Mr. Mac-Graff?"

"She always makes me lunch at exactly twelve. I walk

into our cottage on exactly the last stroke of the village clock and there my lovely Jenny is, smiling and leading me to the table. She wasn't there. There was no food."

"You've spoken to all the neighbors?"

"Of course, my lord. There was no reason for her to leave. She was whistling—whistling—last night, all dreamy-eyed because she was going to marry *him*, that little bastard." Teddy MacGraff took an angry step toward William.

"I didn't harm her, Mr. MacGraff. I swear it to you."

"Where were you last night, William?" Thomas asked mildly.

William looked down at his feet. "I was with Lord Kipper, sir. I fear I was a bit drunk."

"Will Lord Kipper tell me this is the truth?"

"It is the truth, Thomas. I wouldn't hurt Jenny. Really, I wouldn't. I like her."

"All of her clothes were still there, Teddy?"

"Mrs. Ezra said they were, my lord. I had her check Jenny's room and all her gewgaws that belonged to her dear mother. Everything were still there, and in place."

"We will organize a search immediately," Thomas said. "William, you will lead the search."

"What will you do, my lord?"

"I am going to speak to Lord Kipper."

An hour later Thomas was standing in Lord Kipper's drawing room, an elegant eighteenth-century array of gilt and white furnishings that dazzled the eye. Lord Kipper looked right at home amidst the fabulous beauty.

"What William said is true, Thomas. He was with me. I was trying to, er, reconcile him to his fate, not a bad one, I assured him. Perhaps a wife would steady him, that's what I told him."

"Did he get drunk?"

"Just a little. I don't like to see young men drink too much, Thomas, you know that."

"No, I don't."

"Well, it's a fact. William didn't leave until well after

midnight. He returned this morning at about ten o'clock. I had a gift for him, a wedding present."

"What would that be?"

"A lovely epergne that belonged to my mother, to set in the middle of his table. Ah yes, I realize it will be, in fact, in the middle of your table, but it is nonetheless a lovely gift that his bride will cherish."

"That is very kind of you, Niles."

Lord Kipper just nodded. "Where do you think the girl is, Thomas?"

"I don't know."

"Ah, in case you're wondering, my man, Trupper, saw William arrive. He showed him in here. My servants don't lie, Thomas. As you know, Trupper was at Waterloo. The man wouldn't accept a lie from anyone."

Thomas knew it was true. He nodded.

"Where is the epergne?"

"William took it back to Pendragon. It was very well wrapped because he was riding and wanted it protected."

Now that he recalled, Thomas had seen a bundle set just inside the front doors of Pendragon.

Well, damnation.

Thomas returned to Pendragon. Teddy MacGraff said Jenny hadn't been found as yet. The search for her continued, William leading it.

Thomas went to see his wife, who appeared to be deep in thought. He watched her from the doorway for a moment, so grateful that she would be all right, so absolutely grateful to every power that be that she hadn't been killed, that he nearly shouted with it.

He said, swallowing, "Meggie."

She looked up, her brow clearing. "Did you find out anything?"

He shook his head.

She chewed her bottom lip a moment, then whispered, "Could you perhaps come here and hold me for a little while?"

He held her until she lightly shoved against his chest.

He eased her back down against her pillow.

He told her what Lord Kipper had said.

"So William couldn't have anything to do with her disappearance."

"It appears not."

"Who, Thomas? Who could have taken her?"

He shook his head. He knew it was driving her mad. It was driving him mad as well.

Two days later Meggie was reclining on the once gold sofa, now showing as dismal grayish yellow in the sunlight that filled the drawing room, when her father and Mary Rose appeared in the doorway.

She started to jump up, realized if she did, it wouldn't be a good thing, and gave them her biggest smile.

Tysen felt a leap of love and relief at that beautiful smile. She was alive; she would be all right. He'd had to see her, see that smile of hers, to really believe she would be all right. He made it to that ugly sofa in under two seconds. He held his daughter gingerly, then more closely when he realized it was her left shoulder that was bandaged. He kissed her cheek and breathed in the rose scent of her.

"Oh God, I prayed and prayed, Meggie." He kissed her forehead, her nose, hugged her as close as he could without hurting her. "Everything will be fine now. You're coming home with Mary Rose and me."

"I'm very glad to see both of you." Meggie raised her face from her father's neck and smiled at Mary Rose. "Are the boys all well?"

"Oh yes. They can't wait to see you. They hounded us to let them come, but I didn't want to take any chances."

"You look beautiful, Mary Rose."

"Thank you, Meggie, but that's just my outsides. My insides have been a boiling cauldron of mushy fear for you. You're looking much better than I'd thought you would, thank the good Lord."

"Meggie."

Meggie slowly raised her head at the sound of that

voice. Jeremy was standing in the doorway, Thomas behind him. There was absolutely no expression on her husband's face, but those dark eyes of his were as flat as a calm sea.

"Jeremy."

"We are relieved to see you alive."

"I am as well." She got hold of herself. "Now, what are you doing here?" And she cursed the fact that he was here. She wasn't glad to see him. However, the sight of him hadn't made her heart speed up, hadn't made her want to cry with the endless wanting of him. No, seeing him had made her want to frown, and tell him to go away.

It was quite true. She savored the lack of feelings for this man she'd believed she would love forever.

"I wrote them about what happened," Thomas said.

Tysen said, "Thomas also wants us to take you back with us to the vicarage."

"Oh no," Meggie said, separating herself from her father. "Thomas wants me right here. He's just afraid that this person will get me on the third try. I'm not leaving Pendragon."

Thomas said nothing, merely walked to the sideboard.

"Come with me to Fowey then," Jeremy said, and Thomas stiffened but didn't turn. "I have some stable cats, tough and mean, all of them. You can train them to race. If that bores you, then I've some horses that could use your fine touch."

"No, thank you, Jeremy. Pendragon is my home. I'm not leaving my home. Now, how is Charlotte?"

He smiled, splitting his face from nearly ear to ear, and Thomas turned to see it, and imagined Meggie crumbling in pain at that smile, in the knowledge that another woman was responsible for that smile, but she didn't appear to be at all disturbed. He frowned. Yes, she was simply looking at her almost cousin with a slight smile on her own face. It was an affectionate smile, no question about that, but he didn't see anything else.

"She is very pregnant," Jeremy said, and Meggie thought he would rub his hands together, he was that proud of himself. "She tells me she is fat and ugly and I just laugh at her and kiss her."

Meggie turned to her husband, who looked more like a statue than a breathing man, and said, "Thomas, will you laugh and kiss me when I am fat and complain?"

He nearly dropped the brandy bottle. "Yes," he said slowly, "I will. I think you would be safer back at the vicarage, Meggie, or at Fowey."

"That is possible. However, I'm not going anywhere. If you've forgotten, I'm not yet quite well enough to get up to dance with you just yet, so I would imagine that travel is equally beyond me as yet."

She was loyal to her toes, he thought, and poured the gentlemen some brandy. He'd eyed Jeremy Stanton-Greville, seen he was still a handsome man, a man he would probably like in any other circumstance, but not this one. No, he would just as soon stick a sword through his belly, curse him and curse Meggie, who was trying her best to show him that she still didn't love the bastard. Hmm. The fact was, she wasn't acting at all like her heart was in danger of crumbling. Not at all.

When Jeremy walked toward him to get his brandy, Thomas saw that he limped. He supposed that he'd noticed before, but it hadn't registered in his brain. Now he wondered why, and hoped it was from nothing that a female would consider vastly romantic.

"Meggie, love," Tysen said, stroking her hair, "we all think that you should come back home, just for a little while, until all this is resolved."

Meggie looked into her father's beloved face, then at Mary Rose, who was nearly wringing her hands she was so very worried for her, and smiled. "I love you both for coming here. I will be fine. Thomas will make certain that I will remain fine." She looked over at him, standing there so still, holding a glass of brandy in each of his hands. One for her father and one for himself, she supposed.

"Won't I, Thomas?"

Slowly Thomas shook his head. "I think you should go back to Glenclose-on-Rowan, Meggie. You will be well enough by next week. If you wish, you can stay at Bowden Close. The servants will take very good care of you."

Then Meggie looked straight at Jeremy. She was aware that Thomas had stiffened. She smiled at her almost cousin. "Tell me something, Jeremy, and tell me the truth. Would Charlotte leave you?"

"If I told her to, she would," Jeremy said, and it was said with arrogance, those words. He sounded infinitely obnoxious.

Meggie just grinned at him. "Give over, Jeremy. You can't pull that ruse on me anymore. The truth now."

Jeremy gave it up and said, without hesitation, "She would stand beside me and fight to the death."

Meggie said, "Good for her. You know, truth be told, I did hate her. I wanted to remove her from England entirely, perhaps even smack her in the jaw before I had her kidnapped aboard a ship bound for far-distant places. But now she doesn't seem so bad at all. I dare say I will even come to like her a lot, particularly if she's as fierce as you say she is.

"When you and she visit us here at Pendragon, Jeremy, I dare say we will have tea and I will tell her about the racing cat competition we're going to hold here, just as soon as all this mess is cleared up."

"Perhaps," Thomas said slowly, never taking his dark eyes off his wife, "you will have some entrants in the competition."

"You never know," Jeremy said, shook his head at Meggie, and laughed.

"I'm not leaving, Papa. However, I would very much like for you to remain here for a while. With all of you here, why, what could possibly happen to me? Now, I cannot wait for you to meet my mother-in-law, not to mention William and Aunt Libby. Oh dear, Jenny is missing. Nothing is going well at the moment." And Meggie lowered her face into her hands and sobbed.

Thomas handed both snifters of brandy to his father-in-law and gathered his wife onto his lap. He lay his cheek against her hair and rocked her. "Everything will be all right, Meggie, you will see. We will find Jenny."

There was no sign of Jenny MacGraff by dark that night. The search was called off until dawn the next morning. In the meantime, Thomas sent Paddy to question everyone in the village. Surely someone must have seen something. Jenny couldn't simply have disappeared.

33

REVEREND TYSEN SHERBROOKE, Baron Barthwaite of Kildrummy in Scotland, looked at Thomas's mother, his head cocked ever so slightly, and said in his deep elegant voice, one brow arched, "I beg your pardon, ma'am, I am not exactly sure I heard what you said."

"I said, my lord, that your daughter—well, perhaps it would be for the best if your darling daughter did go back to England with you, don't you think? It simply isn't safe for her to remain here, now is it? No, she'd be far better off away from Pendragon."

Compared to what his mother had first said, this was a capitulation indeed, Thomas thought, turning an admiring eye to Meggie's father. Just maybe her father could turn Madeleine into a diplomat. That thought would surely give him a headache.

"Evidently not," Mary Rose said, ready to hit the old harridan in the nose even though Tysen had managed to get her to change her tune quickly enough. "However, I am very certain that you, ma'am, have made her welcome."

"I would welcome her even more excessively if she would just get herself pregnant."

"Quite a feat that would be," Thomas said, rising. "Now, Mother, I don't think you should embarrass Meggie's father in exactly this way. You need to learn to pick your moments. Until that happens, why don't you sip your tea until it is time for you to partner Mr. Jeremy Stanton-Greville in whist. I understand all three of our guests are superb players. You are always saying that you would like some competition. You have it. Sir," he added to Tysen, "thank you for coming. Now, I will bid you all good night and see that Meggie is settled in."

Thomas nodded to his three guests and took himself upstairs. He was whistling when he went into the White Room to see Meggie lying on her back, her hair spread on the pillow, lace and satin to her chin, her eyes closed.

He sat quietly in a chair beside her, crossed his legs, and thoughtfully began tapping his fingers as he looked at her face.

"Stop that."

He'd thought she was asleep and jumped at the sound of her voice. "How do you know what I'm doing?" he asked.

"You're watching me."

"It gives me great pleasure to watch you, Meggie." He paused a moment, continued to tap those long fingers of his together slowly, saying thoughtfully after a few moments, "When I arrived in Glenclose-on-Rowan to assume my father's responsibilities, to fit myself into my new title, the last thing on my mind was taking a wife. However, it seems that when I saw you, everything just seemed to fall into place."

Her heart was pounding, slow deep strokes. She didn't say a word.

"The first time I saw you, you were peeling your little brother's sticky fingers off your skirt. Evidently you would give him candy to keep him quiet during your father's service."

"I remember. It was a new gown. Poor Rory, he was so dismayed that he'd upset me. Oh goodness, then he tried to lick the sticky stuff off the skirt."

"Yes, and you laughed and laughed, held him close, and the sun burst upon my head."

Meggie's heart felt suddenly so very full that she

wanted to cry. She wanted to leap from the bed and tell him he was a wonderful man, that she would never leave him, that he was hers, forever. But that meant telling him straight in his beautiful dark eyes that she loved him. She wouldn't lie, not about something so utterly important as that. But she knew she wanted him, wanted him to be happy, with her. She knew he was as fine a man as her father was, as her uncles were. He made her wild—no question about that. But the other—that heart-wrenching excitement when she saw Jeremy for that first time so very long ago in London, that soul-wrenching near-pain when he'd smiled at her—no, she'd never felt that with Thomas. She'd never felt it with anyone but Jeremy.

On the other hand, she hadn't felt any of that heart-pounding, near-nausea, light-headed, utterly out-of-control excitement when Jeremy had walked into the drawing room this afternoon. Not a bit of it. Nothing at all. She said to her husband, "Thank you for making me remember that wonderful moment. I also thank you for writing to my father and for telling me that the sun burst upon your head."

"You're welcome on all three counts. I hate this, but I really do think you should return with them, Meggie. Actually, I'm here to talk you into it."

"Very well, I'm not stupid. I don't wish to be shot again; maybe the next time it would be just my luck to be low tide. I agree. I will do as everyone wishes."

"I don't believe you," he said slowly, staring at her. "You would never agree to leave me."

Meggie laughed. "It's about time you believed that down to the soles of your big feet. You're perfectly right. But don't you see? It is very easy to agree. By the time I am well enough to travel, all this will be resolved."

"That is another thing about you—you are an optimist beyond anything I have ever seen."

"No, listen, Thomas. The person responsible for all this misery, he or she must be becoming quite frantic—nothing has worked. I'm alive and three more people are here to watch over me. I have this feeling that something is going to happen very soon simply because this person will burst if he doesn't try to finish it. Now, come to bed, Thomas, if, that is, you can swear to me that there isn't murder being committed in the drawing room."

"Actually, there might be, depending on how competitive your father and mother are when playing whist."

"Oh dear. Your mother is partnering Jeremy?"

"Yes."

"They will win; my parents don't stand a chance. You see, Papa and Mary Rose will keep laughing and comparing hands and gossiping about this and that. It drives serious players quite mad."

"I don't like the sound of that. My mother is very serious about her journals and about whist. What about Jeremy?"

"He's a killer at whist. I do hope that Charlotte plays well."

She sounded like Jeremy was nothing more than an acquaintance, perhaps a distant relation. It made him feel very good indeed. He said, his voice light, easy, "Isn't it nice that we're not involved in any of it?"

"Very nice." She smiled at him.

Thomas eyed her one last time, rose and stripped off his clothes. When he was naked, he walked back toward the bed, in truth, thinking about where they would search tomorrow at dawn for Jenny MacGraff and also trying to come up with some way to draw out the killer and stop the madness.

"Oh my."

Those two very short words brought him back immediately to the fact that he was standing naked and that his wife was staring at his groin. He looked down at himself. Predictably, he was hard as the peach pit he'd seen Barnacle throw across the entrance hall for Miss Crittenden to chase down this afternoon. A training technique her ladyship would surely approve, Barnacle had told him.

Thomas took a step back. He stayed hard, got even harder. He was very pleased that his wife admired his body. He was now so hard he hurt. He wanted to weep

as he said, "You're not well, Meggie. Forget all your lust-
ful thoughts. To help you get a grip on your self, remember that your father, who just happens to be a vicar, is
seated downstairs in our drawing room."

She smiled at him, a smile he didn't trust for a minute.
Well, damnation, who cared?

She said, "You're right. At least you will hold me, will
you not?"

Oh yes, he would certainly hold her, dammit.

When she was settled against his side, her breath warm
against his flesh, no, her breath was really quite hot now,
he felt her hand glide down his belly.

Oh God. "Meggie, you really don't want to do that."

"Do be quiet, my lord," she said, and he nearly wept
again at the sound of those wonderful words of hers.

He had to be noble, he had to stop her. It nearly killed
him, but he said, "But you're still not well enough, you're
not—"

"It's just my hand, Thomas. I won't hurt myself."

"All right."

"I've been thinking quite a bit of taking advantage of
you," and she did.

Before he fell asleep, Thomas found himself thinking
for the first time that his mother could be the one who
wanted Meggie dead. She could be determined and vicious, he'd seen it too many times over the years. Her
mind didn't really work like other people's did. She went
to extremes, both in her speech and in her actions. But
why would she hate Meggie enough to kill her? And if
she did have a reason, why then, who would she have
hired to shoot Meggie off the cliff?

No answer.

At the end of the next day there was still no sign of Jenny
MacGraff. No one believed she had run away to Dublin.
Everyone believed she was dead. Everyone believed that
someone had killed her.

It became clear that everyone believed it was William

Malcombe who had lured Jenny from the MacGraff cottage and killed her.

Since Meggie was still weak, Thomas carried her to the drawing room, where his mother served everyone afternoon tea.

It was a quiet group. Every few minutes Madeleine said, "I had rotten cards last night. You, Vicar, never should have won."

"That is indeed true," Tysen agreed pleasantly for the third time, giving his hostess his best social smile.

Mary Rose, her beautiful red hair corking out about her head, was pacing, something Thomas did with great regularity, more now since all the bad things had started happening. Every once in a while Mary Rose paused, looked at Meggie, who was, in truth, still on the pale side, still suffering some pain in her shoulder, and still refusing to take more laudanum. Mary Rose looked nearly desperate. Thomas knew the feeling well.

He also had finally come up with an idea.

Mary Rose turned toward Lord Kipper when he came into the drawing room. He said, standing on the threshold, "Barnacle seems to have taken a brief conge from his post at the front door, Thomas, so I allowed myself to come in."

"Welcome, Niles," Thomas said. "You are just in time for tea."

Lord Kipper opened his mouth, doubtless to say something amusing, when he stopped cold. He stared at Mary Rose, who was standing with her back to the window. The afternoon sun was pouring in, making her hair look like fire.

"By God you are beautiful," he said slowly, and strode toward her. "Who are you? Where have you been? I—"

Tysen rose and stepped in front of his wife. "Excuse me, sir, she is my wife. I am Lord Barthwaite, Meggie's father."

Lord Kipper came to a complete and very chagrinned halt in the middle of the drawing room.

"Ah, your wife. I see."

Meggie, who had never before heard her father introduce himself by his Scottish title, gaped. Here was her father, facing down another man who very much wanted to poach on his preserves. Every bit of Sherbrooke arrogance sounded in his voice, every ounce of Sherbrooke blood in him was ready to boil. Her father, she realized, was ready to take Lord Kipper apart. It was an amazing thing.

Mary Rose suddenly leapt into action. She held out her hand. "I am Lady Barthwaite, sir. And you are?"

Thomas said, "This is Lord Kipper, everyone. Niles, you will doubtless meet Meggie's almost cousin a bit later. He is right now at the stables, eyeing my stock."

It was then that Lord Kipper noticed Libby was there, seated quietly some twelve feet away. She didn't look at all happy with him. Actually she looked ready to shoot him. Lord Kipper was a man of great experience, a particularly fine thing when, upon rare occasion, he made a sterling gaff, such as now. He didn't pause a moment, didn't appear the least embarrassed. He swept down upon Libby, took her hand, caressed her fingers, lightly touched his fingertips to her lips.

"He is amazing," Meggie said to the room at large.

"Of course," Madeleine said. "What would you expect?"

When finally everyone was drinking their tea, Thomas cleared his throat and said, "Mother, why do you think someone wants Meggie dead?"

The sound of sudden silence was deafening. Everyone froze in place and stared blankly at Thomas.

Thomas didn't look away from his mother. She slowly set her cup back onto its saucer. "I have thought about it," she said at last, the look in her eyes very sharp, very cold, "as I'm sure everyone else has as well. I think it must be a man who followed her here from her home. He is jealous because she chose Thomas over him. It is this man who is now enraged because she won't leave you, my son. He wants her dead. He is deranged. Ask her, my son, who this man is."

Thomas said, "Meggie, who is this man?"

"I haven't seen him, Thomas. If he had followed me, surely I would have seen him. Also, wouldn't a stranger stick out like a Stonehenge boulder around here? No, it can't be him."

"She is mocking me, and I won't have it."

"Forgive me, ma'am," Meggie said, "you're right. That wasn't well done of me. However, there is no man."

"Humph. What about this Jeremy Stanton-Greville who plays whist very well but had rotten cards, just as I did last night?"

"No, ma'am. It isn't Jeremy. He's quite in love with his wife."

Thomas felt positively mellow at that.

"Aunt Libby," Thomas said, "why do you think someone is trying to kill Meggie?"

"Madeleine is the one," Libby said with a voice filled with spite, "but she's torn about it. She doesn't want to be replaced, particularly by a little twit like Meggie, who's always laughing, and is young and beautiful. However, she also wants you to have an heir. She is betwixt and between. Perhaps Meggie is still alive because Madeleine is uncertain about what she really wants."

"You witch!" Madeleine yelled, leaping up from her chair. "You betraying cow! I want you to leave Pendragon this very instant, your murdering son with you! You called me a pernicious tart, and now this! Out, out, I say!"

"Actually," Libby said, "I called you a pernicious *old* tart."

"This," Thomas said to his wife, an eyebrow elevated upward a good inch, "isn't turning out to be quite what I expected."

Tysen Sherbrooke held up a beautiful hand and said in his deep compelling vicar's voice that brought immediate silence, all eyes now on him, "I think it could be very helpful, Thomas. I would like as well to hear what everyone has to say. Lord Kipper, why do you think someone is trying to kill my daughter?"

Lord Kipper walked to the fireplace, where he leaned

his shoulders against the mantel. He looked immaculate in his riding clothes, those black riding boots of his so shiny he could see his face. He looked as calm as the sea at dawn, and utterly beautiful. He said, "I believe it to be someone who perhaps despises Thomas, someone who wishes him ill, someone who knows that if he kills Thomas, he will be discovered, thus he is trying to kill Thomas's wife, in order to have Thomas blamed for it. That is the most likely. Perhaps it is revenge this man wants. Even though he is very young, Thomas has certainly made enemies, inevitable since he is ruthless and successful, particularly in his shipping endeavors."

Tysen said, "Can you think of anyone in your business dealings who would wish you ill, Thomas? Who would hurt my daughter rather than you? As punishment or revenge?"

"No," Thomas said.

Tysen turned to William, who was standing still as a stick of furniture against the far wall, obviously wanting to go unnoticed. He said, "What do you think, William?"

"I don't know, sir. But I do believe that it must have something to do with Jenny's disappearance. Don't you think?"

"It seems likely," Tysen said slowly, "since everything is happening at the same time."

"Perhaps this someone," William said, more forcefully now, the worry plain on his face, "didn't want Thomas to marry, but since he did, now he's trying to get rid of Meggie. In my case, he doesn't want me to marry either, thus he's taken Jenny away. But who would want both Thomas and me not to be married?"

"That," Thomas said, giving his half-brother a look of respect, "is a very good question."

"I agree with William," Meggie said, and that set both Madeleine and Libby off. "Someone wants two unmarried men in the house. But why?"

"Perhaps the two mothers," William said, and took three more steps away from his own mother. Predictably, voices went up, tempers rose and tangled, a teacup smashed to the floor.

Once again Tysen said in a voice of honey and iron, "That is quite enough. Thomas has given us a lot to consider. I suggest we do just that." He paused a moment, looked briefly at his son-in-law, and said, "One of the persons in this room is very deeply involved in this. I wonder which one of you it is."

There were dark mutterings.

The party broke up quickly after that.

34

That Night Meggie's shoulder hurt, to be expected Dr. Pritchart had assured her, but still Thomas was worried. But he didn't say anything, simply poured a tincture of laudanum in some barley water and handed it to her. He didn't move until she'd emptied the glass.

He held her until she eased into sleep.

It was very late, dark clouds obscuring the quarter moon that cast a watery light through the window when the cloth slammed down over his mouth. It took him only an instant to realize that it wasn't a dream. He lurched up, ready to fight, but something struck him hard on the head and he slumped back. The cloth was back, covering his nose and mouth. He was aware, on some level, that he was breathing in a sickeningly sweet odor that seemed to fill his lungs, that snaked to his belly, and that odor, even more than the blow, sent him deeper and deeper until he knew no more.

Meggie felt heavy, as if her body weighed more than one of the boulders on the Pendragon beach and someone was sitting on top of it. She didn't think she could move. She wanted to move. She managed to lift a hand, moan, and then her eyes flew open.

She felt light-headed and dizzy, a bitter taste in her mouth. At first she thought she was simply waking up in her own bed. She quickly realized she was wrong.

She didn't want to open her eyes, but she did, finally, and looked up into a man's face. At first she didn't recognize him. Then she said slowly, "The last time I saw you, you were lying on your kitchen floor, blood on your head and flour all over your apron."

"Ye're right smart, yer ladyship. Aye, the Grakers got me, now didn't they?"

"You're Bernard Leach of the Hangman's Noose at St. Agnes."

"Good memory in yer smart head. I remember thinking how purty ye were, and all fresh and innocent since ye'd been married jest the day before."

"We were going to stay at your inn. But it was deserted, just one lit candle in a front room. Thomas and I discovered your wife murdered, hanged. There was no one else there, just you, lying unconscious on the kitchen floor. It was the Grakers who did it, you said, then and you said it again. Then the next day you disappeared and so did the stable lad. Thomas and I remained with Squire Billings, but we couldn't find out anything more. Why are you here? Where are we?"

"Aye, it was the Grakers what brought ye here," Bernard said, and laughed, deep in his throat, and that laugh led quickly to a cough, a nasty watery cough that made Maggie's insides crawl.

"Them Grakers—bothersome little pixies, the lot of them. Don't they travel a lot, eh?" And he laughed some more. He started to cough again, stopped his laughter fast.

He looked even skinnier than he had before, his gray hair even more tufted and grizzled, so dirty and lank with oil it was matted to his head. He wasn't wearing a huge white apron now, but rough homespun that bagged on him. He wiped his hand over his mouth, trying to catch his breath, and Meggie saw a streak of blood on his palm. She said, "You're sick, Mr. Leach."

"Aye, that's as may be, but at least I'm not dead, not like ye will be, my little lady. It shouldn't o' been high tide, but it was. Then ye should o' broke yer back when ye hit the water. Bloody hell, that bullet should have laid ye out, but it didn't, now did it? Yer too lucky by far, ye are. Funny how I never considered high tide. A mistake, sure enough. Aye, I should have shot ye right through yer heart, but I didn't manage it. Nothing went right. Nothing seems to be going right for me these days. It's a right puzzle."

"My husband has known you all his life. Why would you wish to harm him by killing me?"

"Well, ye see, it's like this—"

"Do be quiet, Bernard."

Meggie looked beyond Bernard Leach's right shoulder to see Lord Kipper standing just inside the doorway, his arms crossed over his chest, wearing riding clothes, holding a single lit candle in one hand.

"Eh, she woke up, milord."

"Yes, I see that she did. You may go keep watch, Bernard. Oh, by the way, did you kill Thomas?"

Bernard Leach grunted, not looking at Lord Kipper.

"Did you, Bernard? While he was sleeping? While it was so easy since he was helpless, at your mercy?"

Bernard Leach darted a look at Lord Kipper, then his eyes slid away again. He was shaking his head, back and forth. "Oh no, my lord, I jest couldn't do that. Known him all his life, little Thomas. A fine boy, an excellent man. Only her, my lord, only her, and here she is. Not Thomas, I'll never kill Thomas. I'll jest not do it."

Lord Kipper sighed deeply. "We will speak of this later, Bernard. Go keep guard."

Thomas was alive. Meggie was so relieved, so very grateful to Bernard Leach that she would have given him everything she owned. Because he'd refused to kill Thomas even though Lord Kipper had ordered him to.

Bernard Leach nodded and took himself out of the room. It was a single room, rude, bare boards forming the walls and ceiling. A cottage of some sort, likely abandoned given the filth she now saw. It was dawn and gray light was seeping through the dirty windows. Years upon years of dirt.

"Where is this place?"

"Actually, you are in a storeroom just behind my stables. No, don't think you'll be rescued. No one ever comes here, particularly the men searching for Jenny MacGraff. Why would they? I am Lord Kipper, you know."

"Why do you want both Thomas and me dead?"

Lord Kipper shrugged. "I realized yesterday when Thomas and your father went around to ask each of us why we believed someone was trying to kill you that everything was collapsing about me. Someone, sooner now rather than later, would realize it had to be me."

"Someone?"

"Yes, Libby, of course. Even though I have her in my bed again, I knew I couldn't completely trust her to keep quiet if she did realize what I was doing. She's got an odd streak of honor. It only shows itself on rare occasion, but I really couldn't take the chance."

"I don't understand. Why did you think Libby in particular would realize the truth?"

He only smiled at her. "It's been a very long night, a night that has kept me quite on edge. I'm really not used to that. But the night is over and soon all this will be as well."

Meggie heard a noise. It was a soft moan, just a soft whisper really, the sound of someone barely conscious, moving around just a bit. Meggie tried to sit up, but her shoulder hurt very badly and she fell back. The dizziness hit her again, hard, made her feel as if she were floating for a moment. When the dizziness finally eased, when she saw him clearly again, Lord Kipper no longer looked remotely beautiful. His eyes looked dark and flat, he looked a bit mad. Lord Kipper, the person responsible for all this misery. At least it wasn't either of the mothers, thank God.

She licked her dry lips. "Who was that?"

"That was Jenny MacGraff."

Thank God was all she could think, *Thank God*. Jenny was still alive. "Why did you take her? Why is she here?

Did Jenny discover what you were doing and you were afraid she would tell everyone?"

Lord Kipper laughed. He pinched out the candle because the room was filled with the dirty light filtered through the filthy windows. "Jenny MacGraff is incapable of finding out anything, as you mean it. No, she is merely a simple merchant's daughter. She knows nothing, she is nothing. Nothing at all. Well, she is reasonably pretty and clean, her brain not too dulled by her breeding, and that does surprise me. No, she didn't discover anything. I merely wished to kill both of you together, when all the damned searching was finally over. I even plan to bury you together. I think that is quite fitting."

No, she wouldn't let his words freeze her, terrify her into madness, she wouldn't, but the paralyzing fear was there, deep inside her, taking hold, growing, getting stronger. Thomas knew she was missing. He would figure it out. She just had to stay alive. She had to use her wits. What were wits anyway? She had to try. Meggie drew a deep breath, said, "I don't understand, Lord Kipper. Why the two of us? Was William right? For some reason, you don't want either of the men of the house to be married?"

"William was close enough, actually too close, which surprised me, and perhaps, even remotely worried me. Yes, it was just a matter of time until the truth was out. But now, your time, my dear, has finally come to an end. As has Jenny MacGraff's."

Thomas wanted to kill the man who was shaking him so hard he knew his brains would fly right out of his head. He knew it was a man; the bastard had big hands and he was strong. Nausea rose in his throat, momentarily choking him. His belly was on fire. And then there was the damned voice that nearly sent him back into oblivion— too loud, too loud, that voice.

"Thomas, dammit, wake up! Someone struck you. Oh please, Thomas, open your eyes!"

Finally, giving it up, Thomas managed to open his eyes. He stared up at William.

"Stop pounding me or I will kill you."

"I have to pound you. Wake up. You must wake up, Thomas. Now."

Reason seeped back into his brain. He said, his voice raw, his words slurred, "What's wrong?" What the devil had happened to him?

"You're what's wrong, dammit. There's blood on your head. There's this cloth on the floor that smells like something vile and sweet—some sort of drug. No, Thomas, get yourself together. Meggie's gone. Do you want me to get Reverend Sherbrooke?"

"Yes. No. Just a moment. Help me sit up. Oh God, Meggie. She's gone? How is that possible?"

"It's the truth. She's gone, I just told you that."

His head ached like the very devil, but now who cared? Nothing mattered but Meggie. Gone? Someone had come into the White Room, struck him, and taken her? Then he knew, of course. It was because of yesterday at tea, because he'd scared the person responsible into acting immediately.

"Damnation. What time is it?"

"It's just past dawn. I was awake, just couldn't go back to sleep. I've been thinking and thinking about all this, and I wanted to see if you were awake so we could discuss it. God, Thomas, and here you were unconscious and bloody and Meggie was gone. What shall we do?"

"I'm going to dress. Get Meggie's father. Quickly, William."

William was out the door on a dead run, slamming it behind him. Thomas managed to pull himself out of the bed. He stood there a moment, realized he had blood on his head and face, and walked to the commode. He gingerly washed the wound with the cold water in the basin. At least now the blood was clotted and wouldn't run down his face anymore.

He closed his eyes a moment, Meggie's laughing face in his mind's eye. Oh God—she'd been taken, right out of their bed, and it was his fault that it happened. He hadn't been vigilant, taking not a single precaution, even though he'd known he'd stirred the viper's nest. Maybe she was already dead, maybe shot again, hurled over the cliffs. No, no, dammit. He had to stop it. She was alive, he knew it to his soul.

Why hadn't the person killed or taken him as well? Had the person who'd struck him believed him dead and just left him be in the bed? Why take Meggie?

Thank God William had come.

A few moments later the door burst open and Tysen Sherbrooke ran into the room, Mary Rose and William at his heels. Thomas had just fastened his breeches. He sat down to pull on his boots. He said, cold, calm, in control now, "I was struck down while I was sleeping. Meggie was taken. During our afternoon tea yesterday, someone said something that was close enough to the truth, so that person was forced to act immediately. Now, I think I know who it was and why he's doing this. I think William does, too. Let's go see my mother and Aunt Libby."

"No, Thomas, I don't know, not really."

"I think someplace deep inside you, William, you know. It's simply too painful to admit it. Everything is going to come clear soon enough." He took his half-brother's hand. "It will be all right. No matter what the truth is, I won't let you stand alone. Trust me."

William looked pale as death; slowly he nodded.

Tysen awakened Jeremy, helped Mary Rose fasten her gown, then herded the three of them to the dining room. Barnacle, Cook, and Mrs. Black were there as well, lined up like troops ready to be deployed.

Thomas said without preamble, "Aunt Libby, who is William's father?"

"His father was the earl of Lancaster, Thomas. He is a Malcombe, just as you are a Malcombe. The only pity here is that he is the younger, not you. He could have been the earl, not you, but Madeleine came along too quickly. That was an impertinent question. You will apologize."

"Mother, it's too late now," William said quietly and laid his hand on her shoulder. He was ready to face it now, had to be ready. He added, his voice thick, "Mother, please, it's time for the truth. If for no one else, then for me."

"My dear boy, Thomas is lying. Your father is the earl of Lancaster."

"Aunt Libby," Thomas said patiently, "you know that neither William nor I in any way resemble the earl of Lancaster. Both of us look more like our mothers than anyone else. It is up to you, ma'am. Who is William's father, Aunt Libby? Tell us now. Tell William now. There's really not much time. Meggie's gone and we must find her before it is too late."

She stubbornly shook her head.

"Madam," Tysen said, rising from his chair. "My daughter is in grave danger. You will tell us the truth now or I will do something I will probably regret. Now, madam, the truth, if you please."

William said very quietly, pain and dread mixed in his voice, "It is Lord Kipper, isn't it, Mother?"

She turned utterly white, froze in her place, her eyes fastened on her folded hands.

"Lord Kipper," Tysen repeated slowly.

"Yes, William," Thomas said, "I believe he is your father and that explains everything, now doesn't it?"

Madeleine said, "But William is not beautiful like Lord Kipper is. What a wretched thing. How very unfair."

"But, Thomas," William said, ignoring her, "I was with him. I swear it to you, when Jenny was taken. That's why I believed I must be wrong. You see, I was beginning to wonder why he gave me so much attention, wonder why he always inquired so closely into what I wanted to do, how I felt about things. He was acting like—a man who was related to me, like a man who wanted to claim me somehow, to teach me, to guide me."

"Like a father," Thomas said.

"Yes, and it scared me to my toes. That's why I came to your bedchamber early this morning. I knew I couldn't wait. But I wanted you to tell me it was nonsense, I really did."

"Yes," Thomas said, "I know Lord Kipper was with you. That just means that he hired someone else to help him."

Libby said very quietly, "I didn't want to believe it, truly, I didn't. I forced myself not to think about it. When Jenny MacGraff disappeared, I was relieved, pleased that she was gone, that she wouldn't drag your name down by marrying you. I wanted her to have run off to Dublin. I prayed it was true. I was lying to myself. And look at what has happened. I'm very sorry." She looked up at her son, closed her hand over his. "I'm very, very sorry."

William was shaking his head, not looking at his mother.

Libby said, "Niles has had Bernard Leach here for a good long time now."

Thomas said, cocking his head to the side, his voice puzzled, "But Lord Kipper bedded Marie Leach, he said so, said that Bernard was a sot and a clod. It was obvious to me that Lord Kipper had nothing but contempt for Bernard Leach. Why would he let Bernard stay with him?"

Libby shrugged. "I saw Bernard. I wasn't supposed to, but I did, out by the stables one morning when I was leaving. Why was he there? I don't know."

"He was there as Lord Kipper's tool," Thomas said. "That's it, then. We know enough. William, sir, Jeremy, are you ready?"

35

THOMAS WOULD COME, her father with him. Perhaps even Jeremy. She had to keep herself alive, just had to. She remembered she'd sworn to Thomas she would never leave him. She wasn't about to break that promise.

Lord Kipper had fallen silent. He was standing over Jenny MacGraff, a thoughtful expression on his face. He looked suddenly vicious. She watched him lift one of his riding boots and kick her in the ribs.

Meggie saw red, reared up onto her elbows. It hurt, but she didn't care. "You bastard, don't do that again. Damn you, you miserable coward!"

Lord Kipper ignored her. He said, both his voice and his expression utterly dismissive, and listened to Jenny moan, "She is so very common. I could not allow her to marry William. A travesty, that's what it would have been."

Meggie saw that Jenny was lying on her side, huddled in on herself on the bare floor. She was slight, her hair pale, her skin very white. She was very young and very pretty. She was also alarmingly pale. She was wearing a simple muslin gown that was twisted about her knees, woolen stockings, and one black slipper. The other one had come off her foot and was lying several feet away from her.

"No," Lord Kipper said, his voice meditative now, as

if he were speaking to himself, "I could not allow her to marry William." Then he looked over at Meggie. "Don't you understand yet? This merchant's daughter couldn't be the next countess of Lancaster. Any fool in his right mind would realize what a bitter jest that would be. Thomas forced my hand when he ordered William to marry her on Sunday. I had to do something, and so I did. And then yesterday at the damned tea party your husband set up—William was so very close. And I saw that everyone else was now thinking about that. Everything would soon come down on my head and I couldn't have that, not until I'd fixed everything."

Meggie said slowly, "You are willing to kill three innocent people because you want William to be the next earl of Lancaster? Blessed Hell, why would you care who is the earl of Lancaster? It's nothing to do with you."

"What a stupid question, Meggie. Haven't you yet realized that I am William's father?"

Meggie said nothing for a full minute, then quietly, nodding slowly, "You should be ever so pleased then that he got Jenny pregnant. He also got another girl in Glenclose-on-Rowan pregnant. He is just like you, isn't he? Like father like son. Do you hate the women you have despoiled?"

"Don't be ridiculous. Women are women, they are to be used, to be enjoyed. All of you are silly creatures, at least most of you are. As for my son, in that William much likes to bed woman, yes, he is like me, actually like practically all men, truth be told. Some of us are masters at it, most aren't. Unfortunately, William is one of the latter. He does not have my charm or my brain, but I will teach him. Surely he will improve once he knows that I am his father, once he knows what I have given him. Yes, once William knows that the old earl of Lancaster was so obsessed, so gripped with the belief that he could not trust a woman to bear his son and not another man's, he will thank me, he will bless fate that gave me him as his father and not that miserable old man. Interesting, isn't it? The old earl sewed the seeds of his own destruction. His father was the same way, I understand."

"Evidently, the old earl was right not to trust Libby, wasn't he?"

"He shouldn't have distrusted her, she never gave him a reason. Our brief liaison was discreet, William the result. No, Titus Malcombe was a mad, stupid man. At least I had Libby come here to Pendragon after he booted her and William out. I've looked after both her and William over the years. I expect William will be so relieved that Lord Lancaster isn't his father that he will fall upon my neck." Lord Kipper grinned at that thought, and for just an instant, there was a warmth in his eyes. "I will bring him to live with me for a while, to complete his education."

"The earl of Lancaster was Thomas's father, wasn't he?"

Lord Kipper shrugged, eyes dead again. "I know that Madeleine played him false one time. Was he Thomas's father or was his father Madeleine's lover? I don't know. I don't really care. Yes, William will learn everything from me, his real father. He is still very young. He will not disappoint me."

Meggie said, "If he doesn't learn, will you kill him, too?"

"Shut up, you stupid girl. You paint me as a monster, but I'm not. I want my son to have what should be his. I've been planning this for a very long time. Once he is the earl of Lancaster, I will marry Libby and adopt William, so that when I die, he will also gain my title and lands. No one will ever know that he is a bastard. It will be our little family secret."

"Is William, I wonder, bereft of any sort of human decency, like you, his father?"

He stepped toward her, his fist raised, then stopped. He shrugged. "It doesn't matter what you think, what you say. I merely do what I must, no more, no less. Actually, as it turned out, it wasn't such a bad thing that Thomas met you and fell in love with you—ah, that's a stupidity, isn't it? This love business that doesn't exist in this benighted world. But that's not at all to the point. You brought him a splendid dowry—that is what's important—and that will mean all the more money for William and his heirs."

"I will wager you that right this minute Thomas knows you are the evil behind all this. He is right now searching for you."

"No, you're wrong, not yet, not yet. But it will be close. I will mourn your loss, Meggie, you may count on that. Yes, I must move quickly now. I'm sorry for your death, but in the long run you're not really important." He saw that she was shaking her head at him, that she was so pale, she already looked dead. Such a pity, but no choice. "Listen to me," he said. "I could not allow you to have a child, and the good Lord knows that would certainly be the outcome since the two of you are consumed with lust for each other. And imagine, you a vicar's daughter. Yes, you having a child, that would have complicated matters far too much. You must die now, Meggie, common Jenny with you.

"Thomas, well, I suppose I myself must see to his removal since Bernard doesn't have the guts to. Perhaps I will let him go easily, an accident in his curricle, perhaps. That will do nicely. Yes, Bernard is a coward, when all is said and done."

Talk, she had to keep talking, slow down time itself. "What really happened to Marie?"

"Ah, I forgot that you and Thomas were both there, witnesses to our little drama. It was I who had to string Marie up by her neck after that fool Bernard had killed her when she dished out too many insults on his head—not that he didn't deserve all her rage—the lazy sod. No, he strangled her, then didn't have the guts to hang her up. He cried and carried on the whole time. Then when I saw the carriage stop outside the inn, I hit him on the head and left him on the kitchen floor for you to find. Imagine, it was Thomas and his new bride who walked in the inn. I have smiled a bit over that."

"You decided to blame it on the Grakers."

"That is what Bernard wanted to do. I told him no one could be so stupid as to believe any of that nonsense, but he insisted, said the legends claimed the Grakers hanged their enemies. The next day he was evidently consumed by guilt and got himself blithering drunk, and spewed it all out, luckily only to that wretched stable boy, and he knew he had to escape, and so he did. He came here. I will remove Bernard when all this is done and over."

"What happened to the stable lad?"

Lord Kipper shrugged. "Bernard strangled him and buried him behind the stable, at least that is what he told me. Now, enough, Meggie. It's time for you to say farewell to this life. Your father is a vicar, a man of God. I assume he raised you in his beliefs. Do you believe in God, Meggie? Do you believe in a splendid afterlife for all those who are worthy?"

"Yes."

"I'm glad you will have some comfort. Now, I will shoot cleanly this time, and then it will be over."

"I don't believe you. It was you who killed Marie, wasn't it, not poor Bernard."

"No, she pushed him over the edge, finally. Now, you're trying to distract me, and it is a paltry attempt. It's over now, Meggie."

Meggie stared at that black ugly gun he was lifting in his hand. She couldn't look away from it. She didn't want to die, she didn't. With all her strength, she lunged toward him, her hands out, clutching for that gun. She managed to grab his hand, twisted it upward as he pulled the trigger. It was an immense explosion in that small room. She heard a chunk of the wall explode.

He slammed her back with his fist. He was cursing her, hitting her again, hard on the jaw, and Meggie knew she was moaning, knew that she was nearly unconscious, pain from her shoulder ripping through her. She was panting, panting, so afraid, and now she watched him through pain-blurred eyes as he walked out of the cottage. He was leaving? No, he was getting Bernard's gun.

She tried to rise, but couldn't, she was just too weak.

She lay there, wanting to cry because she'd failed, because all she'd done was just put off the inevitable.

Too soon, too soon she watched him come back into the room, and in his hand he held not a gun, but some stout string. He was wrapping it around his hands, pulling on it, testing its strength. She didn't want to be strangled, but now there wouldn't be a choice.

He came closer and closer. "Bernard always carries this stout string. He did kill Marie, this is what he likes to do, strangle women."

He dropped a knee onto the cot and leaned over her. "Now it's over," he said, and lifted her head. She tried to fight him, tried to twist out of the way. She felt the string, knots along its length close around her neck. She was so weak but still she had to try. She was trying desperately to pull the string loose from her neck, jerk his hands away, but it didn't slow him at all. There was no more strength, none at all now. She felt his hands tightening the string, felt the knots digging into her flesh. Obscene sounds filled the room, gurgling sounds, and she was light-headed, the pain in her neck building and building.

She couldn't die, just couldn't, but there was nothing left now, nothing she could do.

Then, suddenly the knots weren't digging so deeply, the string was becoming slack. Meggie opened her eyes to look up at him. His face was a mask of surprise and shock. He huffed out a breath and fell sideways, crashing to the floor.

Jenny MacGraff stood over him, his empty gun held in her hand. He moaned and both women froze. Jenny very calmly went down on her knees and struck him hard against the temple. When she rose, she said to Meggie, "We've won. What a horrible man. Are you all right, my lady?"

"Yes, thank you." Her voice was a croak, and she was pulling frantically at the knotted string. She had to get it off her, had to. Her voice was raw, painful, but there was no hope for it. "We haven't won yet. There is still Bernard. Quickly, Jenny, he's outside."

Jenny nodded and crept toward the door. She opened it, saw Bernard was riding away.

She turned. "He's run again," she said, then walked slowly over to where Lord Kipper lay. She raised her foot and kicked him hard in the ribs.

"Is he dead?"

Jenny shook her head. "No. But he should be. I hit him hard enough that second time."

"Don't you end it, Jenny. Let him hang," Meggie whispered since it hurt so badly. "Yes, let him hang." Then she held out her hand to Jenny MacGraff. "I am so glad you will be my new sister. Thank you, Jenny. I am Meggie. I would have welcomed you to Pendragon, but that bastard took you first."

"How do you feel? Your voice sounds a little bit better, thank God."

"Yes, it's not quite so bad now. Sit here beside me. Thomas will come soon."

When Thomas, William, Tysen, and Jeremy arrived a half hour later, bursting through the door into the cottage, they saw Jenny sitting on a narrow dirty cot holding Meggie's hand. Lord Kipper lay unconscious on the floor, his wrists bound with the knotted string he'd used to strangle Meggie, his shirt ripped off him, the remnants tying his ankles together.

Thomas walked to the cot, stood there over her, saying not a word until Jenny eased out of the way.

Meggie smiled, a very big smile, and said, her voice not as raw now, "Jenny saved us. She hit him over the head when he was strangling me."

Strangling her. Oh God, he was trembling, he just couldn't help it. He stood there like a palsied man, trembling, so weak with relief, with gratitude to Jenny MacGraff that he wanted to shout with it.

Meggie smiled when her father shoved Thomas out of the way, came down to sit beside her on the cot, and held her close. He buried his face in her hair. "My dearest heart, you're alive. This was too close, Meggie. Far too close. Your voice—that will probably take some time to heal. Are you all right?"

"Oh yes," Meggie said, "I'm just fine now," and she looked toward her husband, who was staring down at her, and that look on his face was one of hunger, immense hunger. "Let me see my husband, Father," and Tysen smiled, hugged her one last time and went to stand by William, who was holding Jenny tightly against his side, and there was Jeremy, smiling toward her, nodding, and there was gratitude and immense relief in his eyes.

"Thomas," she said, everything she felt in her voice, shining on her face. "Please come and hold me."

When his arms went around her, when she was pressed against his shoulder, breathing in his scent, when she felt him trembling, she knew everything was going to be all right. She realized in that instant that she felt whole and somehow new. Life was different now because she was different. She saw things in a way she never had before. She knew what was important now, knew it all the way to her soul. It was her husband. It was Thomas. She looked again at Jeremy, saw a man she would like and admire for the rest of her life, her children playing with his, this man, her almost dratted cousin, who cared enough about her to come with her father and Mary Rose to Pendragon.

He was Jeremy now. He was exactly what he should be.

She felt Thomas easing her back in his arms, and she smiled up at him, touching her fingertips to his lips, seeing all of him now, seeing the endless love for her in his dark eyes, the fear that he'd almost lost her this one final time. He was hers now, and she wanted him with all her spirit and heart.

She said, wishing she didn't still sound so very much like a croaking toad, "My throat will be all right. I'm very sorry that you've been so scared for me."

He pressed his forehead against hers. "Don't talk. I don't want you in more pain."

"Believe me, it doesn't hurt me to tell you how I feel.

I have never been more pleased to see anyone in my whole life. When you came bursting through that door, I knew that our life would never be the same again. There would be no more doubts, no more suspicions, you would never again wonder about what your wife thought and felt. I saw you, Thomas, really saw you. I realized that I love you. With all my heart. I love you more than I could ever imagine loving anyone, ever."

He hurt her he hugged her so tightly against him, but Meggie didn't mind. She closed her eyes, kissed his neck, and felt his heart beating, steady and strong, against hers. She looked over at William, who was still hugging Jenny tightly, whispering against her temple, kissing her hair. It made Meggie wonder if just perhaps there might be something worth saving in William after all. One thing she knew for sure, no one would ever know that he wasn't the earl of Lancaster's second son.

Epilogue

❧

$\mathcal{I}$T WAS A beautiful summer morning in late July. Just outside Kinsale, at the edge of Pendragon land, lay the freshly prepared Pendragon Racetrack, newly initiated this very day. The dowager countess of Lancaster, Madeleine Malcombe, was the mistress of ceremonies. Like Lady Dauntry of the famed McCaulty Racetrack, she stood on a dais, surrounded by at least one hundred people.

Cats heaved and panted and tried to escape their trainer's arms.

She called out, loud enough to be heard all the way to Cork, "CATS READY!"

Miss Crittenden of the Pendragon mews, who'd been meowing her head off, struggling to get free of Thomas, her secondary trainer, the only one strong enough to hold her steady, suddenly stiffened like a cannon, every muscle tensed. She was ready to run.

"CATS SET!"

There were twelve new racing cats, some confused, some eager for whatever was going to happen, some bored, some wishing there was food in their trainer's hands, some waiting just to bathe themselves or sleep in a nice shady spot under a bush.

None of the participants, none of the attendees, none of the trainers, particularly Meggie, had any idea at all of what was going to happen.

Madeleine yelled, her hands cupping her mouth, "FREE THE CATS!"

They were off, at least five of them were, Miss Crittenden among them, thank the good Lord else Meggie's credibility would have been sorely in question. She was running behind Jubilee, a howling black beast with witch green eyes, from Jenny Malcombe's new, exclusive training mews, who was running straight and fast.

Meggie felt a moment of base envy. Jenny shouldn't know success this quickly, it wouldn't be fair, not after all Meggie's work, all her dedication.

Meggie yelled, "Run, Miss Crittenden! Get Jubilee, pull him down, chew his neck! Run!"

The crowd, until this moment, not really knowing what to do, took up chants for the racing cat each of them was rooting for to win.

The noise was deafening. This was both good and bad. The noise made Jubilee and Miss Crittenden run all the faster because Meggie had shared with Jenny that they must accustom the cats to cheering, and so they had until all the stable lads were hoarse.

Two of the cats, calico sisters, nearly three years old and fast, suddenly stopped dead in their tracks, sat back on their haunches, stared a moment at all the ridiculous shouting and jumping people, and began licking each other, even though their ears were forward, taking in all the cheering. Meggie knew this was their way of coping with this unexpected chaos.

Butch, a lean and hungry black-and-white spotted mouser from the Witcherly mews, suddenly rose straight in the air, his hair sticking up, an impressive distance up since he was a longhair, and fell flat onto his side, evidently insensible from all the excitement.

Suddenly, out of nowhere, came Brutus, Thomas's dog. He burst onto the track, right behind Miss Crittenden and Jubilee. Both Jenny and Meggie were now standing at the finish line, frozen in horror as Brutus caught up with Miss Crittenden, grabbed her tail in his teeth, and hurled her a good six feet off the track.

No one had thought to mention that a dog anywhere near a cat racetrack wasn't to be allowed.

Thomas shouted at the dog, but Brutus wasn't about to stop this new sport.

Thomas shook his head, looked toward his appalled wife, and said, "Oops." He ran after Brutus.

Jubilee, an intense, sober cat, saw the dog's shadow, knew time was short, girded her loins, and leapt—at least six feet off the track to land on top of small Liam MacBail's back. Brutus was blocked by Liam's mother, who smacked him in the head. Jubilee jerked her claws out of Liam, ran back toward the track, then stopped, confused, until she heard Jenny's voice yelling, "Come to me, Jubilee, you can do it, come to me, run, you little critter!"

As for Miss Crittenden, she was flailing her tail about, thankfully still attached, back on the track now and running straight at Meggie, who appeared to be her only savior amid the chaos and the wildly barking dog she heard behind her.

Meggie hated to admit it, but this was a new training technique to be carefully considered. A dog chasing a cat. It did add motivation. In this case Miss Crittenden had never run so fast in her life.

Brutus was panting, his tongue lolling, hurtling down the track after her, shaking his head now, doubtless to clear it from the smack he'd gotten from Liam's mother, Thomas right behind him.

Miss Crittenden leapt the last four feet, sailed high in the air, and landed right into Meggie's arms, nearly knocking her backward. Brutus barked loudly, and before Thomas could stop him, leapt at Meggie.

Everyone went down in a welter of arms and legs, flying fur and yowls.

Brutus was licking Meggie's face, then barking, then licking some more, then eyeing Miss Crittenden and barking even more loudly, as he tried to get to her.

Madeleine shouted, cupping her hands over her mouth to be heard, "Miss Crittenden is the winner!"

Thomas managed to pull a very excited Brutus off Meggie, peel Miss Crittenden from beneath Meggie's arm, and helped his laughing wife up, whose face was shiny from Brutus's licking.

Meggie looked around at all the loudly cheering crowd of neighbors and villagers. There were yells and shouts;

some people were laughing so hard they were holding their sides.

She hugged Thomas to her. She was grinning so wildly her face threatened to split. "Our first cat race. And there was an actual winner. Isn't this splendid, Thomas? Our Miss Crittenden won, she really won. She beat Jubilee, and let me tell you, I was worried about that cat."

He couldn't help himself. He lifted his wife and whirled her around him. Meggie suddenly yowled as loud as any racing cat. Miss Crittenden was climbing her skirt, fast.

"No obstacle is too great," Thomas said as he eased both his wife and Miss Crittenden down, "for a true racing cat to surmount."

Madeleine yelled out, "The soon-to-be legendary prize for the winner of the quarter-of-a-mile race, is a magnificent set of collars, handmade by none other than the other dowager countess of Lancaster."

More cheering.

Libby bowed and walked sedately to where Meggie had finally gotten herself together and was holding a more composed Miss Crittenden in her arms.

Jenny was standing beside her, holding Jubilee, who looked disgruntled, occasionally spitting toward Miss Crittenden, a very natural thing, Meggie assured her even as she was grinning like a fool. William was patting Jenny's head in commiseration, in much the same way as he patted his new wife's growing belly in pleasure.

"Very easy for you to say since you're the winner," Jenny said. "That damned dog just about scared Jubilee out of her fur."

Brutus sat on his haunches, his tail a steady metronome, fluffing up dirt, Thomas holding him firmly. He was eyeing the cat collar as Meggie fastened it around Miss Crittenden's neck. There were small emeralds sewn into the collar, as green as Ireland's hills after a summer rain.

It was a beautiful day on the coast of southwestern Ireland, the first day a cat race had ever been run there. It wouldn't be the last.

And luckily, there had actually been a winner.

Dear Reader:

Are you ever in for a reading treat—Jaclyn Reding's *The Pretender*. You'll meet Douglas MacKinnon, an earl on the Isle of Skye, the first of three Highland Lords you'll read about in the Highland Heroes Trilogy.

We're back in 1746, after the Battle of Culloden. Douglas finds himself married to an English duke's bluestocking daughter, Elizabeth, and the chances for peace and harmony in this mismatch, don't look so good.

You will really enjoy *The Pretender*. Write yourself a reminder so you don't miss it when it comes out in March 2002.

Catherine Coulter

Early one summer's day in 1746

A MURKY MIST hovered about the crumbling remains of Emperor Hadrian's Roman wall as the Sudeleigh traveling coach rolled sluggishly along the rugged Northumbrian road. Overcast skies blocked out any trace of sunlight overhead and the wind didn't so much as stir the tall moor grass, making it appear as if they were swimming in the breath of the slumbering dragon long fabled to have been hiding in the desolate, heather-clad hills that surrounded them.

Inside the coach were Elizabeth and Isabella; guarding the outside, two of the duke's most trusted men-at-arms, bulky expanses of muscle and brawn named Titus and Manfred. Of course, there was the coachman, Higgins, as well, but he didn't pose any real threat, being barely five feet tall and weighing all of ten stone with his boots on. They'd taken to the road late that morning, stopping once to rest the horses while they enjoyed a picnic dinner made up of cold slices of ham and tart apples from the Drayton orchard in a basket that the duchess had sent along. Now nearing dusk, they were closing in on England's northern border, where they would pass the night at a roadside inn before resuming their journey in the morning. If all went as planned, by this same hour on the morrow, they should have reached their destination, the home of their widowed aunt, Idonia.

And then Elizabeth's punishment would officially begin.

"I cannot believe this is happening," she muttered. She had leaned her head against the coolness of the window-pane and her breath fogged the glass when she spoke.

"You must have known Father would discover the truth about those letters eventually, Bess," Isabella said from the opposite seat. "It was only a matter of time."

They were nearly the same words her father had spoken several days earlier when he'd summoned Elizabeth to his study unexpectedly.

"Deceived! Ridiculed! And by my own daughter!"

The volume of his anger alone had set the porcelain figurines that stood upon his desktop to rattling. "You've done some outlandish things in the past, Elizabeth Regina, but this? How could you have done *this*? And even worse, how could you think I'd not have found out?"

Deep down inside, as she'd sat there facing her father more angry than she'd ever seen him before, Elizabeth had to admit there had been a small part of her that had wanted to be found out.

While she might, on occasion, spark a bit of conversational debate around the breakfast table, in the letters she'd written for The *Female Spectator,* she had expressed ideals even she had not dared to speak out loud. She told herself she had been speaking for every woman who had ever lived a life of quiet acceptance, for every young girl whose spirit had been stifled beneath the cloak of ignorance. She'd wanted so badly to make a difference, yet now, reflecting back on it all, it wasn't any of those things that lingered with her now. Elizabeth could only see the look that had been in her mother's eyes as the duchess sat quietly in the corner chair while the duke had raged that morning. It was a look that seemed to say, "You cannot change the world, my daughter. And you should have known better than to try."

The duke had railed at Elizabeth for nearly an hour that morning cataloguing every one of her shortcomings before he'd finally dropped into his chair, facing her with the most unhappy of scowls.

"Now I just have to decide what to do with you," he'd said with a shake of his periwigged head. "A shame you're too old to send off to a convent."

At that, the duchess had interjected. "Alaric, really!"

"Well, she is, Margaret. I should have done that eight years ago when she first pulled that exploit at Kensington, disgracing us in front of the queen as she did. I should have known then that it would come to something like this one day."

The duke had sighed, twisting the errant end of his snowy white cravat as he pondered his predicament. Finally he'd said, "Well, it may be too late now to change the mistakes of the past, but I can do the next best thing." Then he'd looked at Elizabeth. "I've made up my mind. You're going to Idonia's."

Aunt Idonia, whose idea of occupying herself was to rearrange her stockings in order of color, starting with white and working her way through the entire color spectrum to black.

Elizabeth had blanched at the suggestion. "Father, please . . ."

But the duke had simply shaken his head, "Do not even attempt to convince me otherwise. My mind is made up. I can only hope that a few weeks—or months if that is what it takes—in the north will help you see the folly of your actions."

Elizabeth had opened her mouth to protest, but the duke had held up a silencing hand. "I am doing this for your own good, Bess. At the very least let us hope this visit will expel these rebellious thoughts from your head once and for all. But don't fret overmuch. I'm not such a total beast as to send you off to my sister without reinforcements. Misery loves company, or so they say, so I will allow Isabella to go along with you. If you can convince her to it, that is."

Elizabeth shifted her gaze from the coach window to where her sister sat across from her, head bent gracefully over a book of Shakespearean sonnets. At times, it was a wonder that they could be sisters at all. All one had to do was look at her to see that Isabella Anne Eleanor Drayton had been borne of a different world altogether, one in which faeries frolicked among a sea of bluebells and springtime never ended. Two years younger than Elizabeth, she had hair the color and softness of black silk that fell in loose waves over elegant shoulders. Her skin was pale as the finest ivory, her eyes the moss green found deep, deep in the forest.

In contrast to Elizabeth's fire and rebellion, Isabella was the image of everything that was soft and at peace with the world. She had the soul of an artist, not just seeing, but breathing in the world around her. When she moved, it was with the elegance of a swan. When she spoke, her voice carried a lilt just like a song. Isabella never challenged authority. She was utterly and maddeningly accepting of the ways of the world. At times, Elizabeth envied that quality in her almost as much as she found fault with it. Yet despite their differences, from the day she had been born, Isabella had been Elizabeth's closest confidante; she had in fact known about her sister's writing from the beginning, had even warned her against it while keeping her secret faithfully.

"He'll soon calm down," Elizabeth said not a little hopefully. "Father has been upset with me before and he always forgives me. Remember my Season in London, when I wore breeches to the queen's masquerade ball? Father's anger that night was more fierce than a storm. It blew and it raged and it thundered, but it just as quickly passed, too."

Isabella looked up from her sonnets in disbelief. "How can you honestly say that, Bess, when it was nearly eight years ago, and he hasn't allowed you to return to London since?"

Elizabeth shrugged. "What care I for mincing bucks in powdered wigs and face paint? Father still forgave me that episode just as he'll forgive me this. I'm sure of it. Oh, I'll have to suffer through a fortnight or so at Aunt Idonia's, no doubt ready to yank out every hair on my head by the time we're through, but afterward, I shall be allowed to return home dutifully sorry. I'll even finish that damnable sampler, if that is what it takes. But in the end, all will be well, Bella. You will see."

Having convinced herself of it, Elizabeth turned her attention out the window, glancing at the fast-darkening sky. *Hmm,* she thought, *I wonder if it will rain . . .*

"I'm afraid it isn't as simple as that this time, Bess."

Elizabeth looked to her sister. Isabella's expression had turned suddenly grim.

"There is something you should know."

"What? What is it? Is something wrong, Bella? Are you unwell?"

"No, nothing like that . . ." Isabella looked at her, her eyes threatening tears, struggling, Elizabeth could see, as if uncertain of what to say. Finally she burst out, "Oh, Bess, we are not going to visit Aunt Idonia, not at all. That was only a ruse to get you to agree to leave Drayton Hall willingly. Papa knew if you were aware of where we were going—where we are really going, I mean—you'd never agree to it and they'd have to carry you kicking and screaming out of the house."

Elizabeth suddenly remembered her father's comment about the convent. Surely he wasn't serious.

"Isabella . . . if we aren't going to Aunt Idonia's, then where exactly are we going?"

Isabella blinked.

"Bella . . . ? You must tell me."

"Oh, Bess, we are on our way to the estate of one of Father's associates, a Lord Purfoyle, in Scotland."

Scotland?

Elizabeth was stunned. "Why on earth would Papa send us all the way to Scotland? And why to Lord Purfoyle? We're scarcely acquainted with the man—I believe we met just once when he came to tea. I didn't even know he had a daughter our age."

"He hasn't, I mean, I guess he could have a daughter, but that's not why Father is sending us—is sending *you*— to Lord Purfoyle's estate." Isabella hesitated. "Oh, how in heaven am I supposed to explain this? It is so atrocious. I'll simply have to just say it. Bess, Father means for you to wed Lord Purfoyle."

"Wed him?" Elizabeth felt all the color drain from her face. "But the man is as old as . . . as our father!"

"He's not quite so old as that, but Papa knew it would be your reaction, which is why he misled you into thinking we were going to Aunt Idonia's. Father holds Lord Purfoyle in great esteem and he wonders that a man of his maturity—"

"You mean a man of his *age*, Bella."

"A man of his experience," she went on, "will be a better husband to you than a man of fewer years. Father will not be around forever. Think of it. He has already lost a number of his closest associates to death. He worries for your future, for all of our futures should something happen to him. The title, the estates, we will lose everything."

Isabella's words took Elizabeth aback. Her father had always been so vital, so timeless in her eyes. Her hero. Her protector. She had never once thought of him in such a way.

"Oh, Bess, I'm so sorry. But Papa said if I told you of this before we were out of England, he would make *me* wed Lord Purfoyle in your stead!"

Elizabeth's heart knotted like a stone inside her chest. She felt as if she'd just been betrayed in the worst of all ways, and by her own father, a man who, despite their differences of opinion on some matters, she had still always respected and adored. And Bella, too . . . what of her? She had known all along and yet had said nothing.

"How could you have kept this from me, Bell? Even with Father's threats, why did you not tell me before now?"

Before Isabella could answer there came a sudden deafening *crack* from outside the coach. Isabella gasped. The carriage lurched forward, then tilted perilously sideways, sending Elizabeth tumbling headfirst from her seat amid a jumble of silk petticoats and lace ruffles. She bumped her head against something hard, then struggled to right herself. A moment later, the coach ground to a sudden, bone-jarring halt.

And then, silence.

Pulling herself aright, Elizabeth reached for the limp bundle that was her sister, her breath catching in her throat. "Bella? Are you hurt?"

"No," came a muffled reply from beneath a cloud of petticoats. "Just a bit disconcerted is all. Whatever happened?"

"I don't know." Elizabeth called out to the coachman as she pushed back the lopsided brim of her straw bergère. "Higgins, are you there? Why have we run off the road?"

" 'Twere a sheep standin' in the middle of the road, my lady. I had to turn us off the road to keep from hitting him, but it looks like we've gotten stuck now. Might've broken a wheel, too."

"Oh, goodness!" said Isabella, lifting her head to peer out the window. "You didn't hit him, did you, Higgins?"

"Who?"

"The sheep, poor thing."

"Bother the sheep, Isabella! We could have all been killed!"

"But he does not realize that, Elizabeth—"

"Oh, he's a'right, Lady Isabella. Still standing in the very spot."

Elizabeth glanced out the window to where, indeed, a shag-haired sheep stood watching them from the middle of the road. When he saw her glaring at him, he bleated.

Entertaining thoughts of mutton stew and leg of lamb, Elizabeth reached for the latch on the door. Outside, the back wheels of the carriage were hopelessly mired in what appeared to be a substantial stretch of bog. Higgins was on the ground, standing a space away and scratching his balding head beneath his hat.

"Do you think you can repair it?" she asked him.

"Aye, if I can get to it to fix it, that is. It looks mightily stuck."

The duke's two men-at-arms, Manfred and Titus, circled around from the other side of the lopsided coach. "We best get you ladies out of there and see what we can do to push the coach free."

But when Manfred took the first step toward the coach, he immediately plunged ankle deep in the mire. He moved to pull his foot free, slipping clean out of his boot instead, his toes wiggling through the hole in his stocking.

"Gaw, it's like molasses, it is," he said struggling to get his foot back inside his boot. He twisted his bulk, stretching back awkwardly, lost his balance and fell face-first with a howl, flailing as he went over like a tree. When he gained his feet several moments later, the front of him—his hands, his face, his paunched girth—was hopelessly covered in mud.

Titus was laughing behind him. "Didn't you know ye're supposed to take your coat *off* before you lay it down for the ladies to walk upon?"

Manfred delivered his comrade a lethal glare as he removed his handkerchief from his pocket and wiped at the mud dripping off his face. "I think I'll be steadier if I were t' carry you on me back, my lady, 'stead of in me arms. D'you think you can wrap your arms 'round me neck?"

"I believe so, yes."

Elizabeth reached for the doorway of the coach and pulled herself to stand at the edge, reaching out for where the man had doubled over and was waiting.

It was just as she was bent over Manfred's back, her feet dangling behind her in a most indelicate piggyback pose, that she heard an unexpected and unfamiliar voice coming from behind them.

"*Och*, but you English lassies do have a peculiar way of showing a fancy for the lads, you do."

Manfred turned about—with Elizabeth still draped over his shoulders—to see a stranger who had come unnoticed upon the scene.

He was dressed in Highland fashion, in a belted plaid that left his legs exposed beneath a loose flowing cambric shirt that he hadn't bothered to tie at the neck. His hair was as dark as soot and hung below his neck, tied in a queue beneath a blue bonnet of sorts decorated with a sprig of heather. He carried a broadsword at his side and a peculiar studded shield strapped to his back. It made him look downright primordial. His cocksure grin, however, and his obvious amusement at their situation, touched a raw nerve in Elizabeth.

"I suppose you have a better idea?" she said, mustering as much dignity as she could while trying not to think of how ridiculous she must look hanging as she was over Manfred's backside.

"Aye, I do." He glanced at Manfred then, ignoring her altogether. "Put the lass back in the coach, man. You can wash yourself off in yon burn."

As Manfred helped Elizabeth back to the coach, the Scotsman kneeled, untying the leather laces on his peculiar-looking shoes. He removed them along with his tartan hose, then, without another word, proceeded to walk straight into the mire—sloshing and oozing his way to the coach in his bare feet. In one sudden motion, he swept Elizabeth from the step and into his arms, cradling her effortlessly before him. His eyes, a deep dark blue, laughed at her above his crooked grin.

"In need of a lift, lass?"

Elizabeth frowned. "In England, sir, it is customary for a gentleman to ask a lady's permission before laying any hands upon her person."

"*Och*, but you're no' in England anymore, lassie. And I'm *sair*tainly no gentleman. This is the land o' the Scotsman, and there isna a thing genteel about a Scot."

"Truer words were never said," she remarked to the mud creeping up his hairy legs.

The man continued to stare at her. It was disconcerting, those blue eyes looking at her as if he could see straight to the deepest reaches of her thoughts. His mouth had

settled into a straight line, but somehow she believed he
was mocking her.

"I'll no' have it said a Scot, any Scot, ever took a lass
who wasna willing." He grinned again. "Even if it is out
of a bog. You want me to put you down then?"

Elizabeth glanced down to the sludge that surrounded
them, from which a sour smell had begun to rise in the
summer heat. "No, please, do not."

"I didna think so."

The man turned and trudged back through the bog to
drier land, more dropping her than setting her down before him. He didn't immediately move away, and stood
so close she could see the flecks of gray that made his
eyes so darkly blue. They were peculiar, those eyes, somehow making it impossible for her to tear her gaze away.

He said, "I'll just fetch the other lassie now."

Only when he turned to retrieve Isabella did Elizabeth
realize her heart was pounding. Putting it off as the result
of the mishap in the coach, she took a deep breath and
focused on the arrangement of her skirts while he carried
her sister from the coach setting her right beside Elizabeth.

"Have you ever seen such a man?" Isabella whispered
as the stranger set about helping Manfred and Titus to
push the coach free of the bog. "He carried me as if I
weighed no more than a feather."

Elizabeth crossed her arms, rubbing them as if taken
by a chill. *But was it a chill—or was it him?*

"He is far too forward."

"He was just trying to be helpful."

"More likely he was just trying to sneak a hand against
your bodice, Bella. If Father were here, he would have—"

An idea struck Elizabeth—*boom!*—like a lightning
bolt, an idea of such ingenuity, such cleverness, she could
scarcely believe how brilliant she was.

Three-quarters of an hour later, when the carriage was
free and the wheel had been repaired, Elizabeth walked
over to the stranger, a much different Elizabeth than the
one she'd been before.

"I wish to thank you, sir, for your kind assistance." She offered him her gloved hand. "I shudder to think what we might have done had you not happened by when you did."

The Highlander looked at her curiously, as if seeing her for the first time.

"Pleased to have been of help, my lady."

He didn't move to take her hand. Instead he turned, taking up his shoes and hose as he readied to leave.

Leave? But he couldn't leave just yet.

Elizabeth followed him. "I, uh, neglected to ask your name. I should like to know to whom we owe our debt of gratitude."

The man looked at her but didn't stop walking. "Douglas Dubh MacKinnon fro' the Isle of Skye."

Douglas Dubh? What in the world sort of name was that?

He stopped for a moment at the burn to wash the mud from his feet and legs. As he bent to cup the water in his hands, large hands, running his fingers down the length of his bare calves, Elizabeth found herself staring at the way the muscles in his legs pulled and flexed beneath the hem of his plaid. There was power in those legs. *Male* power. The popinjays in London could stuff cork in their stockings in earnest and never achieve legs that looked like *that*.

When she looked up again, Elizabeth realized the Highlander was staring at her—as she was staring at him.

Her cheeks went awash. My God, she thought, I am actually blushing.

"I am La—" she corrected herself, "I am Elizabeth Drayton. The other lady with me is my sister, Isabella Drayton. We are traveling to the home of our aunt in the north and were waylaid by that sheep over th—"

Elizabeth pointed to the road, but the damnable beast had vanished.

"In any case, we are indebted to you for your kindness, Mr. MacKinnon."

Elizabeth held out her hand to him. The Highlander glanced at her a moment, then bowed, ignoring her outstretched hand once again. "A pleasure, my lady."

He turned then and started to walk away. "Good day to you and your sister. Godspeed on your journey."

He hadn't made it more than a couple of yards before Elizabeth called to him. "Mr. MacKinnon, aren't you going to put your hose and shoes back on?"

He didn't stop. "Aye, after my feet have dried."

"But, uh, may I ask where you are headed?"

"I'm to an inn not far from here called The Reiver's Rest."

She followed him. "The Reiver's Rest, you say? Why we are going to the very same inn."

It was an excellent lie, clearly delivered and brilliant. Although from the way he was looking at her, she wondered if somehow he knew that it was.

"It looks as if it might rain," she said quickly. "In fact, I'm quite certain I just felt a drop hit my nose." She turned her face to the clouds, then nodded. "Yes, indeed, there is another. Please, sir, allow us to offer you a ride to the inn. It is the least we can do in exchange for your kindness."

The Highlander eyed the clouds, hesitating as if considering her offer. "That really isna necessary, my lady."

"But I must insist." Elizabeth rewarded him with her sweetest smile, the one that never failed to get her what she wanted.

And it didn't fail this time, either.

"If you're certain . . ."

"Absolutely, and do sit inside with Isabella and me so we can chat along the way. This is my first time to Scotland and I would love to hear simply everything about it."

Elizabeth waited.

Finally the Highlander nodded once and turned for the coach.

As MacKinnon ducked his head and slid onto the opposite seat, Isabella grabbed the lace cuff of Elizabeth's sleeve and gave it a warning tug. She whispered, "What in the name of all that is sacred are you doing?"

Elizabeth cast her sister a sidelong glance. "Nothing, yet. But if I have my wish, this Highlander might just prove himself very useful in the next several hours."